"Foy's second thriller, successor to the highly praised *Asia Rip,* is written in a style of galvanic energy. . . . Foy can describe a classy cocktail party, an unscrupulous bankers' board meeting and the steamy hold of a doomed ship with equal assurance. He's a master of violent action, expert in the ways of seafaring, and a shrewd observer of human psychology. *COASTER* is a humdinger."

—*Publishers Weekly*

"The storm and the ship's sinking are rendered with enormous energy and sting . . . a rich opening and many striking details throughout."

—*Kirkus Reviews*

"Foy—sailor, fisherman, investigative reporter, and author of *Asia Rip*—has concocted a perfectly plotted suspense tale, played out against well-sketched settings of Wales, London, Antwerp, Cornwall, and Grand Cayman. . . . The novel's final scenes are masterful vignettes of psychological suspense. A nominee for the year's best-crafted thriller."

—*ALA Booklist*

Books by George Foy

Asia Rip
Coaster

Published by POCKET BOOKS

COASTER

GEORGE FOY

PUBLISHED BY POCKET BOOKS NEW YORK

POCKET BOOKS, a division of Simon & Schuster, Inc.
1230 Avenue of the Americas, New York, N.Y. 10020

Published by arrangement with Viking Penguin Inc.
Library of Congress Catalog Card Number: 85-40567

ISBN: 0-671-62326-5

First Pocket Books printing December, 1986

10 9 8 7 6 5 4 3 2 1

Printed in the U.S.A.

ACKNOWLEDGMENTS

MANY PEOPLE on both sides of the Atlantic helped me with this book. Some of them, who gave me precious insights into Lloyd's, requested anonymity. The rest include Bill Strachan, Harvey Klinger, Sarah Molloy, Gerry Howard, Ann, Skye, my parents, my brother, Norma Heyman, Peter Dervis, Adam Shand-Kydd, Betsy Gruet, Ann Lewis, Donna Levitan, Maria Wadsworth.

It began to go wrong when she asked John Penrose to fetch the cream from the steps at her front door.

"It's your house," he protested.

"Go on," she answered. "It's the only chance I get to lie abed, when my men come home from the sea. And you wanted the tea."

"How many men do you have, apart from your husband?" he started to reply, but she twisted around under the covers, drew her knees up, and kicked him gently onto the freezing slate floor.

He looked up at her smile, at this woman he hardly knew, at the "Free Cymru" poster on the wall tacked cheek by jowl with a reproduction of a Constable.

She stared right back, seeing a strong chin and nose accenting direct blue eyes; longish hair that almost hid a circlet of gold in his left ear; below, a hirsute frame of just under six feet, very lean and well-muscled.

"Your neighbors will see me," he said.

"Don't be silly. No one will see you. It's six-thirty in the morning," meaning it was late.

But she was wrong.

The little Welsh seaport Anne Morgan lived in had only one reason to exist, the Port Garth Colliery, a nineteenth-century carcinoma of black and slag that held thrall over the surrounding hills.

The National Coal Board had laid off a third of PGC's men last fall, miners who were used to getting up at 6:00 A.M. for the dawn shift and now had nothing to do but draw dole,

1

drink at the pub, and watch their street, which, like all others in town, led to the colliery gates below.

Today the unemployment office would not open before 9:00, and the pubs were shut till 11:00. The colliery gates, for their part, would close forever in September.

Shivering, Penrose threw a quarter scuttle of coal on the banked fire downstairs. He knew he was naked but it was a measure of his hangover that he could put the fact out of his mind until he opened the front door, picked up the bottles of milk and cream (their gold and silver caps the only brightness in the dawn) and a note from the milkman, straightened up to go back in—and looked directly into the eyes of a man walking down the street on the other side of Anne's garden hedge.

The man stopped. His face, compressed between scarf and cloth cap against the February wind, did not change. His eyes were black and a big mustache of the same color gave him more than a passing resemblance to Stalin.

Penrose nodded civilly. The man broke his gaze and continued his trudge, while Penrose shut the door and chuckled in embarrassment.

"Someone saw me when I fetched the cream," he said when he brought Anne Morgan her cup.

She sat bolt upright at that, spilling tea over the coverlet.

"Who? I mean, what did she look like?"

"It was a he."

"Oh, *hell*." She buried her head in her knees.

"I don't think it was anyone from next door," he said to console her. "He was walking uphill."

Penrose was shaking violently. The temperature in the house would have done justice to an igloo. He climbed back into bed, but she shrank from contact with him.

"Everyone knows everyone else here," she sniffed. "I wish I'd never gone to that pub last night. I wish David hadn't got laid off. I wish he'd not got the tanker job so he leaves me alone for three weeks at a go." The singing accentuations of Wales filtered easily through the layers of blankets that covered her face.

"I'm sorry," Penrose said ineffectually.

"It's not your fault either. It's me, I'm just a p-r-r-ostitute," she said, rolling the *r*'s like ball bearings. She contradicted herself by turning over, hiding her face against his chest, and bursting into tears.

"It's not your fault either," he said generously, trying like the devil not to be aware of the deep warmth and softness of her skin as she pressed herself against him, but now she had lifted her chin and was kissing him through the tears and there was nothing he could do about the physical reaction.

He tried to make it less obvious, curving himself away from her stomach, suddenly conscious of being caught in a small Methodist town, where fornication and adultery still called down Old Testament retribution.

But she moved with him, hugged him even tighter, felt him against her. She lifted her mouth to his and he forgot the man outside.

The rain never ended here, and never began. Instead of falling, it condensed around you. The sound of its dripping hung around everything.

It was only a quarter mile down the hill from Anne Morgan's house, but by the time he got to the colliery Penrose was wet through.

The guard at the gates let him in at 8:30 with a cheerful wave, and Penrose got lost in the maze of pipes and covered conveyor belts that brought coal from uneconomical seams farther up the hill. Everything seemed black—the bricks of the NCB offices and shift canteens, even the looks he got from men walking between machine shops and warehouses. He recognized a couple of the men from the pub last night, but they didn't wave. No one seemed to be having a good time in Port Garth Colliery except the guard, and he'd had whisky on his breath.

The gray-and-white bulk at the quayside, looming between two coal tips, was his ship.

The *Witch of Fraddam* was a 497-ton coastal freighter. She was twenty-six years old, 202 feet long and had just acquired a faulty weld, somewhere in the double bottom around number three port ballast tank, that leaked in rough seas. The leak resulted from a shortcut the Schelde pilot had tried on their way out of Antwerp, a shortcut that ended on a mudbank. The *Witch*'s 950-horsepower diesel was only five years younger than the ship and used too much fuel, yet the sight of her rust-streaked hull—her clutter of vent cowls, radar, signal halyards, antennas atop the bridge, her smooth-worn hatch boards and patched tarpaulins, her aging donkey

4

engine and frayed quarter lines forward—always gave Penrose the feeling of coming home.

When he got to the quayside he saw the whisky had arrived, not in bottles but in two huge sealed cargo containers forty feet by ten by ten, brought as promised from the small Cromarty distillery that belonged to Alasdair Henderson's uncle. It was last-minute freight, a rush order of Henderson's oldest reserves of single malt, and they'd been lucky to get it: despite the way freight rates were dropping, it might yet give him a profit margin for February.

It was close to high tide, and Penrose had to climb the gangplank like a rope. The generator was thudding and a sound of hammering came from forward. He visited the galley for tea and an aspirin, then went down to the open hold.

"Oy!" he shouted for the third time, wincing at the effect on his head.

The hammering stopped.

"Morning, Captain."

Malinson poked his spaniel's head and thick spectacles over the coaming.

"Morning, Malinson."

No one wore uniforms on most British coasters, or called each other by anything other than first names, but there had to be an exception to everything, and that exception was Roger Malinson, his first and only officer.

"Haven't you finished that bulkhead yet?"

"Almost done, sir." No one else on board called Penrose sir.

"Make sure," Penrose said, "that you tape the seams, and nail the tape in."

Malinson nodded. Fine coal would seep through any unplugged cracks in the temporary timber bulkhead they had just put up. This bulkhead would keep flammable coal dust from coming into contact with the permanent after bulkhead, which was warm because its other side was an engine room stuffed with diesel, generator, exhausts, and pumping equipment.

"Make sure," the captain added, clutching his tea mug, "that the pipe leading down from the inspection hatch is taped as well. Tight as a flea's arsehole."

Malinson nodded. "I put the temperature gauge where you wanted," he began lugubriously, when a voice said,

5

"Oy, John! Did yer 'ave it off with yer Gaelic skin 'n' blister? Eh? You know, the nationalist: the one with the nice bristols? You devil, John." The voice stopped, out of breath.

Penrose had to translate for a second, then winced as he remembered Anne Morgan, her taut breasts equally unrestrained, raising a pint high as she toasted the independence of Wales and Cornwall. The miners around had made Cro-Magnon noises when they left together after closing time. He wished Brian for once would forgo the East London rhyming slang he continuously affected.

Brian Jeffreys's blond head came up a ladder on the port side of the hold. Penrose ignored the deck hand.

"Keep the rose box clear, and make sure you brace the shifting boards," he told Malinson. "That bloody surveyor's late. If he comes by, or if the foreman or the ship's agent does, send them straight to my office. They've got to get a move on with loading if we're to leave on tonight's tide."

The Lloyd's surveyor arrived with the ship's agent ten minutes later, and Penrose had Malinson take the surveyor down to the hold, open up the inspection port in the tank tops and show him where the weld had come unstuck. He had no interest in crawling around the double bottom himself, in those dark confined spaces rank with the smell of sea and dead cargoes.

If the inspection took too long, loading could be delayed, costing them all money, but there was no getting around the necessity for having the damage checked. Any hull damage to a Lloyd's-insured ship had to be surveyed in the next feasible port or its classification, its seaworthiness rating, automatically lapsed. If the classification lapsed, so did the ship's insurance policy.

The colliery foreman came on board at 0915 with a shovel and a bucket. Penrose and the ship's agent walked with him down the quay as the foreman methodically sampled four coal tips, taking shovelfuls from different flanks of each, quartering and mixing the dust on the ground before spooning a portion into the shiny stainless-steel milk bucket he carried. The drizzle hung close, soaking them all democratically. The foreman, a large man with no neck and a hat that seemed glued to his forehead, neither spoke nor looked at them. Smoke from lorries and mining engines rose reluctantly among the sea gulls and the blasted hills surrounding the harbor. When the sampling was finished they went to find the manager.

The colliery manager was a Welsh gnome named Llewellyn, grizzled and squat, who came down to lead them around a warren of corrugated iron, brick, pipes, and NO SMOKING notices pinned at ten-foot intervals. Bright industrial work lights only highlighted the layers of coal grime. Finally he stopped at a door that read: SAFETY EQUIPMENT. TESTING LABORATORY.

Testing was one of the reasons Penrose hated carrying coal.

The fine coal dust, or slurry, that he was loading this trip had to contain less than a specific percentage of moisture, or vibration could cause it to suddenly become as liquid as soup.

In any vessel other than a tanker, a cargo of soup would shift loosely in the unconfined hold, back and forth with the ship's roll, adding its own free-surface motion to the destabilizing effects of ocean swells. The overall effect would destroy instantaneously a ship's stability.

Worse yet was the fire hazard. Freshly mined coal absorbed oxygen and combined with moisture to form peroxides, then oxides of carbon. The reaction produced heat, which in turn caused further oxidation and, eventually, spontaneous combustion.

The only way to avoid this was to cut off oxygen by sealing the hold from ventilation, which also prevented any explosive gases from seeping up on deck, and to check the coal's temperature through special inspection ports during the trip.

Llewellyn unlocked the laboratory door, and Penrose became aware of an utterly incongruous sound. As the light came on he saw a small brown room jammed with rows of Blitz-era gas masks, retorts, fire extinguishers, gas sniffers and first-aid kits. The sounds came from one entire wall given over to a fine-meshed wire cage. Behind the mesh were hundreds of tiny yellow birds chirping, flapping and blinking at the sudden light.

"Budgerigars," the manager explained, fondly. He opened a small door in the cage and three birds flew onto his outstretched finger. "Still haven't invented a better coal-gas detector, look you. We stock 'em for all of Rhondda. Morgan!"

7

Penrose started, then remembered that "Morgan" here was like "Smith" in England.

The foreman came up, clutching his shiny bucket.

"Morgan has sampled your coal dust."

"Mr. Llewellyn," Morgan began.

"You did sample the tips with Captain Penrose?"

"Aye," Morgan said, "but we're already—"

"This is from the tips for the *Witch of Fraddam?*"

"Aye," Morgan said, with a quick glance at Penrose, "but we're late already."

Llewellyn stuck out his hand. Morgan handed over the bucket and left without another word. The manager dumped the bucket on a sheet of newspaper, quartered it once more, expertly, and mixed it with a spade. He measured dust carefully onto a steel tray, weighed both tray and dust on a brass jeweler's scale, then put them in a huge autoclave of chrome and Bakelite that looked like it had been thrown together by Thomas Edison on a day when he'd been as hung over as Penrose. Llewellyn switched on the heat and a fan, and walked over to the birdcage.

"Lovely little things, budgies," he remarked. Nobody else said anything. It was very hot in the little room, and the smell of bird droppings was strong.

In ten minutes the autoclave had baked all moisture out of the slurry. Llewellyn reweighed the tray, subtracted weight two from weight one, divided the difference into weight one and came out with a percentage well below the danger mark. Penrose noted the figure on his bill of lading and headed for the ship.

When he got back to the bridge he found the Lloyd's surveyor seated, listening patiently to the agent telling him where to go on his Caribbean holiday. When he saw Penrose, he rose from the pilot's seat with an ill-concealed sigh of relief and handed him a clipboard.

"I've issued you a certificate of seaworthiness," he said without preamble, "till you get to Holland."

"She's not about to founder with all hands, then?" Penrose asked, with a smile, as he countersigned the certificate.

The engineer—a thin man in horn-rims with a briefcase that looked too heavy for him—just stared at him. "No indication of metal fatigue, if that's what you mean." He looked around the old-fashioned bridge, with its dark paneled bulkheads and brass voice pipes. "Although it's surprising in a ship as old as this."

Penrose kept his voice neutral. "She's not the *QE 2*, but she's not the ark, either, you know. And Clyde-built."

"Yes. Before the Tories shut down Glasgow. And the Scots steel was, of course, almost as good as the Welsh."

Penrose looked up in surprise from stowing the certificate in a locker by the steering station, but not a flicker of humor showed on the man's face.

"Till they closed the mills."

"Yes, till they closed the mills, indeed. Well, I'll be off, then."

"You're welcome to stay for breakfast."

"I don't eat breakfast. Please have the ship immediately dry-docked in Rotterdam, after you unload the cargo, or the classification will lapse, Captain."

The surveyor shut his briefcase with two loud snaps and put on a brown overcoat. Penrose escorted him to the gangway, trying not to think about it, but at 600 pounds a day it was hard to forget the effect dry-docking the ship would have on Cornwall Shipping's fragile bank balance.

III

— — — — — — — — — — — — — — — —

They were all in the main saloon except for Tommy Gowans, the engineer, who was watching over his main pump as it discharged water ballast in preparation for loading. The pump, like the engineer, had a tendency to heat up in times of stress, and Tommy had a secret stash of Newcastle Brown Ale that he liked to visit around breakfast-time.

The galley door opened, and a burst of the R & B music Brian listened to swept over the saloon—a sharecroppin' voice mumbling "we gotta get it together babeh" backed by a hiccoughing base.

Brian leaned out the Dutch door leading to the pantry and tapped his spatula on the counter. The ship's agent, a roly-poly white-bearded little man, smiled as he reached for another sausage. Henry Permuen, the other deck hand, was eating breakfast as if it were his first meal in days. A milquetoast sun squeezed a ray of light through the clouds and into a porthole. Penrose poured brown sauce over his fried bread, fried sausage, fried tomatoes, fried eggs: it was the only way to cut the grease.

"One of our china plates got an announcement to make," Brian announced, his East London accent whining in the morning calm. There was no answer but the clink of crockery and a polite mumble from the agent.

"One of us, for the first toim, got his hands on a nice pair of Alan Whickers. Knickers, to you Welsh illiterates. Spent the night wiv a bird, innit."

Penrose sighed. Henry stopped eating.

"An' it wasn't our beloved guv'nor, wus it, wiv 'is married Welsh trouble, nor our revered mate, neither."

10

Penrose looked up in surprise. Henry Permuen was nineteen years old and came from the town next to his own, in Cornwall. He was a quiet, unassuming kid, a good deck hand whose mother was always standing at the pier next to her blue Ford Escort whenever they docked in the *Witch of Fraddam*'s home port.

Henry was blushing.

"Well, fuck me pink," Penrose exclaimed, getting to his feet and walking around the saloon. "Fuck me, it's Henry!" He grabbed the kid's hand, slapped him on the shoulder. "Great, mate, that's just great," he repeated delightedly, "that's just great." Henry looked around, shy, tousle-headed, proud. Brian was grinning like a dolphin; the ship's agent nodded uncertainly. Even Malinson gave a small salute.

"First time, wunnit," said Brian, unnecessarily.

"Who won the sex pool?" Malinson asked.

Henry gaped.

"We had a little bet going," Penrose explained, "on when you'd, well, have it off. I think Tommy was closest?"

"Who cares," Brian said. There was a popping sound from the galley. "Champagne poor toot le monde," he added, pouring sparkling wine as he massacred the French, "eh, John?"

"Why not?" Penrose agreed.

Evening smudged what corners of Port Garth had escaped the endless pall of coal smoke, and still the colliery had not finished loading.

From the radio-shack porthole Penrose could glimpse men working around the prehistoric snout of the coal chute as he fine-tuned the receiver to BBC4.

"This is the BBC shipping forecast, issued by the met office for 1755 hours GMT. Gale warnings are in effect for the following sea areas: Shannon, Fastnet, Sole, Biscay and Finisterre. General synopsis . . . a low-pressure zone 150 miles southwest of Ushant will be stationary or proceed slowly westward. . . . Forecasts for areas Viking, Forties, Cromarty, Forth, Tyne, Dogger, Fisher, German Bight . . ."

Penrose turned the volume higher and wrote, "Lundy: east-southeast, 20–25 knots, visibility 3–4 miles drizzle. Plymouth: southeasterly 20–25, visibility 2–3 miles, dropping to 1 in haze."

Malinson slouched into the radio-cum-chart room, brushing drizzle from his forehead.

"They just finished loading."

"About bloody time." Penrose noted the barometer reading and clipped the forecast summary above the chart table. "What took them so long?"

"They couldn't find one of the tips."

Penrose snorted.

"And they wouldn't top the fresh-water tanks."

"Why not?"

Malinson shrugged. "We've all we'll need, anyway, for this trip."

The ship's agent and the colliery manager came in together. Penrose signed the final bills of lading for Llewellyn; the clearance outward papers and the Lights List for his agent.

"I understand you're taking the slurry to a plant where they make charcoal bricks, for barbecues," the colliery manager said, to make conversation.

"Another American fad," Penrose said. "And the whisky's going to Rotterdam for shipment to Yokohama so the bloody Japs can learn to make it better and cheaper than the Scots. Incidentally, where's the bill of lading for the whisky?"

"There wasn't one," Llewellyn said.

"All I got was a mate's receipt," Malinson said.

"Your office told me it was a rush job and they didn't have time to send up bills of lading," the agent said.

Colin had mentioned that last night. The distillery had tried all the big companies and none could fit them in at such short notice.

But Cornwall Shipping could, because Cornwall Shipping needed the money. Colin had even arranged for quick, cheap cargo insurance on the whisky, using the Lloyd's firm that insured the *Witch of Fraddam*. "We can always find extra cargo from Rotterdam or the Schelde," Colin had said.

Colin, Penrose thought, had better be right.

It was almost two hours past the turn of the tide when they were finally ready for sea. While they waited for the pilot Penrose took a sledgehammer and made his usual tour of inspection, whacking the hatch battens, bottle screws and ventilator cowls to make sure everything was tight. Malinson had done a good job of securing the whisky containers on the hatch: the cables ran tight as bars from every corner of the huge steel boxes to ringbolts on the deck. Henry had not swept down the portside deck, but the Bristol Channel would soon take care of that. There was less dust than he'd expected, anyway.

They cleared the mud bar at the entrance to Port Garth harbor with several inches to spare at 1955, and dropped the pilot ten minutes later.

—————————————————————————————— **IV**

At 4:30 P.M. on January 4, nineteen and a half hours out of Port Garth, Penrose woke up in the certain knowledge that something was wrong with his ship.

His eyes instinctively went to the compass recessed in the deckhead above his bunk, but the course was right for the time: 88 degrees magnetic for the run from Lizard Point to Beachy Head.

He forced himself to lie still for a moment while he drove sleep from the last corners of his brain. The engines ran smoothly, but the ship's movement was different: the seas had obviously built up since he'd turned in, and they were pitching, corkscrewing a little, which meant the wind was probably still on the starboard bow. But it was the movement—*the movement was sick.*

The ship was listing to port.

Penrose immediately guessed what had happened but jammed the thought to the back of his mind as he threw on some clothes and slammed out of his stateroom. The door whacked Malinson in the face as he came to wake Penrose, and his glasses smashed to the floor.

"Sorry. What's going *on*, Malinson?" Penrose asked.

"We've developed a list, sir. I was coming—"

But Penrose was already halfway up the bridge-deck companionway.

It was dusk, a typical Channel dusk: the sky hazy, very dark gray. Waves rolled in like navvies passing the ship from back to back and flexing white muscles as they did so. Greenish foam creamed through the freeing ports when the

14

Witch of Fraddam bit into a swell. To port, a buoy winked on what passed for a horizon.

Penrose estimated the wind at 30 to 35 knots, south-southeasterly, which meant the circular depression was edging slowly toward them.

The *Witch of Fraddam* pitched mostly and rolled a little, port and starboard, but never quite came back to its center of gravity. They were still listing, perhaps five degrees to port.

So small an anomaly, Penrose thought, to signal so great a peril.

Malinson's eyes blinked foolishly behind his cracked lenses.

"Is it?"

Penrose looked furiously at the mate. "Wake up Brian. Where's Henry?"

"In the galley, making sandwiches."

"Get him up here."

Tommy Gowans was probably sleeping happily in the engine room with his diesel and his ale.

Penrose ducked into the chart room.

Dead reckoning for 1645 put them eighteen miles east-southeast of Lizard Point. Jesus, he thought, they were almost home.

Henry and Malinson were shadows against the binnacle light. Penrose adjusted the autopilot to bring their course directly into the waves, and rang the engines down to quarter speed. There was an immediate squawk in a Newcastle accent from Tommy's intercom.

"Tell him to start flooding the ballast tanks," he told Malinson. "Start with number two starboard." Penrose grabbed a hammer and a light from the port locker, beckoned to Henry and went out into the gathering night.

The elements were more impressive out here, where you could measure them against the ship.

Penrose knew that from where he stood on the starboard bridge wing he was a good thirty feet above the mean surface of the sea, but every time they rolled or pitched the wave tops grasped hungrily only ten feet below the bridge windows. The wind abetted the waves' attempt, shaving razorfuls of freezing spume off the top of each to slash it instantly into cringing eyes. Spray colored the night green as it exploded around the starboard running light at every clash between hull and sea.

They slid gingerly down the slippery companionways to the lowest accommodation tier. Here, on saloon deck, the foam loomed to eye level, flooding the cargo deck, six feet below, and racing around madly before the *Witch of Fraddam* rolled again and sent it jetting out of the freeing ports. Only the cargo hatch, five feet higher than the main deck, with its two huge cargo containers lashed on top, avoided being sluiced every time the ship hit a wave.

Penrose and Henry made their way to the hatch with no more than a soaking, caught their breath for a second in the lee of the bulking whisky containers, then hammered open the lugs on the after inspection hatch.

The hatch only gave access to a narrow strip of space, a cofferdam that ran four feet wide across the breadth and height of the ship's hold.

Penrose flashed his light down the opening, and caught his breath at what he saw.

The temporary bulkhead was made of three-inch-thick planks taken from the hold's spar ceiling, a protective blanket of wood they had to strip anyway before loading coal. The planks were bolted onto four-by-four iron frames that were in turn bolted to brackets welded onto the deck and frames and hatch beams. The planks were braced, and shored at intervals against the engine-room bulkhead with lengths of four-by-four.

And yet the temporary bulkhead was bulging. The lower five or six planks were visibly breathing, bending in and out whenever the *Witch*'s bows tilted up or down against the sea. The angled struts had already bent; three or four of the shoring timbers had fallen loose. A thin lake of liquid coal had seeped out of the working cracks and puddles on the tank top, but it wasn't what Penrose had expected, or, rather, feared least. It wasn't the faulty weld under number three port ballast tank that had somehow cracked and flooded the cofferdam; it was the coal itself that was faulty. It was becoming liquid.

Liquid cargo. And the cargo was *shifting*. No wonder there hadn't been much dust on the decks.

There was a sound beside him. Henry was peering down the beam and his face was ghostly in the back-light.

"Oh, my God," he breathed.

Penrose forced down the feeling of sick horror, made himself think. If the bulkhead's uneven movement was any indication, it meant that only the lower part of the cargo had gone liquid, the part subject to maximum vibration and pressure. They still had a chance.

"Get a ladder."

Henry crawled forward and unfastened the inspection ladder from where it was tied to cables lashing the containers tight with bottle screws against the ship's movement. They levered it upright, fighting the wind, down the hole.

"Where are you going?"

"To replace the shoring timbers. To check if the rose box is clogged, in case we need to use the pumps. I could use your help with the timbers."

"But it's *moving*. It could go."

"It won't go, lad."

Penrose looked at Henry's features stretched shiny in fear and felt a sudden rush of affection for this kid.

"You look like you saw a fucking skeleton down the hold, lad," he said kindly. "It's only coal."

No answer.

"Well, I won't force you to come. At least shine the light so I can see."

But for all his brave posturing Penrose had to will himself to go down the rungs.

The cofferdam was twenty feet deep and pitch dark: all the lights were forward of the temporary bulkhead. The waves boomed and rushed, hollow, amplified by the steel compartment as by a drum box. The engine pounded. Steel plates worked and creaked, but through it Penrose could hear the sound of planks groaning in agony as 39,000 cubic meters of mineral three inches away tried to follow where gravity led.

Penrose took two of the shoring timbers. He wedged one between one of the planks—fucking hell, it was already *cracked*—and the engine-room bulkhead, and pounded it into place with the second timber.

His heart was beating like a jackhammer, and he was hyperventilating uncontrollably, as he always did in deep tunnels or on the rare occasions he had to worm his way into the ballast tanks. But this had never happened to him in his own cargo hold. As usual, the feeling brought with it flashes of his brother's face, and something too nameless to confront—(*the tunnel*, he thought. *Benjie—*)

17

A large bang caused him to shout. The third plank up from the deck had cracked, and a dribble of black vomit came out from the seams above and below it.

Something grabbed his shoulder, and he dropped the timber on his sea boot. "Yah!"

Henry shone the light at his face. The deck hand and Penrose looked at each other, two ghosts in black oilskins in a leaking steel coffin ten feet below the surface of the Channel.

Each drawn face acknowledged the other's fear.

"You really are an idiot," Penrose gasped. "Get the timbers."

The list worsened appreciably an hour later. Except for Tommy, they were all on the bridge, all wearing life vests, listening with their inner ears and they could feel the soggy shift. Again to port.

Penrose was at the wheel, using everything he knew as he steered to keep the ship's movement easy, but the wind had picked up and there was nothing he could do about the steadily increasing seas.

After sixty minutes of steering, he felt that each comber had its own personality, one a slab-sided hunk of black that the *Witch* handled like hitting a brick wall; another fancy, coming in with a curve, slapping the cheeks of the ship's bows and then twisting away unexpectedly so that the ship's entire bulk dropped as if a hole had opened in the ocean. And once in a while there'd be a monster, two waves in one that reared so high the crew looked *up* through the Kent Clearview screens at a dark curtain of water that shut out what light there was and fell on the ship's bows and cargo deck and all the way aft to saloon deck as if wanting to drink them clean out of existence.

Inside, the bridge was silent except for clicks from the echo sounder, a humming from the radar sets, whispers from the radio shack.

The cozy sounds of inboard measurements tried to ascribe rhythm and meaning to the increasing entropy of screaming wind and pounding sea outside, and failed.

Night had fallen without compromise.

The BBC now gave gale warnings for Sole and Plymouth, Portland and Wight.

When the list worsened, Penrose checked the chart and asked his mate to put out a "sécurité" alert on the radiotelephone notifying nearby traffic of their predicament as well as the Royal National Lifeboat Institution stations at Treg, Fowey and Lizard Point.

Treg was their home port. In a funny way the coincidence made their peril that much the starker.

RNLI acknowledged. A blip on the radar screen was the *Cambronne*, a French coastal tanker ten miles away, which offered to stand by should they need assistance.

Penrose accepted the offer as a matter of principle. His crew might need assistance, but he had not yet made the distinction between his own life and his ship's. His mind still weighed options: they could turn and run with the waves, but assuming they survived the violent rolling as the *Witch of Fraddam* came around 180 degrees, presenting its beam to the swells, they still would have only ten miles or two hours' worth of sea room, at which point they'd have to come around at maximum risk again.

At 1935 Penrose went alone with a fire axe to the cargo deck.

The waves had grown since his earlier visit: they were smashing high over the bulwarks now, so that even at their reduced speed of three knots the *Witch* was hitting waves every six or seven seconds, which no longer left enough time for the decks on each side of the hatch to shed their burden. Penrose timed the waves, then slid into the three feet of icy foam sluicing back and forth on the cargo deck, and immediately realized he wasn't going to make it across the six feet separating him from the hatch before the next wave hit. His sea boots filled, and it was all his thigh muscles could do to wade them against the rushing brine. Pushing as hard as he could, he managed to get one knee up on the hatch coaming. Then the *Witch* took another sea slightly on the starboard bow and a muscle of green-black water knocked him smoothly across the hatch cover, sliding across the slick tarpaulin, convinced he would wash right over the port side to his death, until he was folded violently over the container cables.

Winded, trembling, holding onto the taut cables to brace himself against the waves, he waited for some smaller seas before throwing open the hatch cover and wrestling the ladder through. The wind hurt his ears as he struggled, and water slapped him continuously, until he felt isolated in a private movie of salt and cold and numbing noise. Every piece of exposed flesh felt as if it had been whipped raw. And when he finally shut the cover above his head, the feeling of being buried alive returned to almost overpower him.

The coal slurry rose to the top of his sea boots. More planks had cracked, but none had broken yet, thanks to the shoring. He opened the fire and wash-down coupling, then, methodically, keeping dread battened down by force of will, holding the light with his left hand and the axe in his right he began to swing one-handed at the third lowest plank on the temporary bulkhead.

He was freezing, soaked, but sweat poured off his face. Five chops, ten, and the plank splintered lengthwise, then burst in two with a loud report.

"Fucking bloody hell!" Penrose yelled as liquid coal invaded his lamplight. Another plank burst open in a wash of slurry, muddy and stinking of bad eggs. The ooze was up to his knees. He stumbled backward and fell, dropping both light and axe. Total blackness. He had a quick vision of the bulkhead giving way to bury him in wet coal dust. Shouting, cursing without a break to dispel the image, he half swam, half slipped till he ran into the ladder. The slurry was up to his chest by the time he managed to climb out of its grasp.

When he got to the bridge he grabbed the engine-room intercom.

"Right, Tommy," he shouted, ignoring the rivulets of freezing slurry that were gritting his lips, stinging his eyes and pooling on the deck at his feet. "Flood it for five and then overboard discharge with the bilge suction." And almost as an afterthought: "Use the auxiliary pump; keep ballasting with the main."

Flooding with seawater would further liquefy the coal, reducing its chances of clogging the pump when the slurry was sucked overboard. It would take two days to get rid of the cargo this way. The pump surely would clog, but it was better than doing nothing.

They watched the seas get bigger. Penrose took over the wheel from Malinson, and at 1950 the lights of the *Cambronne* hove into sight. They could see waves breaking clean over the loaded tanker's waist as they made contact with the Frenchman over VHF.

At 2020 Tommy called up to say the auxiliary pump had clogged and overheated and the impeller was shot.

Penrose steered in silent concentration, watching the ocean slowly unwind its reserved power, looking at the waves rise and disintegrate on the *Witch*'s bows to be picked up by the wind and hurled at the whirling Clearview screens, hypnotized by the interplay of ship and sea and righting lever. It was becoming impossible to steer with precision—the lag between spinning the wheel, operating the gears and tensing the rudder chains was too great; the time it took the ship to answer when its rudder finally turned and bit was too long—but Penrose tried anyway, peering far ahead through the varying shades of black and white and green to discern what was coming at him and impose his own lead time, enough to choose an angle that would minimize the waves' impact. His hands blistered where he gripped the wheel, twirling it back and forth till the spokes blurred, sweating as he tried to hold off the inevitable. Every minute, every movement was a tension demanding release. At 2043 the ship hit a particularly large sea, pitched heavily, and took another five degrees to port. Everyone hung on. No one said anything.

Another wave, and the *Witch* dipped farther to port, hesitated for ten agonizing seconds, and suddenly whip-lashed violently to starboard through twenty degrees over the next wave, then snapped back to port with bulwarks and the lower main deck awash.

Brian and Malinson were thrown in a heap near the door. Penrose crashed into the radar set and hung on grimly, his nose streaming blood: it was impossible to stand on the steeply canting deck.

Charts and broken mugs, binoculars and pilot books littered the bridge's deck and a smashing noise from the radio shack meant the radiotelegraph had been ripped from its moorings.

A horrible gurgling noise rose from the ship's bowels, seeming to indicate this time it had settled for good.

Penrose managed to pull himself to the engine-room inter-com. Tommy Gowans answered on the first ring, and the captain felt a small glow of gratitude beneath the fear. He'd been standing by: the Geordie was a real seaman.

"Switch the bridge controls on and then come on up. *Now*, Tommy," he yelled.

"Piss off," came the reply.

"Get up here NOW, Tommy," Penrose insisted, then slid back to the wheel.

Brian was crawling over to the door.

"Not yet, damn you," Penrose shouted.

They all looked at the captain as if he'd gone mad, and Penrose felt the whites of his eyes showing and his teeth clamping, desperation taking control.

"Not yet," he repeated, almost to himself.

There was one chance left, so small it almost didn't exist—a chance that he could use the waves themselves to pound his cargo back to an even keel.

Penrose rung for half speed and spun the wheel hard to starboard. They were still heading into the wind but waves were soughing way up the port side of his cargo deck and the canted rudder had trouble biting. Then the diesel picked up and the ship began vibrating like a woman with fever.

Slowly, slowly the dark shape that was their tilted fo'c'sle began to come around. The vibration increased, pervaded. Broken crockery started clinking in period, and that sound—symbol of shattered order—bothered Penrose almost more than anything else.

Now the waves pounded directly on the port side, fragmenting into and over the angled bow, then, as they came around farther, the waves took over the cargo deck as if this were the chance they'd been waiting for, swamping the weather side, coming halfway up the whisky containers, foaming into the lee-side scuppers, trampling the ship down but doing nothing to shift the treacherous cargo from where it lay, fatally off balance, pressing the *Witch of Fraddam*'s port side into the sea.

And in this position they'd never get the lifeboat clear.

Penrose spun the wheel back to port. The ship was taking water somewhere—perhaps the windows on the saloon deck had smashed—and it was even slower to come around this time. The strain of a lopsided cargo, the weight of tons of water crashing every five seconds onto its main deck made the ship's movement sicker, more sluggish.

Tommy Gowans arrived half soaked and with a deep gash across his forehead, cursing furiously in his distress. Strain sewed seams around his grizzled face.

Penrose could feel the eyes of his crew trying to pry him from the wheel, but not one of them said a word.

The bow came head into the waves, and finally fell off a little as the wind raged at their starboard bow, the side that was tilted up.

Penrose still stood at the wheel after the *Witch* had steadied on the course he wanted. He watched the way his ship refused to ride, handling the waves as though she had already given up. The list was worsening steadily, but he had to force himself mentally to accept that she was finished.

Then he hit the engine "kill" toggle and dragged himself, hand over hand, to the VHF.

"*Cambronne, Cambronne,* this is the *Witch of Fraddam.*"

His voice came out loudly as vibration died. Then the screaming wind took over the background.

"*Weetch of Fradamme,* this ees the *Cambronne.*"

"Mayday, Mayday, Mayday," he said. "We are abandoning ship. Please stand by to pick us up."

Brian, Malinson, and Tommy pulled themselves off the deck and crawled aft for the lifeboat.

Penrose got to the chart room, grabbed the briefcase and stuffed the log and the most important ship's papers in it. He remembered to break the glass and take the ship's certificate of registry. Then he switched on all the deck lights and searchlights. After a brief hesitation he flicked on the two red masthead lights that signified the ship was "not under command." Then he hesitated again, feeling a strange temptation to remain on his bridge and not worry about the cold and shame and effort of saving himself while losing the *Witch*. It would be a quick death. He imagined dark waters creeping toward his nostrils, covering his face

Henry was waiting for him in the chart-room companionway, hanging on as the *Witch of Fraddam* settled deeper, tilted farther.

"Get the fuck to the lifeboat!" Penrose yelled. It was no time for heroics: the deck was now angled at thirty-five degrees and waves exulted over the port bridge wing. They scrambled aft, clambering against walls, and almost fell out the port companionway.

From the stern railing of the saloon deck it looked like they were sitting in a roller coaster as each mountain of water appeared from under their disabled ship. The *Witch of Fraddam*'s waterlogged bulks lifted and subsided sluggishly, but the lifeboat bounced crazily in relation to the ship, one minute bobbing at deck level as a wave came by, then dropping like an elevator until it hung suspended from its rope falls ten feet below as the wave disappeared into wind-driven rain astern.

Brian and Tommy were already in the lifeboat, Malinson standing by the davits. Brian was doing his best to fend the boat off the ship, but if they didn't get away within seconds it would inevitably be pulled too close under the ship's counter and smashed by the following wave.

Penrose decided that he and Malinson would have to carry out the launching, then take their chances in one of the life rafts. Another wave almost knocked Henry off his feet, and Penrose yelled to him, "Get in the boat!" To the mate he shouted, "Lower away. We'll take the raft."

Malinson nodded, cranked the winch handle to lower the lifeboat, and gestured at Henry to wait by the rope falls.

In the boat Brian had knocked the pin from the aftermost fall and was trying to keep the craft from crashing into a deck railing or flagpole whenever a wave came under the counter.

Tommy slaved to start the tiny diesel. Malinson had chucked his useless spectacles and was trying to gauge the waves by feel instead of sight.

Henry hung onto the bridge-deck railing, waiting for the perfect conjunction as ship and boat came together in a reverse waterfall of spume.

There were life lines hanging from the davits into the lifeboat, but the angle of both davits and capsizing ship put them out of reach.

The lifeboat's diesel threw up a wisp of exhaust, stalled, fired, and ran.

"Come on lad, jump!" Malinson yelled in encouragement against the banshee wind.

Henry took it as an order.

He jumped too late, as a wave dropped the lifeboat from deck level, and fell ten feet. His legs missed the boat entirely, and he splashed straight into the widening gap between boat and ship, one arm hooking around the boat's gunwale. Brian tried to grab him but slipped and was knocked into the bilge. For a space of four seconds Henry struggled against his own sea boots, trying to climb out of a dripping cave formed by the ship's transom towering above him, a hole of bottom paint and barnacles, the top of the ship's massive rudder on one side and the frail lifeboat on the other. Then the cave disappeared as the ship smashed down on its lifeboat, crushing Henry between the two hulls.

When the lifeboat came back down, Henry Permuen had vanished in the black waters.

"Oh, Christ!" Penrose roared. "Get the boat away! Brian, get away and search for him!"

But Brian was leaning dangerously over the lifeboat's gunwale when ship and boat swung apart. Suddenly he loosened the belt on his life vest, ripped it off, climbed up by the forward falls and jumped into a huge roller to hang onto the looped ropes over the lifeboat's side.

"Brian!" Penrose yelled. "Get back on board." But the wind swallowed his words, and when the lifeboat fell off on a wave Brian ducked his head under and dived into the ice-cold water.

Malinson started to climb over the railing.

"Get back here!"

"The lifeboat's better," the mate began, but Penrose simultaneously jammed his briefcase behind a gooseneck vent, grapped the mate by the belt and hauled him inboard.

Then Malinson yelled, "There he is!" The deck hand's blond head had reappeared on the lifeboat's port side, away from the ship. He was alone. Brian appeared exhausted, and Tommy had to drag him into the boat.

"Get the boat away and search downwind," Penrose shouted. He thought about the force with which ship and lifeboat had come together over Henry, and felt sick to his stomach.

The nausea gave way to a sudden irrational longing to wake up: to treat everything that had happened in the past three hours as a child's nightmare, to forget the agony, to retreat into any fantasy he chose. But he was an adult, and the bad dreams came when you were awake, and the cold would never let him be.

There was another lurch as the *Witch of Fraddam* embraced the sea.

Searchlights from the *Cambronne* played uselessly through the wrack. They were having trouble getting their own lifeboat into action.

Tommy fumbled with the second falls release, but with Brian's help knocked it free. The lifeboat was clear, yet too low on one wave and too far on the next for Penrose and Malinson to jump aboard. Tommy tried to bring the boat around, but the tiny diesel could not push the boat's bow against the elements. Brian was bailing furiously to keep the boat from being swamped. Large waves surfed the boat downwind, and within a minute they were lost from sight.

Alone.

Malinson materialized by Penrose's side where he stood at the half-submerged railing of the saloon deck, wedged against the almost perpendicular angle of the deck plates, pushing back against the waves as he quartered the night for his vanished deck hand. There was a huge crash of falling crockery from the galley porthole as Malinson yelled through chattering teeth into the captain's ear.

"They're away. Come on."

"I'm not going yet."

"It's over, John."

The ship lurched deeper, as if in agreement. "Henry!" Penrose yelled, desperately, but the waves were empty of anything alive, and the wind broke his words and dispersed the fragments.

The *Witch* was lying completely on her side now. Waves smashed on her bottom, sending heavy blankets of spray over the starboard side. Malinson lifted the inflatable life raft from its cradle, grabbing its safety line with one hand. Penrose finally gave up the hopeless search, retrieved his briefcase and helped Malinson throw the casing over the rail. The mate jerked the lanyard, and the raft inflated with a hiss. He held onto the lanyard as the wind tried to make off with their raft and Penrose hesitated.

Then the *Witch* began to move. Faster and faster she turned turtle, and they both had to enter the dark waters. The cold was mind-numbing, near fatal. They swam desperately to clear the lowering superstructure, diving blind into a welter of spume as the waves dragged them close to the prop, then shot them skyward to knock their heads into railings and ventilators two decks up. Penrose felt his left foot tangle in a line from the loose falls of the lifeboat davits, and for a brief, panicked second, he was dragged under before he could pull the rope off with his free hand. He surfaced miraculously clear of the ship, in a valley between two waves, right next to Malinson, who had lost hold of the line connecting them to the raft. They thrashed on, their strength ebbing. The *Witch of Fraddam*'s huge brass propeller lifted half clear of the water, and its swinging rudder, eight feet tall, began smacking like cannon shells into the wave tops behind them.

Malinson finally caught up with the raft, but it took all of Penrose's reserves to swim the distance one-handed, crawl aboard, and collapse inside its nylon shell.

The *Cambronne* lost them as they drifted in the steep waves. Penrose jammed his torso through an opening in the raft's canopy and tried to rip the top off a distress flare with frozen fingers.

As he watched for any sign of Henry's body, he could see the *Cambronne*'s searchlights hunt for them, see the *Witch of Fraddam*'s deck lights wink out one by one as his ship completed her roll and the wind, howling its triumph, pushed their life raft northward toward land.

The first flare would not light, nor the second. Their caps were supposed to spark on phosphorus when cap and flare were rubbed together, but they had been soaked in the interior of the life raft, which was half awash. By the time the third crackled into life, reaming out their retinas with pink light, the *Cambronne* had vanished into the night.

Penrose closed the canopy, found the flashlight, and looked for the emergency drogue.

In the light he saw tears streaking down Malinson's jowls, matching his own.

When first light came they were weak from exposure. The wind had abated somewhat, but the waves were steeper, more vicious, indicating that the wind, which had shifted southerly, was pushing them into shallower waters. The water had changed color as well, become milky from the china clay deposits that extruded in cliffs along the coast of southwest Cornwall. A lee shore.

Penrose opened the canopy and half stood in the opening. He saw the rock immediately. He knew it by its huge size and anvil shape, by the tunnel that storms had carved in its eastern flank. He could hear it as well; the storm waves crashing into the tunnel made a weird juddering sound. It was as big as a three-story building and it had killed more Cornish fishing luggers than anyone cared to remember.

Merlyn Carn. They were being washed directly toward a set of rocks called Merlyn's Teeth leading southeast from the Carn. Penrose lit the last flare. They had a quarter mile and maybe twenty minutes before the breakers bounced them to

27

their deaths against the rock. There was nothing they or their sea anchor could do to prevent it.

But the juddering sound was too loud, too regular, increasing too fast to be waves. Penrose looked up and saw a yellow Wessex helicopter with RAF roundels and AIR SEA RESCUE stenciled on its side, hovering closer, then circling against the gale as if only to mark their position despite the mortal peril they were in.

Ten minutes later, and only two hundred yards from the first of Merlyn's Teeth, the Treg lifeboat came pounding out of a grimy dawn with its blue light flashing like it was Christmas.

V

The fire popped and hissed in the stove, turning the small whitewashed room into an oven, but the stinging smell of coal smoke only filled Penrose with revulsion as he and Malinson huddled in blankets by the chimney.

Men came and went, hanging up slickers, stowing rescue equipment, maroons, and Schermuly rockets in lockers against the wall, hanging life jackets among the confusion of tarred hemp and oars that festooned the rafters: RNLI volunteers going back to selling postcards or mending nets. Penrose had known some of them all his life. They gave him sympathetic nods and smiles whenever they looked toward his corner, but he noticed they avoided coming near him, as if afraid of contracting a communicable disease.

Rain slashed at the windows. Penrose felt like it had been raining forever.

The Treg lifeboat coxswain came in, a barrel-chested, red-bearded fisherman named Roger Toms. He uncorked a bottle with no label and topped up their tea mugs. The smell of Navy rum vied with coal fumes and the aroma of tar for hegemony. The rum won, by a nose.

"The RAF are still searching," he said, "but they'll not find him. With this cold water, he'll be on the bottom for a week or more, and the currents will take him to Sennen. I'm sorry, John," he added, seeing Penrose's expression, "but there it is."

Colin Lovell entered with the lifeboat mechanic.

"Caught a glimpse of the distress light on their raft but 'twere gone and reckoned 'twere only Jack Harry's lights, ghosts, like, 'cause of the wreck. 'Course I didn't believe that," he finished. "They'll be dropping off Gowans and Jeffreys with Dieppe pilots. It was on the radio."

Penrose did not answer. There was nothing to say, and despite the rum, his teeth were still chattering, which made talk difficult.

Colin, a square man who walked like a cube, swaying from corner to corner, sat down facing him. He had a right-angled jaw and shoulders, a nose drawn by a T square, warm gray eyes and thin white hair. He had owned and commanded the *Witch of Fraddam* for fifteen years. When Penrose left the Navy, Colin had trained him as an able seaman, mate and captain for seven, and at the end sold Penrose fifty out of sixty-four shares in his ship and stayed on to manage the shore side of their coasting company.

"Tell me again, John." The gray in his eyes always paled under stress.

"Why don't you f-fucking well leave me alone, Colin," Penrose said quietly. "I've already told you twice. It won't change anything."

"No, it won't change anything at this stage," Colin agreed. "But I would like to be sure who let a nineteen-year-old lad die, so I can tell his mother what happened to him. And I want to know just who killed my ship that I spent my life working for."

Beside them, Malinson had fallen asleep.

"I already told you. It was the colliery. They gave me the wrong coal slurry."

"But you said you tested it."

Their eyes fenced back and forth.

"You think it was me, don't you?" Penrose accused. "Maybe not directly, but you think you'd have saved the *Witch*. Well, I told you I tested it, but the coal went liquid. I don't know how it happened, but it was sloshing around the hold like water. The hold was filled to the coamings, but when that happens it subsides and it must have had hundreds of cubic feet of free surface movement."

"You hadn't put shifting boards in, then," Colin said with grim satisfaction.

"I had put shifting boards in, right up and down the keel line."

"Why couldn't you bring it into harbor?"

"Sod you, Colin! It was blowing force seven! The ship was listing just from going head to the bloody waves!"

"How did you know?"

Toms poked his head in the door, his face blank.

"It's Henry Permuen's father, on the telephone. He's been calling every half hour."

"I'll take it," Colin said.

"Like fuck you will," Penrose said. "It's my responsibility, I'll talk to him. But I won't talk to him over the telephone; it's not fair. I'll go and see them now."

"You could have ballasted her," Colin accused.

Malinson began to snore.

"I started to," Penrose said as he got to his feet, clutching the blanket around his bare chest, "but there wasn't time to finish."

On his way out of the station he tried to shake hands as he thanked the coxswain, but Toms only said, "Were normal," and gave him an embarrassed wave, keeping his own hands out of reach.

The Permuens lived in North Treg, on an unexceptional street of summer bungalows that marked their years by what's on telly and April in Alicante. Their bungalow was of ordinary brick, painted an ordinary cream, with their ordinary sedan parked by a prefabricated garage. The very anodyne quality of the scene, by contrast perhaps, imparted density to the tragedy that affected it now.

A bell played eight notes of "Colonel Bogey March," and the door was opened by a sagging, potbellied man with rough hands, a bald head, and eyes that came slightly alive when he saw them, until he took in the expression on their faces.

"Captain Penrose," he said softly. "Captain Lovell. Aye. You'd best come in."

But he stopped them in the hallway, next to a table stacked with old copies of *News of the World* and *Model Airplane Gazette*.

"He is gone, isn't he?" Despair leaked out of cracks in his whisper. "There's nothing. I mean, it's certain."

More than a question, it was a plea.

Penrose said, "I saw him go, Mr. Permuen."

The man only waited.

"He jumped for the lifeboat, and it swung out on a wave

just as he jumped. He thought the mate had told him to. He fell in but caught on to the side of the boat." Colin would have interrupted, but Henry's father stopped him with one raised finger.

Never, Penrose thought, had anyone listened half as intently to words he was forming.

"Then the ship hit the lifeboat; a wave knocked them together. It must have knocked him out cold. He just disappeared before anyone could do anything. He couldn't possibly have known."

Henry's father manufactured a trembling kind of smile, looking at Colin now.

"Ever since he was five, Mr. Lovell—I mean, Captain," he whispered. "We used to go down to the harbor Sundays. He didn't want to be a bricklayer like his old man; he wanted to be a captain. We used to watch your ship docking. She'll want to know," he said almost apologetically. "You'd better come in."

He left them alone in a living room with a gas fire and a large television that had color snapshots of Henry and his sister in Lucite frames on top of it. There was a three-foot model of a Hurricane fighter, with an antenna for remote control, hanging near the chimney, and Penrose had a sharp flash of Henry sitting on his bunk with a model-airplane catalogue on his knees.

Muffled noises seeped from a door, then a long wail. Penrose stood rigid, as if at attention. Colin gripped one large hand in another and squeezed.

Mrs. Permuen rushed in, a plump woman in a nylon bathrobe who trailed her grief like an obscene pet all over the living room, clutching at the rough jacket the RNLI had loaned Penrose, screaming, "Tell me my Henry has a chance, just a chance" as her husband patted her shoulder and tried to keep her bathrobe straps from slipping down while his eyes screamed louder than his wife. A wail of loneliness, tomorrow and forever.

She calmed down after a while, and Penrose took refuge in clichés, attempting to tell her of Henry's courage in coming into the hold with him. But the woman only looked at him with the ancient female messages that said courage and cowardice were disgusting irrelevancies in the face of intervening death. After a while they left.

When Penrose and Colin got back to Wheal Quay later that afternoon there was a Japanese car angled up alongside the decrepit countinghouse that contained the headquarters of Cornwall Shipping.

The wind had backed northerly, meaning the depression had shifted eastward, but it was still skittish enough to corrugate the upper reaches of Treg River and scramble dead leaves from the deciduous hills surrounding it. The clouds had lifted and it had gotten a bit colder, but Bodrugan the Farmer had not yet seen fit to bring in his heifers, which stood shivering in the lee of a ruined orchard uphill.

"Who is it?" Penrose asked.

Colin did not answer. He had not opened his mouth since they left the Permuens' house.

"The car, Colin," Penrose repeated. "Whose is it?"

"The notary's. If it was the cargo that was at fault, we have to make a protest to the Board of Trade."

"I'm aware of that. I'm also aware of the fact that I have another twenty-four hours to do it."

"I don't suppose," Colin said in his heavy voice, "you noted the coal was dangerous on the bill of lading?"

Penrose sighed. He looked away, at the old Georgian countinghouse, with its long warped windows and oaken doors, at the huge stone quay that once had served a tin mine and that now held only the old Baltic trading ketch he lived on when he wasn't aboard his coaster. How gingerly they had brought the *Witch* up here on top of the tide when there were repairs to do or when they were between cargoes and wanted to avoid docking fees.

So empty now.

Penrose took the sodden briefcase with his ship's papers from the rear seat and got out of Colin's car.

"You can tell the notary I'll see him tomorrow. I'm going to sleep."

Penrose turned and strode off as best he could in pants two sizes too small for him.

Colin Lovell stared after him even when Penrose had disappeared through the hatchway of his boat. He got out of his car and started to walk toward the quayside, then stopped.

"Ah, wishness," he muttered, surprising himself with the

old West Country expression for utter melancholy his mother had always used.

He was sixty-one years old and suddenly felt every minute. He turned and went into the countinghouse.

The *Witch of Fraddam* was shining by the quayside. Penrose could not remember when they had repainted her, but she looked wonderful. He climbed up to the chart room and checked their dead-reckoning position. When he tried to go out the bridge wings, he found the doors had locked.

"You'd better come in," Henry Permuen said.

He had appeared out of nowhere and now stood next to Penrose, looking ill: Henry's face was purple, his stomach seemed bloated and his tongue protruded black between his teeth. Liquid coal began spewing through ventilation gratings, flooding the bridge to their knees, to their necks.

"I'll thee you in Thennen," Henry said, lisping around his swollen tongue. The radar's collision alarm began jangling as water covered Penrose's head. He cried out and woke up.

For a minute he thought the sick feeling was all nightmare, then he remembered, and sadness covered him like seawater in the dream.

The *Witch* had gone, and Henry Permuen with it. He was on the *Salope,* and something was ringing.

It had taken many hours and most of a bottle of cognac to find sleep, and now the telephone was waking him at 3:30 in the morning.

"Hallo."

"John?"

There was a fuzz of music and laughter in the background. It took him less than a second to recognize that intense throatiness.

"Selina?"

"John. Oh, hang on." He heard the phone receiver being muffled and, very distinctly, Selina saying, "Oh, do piss off, Quentin."

"John"—she came back bright and cheerful—"thank God! You are all right?"

"Yes. How did you know?" Penrose asked, stretching the phone cord back toward his bunk. The stove had gone out, as usual, and he was freezing in the sweat-sodden RNLI survivors' gear.

34

"It was on the Beeb, about the *Witch of Fraddam*. And I called Treg lifeboat station. John, I am sorry about that boy. And your ship."

"Yes, so am I."

"Please don't go cold on me," said Penrose's wife.

"I'm sorry, Selina. It's only—I haven't talked to you in almost three months."

"Yes, I know. I've missed you." There were whoops in the background, the pop of a champagne cork, and she muffled the phone again, briefly. "Anyway, I wanted to tell you how sorry I was and ask you— *Damn* you, Quentin!— Sorry—"

"Why don't you call me in the morning."

"I shan't be awake," she said candidly. "I wanted to ask you to come up and stay with us in London, now you—now that—"

"Now that I've lost my ship," he finished for her.

"Well, yes. Surely you could use some time to sort things out? Daddy's been asking about you, and I'd love to see you, you bastard. I haven't seen you for ages."

"Aren't you living with whatsisname, the opera singer?"

"Alex? Oh, God, no, that was ages ago. He was beginning to put on arias—" She chuckled. "Sorry. Anyway, no; I'm home again, at Priory. Daddy's fixing the mews place for me but it won't be finished for weeks. There's scads of room, though, and you're welcome, you know."

"It's awfully nice of you, Selina," he began.

"No, John. Wait. Please think it over. I really do want to see you. You can leave when you like."

"I'll be in London next week actually," he admitted. "After the memorial service. Colin and I have to file the insurance claim, get an advance on it so we can pay the men. But it would be for only five or six days."

"Oh, super," Selina said. "You can rest for weeks, all you like, and I promise I'll put a leash on my social life. I must go; tell me when you're coming."

As he tried to go back to sleep, Penrose found himself wondering who Quentin was. He was still wide awake three and a half hours later, when the telephone rang again.

"Yes," he said, expecting Selina.

All he could hear was the long-distance illusion of wind rattling hundreds of miles of phone lines.

"Hello?" he repeated.

"Is this Cornwall Shipping?"

"Yes," Penrose answered. The *Salope*'s phone was really only an extension from the countinghouse. "What—"

"You own the cargo ship the *Witch of Fraddam?*"

Penrose stiffened. The *r*'s in cargo and *Fraddam* had the characteristic, almost Gaelic, roll of a native Welsh speaker.

"Who is this?"

"Never mind who is this. I just wanted to tell the captain"—now Penrose could discern the Gaelic singsong—"that we're sorry about his ship and the man—"

There were rapid "pips" as post office circuits requested more money for the pay phone, the dead air of ten-penny pieces being shoved in the machine.

"Someone here put a tip of wet slurry in your coaster. Not the one that was tested," the voice continued. "On purpose. Are you still there?"

"I'm still here," Penrose muttered, feeling sick again.

"It was the captain's fault, look you, because he had it off with one of the married women, but we wanted to tell you most of us at the colliery didn't know about the wet slurry."

"Who did it?" Penrose said. The nausea had gone: his stomach now was hollow with horror and fury.

"Who did it?" Penrose insisted.

"It was the brother of the man who's married to the woman your captain spent the night with."

It took awhile for Penrose to unwind the Biblical genealogy but at last he breathed, "The foreman. His name was Morgan."

There was a pause at the other end this time. Then the voice said, "So it's you, the captain."

"The foreman did it. It's unbelievable."

"No one here will ever say anything," the voice warned, "not in the court. We just wanted to say we had nought to do with it—"

"For God's sake," Penrose burst out, "you have to! He killed a man with that slurry!"

"Understand we had nought to do with it, and even Morgan did not want a man to die."

"Listen—"

"T'will teach you to keep your organ out of Morgans in Glamorgan, Captain Penrose."

"Listen," Penrose repeated urgently, "I just want to know," but the line went dead in his ear.

"Fucking hell!" He threw the receiver across the cabin.

It flew like kismet toward a black-and-white picture of the *Witch of Fraddam* butting through waves above his bookshelf, and cracked the glass straight across the water line.

VI

~~~~~~~~~~~~~~~~~~~~~~~~~~~~~~~~~

But revenge is so *vieux jeu,* John," Selina Courtenay said as she knocked his ball ten feet into a jungle of pyracantha.

"Thanks very much, Selina." Penrose stuffed his briar full of Latakia and made a cave of his hands to light the pipe.

He hadn't expected croquet when he showed up this morning. It was only five degrees above freezing—Arctic conditions by London standards—but nothing would stop the ancient Courtenay tradition of playing croquet (Cornish rules) on Friday afternoons whenever it wasn't raining.

The other Courtenay ritual—dressing up to do so—only made Penrose feel that much more disoriented, as if he had been sent to two different time zones at once.

It had been only one week since he had seen his ship capsize and sink, two days since Henry Permuen's memorial service. The endless forms and insurance affidavits he had spent the day filing kept the tragedy bitter and cold in his mind, kept him from recalling this other world, where Courtenays dressed up and staged elaborate contests to re-create artificially the stresses of a life uninsulated by money or Debrett's.

They stood together in silence for a minute, an eighteenth-century highwayman and a Belle Epoque hostess, watching Sir Norman Courtenay in a nawab's robe and turban attempt the impossible feat of knocking his red croquet ball around a fountain, over a knoll, and through a hoop.

"Oh, I don't believe in revenge, in the absolute," Penrose said, sucking hard to get the pipe going. "Nor in the social sense, except in the context of much smaller societies—"

"Free Cornwall?" Selina said. She was laughing at him

again, using every wrinkle that thirty years had given to the corners of her eyes, letting her long blond hair trace arabesques in the wind.

Selina had fragile features that always reminded Penrose of strawberries and April rain. She had a wide mouth and large eyes; not quite beautiful, except when she smiled. The first time he had met her she was wearing a black gown and was fuming because a porter would not allow her to wear a matching veil into the examination hall.

Penrose had been sitting in the porter's lodge when she was escorted in, waiting to get approval for the long cutlass and sword belt he had donned over his own gown. He was in his final year of university, she in her first. They had been allies that morning, united against the dean, who doddered in to tell them that Selina's veil was inappropriate and that if Penrose insisted on wearing a sword, as the college's charter prescribed, then it would have to be an officer's dress rapier and not the bloody great proletarian saber with which he proposed to do his tripos.

Selina had protested, claiming that the results of her exams would justify the propriety of her veil. Penrose swore he was only trying to abide by the letter of college law, while his swordless colleagues flouted it, and in any case under the charter he was entitled to a glass of mead with his exam.

From this perspective it all seemed so unreal.

Quiet curses came from farther down the sodden garden; Selina's father had driven his ball behind a topiary. A Javanese peacock that had been using the yew for shelter strode off indignantly, fanning its tail.

"Your turn," Selina said.

Penrose pushed his way into the pyracantha, impaling his cape on a hundred thorns.

"Still," he said, "revenge has personal validity." He twisted himself low to get around a particularly nasty branch.

"It won't bring back your ship, or your crew."

"No—" Penrose admitted, mentally putting another turn on the tight control he had imposed on his grief when he arrived at Priory. Betraying uncooked emotions was not only considered in bad taste here, it was how you lost the complex games Sir Norman played.

With one hand and great care he maneuvered his mallet around a further series of thorns, braced himself, cranked up

39

a massive backswing and cracked the ball as hard as he could. It took off at speed, bounced into a marble plinth twenty feet away and came to rest next to the fountain.

"Damn," Penrose said. "Just what Norman's been waiting for. Damn," he repeated. "Selina, look, help; I'm under attack."

She still laughed with that catching lack of control, as if laughing were the last thing in the world she wanted to do but she simply could not help herself.

"Oh, John," she said, disentangling his cape and three-cornered hat. "It's what you hate most. You've been berried alive. Sorry. Oh, you look like a skewered chicken." She failed to quell her giggles. "Oh, dear, and now your pride is wounded."

Penrose drew his sword and carved a swath out of his opponent. Three feet of thorns and orange berries bit the dust.

"Daddy will have your guts for garters, d'Artagnan."

"That's to be seen. We meet at dawn, just as your father has always wanted. Will you be my second?"

"What did you mean about revenge?"

"Oh, that." Penrose sheathed his sword and fumbled for matches. His pipe had gone out again. "Nothing, really. It's just that, in personal terms—the only ones that count—it's no good being abstract and philosophical. I'd be damming up communications within myself because I'm angry, and he would as well because he's guilty."

"You mean the foreman. In Freudian terms, he wants to be punished?"

"Exactly. His superego would demand it. Cathexis, you know. And yet I know I'm going to end up being abstract again, not doing anything because I believe Henry— Why are you looking at me like that?"

"Because I remember now why I left you. You're so pathetically cerebral, I can't *understand* why you became a sailor."

"But I thought I left *you.*"

She ignored him. "I meant what I said: I've missed you."

"Yes, I've wondered a bit about that," Penrose said noncommittally, looking at the skyline of London where it intruded among the bare branches of Priory.

The Courtenay manor was a former ducal hunting lodge, later converted into a priory. It had been built two centuries ago in what was then farm country between the Middlesex hamlets of Willesden and Kilburn. Its desultory mansion—part Regency, part baroque—and two acres of parkland contrasted strangely with the semidetached immigrant ghetto that had grown up around it.

A very tall, thin figure with a raven's features took his turn. James Hawkes, Sir Norman's friend and psychiatrist for Selina's brother, was, at his own insistence, the only exception to the dressing-up rule. Selina played again, then a chubby type Penrose's age, a man with a pudding face, paprika freckles and a truffle mustache—Tim Harewood. Then Sir Norman hit Penrose's ball and took his extra turn to knock that ball into a deep fountain.

"Sorry, Penrose."

"What did I tell you," Penrose commented to Selina.

They had Indian tea in the drawing room, seated on uncomfortable divans and dominated by an incredibly high ceiling encrusted with chandeliers. The walls were covered with peeling gold leaf and dead Courtenays peeling off canvas in gilt frames. Pramit, the butler, moved like Shiva, reluctantly offering sweetmeats. Only George Courtenay, pale and emaciated, made the effort of taking one before Pramit whipped the tray jealously out of reach.

"Do you feel any guilt over the death of your crew?" Hawkes asked by way of idle chatter.

Selina interjected, "I think John, as a disciple of the university school, would define guilt simply as a poorly framed question."

"No," Penrose said, "not always. Sometimes guilt is simply bad timing."

"Psychobabble," snorted the psychiatrist, who read all the latest journals and knew what he was talking about.

"I'm just being facetious," Penrose said. "In fact, the sinking was deliberate symbolic intercourse with the sea as mother. The ship was a male symbol, naturally, being longer than it was wide."

Hawkes curled his lip.

"Now, Penrose," Sir Norman interposed delightedly, in his best "hail-fellow" voice.

Selina's father had an actor's range and projection that went well with his big nose and jawline and full head of snowy hair poised like an avalanche about to fall. His eyes were pale, piercing. He had a habit of trying to pull off his

41

right ear lobe with the thumb and forefinger of his right hand, as he was doing at the moment.

"Now, James, you're not getting paid for this, you know."

Hawkes nodded and yawned nervously. Penrose wondered once again how the head shrinker had managed practically to live at Priory for years without realizing he was invited so that Sir Norman could laugh at him.

"I would think the Department of Transport would find out definitively what happened," Harewood said, pushing back his National Health wire rims to follow the butler's tray with his eyes.

Harewood was a well-known financial journalist and a frequent visitor to Courtenay's table as well as his press conferences. Penrose had known him vaguely for years—they had attended the university together, even belonging to the same food-and-wine society, without ever rising above the platitudes of acquaintance.

"I-i-i-it doesn't sound like J-John's fault," George said, pulling nervously at his jacket sleeves. Everyone ignored him.

Sir Norman put down his cup, walked over to the crackling fire and stood beneath a picture showing the Royal Indian Navy patrol-craft flotilla he had commanded during the war tearing hell for leather, Oerlikons blazing, toward a Japanese gun emplacement down the Kaladan River.

"Well, I did wonder, Penrose," he said, "what your plans are now that you've got the sea out of your system. You surprised us all—Selina especially, eh? But now that you've done your stint as the only Middle Trade master with a university degree—well?"

"Back to the bank, you mean?" Penrose answered. Selina glanced up from the small watercolor pad she always carried.

"I'm not sure my bank could have you back, my dear chap," Sir Norman said affably. "Hard times at Courtenay's, eh? And we've some liquidity problems with the shipping side. But you had a flair for it, you had a flair, and you certainly had the upbringing. Did you ever pay off the loan we gave you, incidentally?"

"I have another year and a half, as you know very well, but the hull insurance will cover it," Penrose said with a pleasant grin.

Sir Norman smiled back.

Penrose made some excuse about changing and taking Selina out to dinner.

"But you'll miss the gin game!" Sir Norman wailed in mock despair as they walked out, and Penrose felt his sorrow and rage almost—but not quite—breach the weary defenses he had erected.

They had a late dinner at Jarry's and said good night in the hall. Penrose found a birch fire crackling in his room, which was something he'd forgotten about Priory: Sir Norman insisted on personally building a fire in every hearth in every room whenever he was home. Selina's brother laughed regularly to himself upstairs. The old house breathed other memories he had kept at bay for too long, memories that mixed with recent losses and made sleep impossible. Finally he got up and tiptoed down to the costume closet.

Someone had reorganized the whole collection. There were new racks of clothes, labeled "American Indian" through "Zorro." There were even hangers of polyester slacks and jackets. He came across a papier-mâché bull's head and a suit of armor, as well as a donkey jacket and sea boots he must have left behind years ago, perhaps when he'd still been staying at Priory between voyages. At last he found the feathered hat and cloak he remembered, and the French alto sax, beat up and suffering from wonky notes but still with better tone than his own modern instrument. He remembered to disconnect both alarm systems before opening the flower-room door (slowly, so Aqbar, the night guard, would not hear the creaks) and padding through frost to Selina's wing.

> "He played again, both loud and shrill,
> and loudly he did sing,
> oh lady, this is thine own true love,
> no harper, but a king"

he intoned and followed it with a long saxophone improvisation on a theme by Purcell. There was no answer from her window: Penrose shifted knees and resumed singing.

> "The lady looked, the lady blushed,
> and blushed and looked again . . ."

43

He did a quick riff to keep his fingers from stiffening in the chill. He hoped she had not switched wings. He'd look like a real idiot serenading Sir Norman.

"And he hath thrown his harp—"

"Aaah!" A pitcherful of cold water landed with exquisite accuracy on his shoulders.

"Bloody hell, Selina," Penrose gasped, shaking the saxophone upside down to get the water out, "that's one hell of a way to encourage suitors," but the laughter from above, too bubbling, was infectious as always.

"You're lucky. In King Aster's day that would have been slops."

Penrose, busy wringing out his cloak, did not answer.

"Oh, come on up then," she said, still chuckling.

It was not till he had climbed into her fourposter that he remembered the conundrums of making love with Selina. He waited while she rolled up a ten-pound note to sniff a line of powder from a small mirror beside the bed, then she lay there, willing yet passive, alert yet introspective, breathing hard but motionless as he peeled off two layers of blankets to reveal one sheen of moonlight and another of fire glow on her skin. The Picabia above her mantel—distorted lovers, entwined—watched them in the shine. Her collection of antique cricket cages turned in the warm air, casting prison shadows on the ceiling.

The powerful affection he still felt for Selina mixed with the raw hunger her body always aroused in him and made him tremble with its strength. When he finally rolled on top of her and pushed himself gently between her legs she was shivering as hard as he was: her eyes were vacant, fixed on the ceiling above, but her fingers kneaded his back as she felt him clutch harder and harder until at last she whispered "Now!" and moaned twice, three times, pretending to come, as she always did, as if detonated by his own explosion.

They lay silently for a long time after.

Finally she said, "You know, I was afraid you'd forgotten how to laugh at yourself."

"Lost my sense of humor?"

"No," she said. "You fuck too well. It's such a ridiculous

position, it takes a good sense of humor: by laughing you accept your monkeyhood."

He'd always liked the way her mouth did a reverse curve when she smiled, antinomy made woman, but this time it only made him angry.

"I don't feel much like laughing these days, Selina. How often must I remind people I lost a man on that ship? A friend. Can't you imagine how that feels?"

"I know, and I understand that, John." She got up on one elbow, the smile gone. "But earlier, you became so serious about everything after the bank, committed to some great and grim destiny no one else could share, when you used to prefer laughing." She affected a thick Eliza Doolittle twang, "'avin' a barney 'n all, me ole colly—remember 'ow we met?"

"You have the cause and effect twisted, love," Penrose said. "I left the bank because I was sick of playing at everything, the great British amateur, muddling through Courtenay and Company and thinking it life."

"You didn't have to bank on it. Sorry. But if you'd stayed, you'd have become good at it, surely."

"No: I'm not a banker, and I didn't want to play games with your father any more." Penrose practically fell off the bed getting the pipe and lighter from his jacket.

"And that's what I am, isn't it?"

"What?"

"Don't play stupid. With my painting, you know, the great British amateur, all thick tweed skirts and shooting sticks and Windsor and Newton on the Hee-land Moors—"

"Yes." The pipe was tamped too tightly and refused to draw. Penrose threw it back among his ruffled clothes on the floor.

Selina rolled over to face the windows.

"You *are* a bastard, John."

"I've always said you could be a professional; you have the talent."

"If I stopped playing." She reached for her pad and watercolors on the bedside table but it was an automatic act, not symbolic.

"Not stopped: balanced it with single-mindedness, obsession, whatever it takes to finish anything."

"The kind of finish I could have found with you, is that it?"

45

"Maybe. I mean, come on, Selina, you're too talented to spend your whole life organizing anti-blood-sports events."

She still had her back to him.

"There's nothing wrong with fighting blood sports, but taking polish from you—now that would take some getting used to."

Penrose noticed she used the present tense, striking a chord with his own thoughts.

Getting back together with Selina would indeed take getting used to. The prospect went back and forth in his mind, shifting like wet cargo from contentedness to rottenness and back again as he thought about it.

He listened to Selina scrape at her *papier d'Arches* until he fell asleep.

──────────────

VII

Except for a brief preliminary hearing on the sinking at the Department of Transport offices in Plymouth, Penrose spent most of the following week in London.

The crew—what was left of them—were looking for jobs or resting at their respective homes. Colin was sending polite notes to creditors from Wheal Quay. There was little for Penrose to do, once he and Colin had filed the initial insurance report and all the affidavits, except telephone the underwriter every couple of days to ask if the advance on the *Witch of Fraddam*'s insurance had cleared yet.

On February 18, Penrose once again called de Laune and Court Underwriters Ltd., who held Cornwall Shipping's policy at Lloyd's of London. The receptionist put him on hold while she found Mr. Halpin, the assessor who was taking care of his policy.

Penrose had time to light his pipe and get it drawing quite well while he waited. If Halpin put him off yet again with excuses about affidavit confirmations and claim backlogs, he was going to speak with one of the partners. Colin had said these advances were supposed to be routine, and they desperately needed the money.

But Halpin made no excuses this time.

"Captain Penrose?"

"Yes."

"Sorry to keep you waiting."

"Yes. That's all right." Penrose forced himself to be civil, although Selina and her friends had dragged him into partaking of hashish along with champagne and lamb-and-mint

47

mousse at Jarry's and his head felt like it was smoked in heartburn and stomach fumes.

He became conscious of silence at the other end.

"What news of the advance, dear chap?" Penrose said, putting on his best "let-them-eat-brioche" voice and a heartiness he did not feel.

"I'm afraid I have some rather bad news about that," Halpin said.

"What do you mean, bad news? You can't give us an advance?"

"Well, not actually—"

"What, then?"

"There hasn't been a final determination."

The bells of Grace Church chimed rhythms in the telephonic background.

"Mr. Halpin," Penrose said formally, "please tell me, as succinctly as possible, exactly what is going on."

The insurance man coughed. There was the fizz of a match igniting, and he said, "I'm sorry, Captain Penrose, but Mr. de Laune told me this morning not to go through with the advance for the time being."

"Why on earth not?"

"Well, I believe there are some problems with your hull policy on the ship: as you know, we agreed, somewhat against industry practices, to handle forty-five percent of the value of the policy, so we are more than just a lead underwriter here, and—"

"But that policy was fully paid up."

"Yes, but we have to check these things very carefully, don't you see?"

"No," Penrose said in a voice as heavy as his stomach, "I don't see. What exactly is wrong with the policy?"

"I'm afraid—" Halpin coughed his embarrassment—"that I don't know exactly. Mr. de Laune is personally looking into claims now, and, ah—"

"Mr. de Laune is the senior partner?"

"Yes."

"Please tell Mr. de Laune that I'll be wanting to see him in half an hour," Penrose said and slammed the phone down over strangling noises from the receiver.

It was still rush hour, and Euston Road would be vehicular treacle, so Penrose left the car at Priory and took the Bakerloo Line to Bank station. He ordinarily avoided the tube—its deep confinement reacted with something equally buried in his psyche, and its smell of felt-tips made him want to throw up—but this time anger was antidote to the revulsion. It overloaded his gut to the exclusion of all else. It had not dissipated by the time he got to de Laune and Court's offices in King William Street.

Halpin was a nervous, pinch-nosed man of thirty-odd years who wore a school tie and a suit twice his age. He came up fussing seconds after the receptionist announced his visitor.

"I tried to tell you over the telephone. The partners are always in the Underwriting Room at this hour." Halpin took out one of his Embassy cigarettes and a cigar clipper and cut off an inch of rolled tobacco before lighting it. "Luckily I got hold of Mr. de Laune and he's agreed to see you in one of the conference rooms at eleven." His tone of voice indicated that a personal audience with the prime minister would have been easier to arrange. "We can go over there now and wait, if you like."

Penrose liked. On their way down Abchurch Lane, Halpin said, "You're lucky Mr. de Laune could see you. He treats your case very seriously of course. They're always quite busy. It's like a madhouse. It's quite inconvenient for him."

"Not half as inconvenient as it will be for me if you don't pay up," Penrose replied curtly.

He occasionally had passed the old Lloyd's building when he worked at Courtenay's, so he recognized the gray cathedral of actuaries, all bowed façades and arched windows that rose into drab, shut perspectives from its belt of alleys. He was not prepared for the new Lloyd's building—scheduled for completion in 1988—that soared beside it in the promiscuity only interstellar real estate prices could bring: a tall hybrid, ten stories of polymer cracker by Roman atrium, acres of pipes and glass that smacked of imperial ergonomics.

If the old Lloyd's architecture equated British insurance with the divine, the new proclaimed its triumph over the gods of man, whose acts had already been figured into averages by banked mainframes in the basement.

While the computers hummed under new tubes and lifts, the human business of Lloyd's continued next door. Halpin led Penrose into an imposing foyer of streaked marble that looked like Roquefort cheese. Men in top hats and felt cloaks moved among the scalloped lighting. The emergency wheel from a scrapped aircraft carrier hung at one end, a bank of service flags and wreaths at the other. Between them was a brass-mullioned view of what Halpin said was "the Room," the underwriting heart of Lloyd's, a huge airy compression of blues and grays and hustle, a world of five hundred varnished ships cracking on all paper sail in a tossing sea of college ties. The ships were desks, called "boxes." The largest unsupported roof in Europe—so Halpin said—hung like heaven over three thousand men in dark pin stripes like Halpin's.

In the middle of the room rose a pulpit where a high priest of insurance called names into a microphone. Above his head was the Lutine bell, salvaged from a bullion wreck and used for ringing out good news and bad. Penrose wondered if his *Witch of Fraddam* had rated the same single stroke that tolled the loss of such as the *Titanic,* but Halpin told him he had been there six years and heard it toll only once—for the Prince of Wales's son.

They met de Laune at eleven on the dot in a conference room like a Cunard liner's with portholes in its doors and anchors on its carpet and a glimpse of the drabness of Lime Street.

De Laune was pin-striped, overweight and extremely tall—six foot four at least, Penrose thought. He had shaggy eyebrows and sagging lips, and looked like he drank too much and didn't care who knew it because he was richer than most and sharper than the rest. They disliked each other on sight.

"You're the captain of the *Witch of Fraddam?*"

De Laune surveyed Penrose's flannel suit, university tie and Italian shoes. "You don't look it, but perhaps that explains it." The underwriter tossed a sheaf of papers on the table.

"Explains what?" Penrose asked politely.

"Explains the circumstances of the sinking. Why we can't honor your claim, you see."

So it was true, Penrose thought, and suppressed a surge of despair.

"Halpin told me you'd not made a final determination."

"Well, no, of course not." De Laune sat down heavily, looked at his watch and got up again. "I've really got very little time. We're writing a very complex slip on LNG

50

carriers right now, leading the cover actually, and frankly, my dear fellow, this is very small beer."

"It's rather an important brew to me," Penrose said levelly.

"Quite, quite. Do you have a copy of your policy?"

Penrose did.

"I assume," de Laune said, "that like most ship's masters you know very little about maritime insurance. Why isn't this being handled through a broker?"

Halpin said, "It originally went through our brokerage, until the new regulations."

"Ah, yes. The Fisher Act. What an infernal nuisance." De Laune looked at Penrose as if he were personally responsible, and sighed. "Let's run through this quickly, shall we? Look at your policy, Captain."

Penrose did so. He saw the Lloyd's anchor seal over the initials SG, the name the *Witch of Fraddam,* and the words "on hull, machinery, etc., value of £250,000 subject to conditions as attached."

"This is the traditional paragraph," Halpin put in helpfully, pointing to it.

> *Touching the Adventures and Perils which we the Assurers are contented to bear and to take upon us in this Voyage, they are, of the Seas, Men-of-War, Fire, Enemies, Pirates, Rovers, Thieves, Jettisons, Letters of Mart and Countermart, Suprisals, Takings at Sea, Arrests, Restraints and Detainments of all Kings, Princes and People of what Nations, Condition or Quality soever, Barratry of the Master and Mariners and of all other Perils, Losses and Misfortunes . . .*

"We did have a lot of trouble with Rovers actually," Penrose quipped, more for his own comfort than anyone else's amusement.

"Never mind that," de Laune said. "What we're interested in here are the Institute clauses." He grabbed Penrose's copy and flipped over sheets stapled to the back.

"Particular average clauses: deductibles, you'd call them, not applicable. General Average, sister ship, running down, here we are. *Inchmaree.* That's a good example.

"The *Inchmaree* clause is a negligence clause," de Laune continued, his thick finger stroking the fine print, "named

51

after a boiler accident in drydock on the steamer *Inchmaree* in—oh, never mind."

Halpin snipped another Embassy.

"It exempts the shipowner from even such things as gross negligence by the owner's agents, the ship's master and the ship's crew, but—" The underwriter paused for effect.

"But," Halpin put in dutifully. De Laune shot an annoyed glance at his subordinate.

"But," de Laune repeated, "there is an exception to the *Inchmaree* clause. Here. The exception, which is also implied in the standard insurance form, apart from Protection and Indemnity clauses like capture and seizure, is when damage or loss is due to lack of diligence on the part of the assured—in other words, the shipowner." De Laune's eyebrows reared in triumph.

"What's that got to do with my claim?" Penrose asked, and took out his pipe, lighter and tobacco pouch so he too could have something to play with.

The senior partner sniffed in disgust. "You don't see? The exceptional aspect of the *Witch of Fraddam* policy is that you are both the ship's master and the owner of record. You, not Cornwall Shipping."

"I understand that," Penrose said in a soft voice. "There was no need to set up a limited company when I bought the ship. What I don't understand is where negligence comes in."

"Negligence comes with the way you are dressed, old fellow," de Laune said smoothly.

"I beg your pardon?"

"You don't dress like a ship's master, and you didn't act like one when you loaded the faulty coal that sank this ship."

Penrose's shocked surprise gave way to anger. His hands began trembling, so he put away his pipe and jammed them in his pockets.

"I supervised the testing of that coal dust. It was the colliery that got the tips wrong. Halpin here told me two days ago you got copies of affidavits from the ship's agent in Swansea, as well as the colliery manager, saying that I supervised the testing."

"You tested only the coal."

"What do you mean?"

"Was that the whole process?"

"Was what the whole process? The whole process of what?" Penrose said in swelling impatience.

"You know what I mean. The process of loading."

"You mean the testing? Of course not."

"There you have it," de Laune replied, staring at his watch. "We called the colliery, of course. You should have supervised the whole operation, not only the testing but also the choice of coal, the cranes, the conveyors, the hoppers, the loading, Mr. Penrose, the loading."

"But that's ridiculous!" Penrose cried. "No—"

"Not at all." De Laune moved toward the door. Halpin gathered his papers and followed his leader.

"No shipping company in the world," Penrose insisted, "no maritime custom in the world, makes ship's officers responsible for dockside operations once the cargo's already been tested."

"That, Mr. Penrose," de Laune stated, as distant as if all this bored him silly, "is not our understanding."

They were clustered at the entrance now.

Halpin cleared his throat and avoided looking at de Laune, a signal that had more impact than its form indicated.

"Oh, Halpin, yes, all right." De Laune suddenly reversed his course and pushed between his assistant and Penrose back to the table. He turned for Halpin's papers, smacked them on the walnut and looked at his watch again, for effect.

"This is all taking far too much time. However, I must add that the reasons I have indicated are not ordinarily enough for a Lloyd's underwriter to refuse a claim. Just so you don't start bleating about that you've been hard done by, Penrose— No, you tell him, Halpin. Time you earned your wages."

De Laune hooked his thumbs in his waistcoat pockets, lifting himself to his tiptoes and down again, doing tendon exercises till his shoes squeaked.

Halpin, embarrassed, shuffled the papers, missed what he was looking for, groped for a cigarette, could not find the pack. Penrose remained immobile at the door. Halpin began.

"Normally, even if a ship's owner is at fault through error or negligence, assuming he does not, of course, have a long history of this, in which case he probably wouldn't be assured at Lloyd's anyway—normally, as I said, a Lloyd's underwriter would pay most or at least part of the claim anyway. That is because our—that is Lloyd's—reputation is built on integrity. We do our utmost at all times—"

"Get on with it, Halpin," de Laune growled from the window.

"Yes, Halpin, get on with it," Penrose agreed sarcastically, his fury growing again.

A touch of color came to Halpin's sallow cheeks. "Fine, then. I see you understand. Normally, we could have made some form of payment to you, despite your negligence. But, you see, you let your classification lapse." Halpin paused for effect.

Penrose froze.

Halpin looked at de Laune for reassurance, and de Laune did more tendon exercises. "Captain Penrose—" Halpin coughed and continued—"there is no record of your having renewed the *Witch of Fraddam*'s Lloyd's classification after she grounded in the Schelde. This is something no underwriter at Lloyd's can let by. It is too important."

"No," Penrose said.

"Pardon?"

"No. You're wrong."

"I'm sorry—it is the only way Lloyd's can be certain a ship is safe enough—"

"Absolutely not." Penrose threw his arms back, levered himself off the doorjamb, strode to the table and began leafing through Halpin's papers. "The classification *was* renewed. It was renewed by a Lloyd's agent in Port Garth. He issued a temporary certificate of seaworthiness. Late, but within the correct time." There were no classification documents in the stack of policy forms.

As he talked in a hard and certain voice, a soft and sickly doubt began spreading tendrils in his stomach: he had left the certificate on the *Witch* when she went down. But it wouldn't matter, couldn't matter. Surely the Welshman had done the paperwork. He would testify that the interim certificate had been issued, the weld inspected, the ship cleared for the London-Rotterdam voyage. It had to be a matter of paperwork delayed.

"Is that all," de Laune said with no question mark in his voice, swiveling and striding back toward the door. Halpin immediately took his papers from Penrose.

"No, that bloody well is not all," Penrose said, desperately moving sideways to block the door.

De Laune came to attention.

"Get out of my way, Mr. Penrose."

"This is, if anything, a matter of paperwork being mislaid or delayed. I am telling you my ship was cleared by a Lloyd's surveyor from Swansea before she left."

"Do you have any proof of this?" de Laune asked sharply.

"I didn't have time to take all the certificates off the *Witch* before she sank. The certificate of seaworthiness was in a locker on the bridge, I think. But the Lloyd's surveyor will have a record of it."

"There is no record, Mr. Penrose," Halpin interjected. "Not that you're lying, or anything, but without proof, it's too important."

"What the hell do you mean, no record? The Lloyd's surveyor—your surveyor—"

Again that quick glance of Halpin's.

"Together with your overall responsibility for the loss, it means that we cannot pay." De Laune was watching him with a yellow glint in his eyes.

"There's just no record," the younger man repeated smoothly.

"But—"

"There are avenues of appeal open to both you and the distiller, Henderson," de Laune added, moving toward the door again. "In the meantime, I have sent a note to the Department of Transport in Holborn advising an investigation to see whether you, an obvious amateur, are fit to command ships of British registry. I'm sorry." The underwriter finished with a smile that showed no regret whatsoever.

Penrose looked from one to the other, de Laune's eyes still off color, Halpin's now turned away, but the assistant had finally located his pack of cigarettes and had stuck one in his mouth uncircumcised, a sure sign of strain.

"What the hell is going on here?" Penrose said softly.

He stood totally still for two minutes after the Lloyd's men had left, his hands still jammed in his pockets, while his mind took in the enormity of their statements.

Then he left, to walk the halls of Lime Street blindly for half an hour, thinking the stigma of a possible DOT inquiry should not come close to the misery of losing a kid who had absconded into death with his friendship and trust, nor with

55

the absence of that compendium of forms and mechanics, of meshings you could trust and some you could not rely on that made up a whole far greater than the sum of its parts: a sailor's ship.

The woman, the only woman that had replaced Selina—

The insurance money would have scabbed over the hurt, enabling him to help Henry's parents financially, to buy another ship.

Penrose strode faster and faster, trying to coerce his brain into finding an immediate solution to the insurance problem, but no answers came.

Finally he went to find a telephone. He called the ship's agent in Swansea and got the number of the Lloyd's surveyor, but there was no reply at the surveyor's, then or anytime that day.

"It's a very complex business, actually," Timothy Harewood said, trying to chase nonexistent bits of red snapper around his empty plate.

The journalist lifted a hand and called, "Kypros! *Parakalo!* Another flask of that wonderful Samian, don't you think?"

The Cypriot slavered agreement around his single tooth and black *Andarte* mustache.

Harewood had a standing Friday-evening reservation at Kypros, a tiny establishment in Royal College Street that held only four tables, allowed no Turks and only a few aficionados, served what Kypros felt like serving and was booked solid three weeks in advance.

It was thirty hours since Penrose had talked with de Laune.

"And I'm not sure exactly what you want to find out," Harewood finished.

"I just need information," Penrose said, "to understand all this. The only fact I have is what I told you: their reason for denying my claim is absolutely ludicrous. Ask any ship's master."

"But there are channels of redress."

"Yes," Penrose agreed.

"There is the Supreme Council, and the Committee of Sixteen itself, of course, but also what is known as the Joint Hull Committee. And then there are the courts. More wine?"

"Colin has already told our solicitor." Penrose did not add that old Pengerswick, who had handled Cornwall Shipping's affairs for twenty years, was deaf and half-paralyzed from a stroke due to an excess of amontillado and only just fit enought to take care of their small-claims proceedings.

"I would think we could win the claim eventually," Penrose continued, with more confidence than he felt, "but the problem is now, the next three months. I have a legal as well as a moral obligation to pay the crew's wages for up to two months. I have to pay the deductible on compulsory insurance for Henry's, my crew member's—er—death. Then there is the warehouse lease and so forth. Why on earth don't they just pay up?" he ended, much louder than he'd meant to, but the room was crammed with people and noise and no one heard.

The *kefta* arrived. Harewood held beautifully manicured hands five inches from the dish as if he were praying.

"God," he said, "d'you recall the Cretan cook we once hired at Food and Wine? I thought he was quite good, actually, but the way Kypros handles herbs— It's an art, you know, incredibly subtle and difficult to get right."

Ten religious moments later Harewood sighed, adjusted his ascot and said, "Let me tell you what I know.

"Lloyd's," he began, "is a grouping of private, independent insurance underwriters, whose only connection is that they subscribe to a set of strict standards. The investors— they are called 'names'—whom they represent have to be recommended by at least two current members, and have to be worth at least a hundred thousand pounds personally or they can't invest at Lloyd's. Many of the underwriters are also 'names,' but the latest trend is for some names to get together and buy out control in an underwriting firm, which sort of reverses the traditional order of things.

"Let me see," he continued, subduing a belch and lighting a cheroot. "I suppose I should add that Lloyd's is very conservative and relatively expensive, which has hurt them on occasion: but because they have, since the seventeenth century, had a reputation of honoring legitimate claims, they are still the largest single insurance market in the world, and the absolute mecca for marine policies. Oddly enough, they first seduced (if that's the word) the American market during the great San Francisco earthquake: a lot of American firms refused to pay act-of-God claims, but Lloyd's paid. All this of course underlines how odd your own case appears. Although declassification, or outright fraud, is about the only thing that would keep them from making some form of payment."

There was a weak artificial beep. Harewood looked at his digital watch, took out a plastic bottle and washed down two small white pills with a generous draught of wine. "Heart," he explained, "congenital. The one deadline I never push." It sounded like a used joke.

"Where was I?" he went on. "Yes, the way they do insurance hasn't basically changed since they were a bunch of investors sitting around a coffee shop on Tower Street listening for news of overdue East Indiamen or whatnot. The brokers walk around the boxes, which are the booths from the old café, looking for the best deal they can find, negotiating with underwriters. The broker will prepare a policy slip, set out all the terms; then the underwriter will 'write' his firm's initials 'under' the policy. The initials are like code; you see the junior underwriters practicing them for hours. So the lead underwriter subscribes for whatever percentage. The broker then looks for more underwriters for the remaining percentage. The liveried chaps you saw today are still called 'waiters,' from Lloyd's' coffeehouse days. Quaint, eh? Americans love it: except that the slips they carry will likely deal with anything from software patents or jack-up oil rigs to Elizabeth Taylor's eyes.

"Most insurance policies, especially for large percentages, are reinsured, which means an underwriter passes on part of his risk to another, not necessarily at Lloyd's—spreads the losses in case of a claim. They had a problem with that recently, when some firms tried to make a lot of ready cash by reinsuring with a second firm they secretly owned. Gambling by any other name, against the law.

"And that's all I know," the journalist finished. "They've added a few new regulations, especially after the Alexander Howden affair: now it's conflict of interest if a broker and an underwriter are financially linked, and it's flat illegal to reinsure with yourself, as it were, but otherwise things roll on much as they did under King James."

"Why would an underwriter refuse to pay up?" Penrose asked, licking his fingers clean of thin Hymettus honey from the baklava Kypros served for dessert. "Wouldn't that be against his interests, in the long run?"

"Yes, if—" Harewood preened his spotless ascot.

"If what?"

"Well, look, John. Can I be candid?" The journalist's mustache twitched. "We were friends at university, eh? And I knew Alasdair Henderson, and I'm fond of Sir Norman, and I think Selina is super, but that doesn't mean you are not mistaken, or that you didn't make a mistake that could invalidate the insurance, and you are covering it up. It would be human, only too human. You don't mind my being frank?" He took another baklava, as if to sweeten his own honesty.

"No, of course not," Penrose said. "I'm not asking you to take me on trust. I don't even expect you to spend hours checking my story"—Harewood nodded agreement—"simply because we went to university together."

"Ah, university," Harewood said. "Speaking of which, do you remember Little John Douglas?"

"Sort of," Penrose replied, wondering if he could possibly be serious.

"Well, you know he works for the *Telegraph* now. Remember how he was always trying to chat up tall women? I was standing near him at El Vino's the other day and I saw him at it again. He was with Alison Tytler, who's a bloody Amazon about six feet tall, close to sixteen inches taller than he is. I actually heard him tell her, 'I would like to make love to you.' Do you know what she said in reply?"

"No."

"She said, 'Well, if you do and I find about it, I shall be very, very cross indeed.'"

"Yes," Penrose said, smiling a token smile.

There was silence for a minute.

"But, Tim," Penrose continued at length, as if he'd never been interrupted, "what I am relying on is your professional flair. You wouldn't be financial editor for Keighley and you'd never have unraveled that building-society funds thing if you didn't have it. I'm telling you there's got to be something wrong here. I give you my word on it, a source passing on a tip. Obviously if you do find out something, you'll be helping me."

Penrose wetted his throat with a sip of wine.

"I contacted you," he finished, "because it should be to your advantage as well as mine at least to check what is going on behind the scenes at de Laune and Court."

"No promises?"

"No promises," Penrose agreed.

Harewood sighed, and reached for another baklava. "I can't," he said regretfully, retracting his fingers, and Penrose realized he was talking about the pastry.

"I'll look into it," he said finally. "It's time I did another insurance story anyway, and I suppose there's a faint possibility this could be another reinsurance scam. You wouldn't believe the money that can be made that way—" He made a show of reaching for the check, but nodded in a satisfied manner when Penrose forestalled him.

"But you realize I'm doing this for Selina."

"Couldn't imagine a better cause, my dear chap," Penrose gushed, then reverted to his normal accent and said "I'd be very grateful. I mean that."

"Right then." Harewood got to his feet. "Are you going to Selina's thing at Jarry's?"

"I suppose so," Penrose said doubtfully.

"I'll see you then," Harewood said, and left Penrose to finish his wine and wonder if he would, in fact, be invited to the "thing" at Selina's favorite club.

It was the first he'd heard about it.

VIII

The club had the longest waiting list for membership of any in London. It took up three floors of a sparkling white Regency building in Mayfair. The building had been gutted to provide a feeling of great space, as well as a good setting for theater. Members sat at tables on three offset balconies, where they could order from one of the best wine lists outside White's, or sample dishes by Tony LeGascon, inventor of the Nouvelle Cuisine Anglaise, a hybrid of the underdone style of French cooking and recipes dating back to Elizabethan England: heavy emphasis on lamb, cheeses, savories, odd fish and light sauces.

The genius of Jarry's—and the source of its popularity—was to charge its strictly plutocratic clientele huge fees so it could then invite the elite of Europe's avant-garde at reduced rates, the only stipulation being that everyone wear evening dress. The result of this collision of opposed worlds was often satisfying, usually unique and seldom boring. Penrose reflected that nowhere else would you find a piranha industrialist in white tie and tails arguing with a four-foot-tall sculptress in a dress made of aluminum platelets. There were few places, for that matter, where you could find a table like his own: penguins in tails seated on a wrought-iron balcony, Scilly Island flowers bursting orange everywhere, all trying to resolve the great and British contradiction between empiricism and a university accent.

"But university," Harewood was saying, "was the one time when creativity and application could be evenly balanced."

George, high as a kite, pulled up his jacket sleeves, showing Harewood: "Look, no tracks!" Harewood, beginning to look tired, held up one finger to indicate he would talk to Penrose later.

Penrose harangued Sir Norman: "A linguistic free trade, a creole black market to circumvent the kind of imperialism you were defending"; Sir Norman responded: "Information had to be withheld in In-jah; it was the basis of power and accrued to the fittest." Hawkes, coughing, remarked, "Careful; your delusional system's showing," and looked concerned.

Through it all, Selina was in her element: chuckling, animated, rubies burning at her neck, laughing "The aim of existence is to prove God would be a surrealist were he still alive," which left Penrose feeling unaccountably miserable though he knew why she'd said it. Selina told the story of Paul Crével, who died of TB and opium on an abandoned submarine in Toulon, nursed by his princess-with-no-neck. Crével was the author of Selina's favorite book, a novel entitled *Feet in the Plate*.

Quentin, a handsome twenty-five-year-old with lavender hair and a video camera perched like a parrot on his shoulder, showed up halfway through the brochette de cerf. Selina forgot to introduce him until the length of their conversation made the omission rude.

"Penrose. You're the one—you were just shipwrecked, right? Selina told us all about it."

Penrose nodded, feeling his stomach tighten.

"Amazing, right?" Quentin bobbed his head sideways into the eyepiece of his camera. A brilliant light unit came on over the lens, and he filmed a ten-second shot of Penrose, panned to Selina and stayed there for half a minute, then lowered the camera to film her plate, which was, as usual, almost untouched.

"Quentin does video," Selina said brightly.

"Yes," Penrose agreed.

"Amazing experience that must have been."

"What?"

"That shipwreck, right?"

"Yes, I wouldn't have missed it for the world," Penrose said enthusiastically. "Having a man die gave it that much more, you know, impact, *cinéma-vérité*, to what was already a fantastic aesthetic experience."

The video artist only smiled and went off to talk to the band, but later Penrose saw him taking shots of their table from odd angles until the lights went out and the music came on.

The first set was a mix of Celtic instruments: harps, pipes and drums filtered through Moog synthesizers and accompanied by video takes flashed on different surfaces, even, sometimes, on people.

Sir Norman made some comment about the importance of omission in visual art, and Penrose slipped over next to Harewood's chair.

"Sorry to bother you, Tim. Did you have any luck with the insurance thing?"

"I've been meaning to call you," Harewood whispered back. "Did you know de Laune and Court is controlled by the same names who own Eastern Holdings and Godown in Hong Kong? In this case, not only do the names provide the money, they actually own the agency."

"Is it important?"

"Not really. It's public information, if you know where to look. I've found out something rather more interesting, but it's a bit complicated and I'm not sure how it affects you."

"Fantastic."

"We'll see. I'll know more in a day or two and give you a call then. What"—gesturing at the stage—"do you think of all this, eh?"

"I think," Penrose said, "that video is more interested in controlling emotions than explaining them." Harewood glanced at Quentin where he sat by the band and looked wise. Penrose returned to his seat.

Ten minutes into the set the band did an eerie piece introduced by howling pipes and barrages on drums, then harp and fiddle took over in a winding lyricism that Penrose found strangely attractive. There was a long segment of sea shots, waves pounding on cliffs, beaches and rocks, a sequence of storm surf, and, suddenly, flashing roughly between wave shots, Penrose's head looking up from his table at Jarry's.

"Selina," Penrose said through the darkness and set teeth.

"I know—Quentin." Always laughter in her voice. "He does the video for them. He has a computerized mixing box, calls it improvisational video. He has a tremendous—"

· "Did you know about this?" Hawkes interjected in an interested tone.

"Of course not. How could I? I told you, it's improvisation—"

The music came to an abrupt end. Sir Norman's voice came loud in the silence. "It reminds me of 'Bolivar':

"One by one the Lights came up, winked and let us by;
Mile by mile we waddled on, coal and fo'c'sle short;
Met a blow that laid us down, heard a bulkhead fly;
Left The Wolf behind us with a two-foot list to port . . .
Felt her hog and felt her sag—"

"I know the one, Courtenay," Penrose interrupted quietly. "You know, I don't need Kipling to describe it any more."

The lights came up bright.

"You've gone soft, Penrose," Sir Norman said with a grin. "Criticism, competition, needling, what? It's what distinguishes the men from the mice. You've become a claustrophobic little sea mouse, Penrose. You should come back to Courtenay's, London, the real world, eh? So we can see what you're made of. Things have opened up a bit, love to have you."

Penrose had to bite his lip to keep from replying in kind.

"Sorry," was all he said, looking at Selina, who was wearing her little "dare me" smile.

"Your funeral," Sir Norman said jovially. "Let's play gin."

It snowed the night after the party at Jarry's. Penrose stayed up late while Selina went off to visit friends in Chelsea. He walked through Priory Park, watching trees transform out of the sinewed strains of winter to become doorways into another place, a space of white vacuum where cold brought only comfort and nothing was hard any more.

The feeling of visiting another world suited Penrose's mood.

The ten days since he had learned of the insurance problem had been a stretch in limbo—between-worlds, where only loss was real—hoping for news from Harewood, or Lloyd's, where Colin and Pengerswick had filed a complaint, or for reaction to a suit Pengerswick had initiated in Plymouth. But the only word had been an abruptly polite form letter from the Department of Transport, Marine Safety Office, informing Capt. John Redmayne Penrose that an official inquiry into circumstances surrounding the loss of MV *Witch of Fraddam* was being set up and his presence would be requested at a hearing before HM Wreck Commissioners in Plymouth on a date to be announced, at which inquiry "the ship" would be entitled to representation by a qualified barrister.

Beyond the walls of Priory Park the snowstorm swirled yellow beneath street lamps, killing sound, bringing the illusion of death to semidetached streets.

The Welsh surveyor had left on his holiday, leaving no files on the *Witch of Fraddam* that his secretary could find, no forwarding address. The only tinge of hope had come last night, from Tim Harewood.

As he scuffed deepening powder with his city shoes, Penrose thought about his wife, who had become distant again, not laughing as much, claiming she was back in love with him, then bending over her watercolor pad for hours or at least till it was time to go to Jarry's or Tramp's or whatever avant-garde video performance her film friends had set up for her in Barnes or Putney or Fulham. He reflected that the problem of distance between them would be solved just as it had been last time and the time before that, by his going to sea. Penrose had written Everard's, Crescent, Ensign, London & Continental and a couple of other coasting companies, offering his services.

He received two letters back, stating that the firms in question were no longer in business, victim of too much bottom for too little cargo. But he sent more letters, because he needed to work, and because he had spent what little was left of his personal bank balance after paying one week of crew's wages trying to keep up with Selina. All of which had come to a head last night at Jarry's—

Unable to sleep, Penrose finished the night in the banquet-hall inglenook, watching the flames shift shadows indoors while the snowflakes rubbed them out beyond the leaded windows.

Selina skidded back in a borrowed car at breakfast-time, and it was she who answered the phone.

Her voice, dimly heard from the breakfast room, changed from cool polite to perplexed to shocked inside five phrases.

When she hung up, the rattle of plastic soaked into a well of silence that surrounded the breakfast table until she came to the door and leaned on the jamb, her face very pale and vulnerable.

"What is it, Selina?" Sir Norman asked.

Penrose suddenly felt a rush of protectiveness come through his anger, and wondered if he'd ever grow out of it.

"It's—Timothy," she said in a small voice. "He's dead. He died yesterday."

George dropped his fish knife. "Oh, shit!" he said, much too loudly.

"My God," Sir Norman said, his face for once devoid of any role playing.

"Tim Harewood?" Penrose asked stupidly.

Selina nodded, gulped. "They want one of us to come over to Islington. It seems—he didn't go out after Jarry's. We were the last to see him, to talk to him. Oh, poor Tim."

"How did it happen?" Penrose asked.

"His heart," Selina said. "He had a heart attack."

She came over and buried her head on Penrose's shoulder, and suddenly nothing was clear any more.

Timothy Harewood was lying face up on his kitchen floor. It was obvious that the journalist had not died peacefully.

One hand was frozen over his sternum, fingers clawing in a futile attempt to stifle the exploding pain that had taken over first his chest and then his consciousness.

He was fully dressed, with an apron tied over a cashmere cardigan, a French shirt and expensively cut slacks. The apron had little drawings of radishes printed all over it. His eyes bulged, staring up over the sink at a potholder that bore the words "No matter where I serve my guests, they seem to like my kitchen best." The rhyme was bad but even so it could not have accounted for the look of contorted horror on Harewood's face. His nostrils were wide, and his tongue stuck out of a mouth that screamed nothing should be allowed to hurt this much, nothing.

He had knocked over a shelf of spices in falling and lay surrounded by jars labeled "allspice" and "rosemary" and "star anise." His right hand still clutched the jar of fresh turmeric he must have been reaching for when the thrombosis struck.

The room froze in black-and-white still life as a flash went off, mimicking the stage effects of tragedy: eye sockets emptied, mouths grew into pits, reliefs became planes of shadow and blackness marred the perimeter. The police photographer picked up his tripod and bags and followed the police surgeon out to breakfast.

A recipe book on the counter lay opened to *"Mouclade."*

Selina folded like a light switching off, striking her head on the butcher block. Penrose wet a rag and sprinkled water over her forehead and sponged the small cut. A plainclothesman in a long black coat got up from checking her pulse.

"She'll be coming around in a few minutes, sir, I shouldn't wonder. And we don't need *him* any more." He stepped to the front door and muttered a few words to a constable standing outside.

"Did she really have to see this?" Sir Norman said when the detective came back, gesturing at the dead man and frowning his distaste. "I don't see why she came at all."

Three men dressed in white smocks entered with a collapsible aluminum stretcher and began trying to bend Harewood's arms. The kitchen lights played on the dead man's features, giving them an illusion of movement. A small plastic bag held what had been in Harewood's pockets: twenty pence, a felt-tip pen, and a length of waxed, mint-flavored dental floss.

"But she could tell us something you cannot," the detective said, uncapping a fountain pen with long, nervous fingers. "Women remain sensitive to messages men often shut off."

"What on earth would she be able to tell us?" Sir Norman said crossly. "Even if no one else saw him after we did. He was fine when we left him."

The policeman held up the pen like a flag of truce.

Detective Inspector Karyl Radetsky was in his late forties. He had a pronounced stoop, meek eyes and a thin nose that flared regularly, as if he were smelling rubbish, or perhaps his own breath, which was bad. He also had a hint of foreign intonation that clashed with the North London elements in his speech.

"All for the report, sir. Strictly routine I assure you. And the sooner we can all go home, the happier I'll be. I too have business to attend to."

"Surely a police photographer isn't routine," Sir Norman said, but Radetsky shook his head.

"How did you know to contact us?" Penrose asked, making a conscious effort to haul his eyes away from the ambulance men who were levering the corpse onto their stretcher as if it were a household implement. There was a squeal of escaping gas. They tied a label to the corpse's wrist, zipped plastic around the body and carried it out of the room.

"His calendar, sir," Radetsky answered, nodding toward the door at a large "Save the Baby Seals" calendar with a photograph of bloody clubs and pink fur. "Lady Selina Courtenay's party at Jarry's was the last entry. Now." Long fingers snapped a notebook open. He wrote down their respective names and addresses and formally asked them to describe their relationship with the dead man.

They both said, "Friend."

"Next of kin?"

"A sister. In Scotland. Outside Dundee, I think. Married. Can't remember the name," Sir Norman said.

"Not married was he, or divorced, sir?"

"No."

"What time did he leave the party on the night of February—"

"Hang on a second," Penrose interrupted. "Don't you need to know his age, profession, things like that?"

"I already have those, sir," Radetsky said. "From his union card and his national insurance forms."

"Then wouldn't you know he wasn't married?"

"Just checking, sir," Radetsky said in a level voice.

"You've been watching too much television," Penrose said.

"Let him get on with his job, Penrose," Sir Norman growled.

"Quite, sir. Did you," he asked Penrose, "know of his heart condition?"

Penrose nodded. "I'd forgotten about it— I think I remember now he had it when we were at university, but he mentioned it when we had dinner together recently. He was taking pills for it."

"It was congenital, I believe," Sir Norman added.

Radetsky wrote in silence.

"Look here," Sir Norman said, "could you tell us a few things?"

"What would that be, sir?" Radetsky had been watching telly, Penrose thought; he'd got the dialogue down pat.

"Well, when he died. Why he died. My word, he shouldn't have. Poor Harewood, those pills were supposed to—"

Radetsky sighed and buried his notebook deep in a long black overcoat that reached almost to his knees, took out a box of pastilles, popped one in his mouth and replaced the box. A smell of synthetic raspberry pushed against the aftertastes of mortality.

"It happens very frequently, sir," the detective said. He opened the refrigerator door and took out the small plastic bottle Penrose had last seen at Kypros.

"Digitalis glycoside. Very powerful pills. You take too many, or not enough, or forget twice in a row and the party's over. Such a small detail. Especially," he added, "after a wild party. Wild parties can create an intolerable strain on the heart, as you should know, sir."

Selina made a whimpering noise. Penrose kneeled down to hold her hand, and caught a quick glimpse of motion between her closed eyelids. He said, "But he was very conscientious about those pills."

"Yes," Radetsky said, meaning no. "The surgeon says he probably died yesterday evening, while making dinner, as you can see."

Selina mumbled something, then stirred. It was perfectly done.

"Now if you don't mind, I only have a few more questions and then we can all go about our business."

The questions droned on, as routine as the answers. Penrose suddenly felt far more alienated than he had in the snow of Priory Park. Colors swirled, mixed and enhanced by the fluorescent light: the canary yellow and Danish furniture and ultramodern chrome fixtures of Harewood's kitchen; the indigo mussels and white cream on the counter, beginning to smell; the crow black of Radetsky's coat, small black wires from a tape recorder hanging out of the pocket; the stark marbling of the snowy London street outside long windows; the piercing blue of Sir Norman's eyes and the pallor in his daughter's face. Sir Norman and Selina; Selina and Quentin. The memory of the night at Jarry's flooded back in all its bitterness, so that when Radetsky asked, "And what were your impressions of Mr. Harewood at

69

Jarry's?" he looked up at the policeman with something like shock in his eyes.

Selina "came round." Radetsky made her sit down and sip water as he asked her a few deadpan questions. Then he told them they could go. They filed gratefully past the huge Hockney print in the journalist's front hallway, but when Penrose hung back to question Radetsky further, the detective said, "I was just going to request that you stay, sir."

Outside, the ambulance had left deep blue tracks in the slush, and Sir Norman was brushing frost off the Bentley. A big spruce dominating the yard dripped melting snow on their necks.

"You coming, Penrose?"

"No," he called back. "I want to ask Mr. Radetsky a few more questions. I'll take a taxi."

Sir Norman hesitated, shrugged, nodded and drove off with Selina, who had retracted into her fur coat like a turtle.

"What," Radetsky said, "really went on at Jarry's, Mr. Penrose?"

And Penrose realized that what he had mistaken for vagueness in Radetsky's eyes was there to conceal a much harder substance.

"And you don't mind this sort of emotional aggression?" Radetsky asked curiously, putting his notebook away again when Penrose had finished.

"It's only verbs," Penrose replied. "And I know what lies at the root of it."

"Still." The inspector popped another pastille in his mouth, clicking it against his teeth as he spoke. "I would have thought that you, sir, a ship's master used to handling men, giving orders, would have—would perhaps—" The inspector let the sentence hang.

"Shown a little more backbone?" Penrose suggested.

"You must have your reasons, sir?"

"I have one good reason," Penrose said firmly, "but it's completely irrelevant to all this. Why are you so interested in what happened at Jarry's?"

"Routine paperwork, sir," Radetsky began, his bluff-constable's accent returning thicker, but Penrose said, "Rubbish. The only bearing these questions would have is if foul play were suspected." Penrose deliberately rounded the cliché's consonants.

70

"No, sir, but with journalists we always check carefully: you never know who might wish them harm."

"Rubbish," Penrose repeated. "This isn't Chile. Or Warsaw, for that matter. And I know the way you fellows operate: normally there'd be a uniformed constable here, not a detective and photographer. And you'd do your interviewing at the cop shop."

Radetsky looked at him for a while, expressionless.

"Would you mind stepping this way, sir?" he said at length.

The dining room was lined with flower prints. Sliding doors faced a small garden with a pint-sized hothouse, a stabile and picnic chairs, all mounded gray under snow. The table looked like a genuine Hepplewhite and closer inspection revealed it to be an excellent reproduction. Roses were dying in the middle of the table. Two places were set with bone china.

"Aha!" Penrose said in mock "Eureka" tones. "He was expecting a guest: the plot sickens."

"Yes, sir."

"But you said the daily found him this morning."

"Quite."

"So the guest—"

"Never showed up," Radetsky finished. His black notebook was out again.

"Unless he had set the places well in advance. You don't seriously suspect there was something odd about his death?"

"The surgeon said it was cardiac arrest," the detective answered. "Nothing odd about that. It is only that I dislike loose ends, like a Chopin prelude without its final chord." He sighed. "Frankly, I didn't ask for this job; the inspector put me on this because I wouldn't take a political, but I'm not going to skimp on it, for all of that. What did you discuss when you had dinner with Mr. Harewood ten days ago, sir?"

Penrose told him.

They went up to Harewood's study, which afforded an aerial view of the stabile and picnic chairs as well as gray shrouded gardens on either side. Across the alley two children in duffel coats were lobbing wet snowballs over surrounding walls.

The study was modern, with Formica tables and white bookcases and herbal prints. Everything was scrupulously clean, paper clips in a magnetized box, pens in a marmalade jar, a covered IBM typewriter and virgin paper stacked to one side. Radetsky looked through all the file cabinets and then the bookshelves, but though there were twenty or so folders labeled "Teledyne" and "Building Societies" and "Overseas Securities" and "British Steel," there was nothing even remotely connected with insurance.

A crash came from downstairs; an ice ball had gone through the hothouse. The children's faces held two *O*'s of horror, then disappeared.

Radetsky sighed, and did nothing.

"Time to pack all this up. You can go now, if you like, sir."

Penrose asked if he could call a taxi, but when it came he decided not to go to Priory after all.

He spent the rest of the morning walking Hampstead Heath, soaking his shoes and watching mothers drag children uphill on sleds, wondering why he felt so miserable about Harewood's demise. It wasn't just the way sudden death tore the wrapping paper from the short joke between sperm and worm; it was more than just the off-key manner of his going—

Later he saw *Un Chien Andalou* at the Everyman again, which didn't help his mood. He finished the evening back in Islington, drinking for shilling pieces at the King's Head. It was 11:45 when he got home to Priory and he had to ring to be let in: everybody was asleep, and he went to bed without seeing anyone but Aqbar.

The next morning Penrose woke to find Selina standing over his bed, bearing tired eyes and a tray of smoked oysters, coddled eggs, crumpets and coffee.

He sat up while she opened the curtains. Sunlight invaded the room, vibrating through icicles. The aroma of oysters and Kenyan roast went through the scent nerves and tickled his underlying memory centers; she used to bring him this breakfast in Cornwall.

Standing at the window with her back to him, she said, "I've been acting like a beast again, haven't I?"

Penrose mumbled through a bite of crumpet. Selina was in her contrite emotional mode, but for once he didn't feel like playing straight man. She came and sat on the counterpane.

"I can't stop thinking about Tim. It's so—unfair. I've never seen Daddy in such an ugly mood; he couldn't even finish the *Telegraph* crossword puzzle."

"There's a lot of it about," Penrose said neutrally, thinking about Henry Permuen again.

She gave him a long look. The high spot was back in her cheeks.

"You and him. You're both about as demonstrative as lizards." She looked away again. "Did you go visit the child when you were at Wheal Quay?"

He shook his head.

"I hate it when it snows and gets cold," she went on, drawing up her knees and hugging them. "I think she'll be cold, and lonely—I know it's irrational."

"She's dead, love," Penrose said, meaning more than the simple fact.

"And I'm alive, as you've so often told me. There's a letter for you."

She handed him an envelope. It was postmarked Treg and addressed in Colin's copperplate but enclosed a second envelope, from Henderson Distilleries, Ltd., of Aultguish, in Ross and Cromarty.

Dear John:

Thank you for your telephone call of February 2.

I'm sorry to have to give you this news, but I must tell you my uncle, James Henderson, will be filing suit against you should the Lloyd's underwriters de Laune and Court not reverse their position on your insurance claim within the week.

This is a poor sort of return for your Mr. Lovell's taking out insurance on our cargo containers, but it appears, due to the rushed circumstances of the Yokohama contract, that Cornwall Shipping is the assured in name, and therefore the claim is invalid on the same grounds as the insurance on your ship. Or so I was told by a Mr. Halpin when we telephoned him subsequent to your letter.

Unfortunately, there is no hope of salvage, despite Mr. Lovell's suggestion: although I understand it might be technically feasible, we must assume that the whisky will be tainted, because the oak cases it was contained in were ancient and built to withstand pressure from within, not from without, as would be the case at the bottom of the English Channel.

The high amount of my uncle's claim takes into account not only the three million pounds the whisky was assured for (as you know, it was the very oldest and best of our reserves), but also the estimated loss to my uncle's distillery from losing the Japanese contract. Because of the cargo's value, it was a condition of the contract that the whisky not come under the normal terms for deck cargo. Your ship's agent in Aberdeen agreed to this (he must have known you were assured) but again, under the standard Baltic Conference charter form, this makes Cornwall Shipping liable.

Once more, I am sorry about all this, but I too have

74

*a personal stake in the loss: as a result of my recom-
mending your ship, my uncle will be removing me from
the board and the distillery will be sold out of the
family at his death.*

Sincerely, Alasdair Henderson

Underneath, in Colin's hand, was a terse "Copy to
Pengerswick."

"What's the matter, John?" Selina asked. "You've gone
quite pale."

Penrose handed Selina the letter.

"He's suing you for thirteen million?"

"Yes."

"Blimey, that *was* good whisky!"

"Yes. Apparently it doesn't come under the normal deck
cargo terms, which is always freight owner's responsibility.
There was some kind of balls-up." Then Selina's words sank
in. "Bloody hell," he breathed. "Thirteen million pounds."

"Poor John. What will you do?"

"I've no idea," he said aloud, but thought he would have
to use his anger; with his back to the wall, he had no choice
in any case.

"Yes, I do," he added. "I'm going to find out if there's
some other reason why de Laune and Court aren't paying
me."

Selina looked up with a half-smile.

"Well," Penrose said defensively, "Harewood said he had
found something. For a start."

"I'd say your plans have been scotched. Sorry. And then
what?"

Penrose poured more coffee. "I don't know. It might
come in handy when this all gets to court, if it ever gets to
court—but I've got to do something while I'm waiting or I'll
end up like your brother."

"John—damn you—that's unfair." Her eyes collected liquid refractions.

"Oh, hell, I'm sorry, Selina, I'm sorry," Penrose said
unhappily, putting his arms around her.

The tray slid off his bed, spilling breakfast all over the
Shiraz.

The offices of Harewood's newspaper occupied all of a massive brown block, eight floors of lib-lab architecture. A tall sign spelled the paper's name to Fleet Street in five-foot letters: THE EVENING.

Penrose followed a stream of people swinging through massive doors with handles shaped like mermaids. He asked for the managing editor's office.

He didn't have an appointment but when he mentioned Harewood's name the editorial secretary said she'd get him past the guard.

"Shocking thing," she whispered as they stood in a crowded elevator. "So young and all, and so—" she searched for the word while patting dyed hair—"committed, you know."

Penrose waited in the bright newsroom, watching men and women in shirt sleeves rush around ignoring him. The snicking of video display terminals filled the air. People ate sausage rolls and drank coffee by a rack filled with copies of every newspaper in Britain. Another corner was covered with scaffolding and canvas. The general impression was of lateral febrility: different efforts scattered over a low, wide area and all coming together only in the layout room downstairs.

A tall, skinny, stooped man with eyes whose intelligence was only partially masked by a very loud tie and spectacles came over to the secretary's desk and spotted him.

"Mr. Penrose?" They shook hands. "I'm Allan Clift. Managing editor, they say. Time restricted to a minute or two." He lit a cigarette, shoved it to the left side of his mouth and forgot all about it. Energy burned off him visibly like haze in sunshine. "Friend of Tim Harewood's?" he asked.

Penrose explained how he'd known the journalist.

"People cited trouble in reaching Tim," Clift commented, "much effort involved, but worth it. Bloody good journalist; never missed a deadline. We'll miss him. Feel angry at death. Silly, isn't it?"

They observed a silence due the dead.

"Martha noted your interest in Tim's current stories," Clift continued.

"It wasn't a story as yet," Penrose answered, wondering what struck him as being so familiar about Clift's way of speaking. "I'd given him a tip on a Lloyd's underwriter."

"Ah, the Lloyd's Affair," Clift nodded.

"You know about it?"

"No. Recall insurance led list of potential stories: colleagues knew he was working on it. Let's go to my office."

"I saw him the night before he died and he said he'd found out something interesting," Penrose said when Clift had closed the door. He summarized the de Laune and Court problem in snatches, as people barged in and out to talk with the editor.

"And you seek a lead on insurance problems related to sinking," Clift said when he'd finished. "Newspaper's not a research agency, you know." He lit another cigarette, and remembered to take the crisping filter out of the corner of his mouth before replacing it with a freshly lit one. "Cigarette? No? Small harm in looking," Clift said, and Penrose suddenly exclaimed, "Got it!"

"Got what?" Clift looked nonplussed.

"Sorry, but it's the way you talk—it's in *Evening* headlines."

"Damn it!" The editor smacked his left fist into his right palm, but it was an act: he was not really surprised, or even embarrassed. "Doing it again. Can't stop myself. Sorry." He grinned, unsorrowful. "Let's look in Tim's office— Right, Gerald, conference to be held in five minutes— Then I've got to go."

Harewood's glass-enclosed cubicle at the *Evening* was as neat and modern as his office at home. It had a six-foot-long tray of potted plants under an ultraviolet light, which a teary secretary came and switched on as soon as Clift unlocked the door. The soundproofed walls were lined with shelves that groaned under *Economist Intelligence Reports* and Her Majesty's Stationery Office statistics and files crammed with story folders, but the dozen labels having anything to do with insurance or Lloyd's concerned stories about Iran-Iraq War (profits), computer leasing (losses), LNG (ships), the new Lloyd's Act and Alexander Howden.

"No link suggested with 'Goldfinger' Posgate?" Clift asked, then said, "Damn. Sorry." He started again. "Tim didn't say this affair might in any way be related with the underwriter Ian Posgate, a.k.a. 'Goldfinger,' or Alexander Howden? Or Alexander and Alexander of New York?"

Penrose shook his head. "He only mentioned Howden as one of the last things he'd done."

"Well." They went out, and Clift locked up. "And nothing

found in his office at home. As you can see"—he gestured at the scaffolding in the corner—"we had a fire here a couple of days ago, small blaze, little damage, but those were back issues only, no personal lockers affected."

A handsome woman in a tweed coat shouted, "Allan!"

"Coming," Clift replied, and said, "Sorry, really have to go now. I'll see you at the funeral?"

He showed Penrose to the elevators and disappeared into a conference room.

Feeling disoriented again, Penrose had a couple of pints in the public bar of the Cheshire Cheese. The beers helped stifle the irrational twinge of unease he had first experienced after leaving Harewood's house, so he took a bus down Piccadilly for a quarter-pound hamburger and a couple more pints at the Hard Rock Café. As he ate, listening to Lou Reed blasting through the sound system, he finally decided he would go back to Cornwall the next day: Selina was old enough to look after herself and if he wasn't going to live with her again he would have to stop holding her hand.

If he wasn't going to live with her again. There were times when he still ached to; then she'd do something like the other night and he wanted nothing more to do with his wife, ever. The memory of her smile after Quentin's "improvisation" at Jarry's still burned. She didn't need Penrose. Quentin could hold her hand and tell her everything was okay and praise her tiny watercolors and put up with Sir Norman's idea of a joke.

When Penrose got back to Priory at four that afternoon there was a telephone message from London & Continental Steam Packet Co. Ltd. He called back from the hall phone and was connected to a Captain Gunn, who was chief of operations for London & Continental. Gunn had a deep voice with a hint of Devon burr in it that sounded good to Penrose.

"I understand from your letter that there's the possibility of an inquiry into the sinking of your ship, due to the way the coal was loaded?"

Penrose acknowledged this to be the case. Gunn asked him a few more questions about Port Garth Colliery and how the *Witch* had been loaded with wet slurry.

Finally he said, "I'll be honest with you, Captain Penrose. I don't much like the idea of hiring a man under inquiry. But I know Colin Lovell, and he still thinks the world of you, even now." Penrose registered this fact with some surprise: Colin was still treating him coolly. "You also have a decent reputation along the coast." Gunn hesitated. "And also, we're in a bit of a jam. The regular captain for the *London Princess*, that is, his wife, has gone and had a preemie, and the two relief masters are at sea till next week at least. So we'd like you to fly out to Holland tonight."

Penrose hesitated.

It would mean missing Harewood's funeral and leaving without a word to Selina. But Harewood was past caring, Penrose was getting sick of funerals anyway, and Selina— Selina was half the reason he wanted to leave in the first place.

"Well?"

Above the hall phone hung a photograph of the bank's yacht, a clipper-bowed eighty-footer called *Selina* that usually was moored in Treg Harbor. The picture showed waves of silver halide exploding at her forefoot while a crisp emulsion wind snapped smoke from her stack.

"Yes," Penrose said simply.

"Can you pay for the flight?"

"I've got a credit card."

"Good. We'll refund you, of course. We have a reservation on a flight from Gatwick to Amsterdam at 2100. You'll be loading general cargo for Ipswich. Rolled steel, ready to go as soon as we get you over there. We've got to get another AB as well, of course, because one of the crew's paying off in two weeks, but that's not your concern."

"You mean you haven't got one spare, then?"

"We've two, but one's sick and the other's in Birkenhead and his mother won't answer the telephone," Gunn replied, irritation in his words. "He's on leave, so he probably told her not to."

"You're welcome to use one of mine," Penrose said. "I mean"—letting the guilt pass through unrestricted—"the only one I've got left, actually. If you can get through to him, he's in London."

"Yes, well, that's an idea," Gunn said noncommittally.

"For God's sake," Penrose said, letting go for an instant. "I haven't got the plague, nor has Brian, my deck hand. We had nothing to do with losing my ship." He drew breath, and paused. It would do no good to upbraid his future employer, who was listening in what Penrose imagined to be grim

79

silence. "Sorry, but if you can use him, Colin's got his number."

Despite his outburst Penrose felt something close to contentment as he hung up. This was exactly what he needed. Only at sea could he put the troubles and confusion of land in perspective. He'd had more than his ration of those in the last few days.

Penrose went upstairs to pack and write a note to Selina, feeling better than he had in weeks.

The lights of Sussex twinkled faintly, tilted, and began to recede more slowly and in two dimensions as the KLM pilot brought his Airbus to cruising height. The NO SMOKING lights blinked off and a soft voice welcomed them to something in Dutch. The businessman across the aisle had a watch that beeped, like Harewood's.

Penrose stretched and reached automatically for his pipe, then remembered he had left it at Priory with the rest of his city gear, and ordered a pack of Virginia cigarettes and a beer from the stewardess. She came back almost immediately with his order balanced on a tray full of Indonesian snacks, a throwback to the days of Holland's Far East colonies. There was only a handful of people on the plane.

Penrose pulled off the cellophane wrapping and began to eat, delighting in the feel of flying, the hum of a tight world traveling with purpose, the illusion of leaving shopworn stalemates on the ground below. The snacks were a cut above ordinary airline food, spicy and hot, and it was the spiciness that finally brought his doubts to the fore.

Spicy, he thought.

On the evening he died Tim Harewood had been preparing one of the finest, most delicate seafood dishes in the French repertory. Properly done, *Mouclade* was a blend of the most subtle flavors: wine, mussels, cream, with a suggestion of rosemary and garlic.

Hot.

There was no place in a *Mouclade* for the slightest hint of the turmeric he'd been clutching when he drew his last breath.

So what? Penrose thought as he chewed. He had knocked the entire spice cabinet down with him when his heart had failed. The turmeric was probably the first to fall and he had clutched it automatically.

80

Yet surely he would have let it go, if only to hold his chest or reach for the phone.

Penrose shook his head to clear it of farfetched suspicions, but the first doubt, like a Fury from Pandora's box, seemed to drag out other discrepancies flitting around the edges of his consciousness.

Or perhaps he had been using the wrong spice. But that would be unlike Harewood, whose house and office had epitomized fastidiousness. Even at university Harewood had been the type to change clothes before and after punting.

Fastidious people did not go around using the wrong spices when food was their main after-hours obsession. Nor did fastidious people go around forgetting to take their pills; not when such an omission could place their lives in jeopardy. "The one deadline I never push," Harewood had said.

Clift had put it more strongly, if more generally: "Never missed a deadline." By way of epitaph it was as good as any.

Harewood even had a digital watch that beeped to remind him when to take the pills. Harewood also had three file cabinets full of neatly lined folders for stories he had done, was doing or was about to do. He had told Penrose the night before his death that he had an angle on the de Laune problem, and Clift confirmed he'd been working on it; yet he had no file to match.

Only now did Penrose realize how much that simple fact had been bothering him.

There was something else missing from Harewood's desks, Penrose realized: a calendar or desk diary with interviews and appointments. The pro-seal calendar in the kitchen only listed events like the Jarry's party.

"You do not like our Indonesian menu, sir?" the stewardess asked with professional concern. Penrose realized he had been staring at the seat in front of him like a zombie. He ordered coffee and let her take the half-finished food away.

And finally, there was the mysterious dinner guest, the second place at the table that had so bothered Radetsky. The copper might not have chosen this case but he was no fool. Why had the dinner guest not shown up? Or had he? Or was it a she?

Penrose lit one cigarette, then another, staring blindly out the window as the lights of Schiphol Airport came out of the polders. "Hell for ships," the word meant. By the look on his face Harewood had found a hell for men in the last two minutes of his life. The possibility that someone had sent him there deliberately was unnerving.

They landed at Schiphol at 2200 Dutch time. He took a bus to Rotterdam and boarded the *London Princess* at a quarter to one in the morning.

Penrose woke up to a knock on his cabin door and a nasal Gladstone Docks accent announcing his tea. The face above the fist around the mug was young and pitted with acne.

"They'll begin loading in thirty minutes, and I think the agent will be wanting to see you."

Penrose had never been the type to wake up disoriented, wondering where he was and what he was doing in a strange place, but even if he had the clues were there to remind him: the gray light infiltrating his porthole, three faraway farts as a large ship announced its intention of going astern, encouraging pipes from tugs, the crisp walk of dockers up the quay, their yells of greeting in guttural Dutch. And over everything, like Catholic guilt, hung the smell of coasters; a mixture of forgotten cargoes, sea salt and rotten mud from a hundred penny-ante harbors; the flavor of porthole grease and deck wax and the eternal sweetness of diesel oil.

Penrose lay back in his bunk when the boy had gone, deriving comfort from the warmth of the mug. The tea was strong enough to acquire semisolid consistency, thick enough to turn its forty-percent milk the color of Maas River water, sweet enough to set his taste buds popping.

As he sipped he sensed the first small decay in the frustration that had gripped him over the last two weeks.

Selina, de Laune and Harewood were separated from him by more than their distance in miles. The deceits of London and whatever had killed Harewood seemed picayune when measured against the forces involved in moving cargoes: forces like a snapping hawser that could cut a man in half before he had time to cry out; like the sea that had crushed his deck hand and sunk his ship.

If anyone had murdered Tim Harewood—in the dishwater dawn of the Merwehaven docks, it seemed much more farfetched than it had in the jet.

Penrose got up and showered, dressed in work jeans, boots, turtleneck and donkey jacket, and went topside to face the world.

The world was a gray-and-white 400-gross-ton coaster built in Holland twelve years before, when the Dutch still made them to last. She was 180 feet in length, 40 feet in the beam, diesel-powered, with one long cargo hold between the accommodation decks and bridge aft and the foredeck, fo'c'sle and chain locker forward.

Unlike the old-fashioned *Witch,* the cargo hold on this ship was covered with MacGregor hatches, rolling slabs of metal connected by chains, which lay flat in tracks when in place over the hold.

They had opened the hold on Penrose's old ship by unlashing three thick layers of oiled tarpaulins, lifting off, one at a time, 112 cumbersome and ironbound hatch boards, which were then stacked, individually, clear of the hatch coamings. They then hooked up derrick and winches to lift out the eight massive king and queen beams supporting the boards, a task that took four expert men a good hour and a half to achieve.

On the *London Princess,* they simply jacked up the hydraulic wheels under the MacGregor hatches, knocked loose the steel dogs clipping them into place, hooked up the forward set of hatches to a diesel winch on the foredeck and dragged them toward the bow. As each horizontal metal slab came to the end of the tracks it tipped vertically on one offset pair of wheels and stacked itself next to its chained fellows, like a deck of giant steel playing cards.

The process was repeated for the after set via a block on the after bulkhead, then two queen beams were pulled, and the ship was ready for loading. The entire operation could be achieved by one semiskilled boy in forty minutes.

His new crew was already at work. Penrose watched from the wheelhouse, sheltered from the din as the donkey engine thudded and the half-ton sides of hatch rolled and crashed into each other. Dockers dallied like crows on the quay, content to idle, joking and smoking. Above them the huge cranes gawked like herons. A cold wind blew scraps of dunnage around the warehouses and the flatbed railroad cars loaded with three-ton rolls of the best Common Market steel, produced uneconomically and under massive government subsidy for export to a country with its own surplus of uneconomic and subsidized steel. There was a smell of frying fish from a big Belgian *péniche*, or canal barge, moored forward of the *Princess*. Penrose watched a woman pin washing around the wheelhouse while her fat husband watched television. Their big black, yellow and red flag snagged itself around the TV antenna and hung there.

Loading would take most of the day, including a two-hour break for lunch. The ship's agent came aboard, heavy with forms. When he had gone Penrose inspected the ship, and set the crew to cleaning up the paint locker and oiling the hatch wheels.

Mel, the mate, came up to him five minutes after he'd done this and asked him if the men were not entitled to time ashore in Rotterdam, and Penrose told him they would not go ashore while the paint locker was alive with paint fumes and a serious fire hazard, adding that they'd be better off saving shore time for a port with more to offer than Rotterdam.

The mate of the *London Princess* was corded and tough as a short piece of tallowed cable. He had long, greasy black hair, a gold circlet in his left ear, like Penrose, and green eyes, always ready to start into laughter or anger at any moment. Now the eyes burned like starboard running lights.

"They say you're under investigation, for the *Witch of Fraddam*."

"That's right."

"They also say you were an officer in the Andrew."

"Aye."

"And you were thrown out of the bloody Navy."

"Medical," Penrose said, very calmly. "I could not serve in submarines. Report for inspection when you've cleaned the paint locker."

The mate looked at him for a second longer. As he turned away Penrose caught the words "another fucking *Navy* man," muttered just loud enough to carry.

A delivery van arrived with the crew's order of duty-free booze—eighteen bottles of spirits and as many cases of beer, which were sealed in the bonded locker in the skipper's office. The crane whined, and the ship reverberated as 600 rolls were chocked and stacked into place under Penrose's supervision: 175 forward, 125 aft, 300 midships. The mate discharged ballast water overboard to compensate. The Internav repairman came to fix the defective echo sounder at 1500. The pilot came aboard at 1600, and they were queuing to go through the first sea lock at 1635.

Penrose stayed with the pilot as they threaded the morass of mud banks, buoys and traffic in the Maas estuary. Night had fallen on a fifteen-knot breeze from the northwest. A steady pissing of rain, willed by an occluded Icelandic low, departed south and east of them. The flat darkness was punctuated by a thousand marks of light, some flashing, some occulting, some moving, others fixed; a multitude of codes and ciphers of the coast: lights from buoys, tugs, tankers, barges, lighthouses, coasters, pilot vessels, sludge ships, canal ranging lights, lock signals and occasional plumes of raw flame from the giant refineries along the estuary.

The captain kept close track of their course. He also kept track of the red, green, white, yellow and flashing blue of other traffic. He had never trusted pilots, odd amphibian creatures with a reputation for weirdness among seamen. He thought they were men who rented but did not own their position of command, licensed officers with power but no responsibility. The pilot who had run his ship aground in the Schelde had carried the nickname "Hurry-up Harry" among coastermen, and had sneaked in the nighttime shortcut without Penrose's knowledge or consent; but the responsibility for his error was entirely the captain's.

It was the law, just as it was mandatory to carry a pilot in the Maas, although Penrose probably knew the river as well as VanDaam.

The Dutchman set up a huge night telescope as soon as they were clear of the locks and looked for naked women in the portholes of every East European ship they crossed paths with. When he wasn't using his telescope, he persisted in borrowing Penrose's binoculars instead of using his own. VanDaam knew the river, but Penrose had to remind him to answer Europoort and Scheveningen traffic controllers on the VHF as they approached the estuary's end and the North Sea.

It was a relief to put the Jacob's ladder over and close with the swinging red and white lights of the Maas pilot boat to leeward: a relief to be alone on his own bridge at last, as the crossrips from the *zeegats* got confused and lost in the Atlantic rollers.

Mel came up at midnight to relieve Penrose, and the captain told him to wait till 0230, which the mate obviously took as a direct insult to his abilities. He turned on his heel and stalked below: but Penrose, calmed by the relative peace of the horizon, where Goeree light vessel winked in steady company, merely called after him, "Keep your shirt on, mate."

Smoking, listening to the BBC hum faintly from the radio-telephone set, Penrose felt his body lift and roll gently with the ship and felt some more of his London frustration break up and slip away. In five minutes on his own bridge he had plotted a course, allowed for the southerly tidal current, checked where he was by the time they'd been steaming and judged where he was going by the lubber line on the compass. Hazards of sand, salt and onrushing steel could be plotted on the radar, programmed into the Decca, avoided on the chart.

London—and the telephone call he had to make to Radetsky when they docked—was one hundred miles and a sunrise away.

They raised the Shipwash lightship at 0535, picked up the pilot at Cork station at 0700 and docked in Ipswich before lunch.

"The fuckin' bastards came up at about four in the morning where we were tied up to the wreck. Only the mate on the bridge keepin' radar watch, an' he were pissed as a newt, as were we all except for me that could take it. So they cut the line we had aboard her, the bastards."

Mel came from Hull, where he had risen to mate on an Iceland trawler—the kind that spent winters fishing—before shipping out as third on the Blue Flue line and finally running a salvage tug out of Barbados.

Mel took another swig of his Dutch beer and belched. The cook, an old Irish coastguardsman inevitably named Pat, brought out a big plate of pork roast shining with juices, apples and roasted spuds.

"I woke up the next morning and what did I see?" Mel continued. "This fuckin' great Dutch salvage tug next to *our* prize, all shiny and bright and all this fancy satnav equipment and fire hoses and such, and this great huge git with a fuckin' cowboy hat, the tug's captain, conversin' with the master of the *Ilioka*. I couldn't believe me fookin' *eyes*. God, I hate the Dutch, with all their fuckin' clogs on the bridge. I just grabbed the machetes we kept handy in case we had to let go a towin' line in a hurry, woke up the crew, gave 'em each a machete, raised the anchor and we went alongside the tug."

"What did you do then?" the young deck hand said, forgetting to eat in his awe of the mate.

"Simple, lad." The beer was all gone but Mel squeezed the can over his lips to make sure before reaching for another. "We brought out the Trinidadi birds we had below and told 'em to sunbathe naked on the foredeck. They almost roasted themselves on the deck plates, the sun was that hot, but they did it. Then while the Dutchmen were decidin' which to drop first, their fenders or their cocks, we boarded 'em from astern, EEEEYAH, right up to the bridge with our machetes. Their skipper nearly shit himself— I couldn't believe that git, what a right fuckin' poof, he had a toupee on his chest to go with the cowboy hat— No, I swear it, it started to peel off, he was sweatin' that bad while he was yellin'. I nearly died laughin'—but they signed the Lloyd's form that quick, I can tell you." Mel chuckled dreamily, remembering. "But I told that mate he could bloody swim for it, fallin' asleep like that."

Mel looked at the captain speculatively, as if the story were a veiled reference to what he would do if crossed. Penrose smiled and helped himself to another beer from the former captain's supply.

"We had a mate," Sean began, "on London and Continental, who claimed he passed out unconscious on watch near Shellhaven. We were on the *London Countess*. It was on Sea Reach, and she was on autopilot. The ship went straight for the *Methane Atlantic,* this fucking huge LNG carrier that was loading at Shellhaven— Hit it at six knots while it was loading, but only went through the outer hull 'cuz it was a glancing blow; it didn't hit it dead on. They reckon it would have taken half London with it if it had gone up. Later they found a bottle of gin in the mate's bunk. He'd been pissed as a newt, as well—"

Penrose slipped out to find a telephone. There was some

low talk and a burst of laughter through the saloon porthole when he left, and he guessed they were discussing the new skipper.

A misty midday, but no rain. The security guard for Cliff Quay told him there was a pay phone by the pub.

Penrose checked in with Gunn at London & Continental, then dialed Islington police station and was put through to Radetsky.

"Where are you calling from?" the detective asked between chewing noises.

Penrose gave his present and future whereabouts. He could imagine the lugubrious detective penciling the information into his black notebook with one hand while he held a sausage sandwich in the other. The connection was quite good, and the illusion of proximity brought Penrose closer to events in London than he had been for two days—closer, in fact, than he wanted to be.

"I've been thinking about all of this," Penrose added.

"Yes, sir." A completely neutral tone.

"Well, you know, do you think he was killed or not?"

"I really couldn't say."

"Oh, come on, Inspector," Penrose said. "Don't give me the routine again." The telephone made urgent noises, and Penrose had to shove in another series of heavy coins to buy more time. When the connection was reestablished, he said, "The more I think about it, the stranger it seems to me," and he listed the anomalies that had struck him during the KLM flight.

"I'll pass it on, sir," Radetsky said when he had finished, "but frankly I have other work to do."

"What do you mean?"

"Well, sir—" Radetsky sighed—"all I have is reservations about this man's death. The chief inspector needs more than that to go on, which therefore means this will probably, eventually, be listed as death from natural causes."

"But that doesn't make sense."

Silence.

"I mean, here you were, making dark and mysterious insinuations right and left, like a bloody Conan Doyle character, Inspector Lestrade of the Yard or something, and now the police are simply dropping it—I mean, haven't you come up with anything? Anything new?"

No reply.

"Was there an autopsy?"

"We're not dropping it, as you put it, Mr. Penrose, but if there's no new evidence—and in the absence of evidence we do not ask for an autopsy if the family does not ask for one."

"And his sister did not ask."

"His sister did not care."

Penrose thought for a while. He heard Radetsky take a sip of liquid near the mouthpiece.

"You don't believe it, though, I get the impression."

"No, I wouldn't say that, sir. There are disturbing factors—you saw a couple of them, and you've mentioned one or two more, like the desk calendar—but they are pretty circumstantial oddities. You see, there are always loose threads in a man's life; that is really what living is about, seeking to tie them up, so it would be surprising if there were none in his death."

"Why do I still get the impression you don't believe what you're saying?" Penrose began, but Radetsky merely said, "As you like, sir," and did not ask him to keep in touch.

Out of habit Penrose next called Selina to tell her where he would be over the next week, but she was in one of her blue bedridden moods, probably lying around in satin smoking *kif* and painting more and more unfashionable and unsalable watercolors of men with lizard faces, so he hung up almost immediately and went back to the ship.

The next few days passed as they always did in coasting, with a lot of loneliness and a little companionship, a lot of boredom and a little excitement, a lot of beer and some food: the crew was used to spending most of the food money on beer and buying eggs and potatoes with the rest, and once he had determined they would not drink themselves over the limit while at sea Penrose did not interfere with the practice. Living away from women was an unnatural existence that demanded compensation in some form: it was only the imperative of keeping their own self-contained environment afloat and moving and carrying cargoes that imparted meaning to the life.

So they sailed in ballast from Ipswich, southwesterly, up the estuary, past the relics of war: the sunken ammo ship, and the air defense towers rusting on Maplin sands. During the war these towers had constituted the twentieth-century equivalent of the medieval keeps guarding bottlenecks in the valleys of the Rhone, and pumped defiance at Junkers and Focke Wulfs when they followed the river to bomb London, but those heady days of delicious desperation were gone. One of the towers served as base for a pirate radio station that played top-forty tunes, and another had been "liberated" by a crowd of artsy Quentin types who had declared it a republic because it stood outside territorial waters. The towers bore these indignities in stoic silence.

They docked up the Thames at the huge pilings of the English Paper Mills pier in Greenhithe. There the ship lay for a day and a night to pick up a cargo of scrap, zinc ingots, drilling equipment, paper towels and five hundred cases of Scotch in dimpled bottles, all bound from Greenwich to Dunkirk. The EPM berth brought back memories for Penrose; he had often brought the *Witch of Fraddam* here, because the mill used tons of china clay to gloss paper, and Sir Norman, with a controlling interest in Cornish China Clay PLC, had arranged that Penrose be given the contract to carry clay from Cornwall to the Thames.

It was a gesture of magnanimity and gratitude for his separation from Selina. The paper mill had given him a contract to carry newsprint from Sweden as well, until a media conglomerate bought out EPM and shut down half its operations.

In those days Penrose used the local pub, the Peeking Duck, as his unofficial office. It had a sign painted to represent a duck watching Lady Godiva undressing; it was a dingy place, hung with small-craft propellers from a nearby factory, but the landlord let him use the telephone. Leaving Sean to guard the ship, he took his crew there to get drunk on Alfred's strong, dark local ale. They played darts with the mill men and the huge black security guard, flirted with amateur hookers from Gravesend and scribbled bad limericks on the Victorian wallpaper.

They sailed for Dunkirk on Thursday, then, prompted by pied-piper phone calls from Gunn, sailed north to Terneuzen, near Rotterdam. The choking, bitter cargo of ammonium nitrate they took to Plymouth left sea gulls collapsing in the mineral-laden waters. From Plymouth they headed in ballast for Antwerp in steadily thickening fog that made the bow of the ship almost a separate entity, a gray sea creature bowing to a mythical horizon, connected to the men aft only by use and memory.

The fog made every steel deckhead in the ship a condensing point and turned the watch officer into a priest of the microwave, for dead reckoning meant living by and for the radar screen, plotting the course of other ships in the Channel's traffic separation scheme, vessels invisible except for their yellow shades on the orange display. It meant taking electronic fixes at regular intervals from the Decca navigator, listening for other ships on the VHF; but apart from traffic too distant to worry about, there was only some bored third officer with a Spanish or North African accent repeating like some consumer-age mantra the word "Co-ca–Co-la," at regular intervals on the call-up frequency.

In poor visibility the rules of the road said you had to reduce speed to the point where a radar watch would give you certain notice of possible collision, and it was at the point of near-zero visibility that the five-mile range on the Internav set fuzzed out.

Mel was on watch, and Penrose was hanging around on the bridge in case he was needed, when it happened.

"I've lost the five-mile range," Mel said, blinking as he searched through the windows into the gray invisibility ahead: easy swells in a tight little world barely four ship's lengths on every side; cold water, warmish moist air, little wind, fog.

"Fuckin' Internav."

Penrose took over the radar, fiddling with the gain and sea-clutter controls.

"Fuck me. We'll have to get Sean in the bows with his mouth organ. Get him out there anyway, for the record."

Penrose switched to the two-and-a-half-, the ten-, then the twenty-mile range.

"There's that target bearing 065, about seven miles ahead. He's almost on the same bearing."

"Aye. He's on the same course we are, but a little to the east. The bearing's changin' though, a bit. We shouldn't even see him."

Penrose took the grease pencil and marked a new bearing line. "Bring us west to 60 magnetic anyway. I don't want to find him too near at two and a half."

Mel glowered but complied. Pat brought up more tea. Penrose stayed by the radar. Ten minutes passed, with Penrose switching back and forth between the nearer ranges, Mel sounding the foghorn, two blasts every minute.

Sean trudged sleepily up the deck, looking like Banquo's ghost in black oilskins. Penrose could barely make him out by the time he reached his station at the bow.

The target disappeared from the ten-mile range and reappeared on the shorter range twenty minutes later.

"He's even closer to us," Penrose said. "He must have altered course." He twirled the autopilot knob to 55 degrees. "Keep us there for five minutes; then we'll be clear. He's a big one."

Penrose checked their DR position, which Mel had just updated, and took up the VHF mike.

"Calling ship positioned seven miles southwest of Ostende sea buoy, on heading of 250 true. This is *London Princess,* ship two miles southwest of you. Please make clear your intentions."

There was no answer. Then, from a little farther away than before but still quite close, came the words "Co-ca–Cola?" in a more hopeful voice this time.

"This range's beginning to fuzz over now, as well."

Penrose called again, and the voice on the VHF, delighted, repeated "Co-ca–Co-la!"

"Bloody hell. Has his bearing altered?"

"Only a bit. We should still clear him."

"Fuck this," Penrose said, pushing the engine controls to half speed and moving toward the autopilot. "I'm taking her out of here. To 45—"

"There she is!"

A huge shape, grayer than gray. A container ship, headed on an almost reciprocal course, several hundred yards to the east. They would pass, starboard to starboard without difficulty.

An American voice, very distant, came on the VHF. "Pepsi-Cola," it answered faintly.

"Steady as she goes, then."

There was a loud roar; the ghostly shape had sounded her siren. One short: pass port to port.

"They're out of their fucking minds," Penrose exclaimed.

The arrangement of red, green and white lights looming higher and higher over their heads shifted, eclipsed the green, took up more of the horizon. The container ship seemed committed to changing course, swerving across their bows, to pass to the left.

"Hard astarboard," Penrose said, spinning the autopilot

and holding his breath. "The crazy fool! If that's the way he wants it," and he stabbed the siren once, to acknowledge. The *London Princess* heeled over to her left as the rudder shoved water to the right.

The other ship's turn slowed. The green starboard running light reappeared, even higher in the blackness.

"He's turnin' back!" Mel said, with an incredulous out-breath of horror. "He's goin' to port. He's fuckin' *mad!*"

"Fuck him," Penrose said.

"We'll hit!"

"It's too late. He should have thought of that two minutes ago." Penrose continued jabbing the siren button, five shorts: "I am unclear as to your intentions." At the very last minute the other ship slowed its turn to port, steadied on a course that would seemingly take it straight between Mel and Penrose, then began paying off to the west in time to clear their stern deck by at least ten feet. Penrose and Mel both stepped to the port bridge door to stare upward as catastrophe passed by, close enough to see the astonished expression of a steward twenty feet above as he emptied a pail of slops almost into the *London Princess*'s lifeboat. The gigantic stern wave made the coaster's 400 tons rock like a toy ship.

Mel moved over to the after windows to stare up at the container ship fast disappearing in the fog behind them.

"*Arzadh*. Jiddah. A bloody fuckin' Saudi. God I *hate* the Arabs."

"Probably just a cadet on the bridge," Penrose said, trying hard to keep the shakiness out of his voice. He brought *London Princess* back in line with its wildly swinging compass. One hundred forty feet ahead of him, through the forward windows, he could see Sean's face, white enough to cut through the intervening mist, staring incredulously aft.

Mel cleared his throat.

Penrose took the VHF mike and said, "*Arzadh, Arzadh*, God rot your fucking soul, you bunch of fucking cowboys with Panamanian tickets; you shouldn't be allowed to drive a broken moped in the fucking desert."

"Co-ca–*Co*-la," the VHF replied, impressed.

The mate went over to the chart table, and then back to the stern window. He whistled something tuneless between his teeth.

"Listen, skipper."

"What?" Penrose checked the radar screen again.

"I wanted to say—"

"What?" Penrose patted his pockets for a cigarette. God, even his knees were weak.

"What I said earlier. I mean a few days ago, in Rotterdam. About you being a Navy man. I know you heard—and, well, I take it back." Mel was staring into the Saudi ship's wake.

"It's okay, mate," Penrose said. "Give me a cigarette and we'll call it even."

But as he stood the remainder of the watch, shifting neurotically from the fuzzy two and a half miles to ten miles on the radar, plotting fixes and DR positions to make sure they stayed clear of traffic as well as the treacherous girdle of sand bars around the Belgian coast, Penrose realized that for the last couple of days his sadness had been mellowing, distilling into the thin liquor of memory, strong but increasingly smooth.

The grief was still there, rebrewed every time he found the chart table in the wrong place, or tried to read the compass which had been above his bunk on the *Witch of Fraddam,* or confronted the unbidden association with Henry when Sean brought him a cup of tea; but it had changed, flattened from an obstacle to a landmark from which to plot future directions.

Selina had made up a story about grief, after the child died. She said that in the pit of everyone's stomach lived two bugs—a death bug and a life bug—who always fought over things that affected your guts. The death bug was purple, and thrived on grief. He was bigger and stronger than the green life bug, but the life bug was smarter, and usually won fights by distracting the purple bug with irrelevant stories.

The life bug had won this round, Penrose thought.

They picked up the Schelde pilot at 0540 and found their berth in Leopolddok at 1430.

XI

They walked up the quay toward the seedier sections of Antwerp, Mel in a good mood, Pat whistling, Penrose cracking jokes for the first time in days and Sean weaving a little, because they were third in line for loading and would probably be in port for two nights, which meant that there had been no criticism for going a beer or three over the line.

"Did you hear the one about the Antwerp whore?"

"No—"

"Who told the Belgian she couldn't meet him because she was on her menstrual cycle?"

"Oh, no."

"And he said, 'Don't worry, I'll soon catch up on my Suzuki.' "

"Fuck off, skipper." Sean tooted his mouth organ in derision.

The port stretched out before them, kilometer on kilometer of cobbled docks, yellow arc lamps, gray concrete warehouses, viscous waters; cranes perched over freighters, confused hydraulic vultures waiting for the ships to awaken so they could pick out their entrails. Porthole eyes winked, cabin radios played. Refineries danced on the edges of night. Their footsteps were questions asked of darkness.

They took a taxi from the south gate to the seamen's hostel, looking for cheap beer and free billiards.

The hostel obeyed the same rules seamen did the world over: it stank of shore pay and loneliness saved up so long that each cried for release, by which time the repression was so great it set seamen apart from other men, and especially apart from women.

Linoleum and plastic chairs, table tennis and billiards; notices about lashing-time and sickness benefits, vaccinations and church meetings, in seven languages; twenty men, almost all in their fifties, all sitting alone with a beer or a schnapps, all watched by a TV that spoke of goods they could not take with them in a dialect they could not understand.

If the sea provided a replacement for an amniotic fluid that had once provided a replacement for the sea, then the hostel duplicated its function on land, working as a microcosm of salt water, a fishbowl environment in which the men could live out their brief periods as amphibians.

The *Princess*'s crew became involved in a table tennis match against men from a Zairean freighter that was moored two ships astern of the coaster. The Africans alternated between high-pitched laughter and deep grunts of approval as they trounced Mel and Pat. Two plump Germans made low and insulting remarks to each other as they watched. A stooped Chinese came in and signed his name to the list of waiting players.

Penrose, sickened by the neat smells of unfulfilled male dreams, told Mel he would meet them at the 'Vanger bar and took a taxi to Skipperstraat to look for women.

As he paid off the cab in crisp new franc notes changed by the ship's agent, a second Mercedes taxi pulled up, but its passenger did not get out. Penrose, unheeding, set off into the crannies of the street.

Once every major port in the world must have looked like Skipperstraat, a parade of jumbled bars spaced by brothels spaced by tattoo parlors, here sheltered under the crazy stepped eaves of Flemish architecture. Former warehouses, listed over cobblestoned alleys. Red lights—and green, blue, yellow, orange, black and neon—bracketed plate-glass windows to highlight a main attraction, sitting with care and reading a magazine.

One in particular, an Indonesian or Malaysian prostitute, wore nothing except a long ebony ponytail, fake ostrich feathers and sequins around her nipples and crotch. Two stuffed cobras reared suggestively behind her in orange spotlights. Cheap plaster moldings hinted at a plastic Orient of two-dimensional luxuries: the luxuries of touch denied the richness of history, Penrose thought.

The woman had skin like copper velvet and eyes that

pooled when she looked up, which was rarely. Perhaps the shyness was an act. The stack of movie magazines by her armchair seemed to provide for her intellectual needs, the pimp who would appear by the doorbell fulfilling more mundane functions.

Penrose never did more than window-shop on Skipperstraat, never joined the shipmates, notes clutched in moist palms, slipping furtively into the crooked doorways flanking every window, but he did take vicarious pleasure in looking at the various prostitutes, and it was in the Indonesian girl's plate glass that he first noticed the man looking at him.

He would not have thought twice about it—Skipperstraat catered to all tastes, and Danny's Bar, where the women were not, was only five or six doors away—except for the fact that he had seen the Chinese before, in the seamen's hostel, waiting to play table tennis.

It was the same man. He had lighter coloring than the girl behind the reflections, and the fat cheeks of the northeast Pacific. A second glance showed the man's eyes were not angled as sharply as those of most Chinese, which probably made him a half-caste, one of the wandering thousands of the Chinese diaspora who ran the provisions stores and fantan parlors, the shipping companies, banks and brothels in every Third World port from Surinam to San José to Sekondi.

But the man's furtiveness was not meant to attract attention, like that of the port's homosexuals: only the double bluff of reflecting glass had trapped his quick looks.

There was one other category the man could fall into, Penrose told himself. Antwerp, like any seaport, had its share of thugs, pickpockets, con artists and muggers. The only factor that made this man different was the process of selection which had made him pick Penrose, and this process was by definition a mystery to the victim.

It was more impulse than anything that prompted Penrose's next move: he turned into the doorway by the plate-glass window and rang the bell.

As he did he looked directly at the Chinese, who was now gazing into the display window of a tattoo parlor across the street, ostensibly deciding which of the one thousand dancing girls, daggers, snakes, American eagles, dice, anchors, Popeyes and hearts he wanted injected by *machines de tatouage guaranties stérilisées et sans douleur.*

A wooden judas slid open, and a single eye regarded Penrose.

"*Ja?*"

"How much," Penrose asked, feeling more than a little foolish.

"For Marika?"

It was the Indonesian girl's name, in lipstick in three scripts on the glass beside him.

"Marika."

"How long?"

Bloody hell, Penrose thought, he wasn't really intending to go through with this.

"I don't know—half an hour?"

"Thirteen hundred francs."

"Haven't got it. D'you take sterling?"

"Hein?"

"Pounds. British pounds. Livres."

"Yes, yes. Fifty pounds."

"Thanks, mate." Penrose turned quickly and stepped to the cobblestones, looking around him. No Chinese to the north, no Chinese to the south; just a couple of drunk Belgian bargemen pissing in the gutter. The Oriental had disappeared.

"Hey, meester, fifty pounds iss very cheap." The crablike pimp had come out of his shell, sideways, and made clawing movements from the doorway.

"No, thanks."

"She iss number one."

"No."

"Thirty-five pounds." A click of disgust.

His imagination was working overtime, Penrose decided. Two weeks of Selina and the frothy self-abuse of the people she hung out with had interfered with the notions of causality that kept you alive at sea. He walked toward Danny's Bar.

Yellow light spilled into the street through Arras curtains. Penrose hesitated—the pink neon of the 'Vanger was just up the street—but he wanted a beer now, he had francs in his pocket and an unrequited need for human comedy, street comedy as opposed to the conjured dramas in London.

And if he was being followed, he'd find out in Danny's Bar.

Danny's was a great favorite of coastermen, especially

British coastermen suffering from the leftover sexual politics of the age of Rhodes and Gladstone, the awful hypocrisy that made any perversion the immediate subject of fascination. The transvestites who worked and gathered here were as good as or better than any drag queen in London: only if you were listening and looking did you notice a hint of shadow under the jawline, a slight huskiness in the voice.

Penrose was not convinced that some of them were not women, and once, very drunk, he had reached under one of their skirts, to find his hand taken in a metal grip and gently but firmly returned to his beer glass.

"Not good," the waitress had said. "Her" fingers left marks on Penrose's wrist that turned mauve after two days.

Penrose was into his second Stella and wondering what it would be like to be able to change sexual identity at will when he looked at the window and saw, behind the lace, the Oriental's face staring directly at his own. There was another Asian behind him, dressed in a yellow windbreaker. When Penrose met their gaze they looked away in automatic disguise but did not change position; they resumed watching a moment later.

Penrose shrugged and settled back in his chair. One of the waitresses lifted an eyebrow and pointed at his empty bottle, but he shook his head. Another transvestite came in, and there was a silence, a pointed comment, much feminine fussing at the bar. Penrose used the diversion to slip out his wallet, leave enough notes for the beers and a hefty tip, and stride rapidly across the bar, down the steps and out the door.

No one was there.

Penrose began to feel angry, anger that for the first time held a streak of nervousness. He had been ready to confront the men; seaport muggers did not ordinarily do their work in public places like the sidewalk in front of a bar, and here he could have let them know he was on his guard, not an easy mark. But then, these men were not acting like muggers. Muggers were not interested in making contact, just hitting and running. There had been a message implicit in that gaze through the window, albeit a coded one; he was being told something this time. It was a challenge—but a challenge to what?

Fog was still rolling up the Schelde and it had rotted all

hard lines. Buildings curled into invisibility, neon was halo, smoke was king. Howls of outrage came from one of the basement "nightclubs," then a smash of breaking glass and the sound of flesh striking flesh, it always sounded louder than you remembered—and three bouncers dragged a drunk from the Yellow Cat Disco ("Girls! Girls! Girls!") and threw him into the gutter, where he lay moaning for a while, then became violently ill.

Penrose shivered. The damp was almost palpable. He could use warmth, of various kinds, but the Indonesian variety too often carried an unwelcome bonus of corkscrew-shaped bacilli. Whereas the 'Vanger—it was warm, friendly, the crew might be there by now, and maybe, just maybe, Kirsten would be in the mood for men tonight. It was depressing weather, and Kirsten turned to men when she was depressed.

He began to walk.

They were waiting for him in the next alley off Skipperstraat, four of them now. The yellow windbreaker was the first clue, then their common size, or lack of it by European standards, then the light on high cheekbones, a pink glint. They were close enough to his goal to reflect the neon worms of letters that had once read "Stavanger Bar," with the first three letters shorted out, dead and dark. The 'Vanger. Damn!

His anger flared. He had stopped when he saw the men, but now he made a move to continue to the 'Vanger. A hunched figure behind the group made a noise, and they stepped out into Skipperstraat, ten feet away. Five of them.

Penrose stopped again.

"What do you want?"

Silence. The men were clumped together, eyes shining.

The Chinese was not among them, Penrose noticed. In fact, these men were not Chinese, but Indonesians or Malays, possibly one of the enduring breed of lascars who had crewed the Empire's rust buckets and stoked their hellish boilers for a pittance. The crew's list on British ships still held columns for lascars, where their "headman" could "make his mark" when signing on. Now they crewed the ships of new empires, ships with flags of convenience at their masthead and Swiss accounts their true home port.

He looked around, but the only people visible were so far

away as to be part of the mist, so he turned and began to walk leisurely back toward Danny's Bar.

The men were wearing track shoes that made little squeaks as they walked, at the same pace, behind him. He would go into Danny's and call the cops, he thought, and finally he would make it to the 'Vanger. He passed the Indonesian's window: she was still reading a movie magazine, *Star 2000*, with a glossy cover showing an American-looking blonde. Mist swirled out of a passageway two buildings down. It must have come from a door being opened, because four more figures padded out in the channel of draft, blocking his way to the light from Danny's billowing farther down. There was a street lamp here, an old fixture that had once spouted a gas flame, then been converted to electricity, but it was broken, perhaps deliberately vandalized, for this was the darkest part of the street. Only the glow of the Indonesian girl's showcase gave any light, and it was an unreal orange that turned them all into creatures of nightmares.

Trapped.

Penrose stopped once again. Suddenly, what had seemed, despite the discordant messages, like a casual dance of purse snatchers, a ritual so familiar to anyone who knew the waterfront that it was almost a game, had become an unfamiliar ceremony of sacrifice to demons he did not know. Adrenaline flooded his system. The men behind him had stopped, as well. For a space of ten seconds no one moved; even the prostitute had disappeared and her cobras were frozen. His lungs pumped quicker to feed oxygen to tensed muscles.

Then the judas in the pimp's door scraped open.

"Meester! Queek!"

Penrose reacted without thinking, jumped sideways. Three strides took him to the doorway he had knocked at only half an hour earlier that evening.

This time the door stood open. She slammed it shut behind him, and there was the sound of locks being turned, bolts shot. A blue night light up a narrow flight of stairs showed a hallway of peeling plaster, filthy paint, mottled carpet, the girl looking at him in open fear. The hallway smelled of soup. Her feathers fluttered pathetically as she breathed.

There was a crash that shook the walls, but the door held

firm. Penrose noted it was sheathed in steel. Its hinges and locks were big and brassy, as befitted any shop that stocked valuable merchandise.

"Queek." She ran up the stairs, and Penrose followed, a little confused, trying to keep his eyes on the steps, which were uneven. Her body blocked the night light but he could still catch the sheen of her buttocks, twin arcs that pumped her up the stairs three at a time. She was lithe as a circus acrobat, and left a faint whiff of cloves in her wake to mingle with the aroma of cabbage and bay leaf.

She stopped at a door on the second floor.

"He will come. Please, meester."

The girl's eyes were wide; white encircled the pupils. Surely, Penrose thought, with a window like hers, she was used to street violence in Skipperstraat.

"Please. I help you, now you help. You must pay. He will come! *Geld!*"

And Penrose realized it was not the lascars she was afraid of, but her pimp.

"But my mother," he said, for something to say. "You don't understand; it would be the death of her."

She stared at him: her English accent was good, much better than the pimp's, probably she was taking lessons so she could move to Hollywood, but she had exhausted her vocabulary with "please" and "money."

"Look, I have to go, I won't stay. I go, now." One part of him coped with the problem of escaping the yellow peril and communicating with the girl, while another, divorced from the first, took account of how her breasts were perfectly molded.

"L'argent!" She risked a quick glance up the next flight of stairs. "Money! Francs! Pounds! Dollars." Her small palms were cupped in front of her in a gesture that reminded Penrose poignantly of the sculptures of Angkor Wat.

"Isn't there a back way?"

"*Please, meester.*"

The raw fear in her face angered him. What the hell did the pimp do to this child to keep her so scared and obedient? As if he didn't know. He roughly pulled his wallet out and thrust a wad of Belgian francs into her hands.

Without another word she opened a door behind her and pulled Penrose inside. The room was small, warm and dark,

103

and as she shoved past him he took her arm, and she stopped immediately, conditioned to obey men, especially pimps and paid-up clients.

"Don't turn on the light," Penrose said. "Kein licht. Pas de lumière."

He slipped past her, feathers tickling his chin, feeling his way along the wall. An attenuation of black became gray, resolved into what was probably curtains with the cityscape behind them. His outstretched hands hit a lamp, which began to fall and toppled something else. He caught the lamp, but something small hit the floor and smashed.

"Shhhhh!"

He could feel her moving. The smell of cloves was there in front of him. He reached out and touched her skin. It was warm, and unbelievably soft: so smooth it would have made silk feel like jute sacking by comparison. His fingers spread, almost of their own volition. Her hands came to his waist and her grip was small as she pulled herself against him, found his mouth and kissed him.

It was a professional kiss, expert but neutral. She broke it off after the required interval.

"Here, hang on a minute." He strained to listen, but all he could hear was her breathing. His hands, seemingly of their own volition, still caressed the girl's back and he had to drag them away. "For God's sake!" he whispered hoarsely. His fingers were shaking as he stepped around the dresser and the broken glass, pulled aside the curtains.

A tall French window led to a concrete balcony, and cast-iron stairs disappeared into a courtyard bounded by a high brick wall with one wooden door. The yard seemed filled with cardboard boxes. There were no nearby lights: only the glow of Antwerp, irradiating through the mist. A sign above the television antennas read: "Krediet Bank." A radio played love songs upstairs. There was no sign of life in the courtyard or the alley behind.

The girl struggled to twist open a long bar and handle that hooked the window in place, top and bottom. She failed, and Penrose had to help her wrench them open. Night came into the room, dank and cold. Her feathers blew in the breeze.

"Vous partez maintenant?" It was a request as much as a statement. Her pimp might be coming back to check. "Allez," she insisted.

"Easy come, easy go, eh, love?" He gave her a quick peck on the lips and stepped onto the balcony. When he stopped at the bottom of the stairs to listen for intruders in the alley he could hear her struggling with the bar lock again.

A scuffling sound from behind made Penrose freeze; boxes fell and a long furry streak went over them, heading for the wall—a cat. Behind the fleeing cat two dark shapes gave up stealth for speed as they leaped around the side of the staircase toward Penrose, cutting off his route to the alleyway.

"You bastards!" In his renewed outrage Penrose made up his mind to stand and fight the lascars. A blue light had come on up high in the house and he would be able to see what he was doing.

Then the alley door opened, changing the odds: the stooped Chinese he had seen earlier stepped sideways into the courtyard. He had a black scarf around his mouth and a length of black metal in one gloved hand. Penrose turned and sprinted back the way he had come.

The girl was still trying to fasten the bar lock when Penrose burst through her French window, knocking her backward onto a huge waterbed. Her eyes looked at him—wide—then at the window he was wrenching shut behind him, comprehension coming as fast as trouble in Jakarta. The blue love light she had turned on to help in her struggles with the window had also turned on a video that showed two women and a man in athletic poses. The room was a jumble of leopardskin throws, erotic silkscreens and posters of myths: Jean Harlow, Judy Garland, Sukarno.

She rolled to her feet in a flash of sequins and ran out the hall door, just in front of him, down the blue stairs. There was the sound of windows smashing, boots thudding. A voice screamed from the third floor: the pimp. Penrose started to unlock the front door, his heart beating so hard he had trouble thinking, but he still paused at the final bolt and opened the judas and saw—darkness.

At first he thought there was a second slide blocking the opening, but two triangles of light came through, and he realized there were human figures square in the doorway, blocking illumination from the street.

Feet began pounding down the stairs, two pairs, plus the pimp's, higher up. He was yelling "Skata, skata, skata."

The girl was doing her best to become part of the lurid wallpaper. Her eyes were all whites, and Penrose again had the distinct impression she couldn't care less about the Asians; she was in thrall to a far greater fear that kept her obedient in a small room with a back exit.

There was only one other door on the bottom landing. Penrose slammed the judas shut and went through it.

He was in the display area, behind the cobras and the armchair, in full orange view of anyone on the street, but only the backs and shoulders of the lascars outside were visible, as they waited for him to unlock the final bolt. The feet from upstairs reached the landing, and a hand was already turning the door handle as Penrose got his hands around the stacked movie magazines and under the armchair. He straightened his back in one straining thrust to heave the heavy chair straight through the middle of the window.

He threw himself directly after it, his jacket tearing on one of the jagged stalactites hanging over the hole, and rolled in the twinkling slivers of glass among the cobblestones. He could feel his left palm and knees being sliced, but, more important, he could feel the two, no three, Asians reacting in the doorway behind him. Momentum carried him onto one knee, onto his feet, and he took off into the fog.

The humidity made the cobblestones slippery, and he could hear the squeaking of track shoes gain on him. Shouts wafted from the intersection ahead: these thugs were coordinated like an Afrika Korps, but if he could get by that group he would be safe—the 'Vanger was only two doors beyond.

A French sailor turned from perusal of a Zairean window to stare at Penrose as he pounded by. He risked a quick glance behind him: the sailor was doing nothing, just staring at the first lascar, who was only ten feet behind.

His breath was scraping, too fast, at his esophagus, those bloody cigarettes. At the intersection he swung wide away from the lascars, who had come out of the alley and were now trying to cut him off. But at that moment a twisting length of bamboo somehow materialized between his feet, and he went down as if gravity had just called in all its notes at once, so fast and hard he did not have time to get his elbows beneath him or retrieve his tongue from between his teeth.

They were on him in milliseconds, two of them dragging

him off the cobblestones where he was trying to imitate a Ridley's turtle, flipping him to expose his vulnerable underbelly. Penrose managed to get in a good jab at an ear, hard enough to knock the man sideways, and a good kick that landed square in a soft stomach, but now they had manpower to spare, enough to have one goon anchoring each of his limbs and a fifth sitting on his chest, and all the writhing and arching in the world was not going to do him the slightest good.

There were a couple of slurred commands in some Oriental language from the masked figure, then the man who was on Penrose's chest stood up. He was the heavyset type Penrose had kicked in the gut, and he was not wearing track shoes. The rationale for his thick leather boots became instantly obvious as he swung one foot back and kicked Penrose's head.

The sky filled with galaxies previously unknown to man. Penrose's brain tried to retract on itself as it assessed damage. Urgent messages of pain came from his cheekbone and lacerated skin, but there was no dangerous haziness yet, no fuzzy feelings from messages that had been sent but could not get through due to trauma of the neocortex.

Yet.

The boot was swinging again. Penrose shouted, "I don't think I'm—" and tried to heave himself out of the way, tried to tuck his chin down to present his forehead, the strongest part of the skull, but the boot swerved and drove into his shoulder with unbelievable force, leaving it numb. One of the men began twisting his other arm and shouting what had to be insults, which seemed superfluous to Penrose. He kept his face averted, but the man with the boot simply positioned himself over him. The boot crashed next into Penrose's temple, and for a second everything went black; then came stars that did not go away completely, just encircled the face of one of the thugs on his arm, a young face with implacable almond-shaped eyes and a mustache that would not cover his lip.

More conversation, and the boot swung again—into Penrose's ribs. He heard a distinct crack, felt his breathing constrict and prayed the broken bones would not puncture his lungs. His brain, at least, was still functioning efficiently as a damage control center, processing the pain impulses by intensity and origin, though the intensity signals were rising to the point of overload. Another kick came to his ribs, and a third, on the other side.

He began to realize, coldly, unemotionally, that these men were going to kill him. Another dozen blows like these and his insides would be pudding; internal bleeding would finish him off.

"Look," Penrose gasped, "why don't you—check my passport."

There were more mutterings between kicks, and a far-off cry—dissonant, Penrose thought, un-Asian—"Oi!"

One of the men on his legs got up and Penrose lashed out as fast as his neural centers could relay the message, and missed. As soon as he kicked, the pain in his side flashed yellow in his brain and he cried out in agony.

Now the track shoes next to Penrose's head pointed away from him. A rising chorus of yells including one distinct "fucking" echoed through the street. There came the sound of a scuffle. The kid on his arm jumped up and pulled a long wooden-handled knife, and Penrose yelled, "Look out, a knife," which brought another wave of protest from his ribs and head and a bellow of surprise that sounded very much like Pat.

"It's de fookin' skipper!"

"*KILL* 'im."

The track shoes next to his face bounced, danced and jumped to reveal a scrum of six or seven men, a confusion of feet and fists grabbing hair, from which Sean emerged in a low back flip. One of the Asians had Mel in a stranglehold, but Pat had another in the same lock and was stomping on a third. The French sailor attacked someone who was using a bamboo stick on Mel.

The struggle went on, isostatic, for thirty seconds; then came a long, two-toned whistle.

Immediately there were more shouts in the Oriental language, and one part of the violent dynamics subsided, then another, as the lascars broke off the fighting and ran or limped to group around the stooped man in the black scarf.

Pat was jigging and crowing hard on the outskirts of their tight little group, eliciting threatening gestures from the bamboo stick.

Finally, at some silent command, the lascars turned like a military unit (two of them supporting a man who could not walk) and marched down the alley into the mist.

108

A crowd formed; lights played; the Indonesian girl's crab-pimp came over and began screaming in Greek at Penrose, who merely closed his eyes and let Pat hoist him delicately in his fat arms and drag him, at long last, into the welcoming pink glow of the 'Vanger.

XII

"Penrose, you are so damn stupid, you still do not learn how to fight!"

He looked up at the woman insofar as he was able with his left eyelid swollen and both retinas raked repeatedly by the beam from a pencil flash she held in her right hand like a paintbrush.

Kirsten Alnes had clean features and brown curls. She was pushing forty so hard it had fallen over several times already, but she used makeup well enough to keep people guessing. The wrinkles visible around her eyes demonstrated an ability to smile, but those eyes were as blue and cold as glacier water: intelligent, appraising and inexorable.

She put the flashlight down and picked up swabs and bottles.

He tried to move his lips, which were still there despite the cuts and dried blood, and in fact they seemed to have grown noticeably larger, as had the tongue that probed them. An eyetooth had changed shape, and become sharper as well. Half his left cheek had fallen off, sixteen-inch naval guns were firing rounds inside his skull and his entire chest was on fire, which made the lacerations on his palms and elbows that Kirsten was dabbing with iodine seem painless.

"Aaah," he moaned. "You bitch. I need the disinfectant inside, not out."

"You are a child. I always tell you to learn karate, or something. And you are too thin, huh?"

She opened his shirt and lifted one eyebrow, the only sign of emotion she was capable of.

"Sophie."

A very tall Zairean woman uncoiled herself from around a long drink and a high barstool.

"Encore de l'eau chaude." The Zairean ambled over in languid fashion. "Merde, dépêche-toi, nom de Dieu!"

"Christ, Skipper."

Sean looked awed, but it wasn't because of the cut on his forehead. He, Mel and Pat were standing in a half circle a few feet away. Apart from the Zairean, the bartender, and a fat man and a prostitute bent over the jukebox, there was only one other person in the 'Vanger, hunched under a floppy beret at the far side of the bar, next to Kirsten's collection of religious statuettes. You tossed franc pieces into them and they would stick oversized sexual organs out at you and play "L'important, c'est la rose."

Penrose looked down at himself, and quickly looked up again.

"I'd say very late Turner, one of those red sunsets with London burning in front— Bloody *hell*, Kirsten!"

"You may have broken ribs. At least one is cracked, anyway. Here are aspirins."

"What did ye do to get them so cheesed at you, John?"

"Yes, and Elafkadis. Why was he there too, eh?"

"Will someone get me a fucking brandy!" Penrose yelled, and then turned pale from the effect yelling had on his chest. Through the crusted blood on his eye he saw the figure behind the bar look up: a woman, with a very long woolen scarf riding up around her chin. One of Kirsten's stable, he thought, otherwise she wouldn't be here.

Sophie brought water and the muscular Flemish bartender brought homemade brandy, which went down like fire. The fat man at the jukebox selected a German disco rhythm, pounding out "Warum bist du immer, immer so toll?"

When his tears and coughing had subsided, Penrose asked, "So you don't know those people?"

"I did not say that," Kirsten replied.

"Then who are they?"

"There is a gang of lascars that is well known in Antwerp."

"And it were them?" Sean asked curiously.

"And you said somethin' to a girl they were protectin'," Mel added wisely, tottering a little. Then he slipped off as another of Kirsten's women came downstairs with a customer trying to act nonchalant in her wake.

111

"Perhaps," Kirsten replied to Sean's question. "To me they look alike, the same. But the lascars"—the eyebrow went up again—"they would have to have a reason. They only do contract work, for people who pay them to do a job, to beat up someone. So—" her voice rose—"do I have to ask damn Elafkadis, Penrose, or do you tell me?"

"What? Ask who?"

The blue eyes went colder.

"Elafkadis. The Greek who was so angry with you. I am thinking that is why you were attacked. Maybe he phones them. Maybe he has contracts with them, huh? What did you do, you limey pig?"

The Greek, Penrose thought. Marika's pimp. "No." He took more brandy. "The Greek who was yelling— That's how I got away from them at first. His girl let me in when they cornered me."

"The girl."

"Yes."

"The one with the skin."

"Ah, yes, the skin, that skin," Penrose said lightly, trying to come up with an analogy close to the memory, "softer than the wet dreams of a silkworm—" He looked up in surprise, winced as his cheek stretched. Those eyes were so cold they must be freezing over by now, he thought.

"You—er—tried her?"

Kirsten nodded. "Of course."

"But you didn't keep her."

"No." A sigh. "I would have ended up wanting her for myself only," Kirsten continued, "and it is better to have many that are all okay than one who is like Marika. She makes the rest look like damn cows, and that is trouble."

"She is trouble," Penrose agreed, closing his eyes, "but that skin—" Then he added hastily, "But she only helped me to escape. That's why the Greek was so angry, in fact. She let me in, but not for business."

"God, I hate the Greeks," Mel commented loudly, swerving by on his way upstairs.

Penrose said, "Try to find out for me what the lascars wanted, eh, Kirsten love?"

He lay back when everyone had finally left him to go drink or serve at the bar and lit a cigarette. The tobacco tasted like tobacco tasted when you recently had been half killed by strangers for no particular reason. With his eyes closed he tried to assess whether Kirsten was right and his ribs were only cracked, holding his breath deeper and deeper, but he gave up when it felt like his head was going to explode and his lungs congeal. Sophie brought him another brandy and, in a surprising turn of speed, another. He was beginning to feel as if the microscopic harpies who were slowly peeling raw strips of flesh off his chest and face were contemplating a break; in fact, he was almost asleep when a voice said, "Captain?"

Penrose opened his right eye, because his left was gummed shut.

He tried to say "Yes" in a suave manner, but his lips seemed to have become two hunks of unwieldy blubber, so that all he could manage was a hoarse "Bliss?"

He tried to sit up, but his ribs had petrified around bruised nerve endings. He gave an involuntary gasp of agony and subsided on the cushions again.

"Oh, lord, I'm sorry. Don't get up," the woman in the beret said, sitting down on the other side of his table.

The first impression he had had of her sitting at the bar was wrong; this woman was no prostitute, did not carry herself with that kind of calculation. His second impression was based on the smooth line of her jawbone, the set of her eyes and angle of her head: the woman was driven, single-minded. The third took in a mass of very, very light chestnut curls, gathered in a bun at her neck, full lips, a small nose and deep eyes, so brown they were almost violet. Her accent was a nasal Yankee.

"You look terrible," she said.

Penrose probed his left eye with a finger till it creaked open.

"What the hell are you doing in the 'Vanger?" he mumbled.

"Research." The full lips curved a little higher. "I'm sorry to disturb you. I can see you're in pain."

"Too bloody right," Penrose agreed, reaching gingerly for the brandy glass.

"Here, I'll get you some more." She did, bypassing the Zairean, who suddenly looked ready to scratch her eyes out. The fat German fed the jukebox again: "Gar kein SINN, in Ber-LIN."

113

The volume was so loud it hurt Penrose's head and made the fake paneling and real life rings adorning the bar tremble with its strength. But the woman's presence seemed to demand conversation.

"You said you were doing research? In the 'Vanger?" His lips worked better, Penrose noticed, when lubricated with brandy. "Doesn't it scare you, coming alone?"

She smiled. "All good American girls," she said, "carry a can of mace in their purse."

He let that one slide. "What's the research?"

"I'm working on a doctoral thesis. In psychology. On prostitution."

"I see," Penrose said. "You've come to the right place, then." He took another swig of brandy. "What's the supposition you're trying to prove?"

"I'm sorry." She looked nonplussed. He took another sip.

"The supposition. Your thesis. What's the gist of it?"

"Oh, I see. Well, it's about alienation, rootlessness: foreign prostitutes who work with seamen, who I think are rootless by avocation. It's about the long-term effects on these women: anxieties, depressions, neuroses, that sort of thing."

"Trying to prove the importance of having a home?"

She smiled, and shook curls out of her eyes. "Yes. Only in a larger context: why society forces them to live the way they do."

"Seamen or whores?"

Kirsten stamped into the room, glared at Penrose, unplugged the jukebox and switched on the tape machine. The whining sound and punching lyrics of Bob Dylan muffled the drunken protests of the discophilic German. The bartender came over, primed to throw the German out. The woman opposite Penrose gulped.

"Bob Dylan. God! That takes me back."

"To what?" Penrose licked his lips, trying to lubricate the cuts.

"Oh, I don't know. School, college. Whatever."

"I was so much older then," Penrose quoted. "I'm younger than that now?"

Her gaze had turned inward, but when she became aware of her introspection, she made her social defenses whole again.

"Maybe," she said. "It's just a funny place to hear Bob Dylan."

"Well, it's Kirsten's favorite." Penrose nodded at the Norwegian madam, who was yelling at Sophie in rapid French. "She's convinced 'Positively Fourth Street' was written for her. You know, the one about the woman who wishes you good luck but would rather see you crippled. She thinks there is no situation in life that is not covered in 'Memphis Blues'— Why did you come over to talk to me?"

"Because I saw them bringing you in after the fight, and I heard something about, uh, an Indonesian prostitute?"

It was weak, and he had a feeling she knew it.

"You know"—she was changing the subject—"my grandfather used to tell me about places like this." Saying the first thing that came into her head, she looked around the bar, her eyes lighting on the life rings, the cheap linoleum. "He used to be on ships; he went all over. I promise you I keep all my data confidential."

Her eyes were looking very frankly into his, but he could feel her awareness of the sexual background. Penrose felt the brandy beginning to move his pain along, but it wasn't entirely the alcohol or the 'Vanger's pink light that was making him feel better. It was the warm feeling of talking to a good-looking woman with a head on her shoulders, in this of all places; and from that he derived a certain necessity to let her know he was not one of your typical whore-banging foul-talking seamen whom any self-respecting graduate student would not be seen dead with outside business hours.

"I was not a client. The girl helped me escape from that gang. But I can tell you a lot," he offered quickly, "about seamen, and their relationships with ladies of the night, as it were, if you let me buy you lunch tomorrow. Hello, Kirsten."

"Feeling better now, eh, Penrose?" The Norwegian had her arms folded tight, which made her generous breasts that much more so; her eyes had followed the downward trend in temperature evident earlier that evening.

"Pretty woman, eh? Damn you, drinking my brandy. This is not a pickup bar for you; this is a business place. Get back to your damn ship if you feel so good!"

She wheeled and marched back to the bar.

"Bloody hell, what's got into her?"

"I think she's jealous," the American woman said, her eyes crinkling.

"Yes, but not the way you think."

"Okay."

Penrose observed her, and smiled as far as his lips would allow.

"One o'clock, in front of the Brabo fountain in the Grande Place," he suggested, and felt even better when she nodded.

XIII

The next morning he wondered whether he could keep his appointment with the American.

His chest had become a mass of yellow and purple contusions that created a kind of chain reaction of pain whenever one bruise shifted a millimeter to bump another.

His first attempt to get out of his bunk left him sweating, gasping and pale, and he had not even got his head off the pillow. It took him ten minutes to complete the operation successfully, not counting time spent peeling bedclothes off his scabs. Changing the bandage Kirsten had put around him to brace his cracked rib took another ten; forty to shower and dress; and a good minute to shuffle painfully to the saloon.

Morning in port was the shriek of gulls, the growl of cranes and the smell of wet chips, mayonnaise and rain. He consumed one glass of cognac to get to the bridge, and another to catch the weather report, go over the stability calculations, come up with loading schedules and fill out insurance forms for the seven cases of Dimple Scotch that had disappeared in Dunkirk, courtesy of thirsty dockers. He drank two more glasses before even trying to wrench his stiff abdomen into a taxi with special permission to pick him up right at their berth.

Braced in the taxi as they jounced over tracks and cobblestones, lighting a cigarette with hands that hurt from glass cuts, Penrose wondered why everything in the day tasted like new apples. The mere fact of asking a woman out for a lunch date, even if it was the first time in years, should not

117

have that effect on him. But the apple feeling disappeared when he could not find her at the fountain.

He found her by the cathedral under the same beret and in a no-nonsense trench coat. It began to rain in earnest, so they went into the first brasserie they came across, a dark place with polished brass, shining mirrors and black-suited men discussing diamonds.

"It just occurred to me—"

"Do you know—"

"Go ahead."

"No, you."

"It's not important, now I think about it. I was going to say, I don't even know your name, but now I'd rather you didn't tell me, for a while at least. Nothing wrong with mystery."

Her laugh was a little hoarse, and betrayed control. It had been a pretentious comment, he realized. Now that he could see her eyes in direct light, he thought they covered stories with confused endings.

They ate sausages. Penrose drank a lot of beer, using his aches as an excuse; he felt high but in full command. The American sat and listened to his jokes with every appearance of interest. When he began talking about ships and seamen and the women they met in ports, she took out her notebook and began jotting down information, but after a while she stopped and simply listened to him.

Penrose found he had begun ordering Mort Subite beer as a reaction to her relative silence; if he wasn't careful he would blow himself out of the water.

"Look," he said at length, "I've been doing all the talking. I want to know more about you."

"But why?"

"You're being coy." He smiled, to draw the sting.

"Not really. What I do is nowhere near as interesting as roaming the ports of Europe for a living."

"Familiarity breeds contempt."

"Perhaps. But you have something solid to be contemptuous of, not theories and departmental rivalries—who out-publishes whom."

"It's not all wine, women and song. Romantic rubbish, girls in every port. There's a lot of being alone, and worse."

"Such as?"

"Such as losing a ship."

"You?"

Penrose nodded. "And a deck hand—a friend, rather. I'm not trying to garner sympathy, but I'm trying to tell you it's not all Masefield out there."

Her brown eyes shifted gear, reassessing.

"I sensed—something. There's more than just the bluff British sea dog to you. Is it that?"

"Do you want me to lie down on the bench, here?"

She laughed.

"Tell me about yourself," he repeated, forestalling her but secretly pleased with the interest. "You're not the run-of-the-mill yuppie-scum, either, or at least you're the first I've ever seen in the 'Vanger."

"The first what?"

"Yuppie. Young urban professional. An American term, I believe."

"I know the term."

He lit another cigarette. She sighed.

"What do you want to know?"

"Everything."

A distant laugh. "Where do I start?"

"How about the beginning, such as where you came from?"

The cigarette stuck on cracks in his lip. He shifted it to the very edge of his mouth, watching her realign her knife and fork till they were exactly parallel.

At length she said, "I'm from Maine. Brunswick Falls. A seaport, sort of. My father was French Canadian. He worked at the lumbermill, but my mother's family were all fishermen and sailors. So I guess it was genetic."

"Recessive."

"Mendelian." His turn to laugh.

"They had some of the best sailing coasters in the world in Maine," Penrose added, sipping slower at his Mort Subite. "Fast schooners, big, with up to seven masts. Better than Thames barges, faster than Brixton trawlers."

"My mother's father used to own one. He used to go all the way down to the Caribbean."

"I *knew* there was something about you I liked. Tell me about it," Penrose added enthusiastically, but she looked away, pretending to listen to a conversation in the next

119

booth but one, where men in clipped South African accents mentioned "tear cut" and "brilliant," linking them in each case to carats and money and men.

"You mentioned him last night. Your grandfather, I mean," Penrose insisted. "I'd like to know more about him."

She brought her eyes back. "Why?" It came out flat and harsh.

"Because"—it was so long since he'd last played the flirting game he'd forgotten the timing, the moves—"because," he improvised, "he interests me. You interest me, for that matter, and I can tell you care about him. But also, one of the reasons I like working on coasters is because of the history. It's the oldest of trades; they only just started slapping rules on it, shutting people out who don't belong to trade unions or who didn't go to school. So you still find men who've had it in their family for generations. Like your grandad."

"Grandad"—she gave a half smile at last—"is what we called him. He used to call me 'Clarabelle,' " she offered.

"I tell you"—she leaned forward a little, ambushed by the memory, and Penrose froze, anxious not to disturb what he saw, without knowing how, would be a rare opening—"in the whole crummy boring spectrum of my childhood that man stands out like a warm beautiful summer's day."

Penrose waited. Her eyes looked down, stared at the table. One of the South Africans said, "Magtig, it's done," and a silence fell over their booth as well.

"What kind of schooner did he have?" Penrose prompted.

"Oh, a big one." She sighed. Now she spun her coffee spoon with two fingers, following its turns with her gaze. Her voice begrudged him, a little. "Real big. I used to play on it when I was a kid. It was called *Sarah and Beth,* but he hadn't used it for years. He had it tied up at the stone company pier. It just sat there, rotting away, but every day he would go down and sit on the wharf and I would go play house in the cabins. You know, I can still remember how the sun used to come in the deadlights, just the color of butterscotch, and make all that old cracking paint seem real and new. He never used to say much but we always had a good time together, he and I. I was his only granddaughter— It's only now I realize how it must have broken his heart every time he looked at her, but he wouldn't let a day go by without going down to the wharf."

The coffee spoon was spinning faster, 360 degrees with every flick. Her eyes followed the spoon, hypnotized.

"He was the most honest person I've ever known." Her voice eased, and sank to a lower register. "A funny thing: two days after he died, there was a big storm. From up the river. The schooner's ropes snapped, and she floated out into the bay and sank. She had been on that wharf for thirty years."

The spoon stopped. One of the Afrikaners made a comment in Flemish, and they all laughed.

"Are you all right?" Penrose asked gently, refraining, just in time, from touching her hand.

"I'm fine." She looked up at him quickly. Her eyes were very bright, but dry of tears. "Believe it or not, it's still like a ray of sunshine on that old boat, thinking about him."

She smiled, waved her fingers. "My back pages; I was so much older then. I'm sorry to bore you. Where's the ladies' room?"

When she came back her eyes wore guards again. Her manner was controlled, almost frosty. Penrose tried to resume the probing, and she shut down hard and fast. She told him there was a sculpture garden she had planned to visit, so they paid up and left to hail a taxi.

The garden lay behind an old villa redolent of the profits of smokestack industries, blanched in mist and winter and crammed with plastic forms. They strolled down pathways and along narrow canals patrolled by ducks, reacting to different things. Penrose stopped in front of a spiraling abstract horse, while the woman went on to contemplate a high-tech construction of tubes. A series of poles at the edge of a lawn was labeled "Double Progression Green and White," and it was in front of these that she paused and said, "I've been in England, you know. There's something about your language. It doesn't fit. You had a broad West Country accent in the brothel last night but it's all very much BBC now. And you use concepts that don't fit with your having come up the anchorhole."

"The hawsehole," he corrected her.

"Through the hawsehole, then." Rain was beading on the lip of her beret and trickling down her nose. She had very pale skin, Penrose noticed.

"Your language is different," she insisted.

"Most deck officers have a formal education, these days."

"Few are generalists, in my experience. Even fewer get off on Raymond Duchamp Villon."

"Get what?"

"Off. Enjoy. Slang."

They began walking again, around a pair of gossiping pregnant plaster women.

"You should meet my other deck hand," Penrose said finally, "the one I didn't drown. Brian is a Cockney. He is highly intelligent, and fascinated with words, in a funny sort of way. Insists on speaking rhyming slang, which is a sort of East London code that consists of replacing one word with another that rhymes with the first, like apples and pears instead of stairs, or pig's ear for beer, that sort of thing."

A flying Pegasus watched them. Rain pinged on an Art Deco rooster.

"But Brian has been brought up with the wrong codes. Lots of kids in East London, for example, are conditioned to think only their own codes are cool, something others can't comprehend. So they learn slang that only their group knows and don't bother working on their Queen's English. The academics called it a restricted language, as opposed to an elaborated one. Am I boring you?"

"No."

"Well, the trouble with a code is that it only works with your own group. Which means that a kid like Brian can't deal with concepts in a different code—the important code called BBC English. The kind you need to raise your skill level. I've tried and tried to get him to take his mate's certificate, but he won't do it. He knows the navigation cold, better than my old mate, who *has* a ticket in fact. Brian knows the concepts of triangulation without knowing the proper names for them. It's not only that he'd have to catch up on his BBC English. He's been conditioned to think he can't do it. Do you see what I mean?"

"Shoo-wah."

"Pardon?"

"Shoo-wah. It's code, in Maine. It means yes." She took off her beret, wrung it out, and set it back at a more elegant angle. "But none of this tells me where you're coming from: you, Captain John Penruth."

"Penrose."

"Penrose, then. What about you?"

"Me?" Penrose said brightly. "I was educated as a university man, don't you know. Which means my codes are understood only by the people of my milieu, the people who run things anyway. Which doesn't mean they're any less limiting, mind you. I hope you will be coming to England soon, incidentally, so I can show you some of my milieu." He gave a stage laugh, and kicked himself inwardly. It was the Mort Subite talking.

"I'm supposed to be going over," she said, looking at him directly, "in about a week, to do some reading at the British Museum."

Penrose pretended to trip on a sculpture that had its belly to the ground like a snake, and ended up giving his ribs a painfully real twist. So much for clowning.

"Are you okay?"

"Maybe," Penrose said, "we could meet then."

"Maybe I'd like that."

"Soo-per," John Penrose said, hiding his real pleasure under a fake accent.

On his way back to the ship Penrose stopped by the 'Vanger.

It was a long time since he had been in there during the day, and he had forgotten how the pink neon shone too weakly to hold its own against a Belgian overcast. The bar looked seedy; the souvenirs of scrapped ships and dingy ports seemed lost and pathetic, postcards from places like Valparaiso and Yokohama were curled and brown. Sophie was grunting and perspiring as she mopped the floor, and one of Dylan's more lyrical laments was playing softly in the background. Penrose found that none of this affected him.

"You look very damn happy, my friend, even with all your wounds," Kirsten snarled, looking up from a copy of Oslo *Dagbladet*.

"Your make-up's slipping, Kirsten my love," Penrose replied, limping over to a barstool. "You look all of thirty-eight." Now that she mentioned it, his wounds were aching like hell. "Can I have a beer?"

She was still angry, Penrose thought, but Kirsten got up and pulled a Stella from under the bar, snapped the top off, poured it into a canted glass, and set it in front of him in one fluid motion. Then she leaned over to look into his eyes from a range of three inches.

"Damn you, you pig!" she said with real anger.

"She's not for you, Kirsten," he replied levelly. "She's not like you."

"She's not for you either, my friend, not like you either. But I could have changed her. You do not understand her, you never could; but me, I can tell. I could have changed her," the woman repeated, swinging away. "She is a wasteland, anyway. She is like sand castles, at low tide; the water runs in, the water runs out. She lets you build what you want on it as long as she can live there and control it."

"You're one to talk."

"So, I get to you, huh?" Kirsten crossed her legs, hiked her skirt up to her crotch to taunt him and reached for her Oslo *Dagbladet*. "You men are what you think women are like: always you want something, quite cheap."

"Give it a rest, love," Penrose said, his good mood almost vanished now. He took a long slug of beer, lit a cigarette and added, "We've known each other too long, Kirsten, so stuff the political lezzie bit and tell me what I want to know."

"How do you know I got it so fast?"

"Because Veritas would not pay you what they do if you couldn't find out something that simple in twelve hours."

"It's going to cost you money. Sophie, chérie, fais les lits." Kirsten turned to boost the volume on her fancy tape deck.

"Thanks, Kirsten," Penrose said, weary of the interchange. "With friends like you I don't need lascars."

"One hundred francs will be enough."

"Well, what is it?"

"The money first."

He sighed and pushed the notes across the bar.

When she had stacked the money in the register she said, "Someone wants you out of commission, Penrose. Maybe for always, maybe not."

"That's it?"

"That is it. The lascars were paid by someone. They knew your ship, your face, your ETA. My friend thinks the job did not come from Belgium, but that is all he knows. They sent a man over here with money. The man is no longer here."

"Thanks again, Kirsten," Penrose said sarcastically. "I could have made that up on my own."

"Then go make up your own damn stories."

Penrose got up in only three separate stages and headed

for the door. As he pulled it open she called, "You better learn karate, Penrose, and gain some weight. That is what I think. Or else, be careful."

He hesitated, then turned around, but all he saw was the *Dagbladet*. He left the 'Vanger and went directly back to the ship.

XIV

A full-time London & Continental master relieved Penrose of the *Princess* four days later in Great Yarmouth, where they were waiting to unload their six hundred tons of phosphate fertilizer.

Except for the new skipper coming onto what had become *his* bridge—looking around with an appraising and judgmental eye, as if wondering what damage this captain-under-investigation could have allowed in two weeks' time—it was not so different from the quick weekends Penrose had snatched when the *Witch* was waiting to load or unload, tied up at inexpensive, foul-smelling industrial berths where purple sewage stained the rivers. Waiting for cargoes; there had been so many of those waits in her last few months.

And except for the fact that when he left the *Witch* he had usually visited Priory, until two years ago, when Selina had begun stepping out in earnest with the opera singer, it was not so different from the times he had rushed off to whatever station was nearest the harbor, duffel bag on shoulder, to catch the first train to London.

But when he hurried off the platform at Euston Station, he realized he had nowhere to go and nothing to do. It was too early, even, for the pubs.

Priory was out. He had barely thought about Selina and her family and their games in the last few days. Tim Harewood had occupied more of his few moments of reflection than his wife, and even the questions Harewood's death had raised had been bulldozed into the background by the urgency of tides and pilots. Now it all came spating back with the smells and bustles of the capital, and he saw that a resolution had formed in the breathing spaces: he was going to avoid Selina and her world to the extent it was possible.

It was a bright, sunny Friday afternoon in March, and the British Rail digital readouts were flipping to 15. He could make the 15:15 from Paddington, and pray to the gilded gods of Selina's society that she would not decide to spend the weekend at Restormel.

He caught the train with enough spare time to buy some lagers for the ride, and to call Colin and even Radetsky. Colin was out and the inspector was not at the police station.

When he got to the carriage he sank back gratefully in one of the soft blue seats, all of which were facing forward in an effort to con passengers into thinking they were actually flying in a jet plane, the triumph of speed over purpose. He missed the old compartmented trains, where you spread out your coats and luggage, and if no one got on in London you could lie down on the seats and snooze till Reading, Exeter or even Teignmouth because the only entrance to your compartment led onto the tracks. And if there were two of you, well—they had called it Intercity Intercourse in university.

He would have liked to lie down and sleep. He had learned to trust Mel but had stayed up over three of the last watches because the radar had fuzzed out again and the traffic in the shipping lanes around Orford Ness had been murderous—

He awoke with a start to the recessed lighting, the metallic syntax of train wheels, a quarter moon putting silver fingers on paddocks and windrows, the truncated farm roofs of Wiltshire that flitted by at eighty mph as if touched by a spell.

Inside, a warty conductor was parrying scathing verbal onslaughts from a thin kid with dark glasses, drainpipe trousers, a jean jacket and a bush of cyan dyed hair. Other passengers were doing their British best to ignore the altercation.

"Why the hell would ah bluddy well get on in bluddy Lundun if ah live in bluddy Reading?"

Four words from the conductor.

"It's the type of mind-twisting you Tory aliens on British

Rail rely on, learn it in standard textbooks for Beginning State Domination by UFO Crews, ah shouldn't wonder."

"I saw you in London, mate," the conductor repeated, stolid as a locomotive. "You got off for a bit in Reading, that's all. You shouldn't dye your hair blue if you're going to skive. Now pay up or get off, and let's have an end to it."

The kid turned to Penrose with a snort of disgust. "See? Impossible to get any give and take. Yet when his bluddy huge union decides to stop them all dead with a fooking strike, they sit down and take for so many hours their bladders swell to the size of footballs because of all the tea they drink with management."

Penrose laughed, surprised from the sluggishness of sleep.

"Right," the conductor said, his red face getting redder. "You're getting off at Exeter. Come on."

"British Martian Rail. Bug-eyed ticket collectors."

"Get up."

The kid slouched to his feet, feigning a yawn, clutching a Sainsbury's bag full of papers. They both turned to look at Penrose when he said "Here, just a minute," the kid imperturbable, the conductor stiff with the weight of running the Penzance Express in difficult times.

"How much does he owe you?" Penrose asked the conductor.

"Too late now, sir."

"Oh, come on, be serious. You're not going to run this kid off for skiving the London-to-Reading run, are you? It can't be more than a couple of quid."

"It's the regulations, sir."

"Aye, isn't that what Goering said to the Jew, 'n' all."

"Right, that *does* it."

"Hang *on,* conductor."

After two or three minutes of pride-massage the conductor finally agreed to let Penrose pay the difference. The kid merely glanced at his benefactor, gave him a cocky salute, and began rolling a cigarette.

"How can you tell alien railwaymen from earthlings?" Penrose said.

"Easy. The aliens try very hard to talk BBC English. If you talk to them in a Wigan accent, they start foaming at the mouth, as you saw. They are actually only units of a large bureaucratic life form that has been taking over this planet for a century. Here, this will explain it."

He bent down and rummaged through his bag, fished out a paper and handed it to Penrose.

The paper read:

"Saatchi trained us to say, 'oh I'm sorry,'
and 'pardon,' and 'thank you,' and talk like a Tory,
and lick Tribune arses when it's time to vote Labour,
but never for this. Look, do me a favour,
Our planet, Squirg 90, never taught us to friggin'
cope with an accent that hails from Wigan. Get off!
She foamed pink and pulled out a ray gun . . ."

There were two pages of it. They were signed at the bottom, "Genghis Kant."

"That's you, eh? Genghis."

"Yeh. Like it?"

Penrose said, "I know what you mean. I used to work in a bank."

"I'm reading it at a right-to-work meeting in Plymouth. It sounds best when you speak it. Mostly I'm reading anti-Navy stuff, though. Like this one: 'My Mother Was an Argie Ewe.' It starts off:

"From Poona to Port Sudan, it's enough to make
* you weep,*
all the Navy's ever done is to shell the fucking sheep,
as long as they're not British, as long as they are
* brown,*
from Matins on to mutton they will grind us bastards
* down . . ."*

"That about sums it up," Penrose agreed, without adding he used to work for the Royal Navy.

"The sheep are gettin' browned off."

"Like a lager?" Penrose offered.

The kid got off in the Navy town, with four-fifths of the other passengers, and forty-five minutes later Penrose stood in the smell of coal and piss and clover that he always associated with Treg station, noticing how the very first wisteria were poking around the white picket fence, while the station-master phoned into town for a taxi.

The taxi dropped him off at Wheal Quay just before 10:00 P.M. in the midst of a gaggle of Bodrugan's sheep that had got out yet again through the same fence he never mended properly.

The hatch of *Salope*'s after cabin always jammed when it had not been used for a long time. He had to drop his duffel bag and put his shoulder to it, twisting his head sideways as he pushed, stifling the protest from his ribs. The white paper anomaly on the mainmast first entered his field of vision as the hatch groaned open.

He was puzzled for half the ten strides it took him to get to the mast, increasingly angry and apprehensive as he recognized, reached and read the official notice, wired just above the boom jaws and sealed into place with wax and crown.

SHERIFF'S ATTACHMENT, the sign read, adding amid a lot of pseudo-Norman legal folderol that until further notice the sailing vessel known as *Salope,* belonging to John Penrose, Esq., dba Cornwall Shipping of the town of Treg, would be attached by the Cornwall Crown Court due to legal proceedings against said Cornwall Shipping Ltd.

So it was really happening, Penrose thought as he read, his breath coming shorter and shorter, his heart beating more quickly. This was final confirmation that the escape of seafaring was only that, a flight, and as soon as he set foot on land the complications of people and government forms would always be waiting to trap him.

The thirteen-million-pound claim had seemed unreal by the very fact of its size, and he had dismissed it, stored it like awkward gifts in the holds of his unconscious, because of that unreality. How, after all, could they wrest thirteen million pounds from a man who owned a tuppence ha'penny shipping company that had just lost its only vessel?

The answer was here: they could not, but they could take everything else he owned, including the *Salope,* the Land-Rover and his sextants. He wanted to rip the notice off the mast, start the *Salope*'s diesel, hoist the Jolly Roger and head off downriver for France, the Mediterranean, points east.

Instead he paced up and down the dock for a few minutes. This did nothing to cool his seething thoughts, so he walked past the countinghouse, down the lane, kicking at pebbles, punching at branches that Bodrugan never trimmed. He almost broke his hand on one low-hanging oak, which took his mind off things for a while. The vacuum left by impotent rage seemed to require filling.

Finally he trudged slowly over to the countinghouse shed, ground the Land-Rover's engine unmercifully until it started despite itself and drove along the estuary and over the hill to the Anker. He needed a beer.

The pub was old as the hill it sheltered under, built of white stone and black oak. It was far enough from the estuary to be off the tourist track, yet close enough to conceal the entrance to a long tunnel linking it with the shore cliffs near Merlyn's Carn. Jenkins used one end of the tunnel to store local brews (vulnerable because of their lack of preservatives), but in the old days it had been used by men of the smuggling trade to offload Spanish brandy and French lace from their luggers.

There was a skittles tournament going on in the public bar when Penrose walked in; smoke and conversation seemed to pack the room to the eaves. From downstairs came a rhythmic stamp and jingle as Melville's clog-dancing team practiced and drank beer and practiced again. Bodrugan was at his corner of the bar, the one that local gossip suggested fell down whenever he left the pub. So was his even older cousin Tregeagle, the last man around this part of the coast to speak the ancient tongue.

Poodle Crocker was talking urgently to Jenkins in one corner, probably about business, his long nose wagging below curly black hair and a cloth cap. Their conversation stopped abruptly when Poodle saw Penrose hooking his donkey jacket on the stuffed stoat's head by the door. So did everyone else's. Penrose walked with measured tread across the warped floorboards to the counter.

Old Tregeagle was the first to break the silence.

"John Penrose," he cackled, "back from the dead, comin' home with Penny Liggan."

No one else said a word. Penny Liggan meant broke, broken. The *Witch of Fraddam* had been the only large ship based in the river since the war. Corner shops sold postcards of her to tourists, and she had acquired the status of local mascot. Henry Permuen had not been the only kid to base his dreams of faraway palms on the *Witch*'s familiar rusty shape. Her sinking, together with Henry's death, must have been the biggest event in a year in the Treg area.

"Us knew it, John Penrose," Tregeagle continued, pointing an arthritic finger at the captain, his bushy white eyebrows scanning like radar. "The noit afore your ship went down us was by Blackbottle Cliff. And us saw her!"

Jenkins turned away to wash a glass, with a professional landlord's chuckle that disassociated him from any ill winds blowing in with customers. One customer boycotting the Anker could mean ten or fifteen of his cousins going to a rival pub as well.

One of the younger skittles players jingled some coins impatiently. The rest waited for what they knew was coming.

The old man's voice lowered to a theatrical rush.

"The Irish Lady. The Lady with the Lamp. She were walkin' the beach, holdin' the lantern high, a white hare coursin' along behind." Tregeagle paused to drain his pint of cider, then wiped his lips with the sleeve of his black serge coat.

Penrose simply stared at the old man, trying to decide whether to shout him down or ignore him. Everyone knew he was senile.

"Oh, no, course you won't believe it, Penrose: nor the younger of you here, you won't believe. But us old folk remember the wreckers along our coast, and they know she walks of an evenin', just as us saw her, holdin' her lantern high to warn of death at sea. Even if it was far off, it were her. 'Oo else would carry a lantern along the beach in February?"

The eyebrows scanned Penrose again. "It were just at dusk, an' us could see the Carn from Blackbottle Point, an' hear the barkin' and shoutin'." He sat down abruptly on a barstool and shoved his empty pint toward the tap.

Penrose responded by ordering a pint himself, from Jenkins, and mentioning to Bodrugan, as if nothing had happened, that his sheep had got out once again. His anger would keep, and eventually dissipate, just as he had finally eliminated the hatred he felt for the Welsh foreman. He hadn't thought of Morgan in days.

Two of the skittles players, notorious doublespeakers both, came over and told him they were sorry about his ship and Henry and not to mind old Tregeagle, who was always seeing the Irish Lady when he was three sheets in the wind. Crocker sidled up and asked Penrose if he needed a job, now that his ship was gone, the sharp eyes and nose jabbing at

Penrose with every phrase, giving his words a hidden meaning that was fully intentional.

In a way, Crocker, like Tregeagle, was the last link here to the Anker's past, and Cornwall's. He was originally from Polperro, and everyone knew he had gone to the London School of Economics, there to dabble in radical politics. He ran a thirty-five-ton Scottish seiner out of Treg, but it was common knowledge up and down the estuary that his real money came from the Trade; not smuggling brandy or any of its modern equivalents, but illegal immigrants, mostly Asians and Turks, the slave trade of the twentieth century. He also carried on a profitable sideline in pets, bringing in Chihuahuas, poodles and Persian cats for doting owners who could not wait six months for their pet to undergo the rabies quarantine demanded by British law.

People said Crocker insisted on all the proper vaccination papers for the charges, both human and animal, that he brought in through an old abandoned smuggling tunnel toward Blackbottle Cliff, but no one knew for sure. Hence his second nickname: Mad Dog.

Penrose declined Crocker's half-offer with a half-hearted joke about dole queues. Poodle wanted to chat further, as always, but Penrose made some excuse, sank another two pints of Bushells chill-and-foaming bitter and went out the door.

He stepped into the darkness, his eyes adjusting to the moonlight, and a voice came almost at his ear: "Oi'm *warnin'* you, Penrose!"

The captain recoiled without thinking, exclaiming "Shit!" In the next split second he recognized the voice and remembered that its owner had left the pub five minutes ago.

Rooks rose cawing from a prehistoric oak across the road.

"Go back to your dirty mac, old man, and leave me bloody well alone." He could see the white beard now, the eyebrows and spectacles.

"Your father-in-law, educated man that he is, would not want you talkin' so to an old man only doin' you a favor; for there's somethin' else us saw, Penrose." Tregeagle paused for effect, but the wait grew too long, Penrose had stepped away and was getting into his Land-Rover.

"The Borgest, Penrose," he hissed into the silence, "the Yelldogs, the dogs of hell. They came last night, Penrose. I was watchin'; us heard 'em howl."

Penrose put the Rover into second gear to climb the hill over to Wheal Quay, but he could still hear the old man screaming behind him: "You're next. I tell you, that's what it means: it's Henry Permuen comin' to tell you, you're next!"

It might have been the old man's warnings; more likely it was the sheriff's paper and the thirteen-million-pound threat sealed to his mast that made Penrose sleep fitfully that night between dreams of cargoes that were late or never arrived, dreams of fogs, dreams of looking for but never finding a woman in Antwerp who might or might not be the American girl. But when he woke he found fair weather holding and there was a breath of spring that was attributable, but only partly, to some early yellow asphodels garnishing the hedges.

Again Penrose resolutely boosted control. As he brewed coffee he put writs and drowned deck hands, murdered journalists and repressions from his mind.

Focusing on the warm feel of sun on skin he embraced the anesthesia of routine. He opened all of *Salope*'s portholes and hatches, stoked the stove to exorcise dampness and checked around decks, beam knees and bilges looking for dry rot. The *Salope* attracted dry rot like no other boat he had ever known. Finally he locked her up and cranked the Land-Rover to go carry out the only family ritual he had left since he had stopped living with his wife and the endless forms their marriage retained to cover up its loss of substance.

The sun was barely over the eastern tor when he reached Saint Winnoc. Old Jack Tomkyns, the gravedigger, was not yet out; breakfast smoke was coming from the gray stone farmhouse that was the only other building in the hamlet besides the church. A sea pie stalked off down the mud flats when Penrose opened the creaking gate and walked to the little granite headstone that read simply:

ELIZABETH COURTENAY PENROSE
Born June 2, 1980
Died August 21, 1982

Their substance. His and Selina's.

He didn't believe in life after death or reincarnation, did not think it mattered what happened to your remains one way or another, but if a child had to die her body should be laid to rest here, by the tall willows and the slow river, the ancient church and the long hills parting toward the sea. Here, where a dozen generations of children, many of them bearing her name, had lived and died in rhythm with the earth and water around them, with nothing to disturb their reintegration.

It was the only prayer he was capable of.

He did not hear the car come down the hill behind him, did not even hear the gate. When he turned he found his wife standing three graves behind him in a long dress and a patchwork coat that burst wool all over the place, the knuckles of one hand in her mouth. Her other hand was clutching a huge bunch of asphodels.

"Selina." His first reaction was anger; he could never get all the way away from her. "I thought you'd be in London."

He went up to her and touched her shoulder, but she kept looking at the grave, not melodramatically, merely out of preference. Her eyes were dry, and when she spoke her voice was deep and steady.

"I knew I would find you here."

"You followed me?"

"No."

"Selina."

"What?" She lowered her hand. There were white tooth marks on her knuckles.

Their reflex was always to take refuge from the stone non sequitur of the little tomb in pleasantries and small arrangements.

"Did it come to you in a vision of angels? That I was here? In Cornwall?"

She shook her head. "We all came down. It's Courant weekend, remember? Old Tregeagle came by this morning. I thought that's why you were here—I decided I had to talk to you; it was important. And when I saw the Land-Rover was gone—I knew. Where you were."

"Why do you want to see me, all of a sudden? I know, it must have been my sparkling repartee you missed."

He took her hand, the one with the asphodels. She pulled it away, stepped to the little mound, put the flowers down quickly on the grass and turned back to him, shivering.

"Oh, Christ, I don't know, now." She still hadn't looked at him.

135

"Did you hear the one about the Belgian in the grave-yard?"

That brought her eyes level with his.

"You don't understand, do you?" she said, matter-of-fact. "You can fill yourself up with those little jokes till what really matters no longer touches you. I used to do that too. Well, I can't; not any longer. Not here, not with you, not against this desolation that is tearing me apart. How can desolation be so tangible it can hurt me, physically hurt?"

Her voice held the strain of uncontrollable forces striving nonetheless for control, yet the tears remained unshed. Only her hands, wringing and wrenching at each other in the absence of asphodels, told of the struggle within: that and her eyes, drowning and burning at the same time, even in the shadow of the sun.

The quiet graveyard became charged with forces it was never meant to accommodate.

"Selina." He said it like an abracadabra that no longer worked.

"It's all over, isn't it? You know it is." Her voice cracked a little, and she patched it over by clearing her throat. "Things changed when she died, didn't they?" she went on. "We joked more and we danced more. Then you went back to sea more."

Penrose's wife turned back to the grave, then swiveled around again, even more quickly, flaring the wool, shading her vision, fishing out the German shades as if she could not bear the shadow. "What happened to your eye?" she asked illogically, then continued as if it were all part of the same general subject, "That's when the emptiness got so much worse, didn't it? But you won't admit it. Your control, Captain Courageous, leader of men. My God, why won't you admit it?" she practically shouted.

Penrose opened his mouth. Again she forestalled him.

"No. No little jokes, John, please."

He had not seen her like this since the child died. There was something stronger here than the periodic wails of anguish their ruined marriage gave vent to.

"You are in bad trouble, you know," she went on. "Not just your ship: it's the death bug again, it's that hole in your soul."

He shook his head.

"Oh, I don't mean to hurt you, John, I never want to do that."

She held out her hand shyly, like a little girl. It was trembling hard.

"Please shake my hand. We'll be friends, all right? And you can come to the hunt. It's just starting; you'll be late. You've never missed the Courant Hunt. And you can meet Quentin—oh, of course, you've already met." She uttered a giggle that was half cousin to a sob. "He's really a dear; I'm really head over heels." She began walking up toward the gate with an unnaturally affected sway.

She turned around when he didn't follow her.

"Please, John. Daddy wants to see you."

"What's the point?" he called. She was thirty feet away by now.

"Daddy wants to *see* you." She stamped her foot, again like a child. "I think he really does; he wants to help you."

"No."

"Please, John?"

"Selina, you want a divorce, don't you?"

A silence.

"Well, don't you? It's what you've been leading up to. It's why you've got dark glasses on," he said inanely, meaning it, in a different way.

"All right. Yes. Yes, I want a divorce. Yes, I want a divorce now."

The words were out; hysterical or not, they could never be retracted. Relief came with a sadness that was surprisingly bitter, like bile.

"Perhaps it's for the best," he said at length.

"Ask not for whom the biological clock tolls. It tolls for me."

"I see."

"So you'll come."

"Of course not. Why should I come to the Courant? Because 'Daddy' has decided I'm no longer posing a threat to his beloved daughter?"

Selina looked at her toes. He had to strain to catch her next words, they were spoken in so tiny a voice.

"Do it for me, please, Johnny? Like giving me away?"

"What?"

"For my new life?"

"He must want something very badly."

137

Selina sighed.

He stayed in the same spot as she walked through the gate, clanged it shut and drove off, the Jag's twin exhausts only returning a hostage peace to the little valley when they dwindled to nothing over the tor.

Part of his mind wondered for the nth time why she used the Jag only to come visit this grave, while another ranted at Selina, at Sir Norman and Restormel and the bank, and all the socially rotten boroughs they represented.

But later his stomach reminded him that they always had a full table of fresh Colchester oysters at the Courant. Side-tracked, he admitted to himself that it would be much more civilized to accept that he and Selina were finished. Refusing to visit Restormel because he was angry with Selina would be a sign that his emotions had control of him, instead of the other way around.

Finally, expelling a deep breath that seemed to have been held since Selina's arrival, Penrose followed his wife up the hill, north along the river, west into the clay moors and toward Restormel.

After all, he had nothing much else to do today. And it was the Courant Hunt.

When Sir Norman inherited Restormel House as well as the old tin mines and clay pits that provided, in good aristo style, the original underpinnings of an eighteenth-century title, it had been a huge decaying Palladian pile of stone. Endless landscapings by Paxton had been going to genteel seed around a backed-up stream; battalions of marble Dianas had disappeared, victims of the revenge of the vegetable. Even the fake Baalbek temples and the massive nymph's grotto were rotting and sagging.

Sir Norman had used his personal fortune to restore the lawns, the towering ballrooms, the molding antiques, the rhododendrons gone native, to bring Restormel back to its former grandeur. In the process he had taken over a fading hunt club, built up a new pack of beagles and turned the monthly chases into an excuse for the lavish formalities he was so fond of.

But now the weeds were fighting back, Penrose noted with surprise as he drove past serried Land-Rovers and horse vans into a courtyard he had not visited in almost a year. The gardens could not have been tended properly last summer, and there were other signs of neglect redux: paint flaking off fences, a broken Venus Pudica left unmended, old hay in the stable yard. Sir Norman had not been joking about hard times at Courtenay's.

The front lawn was shaggy but the horseflesh it carried had dished profiles, balanced conformation, clean hocks, deep chests, long withers, good space between the forelegs. The animals were curried till they shone; their tack was rich with wax and polish. The men wore tricorn hats, powdered wigs and swallow-tailed coats, as was traditional for the Courant; the women wore top hats and riding skirts and had lace clouding at the throat. Old Mukerjee staggered around in a frock coat bearing stirrup cups of port, trays of Colchester oysters and curried quail. Another victory of form over substance, Penrose thought as he grabbed an oyster and skirted the noise of laughter and clinking stirrup cups looking for Selina, sampling odd fragments of conversation as he went.

"I say, Sally gel! Havn't seen you in *yonks!*"

". . . and that wonderful Beeb documentary about how the Russians are *ruining* the tribal polo they play in Pashtunistan . . ."

". . . do tell me the dreary farmers aren't really setting booby traps for the hunt, are they, Roger? How frightful!"

". . . absolutely not, I said, order an Argentinian martingale after the *Sheffield.*"

"Dear Vanessa, poor thing?"

Penrose nearly tripped over George Courtenay, who was lying on the edge of the crowd, half conscious, head on saddle, with his eyes open and staring at the sun. Just then a voice shouted, "Penrose!"

It was Sir Norman, apparently acting as MFH these days, for he wore the tricorn with the plume. He broke out of a crowd of other tricorns and toppers and strode toward the captain. The crowd parted to stare after him: Hawkes, imperturbable, standing a good head above the others; Lord Askew, from Sir Norman's merchant banking commission; one of the county women—and Quentin, his purple locks hidden under a powdery wig, a video camera slung over his frock coat.

Quentin, the new pretender.

"Why aren't you dressed yet?"

Selina's father wore a broad social smile but his eyes were

139

apparently sincere. He looked tired, and his color was higher than usual.

"I'm not riding to hounds this time—Dad."

Sarcasm was lost on Sir Norman today.

"Not riding, John. But you're always invited, you know, expected even. Isn't that right, chaps? And Mrs. Chandos-Wicke, of course. Penrose," he went on, "is one of the best horsemen in the hunt. What's that—hurt your ribs? Oh, come now, John. Penrose, you know, is a damn good banker as well, has a real flair, yet he wastes his talents running little ships around the ocean, back and forth. A waste, a waste. No wonder you get into accidents, must have been what happened to your eye as well. But when it comes to man's work, eh, like hunting—sorry Mrs. Chandos-Wicke—of course, it's dangerous."

Penrose said nothing.

"Just teasing, of course."

"I'm looking for Selina," Penrose said.

"She ran off into the gardens ten minutes ago, crying her eyes out. I honestly don't know how you two manage to make each other so miserable. Must be an art to it. Just as well it's over, eh?"

Even Mrs. Chandos-Wicke looked away, embarrassed.

"Quentin's riding, of course. Now he doesn't mind a spot of danger, do you, Quentin?"

It was childish taunting, and by submitting to it he would, once again, be playing Sir Norman's game, but there came a point when the primal instincts demanded release from the intellect or they would burst out to wreak havoc somewhere else.

"Is Talisman—"

"Wear lots of sweaters," Mrs. Chandos-Wicke interrupted cattily. "It'll be chilly, and you're so thin."

"I saved him for you," Sir Norman said, grinning in satisfaction, and Penrose knew that, as always, the game had just begun.

Courtenay put horn to lips at 9:30 A.M., and old Mukerjee led the straining hounds down the back lane, with its hellish view of the clay-pit country to the south, past the Chinese gardens, to the West Meadow where the drag hunts began.

The beagles yelped in a frenzy, prancing perilously around the horses' legs until all the thirty or forty riders were inside the gate. Then, at a command from Courtenay, the lead dogs began ranging around the field, tails wagging, sniffing, while the younger hounds churned frivolously around the middle, barking, checking each other's hindquarters, standing on their back legs to look for rabbits, running back and forth and generally adding to the confusion until with a high and suddenly serious baying the oldest dog found the scent and set off straight for the hedge at the north end of the meadow.

The other dogs immediately gave up playing and streaked after him. Sir Norman sounded the "gone away" and, though he reminded himself every year that it was an anachronistic, atavistic and basically primitive feeling, Penrose could not quite repress the surge of gut excitement that told him the hunt had started.

He had been holding back Talisman, a large, rangy, slightly psychotic gelding, giving strong if gentle checks at the reins to keep his head tucked in and under control, but now he let the reins out a little, tightened his knees, kicked him softly with the right heel into a left-leading canter and followed the hounds and fifteen-odd riders in front of him at a disciplined pace.

The Courant had originally been a full-fledged fox hunt, until at age seventeen Selina had informed her father he had a choice: either he give up the wholesale slaughter of foxes for sport, or lose his only daughter. Now, instead of a fox, the hounds pursued an olfactory spoor left by a bag of crushed aniseed dragged along a secret course two hours before the hunt was due to begin.

The first hedge was an old beaten row that saw the beginning of every Courant meet. Talisman used it as an excuse to stretch his neck and take control, and bucked like a colt when Penrose wrestled it back. They swung left, easily, down a long meadow, sheep fleeing on all sides, the riders looking down to watch for rabbit holes as they rode.

The hounds were moving faster, however: Courtenay, Hawkes and a couple of others rode in a group right behind them, and cleared a fence at the end of the meadow. A stream ran there, Penrose knew. One of the horses refused, hard, when he saw the water, and its rider tumbled off potato fashion in a cloud of skirt and lace. It was inexcusable, he told himself, to insist that the ladies ride sidesaddle, inexcusable and dangerous, but the woman rolled back to her feet, unhurt.

They were fifty feet from the fence now. He let Talisman choose his stride, within reason, leaned forward as he felt the big horse time the jump, take two shorter strides to get into position and sail contemptuously over the three and a half feet of stone and wire, just slowly enough to brake and negotiate a slippery mudbank and a ford full of moss and rock.

The hunt diluted over the next meadow, Penrose halfway between the leaders and the rest of the pack, Talisman starting to get into his rhythm. There was a wide stretch of flatland as they followed the brook's other bank, in and out of a dale, and he could begin to canter out. They jumped a low hedge-and-wall combination into moors swampy enough to pepper their clothes with mud, then rode over high drier ground until the hounds tracked left toward a wood. There the scent led across a ditch and a high wall with only one gap that did not have barbed wire across it, and he had to wait for stragglers from the vanguard to jump the gap, standing well back to gain sufficient run-up to clear the obstacle, which was high and clean.

Penrose's ribs were aching a little now, some of his long-unused riding muscles were hurting more, but all was subsumed in the balanced elation of jumping: discipline cut with abandon, courage tempered with fear, man blended with animal, all to rediscover for a fraction of a second the forbidden mysteries of flight and the programmed desire for blood.

The hunt straggled farther through the wood: the dragger, either sadist or novice, had pulled his scent bag down a bewildering number of small trails, and it required real skill and a slower pace to keep one's horse slaloming around the various trees while looking out for branches, holes and beagles at the same time.

Just before breaking clear of the trees Penrose heard a horse literally galloping up on his tail and twisted around to see who it was, throwing Talisman off balance, so that they nearly parted company around an elm. He caught a flashing glimpse of Hawkes, hurling down a parallel path at a reckless pace, pursued by, of all people, Quentin, hat and wig now gone, pushing his own bay, yelling what had to sound like a taunt, given the situation. Hawkes drew ahead by a length.

He held Talisman back while they were in the woods.

Then they were out in the open, chasing the dogs up a long tor in zinc sunlight. Hawkes was a good horseman, but Talisman's neurotic character did not permit being second best, and when Penrose gave him his head he thrust it out and swallowed up the gap. Quentin, jouncing along behind, all knees, elbows and video, was lost in their dust.

They were neck and neck as they came over the crest of the tor, almost up to Sir Norman's latitude. At the top the trail led around the Hermit's Home—six or seven dolmens measuring the expanse of moorland that spread in bruised colors below them. Local legend said they were the bodies of pagans caught dancing on a Sunday by a newer, Puritan god. When they plunged over and into the next valley Penrose was leading Hawkes, with Sir Norman and Lord Askew well to the left and closer to the hounds.

The slope grew steeper, and they had to swerve around thickening stands of gorse. Talisman slipped, recovered, and Hawkes gained ground. The horse was lathering with the effort but his muscles did not slacken and he gave no indication that the grueling pace was depleting his reserves of strength. Penrose, on the other hand, had to grip even harder with his thighs to quell their trembling.

The sound of Courtenay's horn came as they thundered onward, level but even farther to the left; they were heading for a wall that led away from the hunt, into a field parallel to the one the hounds had just entered, but Hawkes had declared the race and seemed to have no intention of giving way. For his part Penrose refused, in this day of challenges and frustrations, to pull back and turn away merely to follow the dogs.

There were only two gaps in the combination of ditch, wall and hedgerow Penrose could see defining the two parallel meadows. Hawkes, to his left, was naturally aiming for the left-hand one, which gave him the right: a not-too-difficult jump with a clear gallop on pasture beyond. He checked the gelding a little, lined him up with pressure on the left flank, judged the distance remaining, took measure of the takeoff ground and what he could see of the landing, then let the gelding go. Talisman gathered up his powerful hindquarters, took a longer stride. Penrose encouraged him with pressure from both legs, and the horse took off, up, over, well clear. There was only a small glint of reflection when an invisible force plucked Penrose out of thin air; punched him right out of the saddle with a stinging blow to the upper chest; held him suspended over the wall and ditch while his horse, reins and stirrups continued their flight into the field beyond; and then dropped him six feet, crumpled, flat on his arse and shoulder into twenty inches of brackish water in the ditch.

For a second he thought he had finally done it, broken his cracked but mending rib and shoved it straight through his lungs. He could not breathe; his lungs seemed able to pump only little breaths that would not have prevented anoxia in a mosquito. It racked his chest with agony to breathe any harder. He rolled to his knees in the ditch water and found himself face to face with the putrid, staring features of a dead crow, beak open and bloody, stiff and floating in the cold, soupy liquid. He used all his strength to straighten up, and the stabbing pain grew worse and then, quite suddenly, subsided. The next breath was already deeper.

He felt for added damage: shoulder bruised but movable, ankle wrenched but ditto. He could look around now for Talisman, but the horse had vanished on the other side of the wall. Two riders were approaching. Hawkes, oddly, was unhorsed as well and limping in his direction.

Penrose got to his feet, using the sides of the ditch for support, and sat heavily on its grassy lip. He was getting sick of accidents that weren't. Holding his stomach he looked up at the wall and hedge, the obstacle that had seemed so clear-cut minutes previously. It took him a couple of seconds to find the thin glint of wire stretched taut five feet above the wall.

Following reflections that moved when he did, he could follow the wires to where they were anchored in posts hidden in the hedge. If the sun had not been shining he might have missed the wire entirely.

"I would advise," he gasped to the psychiatrist as he approached, face covered with mud and scratches and a long tear in one elegant black-and-tan leather boot, "that the Light Brigade approach the Valley of Death from a different direction."

There were noises to the left of them, noises to the right of them. He looked around to find a friendly county type rushing over, features locked in concern, and Quentin, still on his horse, filming away madly with his portable video camera while Penrose picked off mud and crow feathers and tested his various moving parts to see they were all still in working order.

The next hour consisted of a long progression of shocked comments, breathless sympathy, supportive threats. The county type cut the wires down. There was a long, aching slog homeward in the company of Quentin and a couple of other members of the hunt who had seen them diverge from the main drag and come to grief on the wires. Hawkes recovered sufficiently to make barbed comments about Penrose's competitive urges.

Penrose's ribs began throbbing, and his chest bore a thin shallow cut where the wire had sliced through three layers of clothing to lacerate the skin. Wryly he thought that had it not been for Mrs. Chandos-Wicke's advice, he might have been sliced in two.

When at last they got to Restormel House he politely shook off concerned hangers-on and Quentin's whirring machine. He left the impotent threats, the friendly and inaccurate medical advice, poured himself a generous snifter of brandy in the breakfast tent and went to ground in the gun room.

He sat there for a long time, replenishing his snifter from a decanter in the shotgun case, watching the fire reflect on Brescian snaphance pistols, flintlocks by Manton and Lorenschi, as well as duller Bren guns and kukris and captured Arisaka carbines that Sir Norman had brought back from the war.

Hoping Selina would find him, he remained unwilling to go out to look for her. Their words by the child's grave were beginning to permeate his consciousness but understanding did not bring a change in the quality of their effect on him. He still felt torn between relief and a deep, drenching sadness. The thought of the American girl hung around the outskirts of his mind in a shimmering aura of hope that somehow did not add to or detract from his dichotomous feelings about Selina.

It was Sir Norman who found him sitting there, a little drunk but in no great pain, an hour later.

"Penrose." The banker walked over and stood before him, coated with dust but still resplendent in his MFH outfit. He carried the hounds' whip coiled under one elbow like a swagger stick. "I just heard. Repeat what happened."

Penrose complied, mellowed by brandy. Selina's father threw two more logs on the fire.

"Those farmers are going to regret they ever tried a stupid trick like that," he said in a soft voice when the captain had finished. It was a voice Penrose recognized from Courtenay and Company's board room, a voice whose quotient of disinterest was in inverse ratio to the firmness of a decision. Here, at least, was a warning that meant something.

"Look at yourself"—pointing at the red line across the ruffles on Penrose's shirt. "Do you realize that five inches higher that piano wire would have cut your head off clean as a guillotine?"

Penrose did, but wished Sir Norman would leave him alone with the brandy decanter and his nascent acceptance of new emotional realities.

"I'm going to find out who it was, of course. I have a good idea who did it, you know, though of course he's never tried anything like this before. Attempted homicide, by God!" A slight tic had developed in a panel of Sir Norman's cheek, right where it became eyelid. Penrose's mind started to drift again until Courtenay dragged the second armchair over and sat down in front of him in a "man-to-man" attitude.

"You're sure you'll be all right, Penrose?"

Sir Norman was abnormally intent, serious. Penrose began to pay attention.

"I'm fine, Sir Norman. Pain drowned in VSOP, you know? But I don't think that's why you hunted me down, touched though I am by your concern. Not even the piano wire, eh? I think—" he formed the words with care—"you wish to talk to me about your daughter."

"Good old Penrose. Always dead on. Ha ha ha." The laughter was false. Sir Norman could fake laughter when he wanted.

"Partly about Selina, old boy," he continued. "Just talked to her, and, as I said before, I think it's best you two split up, thought so for years actually; you never should have got married."

"You make it sound so simple."

"But it is, it is. Mutual consent, eh?" The implication had to do with alimony. Penrose nodded, suddenly contemptuous.

"But I really wanted to ask you about Harewood."

"Harewood?" Penrose repeated stupidly.

"Yes"—he made a gesture of impatience—"Timothy Harewood. You remember, because Sela told me you've got some cock-and-bull notion he was done away with, bumped off. Well, violence is rampant today, isn't it? It all sounds ridiculous to me, frankly, but if by some off chance there was something amiss in his death it would disturb me terribly. He was, you see"—Sir Norman pulled at his right earlobe—"a friend. Of course, he was helpful in financial affairs as well, but a good man. Your theory came as a bit of a shock, I must say. So—" Sir Norman got up, walked to a standing case of silver pistols, and began taking them out, one by one, to line them up on a square of felt. "I'd appreciate if you'd elaborate a bit."

Penrose explained, surprised but somewhat gratified. Sir Norman listened attentively, his eyes on the guns, apparently following the captain's line of thought. But when the explanations were finished he shook his head.

"No. All circumstantial. Proves nothing."

"Perhaps not, Sir Norman. But there are ways of checking even circumstantial evidence."

"How?"

"An autopsy, for example."

"But there was."

"Pardon? Was what?"

"There was an autopsy done. While you were at sea. Apparently the inspector in charge shared your doubts. But they found nothing. The inquest took about ten minutes. Death by cardiac arrest."

The shock cut right through the brandy.

"But—"

"So you see."

"I didn't know."

"If you've nothing more to add—"

Penrose poured himself another glass of brandy, feeling like he was ten years old and had not done his science homework.

"But Inspector Radetsky—"

"Is a melodramatic Polish refugee who is trying to shore up a dwindling career by turning every case he comes across into a murder most foul," Courtenay said loudly, moving away from the firearms, waving the whip around as he paced.

"When Selina told me your theory," he continued, "I had

147

some chaps at the bank get in touch with someone at Scotland Yard. They knew your so-called evidence, John, backward and forward, and they closed the case anyway. There's nothing to base it on, you see. I even talked to a friend of mine at Lloyd's, and he said there'd be no motive. So, of course one wants to punish someone—that's the natural reaction against the senselessness of death—but— Anyway, Radetsky's been reassigned. He's on his way out. Why do you think he was put on a heart attack to begin with, eh?"

"Are you asking me or telling me?"

Courtenay ignored his remark. "Which brings me back to you."

"I'm flattered." This conversation was jumping around like a flea on a hot griddle, Penrose thought, and covered up his discomfiture by swallowing VSOP.

"No, you're drunk," Sir Norman countered. "But listen closely anyway."

He sat on the edge of his armchair, coiling and uncoiling his whip.

"When you left the bank," he began, "I was a bit annoyed, eh? Here I had given you my only daughter and a responsible, well-paying job in the upper levels of British finance, and you threw one back in my face. Eventually the other as well. That, of course, was inevitable."

"Of course," Penrose agreed, sarcastic.

"Yet over the years, I began to understand you, John." Sir Norman looked at the fire again. "On reflection, I've enjoyed having you around. You're better company than Quentin, at any rate—" Sir Norman almost winced, and for once Penrose did not automatically qualify one of Selina's father's opinions.

"You see, you and I are very much alike. All this posturing," Sir Norman went on, "the hunt, these costume affairs, the Buck House garden parties, this trading superficialities with people like Mrs. Chandos-Wicke—I enjoy them fully, you see, just as I love the parry and thrust of merchant banking, taking risks on the basis of how a man looks and talks, what you find out about what he is hiding. The game's the thing, John. It's no bloody different than sneaking behind Jap lines in sampans during the war, assuming roles in order to find out what people are trying to hide from you, and they are all trying to hide something, they are all playing a deadly game against me, make no mistake, against all of us who hold power in trust by virtue of descent, education and breeding. Listen well, John. I'm digressing, but my point is that, to any intelligent man, it is not the trappings of a role or a job or a game that are important, but the ability to *change*, to adapt, to slip behind your own mask and find out what lies behind someone else's. Why do you suppose I chose the Royal Indian Navy? Because we made our own rules. Fair play is an excuse for mediocrity, of which this welfare state is the epiphany. Look what it's done to England—you know as well as I do—look at the stinking decay of our docklands, our ports, riddled with rot and shop stewards."

Penrose kept his own features carefully blank, as if to demonstrate agreement.

"And that's how I cottoned on to you, John. It was that ability to change that allowed you to drop straight out of class and profession into the docks. I had you checked on periodically, you see—I didn't understand you then. My men told me you'd switched clothes, accent, all the superficialities of class, within three months, and no one outside Treg knew who you really were. You had the ability to change, and it was the opportunity you really desired, the freedom. And you used that freedom to gain control, in your own small way."

The son-in-law had forgotten his brandy.

"Come back to Courtenay's, John," Sir Norman finished, standing up abruptly. "That's what I've been trying to tell you." There was a direction in his voice that contradicted what he had just expounded. "Bygones are bygones, now Sela's happy. I can find a job suited to your talents—related to shipping, if you like. But I'm asking you to come back." Sir Norman looked serene, moving away now as if the response were given.

"I've bared myself to you today. I'll give you time to rest, think about it, get over these neurotic, paranoid conspiracy theories. Come see me in London"—his voice was fading away hypnotically—"and we'll arrange everything."

The door closed with a sharp click behind him.

"But she's not happy," Penrose told the fire.

The fire crackled merrily, as if it had not heard, or understood. Penrose shook himself gently, to see if he were dreaming. Then he remembered the autopsy, and poured himself another brandy.

XV

"Detective Inspector Radetsky has been transferred to another case," the sergeant said, shuffling papers and giving Penrose a careworn look that conveyed how the burden of law enforcement in North London rested entirely on his thirty-five-year-old shoulders and he really did not have the time for civilians injecting their fantasies into police business.

"Yes, I know. And the Harewood file has been closed."

"The *case* is closed. Yes, that's right sir, if that's what the blotter says." Truly right, just and proper, by the tone.

"Okay. I only wanted to go over some of the information with him. I'm—I was a friend of Harewood's."

The sergeant's face was pure sceptred-isle: ginger hair, fair skin, pale blue eyes, freckles. He had a habit of constantly thumbing through his ledgers while he talked, as if he knew there was a regulation for every phrase, had he only the time to find it.

"If you have new information, sir, you wouldn't want to talk to the inspector."

A Ghanaian woman added a long rising ululation of Twi to a cacophony that already dominated the dingy waiting area of Islington police station. Other voices discussed an alleged case of harassment and assault.

"I did not tell him I would punch him. He has been telling me."

"He has been telling me that he will burn down my shop."

"Bleedin' lyin' git. Innee."

"No, we are not lying absolutely."

"Could we all have silence please," the sergeant bel-

150

lowed. "Constable Dobbs!" The din subsided somewhat. Sergeant Reeves returned a small percentage of his attention to Penrose.

"Who would I want to talk to, Sergeant?" Penrose pulled hard at his pipe, making sure it would not go out in the midst of a face-down with the law.

"It's a closed case, of course, but if there's new evidence"—Reeves pretended to thumb through a very long directory—"you'd be wanting Detective Inspector Martin, at New Scotland Yard. His number is 362-3172. Now if—"

The Ghanaian shopowner began yelling at his own wife in frustration. Constable Dobbs tried to segregate witnesses in different interrogation rooms. The sergeant got up to lend a hand. Penrose recognized that he was beaten and left the station.

When he had taken the train at Treg that morning spring had been a reinforcement arriving by sea to relieve a beleaguered Cornwall, but winter was still laying siege to London, and its inhabitants looked it. Only a slight thickening of branches in the gardens he passed afforded some hope of rescue. Thin cirrus clouds were beginning to veil a sulphurous sunset. It was dry but cold, and getting colder. Colors faded in the shadow; streetlights switched on. Penrose tightened his scarf, buttoned his city coat up to the chin, pushed his hands deep in his pockets and turned right on Upper Street.

Depression weather. Siege weather.

He was going to have to find a cheap hotel or a small bed-and-breakfast to spend the night in. Normally, if Priory were closed he would have slept at the University Club, but its rooms, though cheap by London standards, were expensive for a man with less than two weeks' master's pay in his pocket and no immediate prospects of employment. University graduates were supposed to have a minimum level of discretionary income.

Neighborhoods like Islington were generally good for finding inexpensive lodgings, being too out of the way for tourists but still within walking distance of the inner city. Lots of single rooms and bed-sitting rooms converted when Jonny left home; ration-card furnishings and Victorian porticos, shilling in the meter for the gas fire and 50p extra for the bath, loo down the hall and no guests after nine, dear. Penrose had gone out with a girl at Birkbeck College before

Selina, and she used to room not far from here, in Swiss Cottage. They had spent a whole week there together, eating nothing but cauliflower cheese. Penrose wondered for a minute, as he walked, what had happened to her and the years in between.

His thoughts grew darker. He wished he had not been paid off from the *Princess*, at least. Then he could have lost himself in cargoes, not had to think about the *Witch*, or Henry, or Selina. Maybe they could have gone back to Antwerp.

There was a sign, ROOM TO LET, BED AND BREAKFAST. He walked up and rang the bell. A tall older man in a polyester cardigan told him they had let the room last week, that they really ought to take the sign down, but he might try the second street on the left, take a right at the pub on the crescent.

Penrose followed the man's directions, trying not to let February stage-set his mood, consoling himself with the idea that he had made a stand against Henderson Distilleries, against the freak chain of fates that had sunk his ship, against de Laune. It had helped to assume de Laune was a foe: if you had a solid human enemy, no matter how mysterious, it followed that he could be beaten.

He found the crescent and, with a little more difficulty, the bed-and-breakfast. A sign on the door read: NO VACANCIES. The landlady was not home, and the lodger he disturbed from viewing "Coronation Street" was unaware of any other rooms in the neighborhood. Penrose resumed his walk.

Yet if Tim Harewood had died of natural causes, he had not been murdered, insurance files or no insurance files. If Harewood had not been murdered—and the autopsy findings sounded conclusive—then there was no sinister agent at work behind de Laune and Court's refusal to pay his claim. If there was no sinister agent at work, then his problems were probably due to some conjunction of bureaucratic cusps in a huge international organization that Penrose was powerless to fight. By definition, you could not "best" an organization. Especially not an organization like Lloyd's.

In that sense, Radetsky had been his only hope. Navigating by gut only, Penrose aimed left for a high street, and walked left again toward the west till he came to a phone.

The directory listed seven Radetskys, only one of them

152

with the initial K. The rings went on beyond counting as he waited. No one home.

The windows of the telephone box were broken. It smelled of a thousand 11:30 micturations and was colder than outside. The pubs would be open by now, but that would only solve his lodging problem till closing time. He would damned well rather spend the night in Euston Station than wind up like a loser at Priory, begging to be let back in. His psyche winced at the very thought. He dialed another number, prepared to find another door shut or missing, but Brian answered on the second ring.

"Fuck me pink, it's the skipper!"

"Brian!" a voice screamed in the background. "Watch yer fucking marf!"

Penrose pussyfooted around the issue for a polite space of time and then asked the deck hand if he could take up an old invitation to stay the night, as he was skint. Brian told Penrose he was still paying his wages, and would be welcome even if he were not, as long as he could take his mum, who was a right old bag and nosy to boot. Penrose rang off, relieved in a primal fashion to have secured warmth and shelter for the night and looking forward to seeing Brian again, only partly as a bridge back to more peaceful times. He picked his address book off the top of the telephone, and his eyes found the notice advising customers that in case of fire or any other emergency they should dial 999 and tell the operator the box was located at the corner of St. Paul's Rd. and Douglas Rd., Islington, N.1.

St. Paul's Road. It was the first big road he had taken on his trek to Hampstead Heath the day Tim Harewood died. Or, rather, the day they had found him.

If he walked back east up St. Paul's for five minutes or so he would run into the street Harewood had lived on. The more he thought about it, the more he felt an almost perverted desire to return to the house where things had seriously started to go wrong. Just to look at it, as if to come to terms, in his own mind, with the contradictions between immanent, stolid, innocuous objects, and the fizzing banging disasters that could occur among the electrochemical haze that was human consciousness. Just to see it: he could feel himself irresistibly drawn and wondered with a sinking stomach whether he really was neurotically obsessed with

153

some paranoid conspiracy theory about Harewood. Perhaps, as Sir Norman had implied, it was becoming clinical, a schizophrenic escape mechanism for a failed life—

Neurotic or not, he had to start moving before he froze in the coinbox. He pushed the door open and turned right, east, without a second's hesitation.

It was not even five minutes' walk to Northampton Park Road. You could recognize the house easily by the fat spruce that overwhelmed its tiny front garden.

Penrose stood in the conifer's shadow, gazing up at the three stories of stolid brick and trim as if expecting an answer to seep out of the suburban pile. Nothing seemed to have changed, except that the snow had melted. There was no "For Sale" sign, no sign of any kind. Quite possibly no one had been in the house since Radetsky had left, which meant that if Harewood had hidden his file on de Laune and Court somewhere inside, or put it in a place neither Penrose nor Radetsky had thought of, it was still there.

He looked up and down the street. A bulky woman wheeled a pramful of babies into her garden. People fussed with tea behind frames of light or glowing curtains. He unlatched the gate and quickly walked through the side alley, in the shelter of a blind wall belonging to the row house next door. He kicked a rubbish-barrel lid and froze, listening for interest, but none showed.

When he got to the garden in back he saw that the hothouse window had not been repaired. The rear wall sheltered him nicely from all but the bedroom windows of houses opposite. It took only a minute to pick away the last shards of glass, slide over the frame and drop inside.

He found himself reviewing an honor guard of dead plants, their fronds, creepers and stamens lifted in brittle salute as he passed down the central alley. The door from hothouse to cellar was unlocked, as he had hoped. Penrose found his lighter, snapped it on and, shading it with one hand, went inside the house.

He was in a rectilinear rain forest of garden tools, ancient skis, mowers, a bike, twine and water pipes, a cellar exactly like a million others in England. Wooden stairs lay behind a partition. Still keeping the small flame sheltered behind a palm, Penrose negotiated the various obstacles and climbed upstairs.

This door was unlocked as well. When he opened it and

154

poked his lighter inside he found himself looking at a "Save the Baby Seals" calendar on the wall beyond.

The kitchen. Penrose deliberately slowed his breathing, waited for his pulse to settle down and tried to rid himself of this superstitious feeling of violating the abode of an unshriven corpse whose shade would be lying in wait for him somewhere.

He opened a couple of cabinets that contained nothing but pots and pans. Those under the sink held detergents and rags. He tested the walls but they were solid plaster, as expected.

He went into the hallway, feeling less superstitious and more stupid now that he was actually carrying out this ridiculous search, ridiculous because *if* Harewood had been killed for his information, the information would have been stolen. Yet he had to make sure; the killer might have missed something.

The Hockney stared at him in accusing fashion but proved not to conceal a safe. Nor did the hall cupboards, the closet under the stairs or a linen closet on the second floor. He forced himself to look under the bed and in the drawers of Harewood's bedroom. Here he began to feel truly uneasy, as he unfolded the intimate archaeology of Tim Harewood's life: his striped shirts, his silk underwear, his neatly paired socks.

An honorary diploma; two whole drawerfuls of airline soap, hotel cutlery and restaurant matchboxes methodically purloined from a hundred different cities and airplanes around the world; letters, tied in white ribbon; fund-raising leaflets for S.N.I.P., "Society for The Neutering of Islington Pussies"—every object, every choice or action it implied fleshed out the skeleton of a man Penrose had not known that well, defining the dead journalist in more and more facets and dimensions until Penrose felt like he was robbing a grave.

A bedroom closet contained two boxes of papers that set his heart thumping again, but they turned out to be old income-tax forms and mortgage agreements.

The lighter was running out of gas, so he tiptoed gently back the way he had come, deflated and yet elated to be getting out of the house. Perhaps that was the true root of superstition and sacrilege, he thought as he went down the stairs, the fear of ultimate irrelevance catching up, not with the dead, but with *you*. A great breath of swelling air made him freeze between two steps, but it was only the mechanism of the central heating, still plugging away as in a science-fiction story where neutron bombs had stripped the city of all organic life and only the machines still functioned.

His relief was almost tangible when at last he could step over the low wall in front, check once more for nonexistent observers and stride down the street as if he were only late for supper.

He walked aimlessly for a while, seeking to put distance between himself and the taint of decay in Harewood's room, the remote possibility that someone had seen him prowling around.

Despite his circuitous route, after five minutes he began to feel he was being followed. Twice he turned to check. Once, he saw a tallish figure in a short coat walking in the same direction a hundred feet behind him, but at the next street the figure turned into the entrance of a block of flats. A second time, he saw a shorter, rounded figure in a soft hat, about the same distance behind as the first, but this one, too, soon took its own path.

The feeling of being watched persisted long enough to send him pounding down the high road after the first bus that came along. He almost dislocated his shoulder, and painfully tweaked his ribs by swinging onto the rear platform just as a 171-A was leaving. The Jamaican conductor looked at him with contempt for all fools who did not wait obediently at bus stops, and without speaking held out his hand for the fare.

The bright lights in the double-decker merged objects outside into a blur of blacks and grays. Later Penrose told himself it was just his imagination that converted one of those dark shapes into a hunched figure in a soft hat waiting near the corner of the next street he would have come to on foot, turning to watch the bus as it growled down the road toward Highbury.

Brian lived in East Ham in a neighborhood surrounded by the failed hopes of a disused gasworks and the broken promises of Labour council flats. Penrose woke up early on his first morning there, roused by the chill of his tiny room and the loud rantings of Mrs. Jeffreys as she got Brian's sister out of bed in time for work.

He dressed, sneaked by the kitchen while she brushed her daughter's hair, and went down to the corner phone, the only phone for most of the row houses on the street.

A woman with a foreign accent answered Radetsky's phone almost immediately.

"Is this Inspector Radetsky's number?"

"Yes. Who is calling please?"

"John Penrose."

The mouthpiece was covered for a lengthy interval, there was the sound of discussion, then Radetsky came on the line, sounding so rigidly neutral and copperlike that his words effectively put distance between them.

"The chief inspector has closed the case, sir. I am now assigned to a different case," Radetsky said when Penrose had finished.

"Yes, I know."

"It would serve no useful purpose for us to meet, sir."

"But I only want to go over the information again."

"I have been assigned to investigate a series of shopliftings on Holloway Road," Radetsky went on stolidly. "If you have any further information that might be pertinent to the death of Harewood you should contact Detective Inspector Martin at—"

"—at New Scotland Yard," Penrose finished for him, his voice rising. "But I don't have any new information. I don't even know why I want to see you, actually, except that I have a feeling there was something very wrong in the way that man died. I hope—I mean I think it was at least a possibility that he may have been killed, murdered, because of something he found out about my insurance problems. To be honest with you, I hope he was killed, because it would mean whoever killed him had something to hide, which means that if you found out who it was they would have to pay the claim and I would be able to get another ship—" Penrose stopped, out of breath.

There was silence on the other end.

"Everyone has an inner reason," the detective said, "for their theories about the outer world."

"Sorry?"

"I appreciate your honesty."

"Thanks."

"But I cannot help you right now."

"Bloody hell," Penrose said. "You lot are all alike. When

157

the bureaucrats crack the whip, you jump." He paused. "I was attacked in Antwerp, you know. By a gang of men."

"Really, sir?" Amusement in Radetsky's voice. "In the red-light district, perhaps?"

He let that pass. "Someone over here paid for them to attack me."

"How do you know this?"

"I have contacts there."

Dead air.

"It could be anything. Even if it's true." He paused. "There is a caff," Radetsky continued at length, "near King's Cross, on the corner of York Road. It is hard to find but no one will see me there." His wife interjected something in the background. Radetsky said, "No, it's all right," and added words in Polish.

"This one time only, Mr. Penrose," the detective said, then stopped to confer with his wife again. "Only to explain why the case is closed, so you don't bother me again. The rules are strict. Twelve-thirty," he added.

It was a long way by bus to Euston. The fair weather was over, and rain lubricated the streets, increasing the friction on traffic. Penrose picked up his bag at the station, then took another bus to St. James's and the University Club.

There were two envelopes waiting for him. One bore the blurry rubber stamp of Cornwall Shipping and the Treg postmark: it was from Colin. The other was a Continental aerogramme with the face of King Leopold on the stamp and "Anvers/Antwerpen" on the cancellation.

He tipped the desk clerk. Then, after he had bathed, shaved and changed, he went down to the members' library. Encircled by burgundy drapes and books, protected by Persian carpets and a rule of silence, he opened the letter from Cornwall.

Colin's note was folded around an official letterhead. "This was only to be expected," Colin wrote. "Nothing changes. Pengerswick says court hearing due on April eleventh. Surveyor still unavailable. The Department of Transport inquiry will be held in Plymouth. Please see me first."

Thanks a lot for the chitchat, Col, Penrose muttered to himself, his anticipation slipping a couple of notches.

The official letterhead was embossed in gold on rich, heavy bond paper. It read "Tortuga Insurance Company

Ltd.," with an address in the Bank of Labrador Building in Georgetown, Grand Tortuga Island, British West Indies.

The text of the letter stated that de Laune and Court had passed on sixty-five percent of the policy burden, reinsuring that portion of the *Witch of Fraddam*'s hull and cargo with Tortuga Insurance; the Caribbean company was the largest holder of Cornwall Shipping's policies. Furthermore, TIC had no reason to question the expertise and authority of de Laune and Court Underwriters Ltd. in refusing to pay any claims ensuing from the total loss of the *Witch of Fraddam* and her cargo, and would therefore not be paying any of said claims. As a result, Tortuga Insurance Company was a co-defendant in the suit initiated by Cornwall Shipping against the Lloyd's underwriter. The letter was signed Andrew Smith, Secretary and General Counsel.

See you in court, Penrose thought wearily, and opened the letter from Antwerp.

One phrase leaped out immediately from the large rounded penmanship. "I will be at the Cadogan Hotel in Kensington from March 13."

The rest was friendly salutation, written in excellent style and signed "Claire Thibodeault."

Claire. Penrose rang the name in his mind several times, deciding he liked its short purity, the way it went with his memory of her. Thibodeault was, perhaps, a little trickier.

Penrose tried the hotel several times, but there was no answer in her room. He had a glass of the club port and phoned twice more with the same result. Finally he left a message at the Cadogan, with a time and place for meeting, and went to see Radetsky.

He found the transport café squatting under a railway off Caledonian Road. Its plastic sign read: NORTHERN CAFE. The interior was decorated in two different styles, one half of the long room torn between "fine" wainscoting and fading wallpaper with colored fruit, the other half featuring red plastic tiles and snot-colored linoleum. Tables of steel and Formica, ashtrays advertising lager, truck calendars with nude women hitchhiking and crusted bottles of brown sauce shared the area with an aroma of grease, chips and rock cakes. Large men in donkey jackets bartered stolen goods and vented clouds of tobacco smoke that almost obscured Radetsky and another man sitting, backs to the wall, at a corner table. Penrose bought a cup of tea and joined them.

His first impression was that Radetsky looked older, perhaps because of dark rings around the eyes, but otherwise the detective was clad in the same ratty blue suit; the same long black overcoat hung over a plastic chair, earphones from his tape recorder protruding slightly.

His companion, on the other hand, wore a beautifully cut set of pin stripes, gold cuff links and Italian shoes that could have belonged to a merchant banker. He was of medium height, very fit, Penrose's age, with styled hair, a clipped mustache and calm brown eyes. A very long face endowed him with a distinct resemblance to the Prince of Wales.

His name, Radetsky said, was Malcolm Brent and he was a junior underwriter at Dawley and Dawley Ltd., of Lloyd's of London.

"I don't mean anything personal by it, you know," Penrose said when the introductions were finished, "but I'm not certain I wish to talk in front of anyone from Lloyd's. Not until my case has come to court."

Radetsky made a dismissive gesture. "Mr. Brent is all right. He's a family friend. My wife and his mother go to temple together."

"Why did you bring him?" Penrose asked, politeness forcing him to address the younger man as well. "I thought you had given up on this case." To the Lloyd's man he said, "Why did you come?"

Radetsky said, "In case you had something substantive to add, Mr. Penrose. It would only work to your advantage."

"Unless he's reporting directly back to Lloyd's, or even to de Laune. That wouldn't help my suit."

"Relax," the policeman said. "He won't. But then, I thought you said you only wanted to go over old information. Except for Antwerp."

"We're going in circles," Penrose said. "I didn't have anything new, except—"

The detective and the Lloyd's man looked at him and waited.

Penrose looked at Brent doubtfully, decided to ignore him.

"Inspector Radetsky," Penrose began, "when I last saw you in person you were willing to flout police procedure and buck your own superiors because you had an instinct, based on circumstantial evidence, odd clues and such, that Harewood's death was more than it seemed."

Radetsky started to ransack his coat. He located and produced a red box of cherry pastilles.

"A week later I called you from Ipswich, and your instinct had somehow disappeared. You see, I merely wanted to know why you are now satisfied Harewood was not murdered." Penrose stumbled as he tried to recall exactly why he did need to see Radetsky. "So I in turn could stop worrying about it. Sir Norman told me I was psychotically obsessed by it, but an obsession is defined by its inaccuracy. Was I—were you, you know—wrong?"

The detective sucked at his sweet. Brent picked out a cigarette with manicured nails and lit it in three deliberate steps.

"Mr. Penrose," Radetsky said when it was obvious Penrose had come to a halt, "a police department in a democracy is a large organization with the social rules of the community it works within, and also the hidden rules of any large bureaucracy, the rules of power."

"What's that got to do with it?"

"I'm trying to answer your question. I started off," Radetsky continued, "with a handicap, being both a naturalized foreigner and a Jew in a Protestant and British organization. My adopted country, you see, has a historically tolerant caste system, but it gets less tolerant the more you ask of it. I could not be Dixon of Dock Green; still I worked my way as far as I could up the Metropolitan Police ladder. There I was stuck—partly, I'll admit, because I refused to carry out gratuitous investigations of parties our caste system decided were subversive. You may recall the search of a BBC journalist's flat last year? It got publicity, and that was what really botched things up." The detective's eyes checked the café once more, a weary scan. "So they put me on accidental deaths and shopliftings."

"It must have been the autopsy," Penrose suggested in a fatalistic tone, "that changed your mind."

"No."

"Pardon?" Penrose had been so sure of himself that he did a double take. "It was not the autopsy?"

"No. The autopsy proved nothing."

"But—that is—I mean how could he have been murdered

161

if he died of natural causes? I suppose that is really the specific thing I wanted to ask you, you see. What about the autopsy?"

"An autopsy," Radetsky stated with the flatness of expertise, "only proves what is not there."

"But he died of a heart attack. What does 'what was not there' matter?"

Radetsky simply looked at him. Malcolm Brent punched out his cigarette and watched Radetsky. Penrose got the feeling he was sitting for an examination.

"You're implying heart attacks can be faked?" he ventured.

"I am implying no such thing, sir. I am not at liberty to question departmental policy. You are of course free to draw your own conclusions."

"Hell, must you be so bloody Delphic? That would take drugs, or something. Surely they would show up in the autopsy. And he had a heart problem. Bloody hell, what a pair of paranoid twits we are, making up stories to account for the simple fact: he had a heart problem."

"Precisely."

"Bloody hell," Penrose repeated. "Why do I feel like Dr. Watson's thick-as-two-short-planks younger brother?"

"I'm not sure I understand either," Malcolm Brent admitted in a bored but mellifluous voice.

Radetsky sighed. "There are two ways," he intoned, as if reading from a textbook, "to kill a man with chemicals. One, the most common by far, is by adding them to the metabolism. The second, very rare except in hospital situations with people who are very ill, is by removing them."

Memory circuits crossed, linked, created new relationships in Penrose's brain. The process automatically hooked up with the pleasure centers as solutions dawned.

"His heart pills?"

Radetsky blinked his eyes.

"But he could have forgotten to take them normally, even if it's unlikely. The pills were there."

"I would advise that you reflect on it for a while, sir."

Penrose was silent, thinking.

"There's nothing that has been written in stone, nothing proven," the detective continued softly. "It may be a figment of both our imaginations, Mr. Penrose, and we are, indeed, both twits. I know what the Yard told Sir Norman when he inquired: Radetsky is past it; he's honest, but his future is not too bright with the Met, so he's blowing up even the little cases they give him. But it's wrong"—Radetsky leaned forward a little—"to pass over your instincts. That is what makes a good investigator, a good detective, and—" He looked around the café again and back at Penrose. "You are right," he admitted, more softly. "Mine still say that *this* is wrong. A policeman needs his instincts; he cannot rely on seeing patterns that are there in the facts only; he has to make up stories to fit the facts. That is where the creativity of detective work lies; we need it as much as poets or musicians. Where would Chopin be if they told him to stick by the rule book, the facts?" The detective sat back, suddenly conscious of getting carried away, and checked the room for police informers again.

"Another thing too," Radetsky went on in a much lower voice, "is what Mr. Brent has told me. Malcolm."

Mr. Brent lit a cigarette and raised his eyebrows at Radetsky.

"A crime implies a motive," the detective prompted. "Mr. Brent mentioned a set of circumstances at Lloyd's."

"Only in a general way: very circumstantial," the Lloyd's man said.

"You may as well outline it. It puts what Harewood was doing in a different light. You see"—Radetsky turned back to Penrose—"when you mentioned you could not find the insurance files at his office either, I asked Malcolm if there could be any reason for an insurance company fraudulently to avoid paying a single claim. And he said he could think of only one—"

"Reinsurance fraud," Penrose suggested.

"Very interesting, sir," Radetsky said in surprise. "So you already know." He looked almost disappointed.

"Harewood mentioned it."

"Did he, now?"

"I'd still like to know more."

"This is all whistling in the dark," Brent said, and made a smoke ring.

"Go on, Malcolm."

"Well—" The Lloyd's man sighed. "It's only a hypothesis. But Lloyd's had a problem a couple of years ago with companies that reinsured with firms they secretly owned, usually in tax havens like Liechtenstein or in the Caribbean— I see you know about that."

He pulled deeply at his cigarette. "They threw some people out of Lloyd's, including the then chairman, made some new and largely ineffective rules, which had to be passed by Parliament because of the royal charter, and did their best to forget about the whole unpleasant business. Everybody believed them when they said the spiders were all out of the attic. Except"—Brent breathed out smoke— "some of us think this kind of stuff may still be going on."

It was Brent's turn to stare intently, lean forward and lower his voice to conspiratorial levels. "You must understand what Lloyd's is really like. Oh, Harewood was a good journalist—I read his columns—but even he had no idea. He printed only what they told him, the myth: the myth that Lloyd's is some quasi-royal institution, sanctified by age and King James, as solid as Threadneedle Street, as true as the word of the British Gentlemen who run it. Rubbish!

"In fact," Brent said, a bit violently, "Lloyd's is a bunch of arrogant, amoral public-school spivs who control the most formidable marine intelligence system in the world. They control the information because they are all grouped together, and collectively they make up the biggest single insurance company on the planet. They control it because they all know each other; everyone knows who went for whose balls in the rugger scrum at Marlborough and Eton. They are tough, smart, able to react instantly to price the various risks, because that is what the business demands, and they make enormous amounts of money at the business. They have few scruples, yet they supervise each other, because it's like a stock exchange for insurance; everything moves so fast, the paper flow is so phenomenal that even their own underwriters don't know what is going on most of the time."

"What *is* going on, then?"

"What's going on is that if you're willing to take a few small risks, like Posgate did, you can clear well over a million pounds a year, tax free, in an offshore bank of your choice. Or, you can lose your shirt."

Radetsky started looking at his watch and dropping money on the table.

"Well"—Brent straightened up, brushed a few strands of

forelock into place—"of course a lot of people did that, reinsuring good risks with themselves, bad risks with others. The money was phenomenal. Some bought five-million-pound jets or 150-foot yachts or Brueghels. One boasted that he bought a woman for one night for more than Onassis paid for Callas. There was a huge empire of offshore cash, a huge pool they used for all sorts of odd speculative ventures. And because the paperwork is so unbelievable—they paid millions in accounting fees just to nail Posgate—no one can be sure it's not still going on, Fisher Act or no Fisher Act."

"Reinsurance fraud," Penrose repeated.

"Maybe."

"De Laune and Court," Penrose said, "reinsured my claims with a company in the Tortuga Islands."

Brent shrugged his Continental-cut shoulders. "It proves nothing. I told you, Karyl. None of this proves anything. I'd like to be of help, but—"

"It's a possible motive, no more." The detective pocketed keys and candy.

"Hang on"—Penrose tried to stay the motions of departure—"okay, let's admit we have a motive—"

Radetsky held up a hand.

"Mr. Penrose, I must ask you once again not to mention any of this to your father-in-law, or he might pass it on to his friends at Special Branch, and then they will not even give me shoplifting cases." He got to his feet and said, "I must go."

Brent rose as well. Penrose looked up at the two, feeling deflated.

"And I'm back to square one," he said. "All I have now is your opinion that the autopsy might not have been conclusive."

"That's right, sir." Radetsky put on his earphones, switched on the cassette player. "It's one possibility."

"But I still don't understand fully. How would they know he would die simply because he did not have his heart pills?"

The policeman listened to his earphones for a moment, and Penrose thought he had not heard. Then he lowered his lugubrious features to Penrose's level, close enough for Penrose to smell his sour and cherry-flavored breath.

"Boo!" he said. Penrose flinched.

"You mean—"

"I mean nothing. I'll know more when I get the laboratory results."

"The lab results?"

But Radetsky had turned for the door. The midget sounds of tape-recorded Chopin wafted behind him. Brent shrugged and followed.

Two truck drivers came over and took away their chairs.

Scared to death, he thought; that's what Radetsky meant. Penrose was left sitting alone, with five hours to kill before he was due to meet Claire Thibodeault.

He still couldn't get his tongue around that last name.

XVI

It was Friday night and the seafood restaurant off Leicester Square was filled with theater people, as it usually was this time of evening; men with longer hair who wore their jackets draped over the shoulders, women in clothes that hung dramatically onto red-checked tablecloths and into the soup or butter, as often as not. Then there was the publishing crowd, reverse chic in sports jackets and aphorisms.

When Claire finally came through the door, in a rush of haste and silk, she stopped the place. The theater men were smooth about it but they still abandoned all veneer of civilization in a flash and sniffed her up and down from a distance, noses turning and quivering in practiced unison. The women, less subtle, took her in, added her up, spat out the result and bared their sharp white teeth. Sociobiology ruled okay in the few seconds it took the maître d'hôtel to lead her to Penrose's table. The abstract victory of being the leading male both delighted the captain and made him a little nervous.

"Claire." Penrose tried it aloud as he gave her a quick Continental kiss. The pack tucked their tails between their legs and fled to their respective mates.

"John." Her smile almost veiled the immanent sadness. She had her hair tied up in back, emphasizing her long, fragile neck; a sort of fedora hung off a ribbon behind it. A loose pant suit of shot silk somehow emphasized all the curves that counted. Penrose made some feeble joke about escaping from Belgium.

"Now that we've been officially introduced," she said finally, "I have a message from Kirsten."

167

"So you went back to the 'Vanger?" Penrose signaled the waiter, ordered Sancerre, Colchesters and fried whitebait, and ignored the tiny feeling of jealousy as he remembered Kirsten's unsubtle challenge.

She smiled. "Don't worry. Only once. To talk to some of the women." Claire took a folded pink slip from a tiny purse and handed it to Penrose.

It was a cable form, unused. On it, in Kirsten's erratic but delicate hand, were the words: "The man with the money who employed Tewfik and his men came from UK. He works for a man in London who wanted you damaged badly, in the hospital. My contact says he must have you out of the way for two weeks, or kill you. You owe me 200 francs. Learn karate. Kirsten."

"She must have been depressed," Penrose said lightly, though the words had spread unease in a different direction.

"Sorry?"

"Nothing. An interesting woman."

"We talked about you," Claire said, curving the glass to her lips with a graceful twist of her long wrist and fingers. "Why does she say you are in danger?"

"Because of something I asked her to find out," he said, wondering if he should tell her, if he wanted to tell her.

"She must have good connections."

"It's her job," Penrose replied absently, thinking that he did want to tell Claire, that there was no one else that he could confide in.

"Her job? As a madam in a sailors' brothel?"

"Her other job. She's also on retainer for Veritas, which is the principal insurance and registry firm for the Norwegian merchant marine—rather like Lloyd's, funnily enough. She collects news and gossip for them, about ships and cargoes and seamen, possible cargo fraud, that sort of thing. She's worth her weight in gold."

"So she knows what she's talking about. Which brings me back to my first question."

"It's a long story."

"We've got all night."

Penrose looked up at her with an exaggerated leer, and she colored.

"I didn't mean—"

"I'm sorry," Penrose said. "It was stupid," and found he had already made up his mind. "You won't be bored?"

It took him only fifteen minutes to blurt out every detail that counted, every hypothesis and suspicion right up to the meeting with Radetsky, as if he were puncturing an abscess, which according to Sir Norman it was.

She listened with her lips slightly parted, moist from sipped wine, her brown-violet eyes intent on his. As he talked Penrose became absorbed in the questions he saw bottled up behind those irises, in the way she used her tongue to scavenge the last drop of juice from an oyster.

"The ports," she commented when he had run it out. "The violence never stops."

"That's right. You grew up in one."

"I don't want to talk about my life tonight. We did that in Antwerp. My research is getting me down, I think. So much goddam waste! But I do want to hear about the murder. My God, it's unbelievable."

But Penrose, his suspicions released now, found himself unwilling to go back over the more recent events. Perhaps the violence, the doubts and the heartache were bad omens he no longer wanted touching this part of his life.

Instead, he talked about the *Witch*, London and his time in the bank, the Navy. He played the fool, told her stories, like the chestnut about the old Kensington newspaper Courtenay's had loaned money to before the war.

"When Zog the First, King of Albania, was booted out by Mussolini's Fascists," he began, "he came over here and bought a huge house in Kensington, not far from where you're staying, and started sending out ten-page diatribes excoriating the invaders, saying the Italians were Turks in disguise (the worst possible insult in Albanian), extolling the benefits of the dynasty of Zog and so forth. No one paid much attention, of course; there were minor details such as the invasion of Poland, and no newspapers would print his epistles, so one day he showed up with his retinue of *bachi bouzouks* and eunuchs and whatnot on the doorstep of the *Kensington News*, a genteel weekly with a gardening column. He offered the bemused ancient editor there an incredible sum in gold, and took over the paper on the spot, with the blessings, of course, of Courtenay's bank. The next morning every sedate bourgeois household in the royal borough woke up, as usual, to the folded *Kensington News* next to the milk. Instead of gymkhana awards and news about geranium shows and rates, there was a nine-inch headline: ZOG SPEAKS!"

She only smiled at that one.

"It's sort of funny, anyway," he defended himself.

"Oh, no, I liked it," Claire said. "My great-uncle had a newspaper once, a weekly as well, but everyone in town, even the dogs, ended up emigrating to Bath and Bangor, till he was the only one in the township. He kept on printing the paper, though. In fact, he had himself elected selectman, treasurer, dog catcher and everything else. He was making his own Fourth of July parade, toward the end. People say he went a little crazy, but it's hard to tell for sure in Maine. Why did you leave the bank?"

"I got claustrophobic, in a way. I really am claustrophobic, physically, in the sense that I hate tunnels, tubes, lifts, confined spaces. I can ride the tube, but I get this overwhelming urge to brace the roof over my head with my arms."

The fried whitebait came.

"Surely your bank wasn't underground."

"No. That's my other kind of claustrophobia. But I think it's related to the first. I don't like crowds of people, I don't like them interfering with my life, all the little politics, the tiny confining squabbles that dominate people's lives day to day. Courtenay's was all that: money, greed, despair; and all the conflicts arising out of that not being solved logically, in controlled fashion, according to need, but by the political factors, who knew whom, who went to university with whom, who was willing to go behind whose back. At sea you have some politics, especially in the larger shipping companies, but it's kept in firm control, because there are more vital imperatives. The master has to be in total command, the ship has to stay afloat, the cargo has to reach its destination intact. The sea is still dangerous enough that it will kill you if you start playing politics on it."

"So you went to sea."

"So I went to sea."

"Was that the only reason?"

"No. There was a marriage, as well. Is, still, though we're getting a divorce, I suppose," Penrose continued quickly. It was the first time he had said it to himself.

"You know what Michelsen says about marriage, love, all that."

"Who?"

"Michelsen. American poet, very minor. He says it's a self-fulfilling prophecy of decay. What caused it, anyway?"

"I'm sorry." He didn't want to talk about Selina.

"The claustrophobia."

"The claustro— But, what do you mean? It's just the way I am."

"No. What I mean is, usually there's something behind it, some trauma."

"Like Freud's phobia case—the woman who was scared of knives?"

"Yes."

"I don't remember."

"You blocked it out."

"Perhaps." He smiled inwardly at being psychoanalyzed in this fashion, but at least they'd got away from the other subject. "I do know it was something in my childhood, probably too early for me to remember. I get nightmares about it, but that's all. Something to do with my brother, Benjamin, who's in New Zealand now with my parents. No one remembers. I've been like that all my life."

"It's there, somewhere."

"The couch, doctor?"

She laughed. "How about music, instead? The Royal Philharmonic is doing *Das Lied von der Erde*."

He didn't like Mahler, and thought he was off the hook when her attention was distracted by a pair of gypsies who came in the door and headed straight for their table, which was closest.

They readied their instruments, but the American seemed to resent the intrusion, willing them to leave her table alone. They played anyway, two comic-opera types in morning coats, one a violin, one a guitar, singing a Spanish song with the Hungarian czardas beat that was supposed to make *gajos* feel wild and carefree and run off to be raggle-taggle with campfires and horses and men with gold earrings.

"Madam." They bowed when they had finished.

Claire turned her back on them. Her lip muscles dragged down, and her eyes burned.

Penrose watched her with his own jaw slack, and gave them a larger tip than usual.

"I thought you liked music."

She did not smile.

"Sorry," he said.

"Don't look so disgusted."

"I'm not disgusted."

"You're not?"

"Hell," he said, "it was a joke. Let's forget it."

She took a sip of wine, still pouting.

"It's all right. A lot of people are uncomfortable with gypsies."

"Look, John. I don't like beggars. And I don't like people interrupting me when I'm eating. If you must know, I didn't always get much to eat when I was a child. When we did, it was mounds of potatoes. I worked my way up to where I am by my brains. I never asked for charity. Now I get enough to eat. End of conversation."

"End of conversation," he agreed, wondering.

The Royal Philharmonic was sold out. They took a taxi to a wine bar that specialized in good jazz music and a view of Putney Bridge, broken and scaffolded after having collapsed ten days before.

The half moon soldered racing clouds and electroplated the river. Men from the Rowing Club and film people from across the Thames asked for specific wines and made sure they were first to applaud when the saxophonist or the drummer finished a riff.

Penrose and Claire, the gypsy incident forgotten, went down the list alphabetically, glass by glass, finding more sociological common ground in their remarks to each other, exchanging coherence for camaraderie as they went through Bordeaux, Bourgogne, Châteauneuf, Dôle du Valais, Engadiner Weiss. A white-faced woman with huge teeth and long jet-black hair kept crooning a song she had written about "the sandman," over and over, to a TV producer on her right. Watching the film types, Penrose trotted out his Quentin theory, about video and drunkenness both having reduced peripheral vision in common. She agreed with him, politely.

The saxophone led into a long, slow set that had some of the trendies up and dancing around a wrought-iron balcony over the embankment. Barges and tubby little yachts nodded black-on-silver outside. Penrose and the American got to their feet and joined them.

He found the slope of her nose and cheekbones fascinated him as much as the way she controlled legs that were as long as a colt's. Shared interests implied friendship; her unexplained sadness implied an ego that had tried to conquer the condition of being alone, and failed. It all made him want to protect her against the wolf packs and other predators. The combination of emotions and the excuse of cold air allowed him to draw her tightly to him, and she did not resist. When he lifted her chin with one finger and kissed her she responded, lethargically at first, then with increasing enthusiasm. The saxophone moaned and howled in sympathy; the moon went down on a big bank of clouds. They got to her hotel in Cadogan Square at three in the morning, and she waited for him to pay off the taxi, peacefully accepting conclusions reached earlier that night.

The hotel was technically a bed-and-breakfast, but the kind whose porter knew your name and how long you liked your caviar chilled when you came back ten years later. A tiny Vermeer hung by the staircase, and there were cold Krug and fresh grapes next to a freshly ironed *Times* at the door of her room.

"Psychology must pay well."

"This foundation does. Carnegie money."

A radio-and-tape system was built into the headboard. The first thing she did after dropping her coat and hat on the chair was slip in a cassette. The Nordic heartaches of Grieg strained into the room. A large bunch of roses scented its warmth.

He opened the champagne; she let down her hair. Neither of them felt any urge to talk.

They closed standing up, as if obeying a cue from offstage. He began picking at the buttons in her silk and she started to tug at his belt. Naked, they held each other harder and harder, until he picked her up.

They fell into the bed with her legs entwined about his. The Grieg unfolded, rhapsodies on cold blue snows and deep blue fjords and the triumph of winter over myth. The piano sounded the concerto's theme, closing the circle, and the strings responded, voice answering voice more quickly, more strongly. Her eyes flew open suddenly and a great gasp escaped her. The concerto went critical in sforzando and glissando, and she began to climax uncontrollably now, biting down on sobs, the sobs tearing out nevertheless, louder and louder, bringing him with her in wave after wave of growing deliverance, her hands scoring his back and tears streaming from her eyes.

"Why were you crying?" he asked afterwards, wiping her cheek with the side of one finger.

She did not answer. Her eyes were closed and she appeared to be asleep. But when the music stopped she eventually whispered, "Grieg. It always affects me that way."

Penrose grunted noncommittally, and rolled over to find his pipe, but he wondered what the hell was wrong with him when the women he picked needed drugs or romantic composers before they could gain any satisfaction from sex.

Neither of them spoke much in the morning; they just observed each other warily, wondering what might have been let out of the cage. The apple feeling was gone, Penrose realized: in its place was a sort of helpless excitement.

Beast emotions ranged back and forth, snarling at their nakedness. They got dressed in separate rooms. He wondered if he was falling into her sort of love, the self-fulfilling decay kind. When he mentioned the four-letter word once, in jest, she winced as if he'd slapped her.

They left the hotel together at nine. Claire took the tube to Great Portland Street and the British Museum, where she was to spend the day over hoary population surveys of British cities.

Penrose walked to King's Road, making phone calls from coinboxes on the way: one to Gunn (he might have to relieve the *London Princess* again); one to the University Club (no messages); one to Colin (no answer); one to Brian. He splurged on cappuccinos at Picasso's for an hour, relieved that he might be working again soon, daydreaming vaguely about Claire, about Selina.

His previous suspicion was confirmed: the new emotions in an odd way sharpened the old, as if they shared a common source of energy. His musings led him back to Priory, to Harewood, to Lloyd's. On an impulse he tried calling Clift, to see if anything had turned up at Harewood's office since his last visit, but the editor would not be in for an hour.

He had nothing better to do, Penrose thought, so he paid

his bill and took a number 11 bus to Fleet Street. He got there fifteen minutes before Clift was supposed to. He balked at the lift, so a porter escorted him up the stairs to the same newsroom and placed him under the custody of a young temporary secretary with a green streak in her hair who could not have cared less what he did. The big room was buzzing exactly as it had on his last visit.

There were shelves of bound issues going back five or so years near the reception area. While he waited Penrose leafed through the Sunday financial sections, where Harewood's long pieces used to appear.

He found one fairly quickly, a three-year-old article dealing with proposed reforms at Lloyd's, but it was as Brent had said: Harewood had done a straightforward job of reporting but had not really dug behind the official persona of Lloyd's or under the *mea culpas* of the Posgate affair. There was little of interest, little that even swelled his rudimentary knowledge. De Laune was safely gone to ground inside the corporate mass of Lloyd's, and Lloyd's presented a seamless front. Radetsky was all instincts and leading hints, but no hard clues. Brent had his suspicions, but no solid facts.

Penrose had only £13 million in debts.

He almost missed Clift, as he moved into the newsroom at speed, shucking his trench coat as he walked, a contrail of cigarette smoke behind him.

"Mr. Clift."

The man glanced over his shoulder, waved vaguely and carried on.

"Excuse me," Penrose said, chasing after. The temp did not even look up as her charge took off.

Clift stopped, puffing at his cigarette in annoyance. "Yes. Very busy. Time limited to— Oh, it's you. Penrod. Penheath. Penflower. Pen*rose*. Friend of poor Harewood. *Captain* Penrose. Missed you at the funeral."

"Yes. Could we—"

"Sorry, not now. Later perhaps. What did you want? Don't mean to be rude."

"I only wondered," Penrose said, "if you'd located the files or anything on the story Tim Harewood was working on when he died?"

Clift automatically patted his pockets for cigarettes and said, "Lloyd's, right? Now where on earth— Ah!" He gave a boyish grin as he located the pack and took out a cigarette. Penrose decided the boyishness, like the headline style, was simply a habit the editor did not mind keeping for effect.

"Lloyd's," the editor mumbled as he lit up. "Yes, there was something, but not files. What was it? Ah, tragedy of a young mind swamped by excess information. Look here, come back later." He held up a hand, moved away under its protection. "Half an hour. I'll have got it by then. Promise. Okay? Jack!" he shouted to no one in particular. "Editorial meeting!"

Penrose returned to his back copies, fully prepared to wait for an hour before he tracked down the editor again, but Clift came charging down the newsroom forty-five minutes later, with a very fat middle-aged man in a blue smock waddling mightily to keep up. The pair took a left by the reception area, Clift beckoning to Penrose to follow. They ended up in a small conference room with a large table, a view of Fleet Street and the I in EVENING on the sign outside.

"Remembered halfway through the conference. Of course. Captain Penrose, Alf Swikes, director of photographic services, card-carrying party member, shop floor coordinator, perpetrator of strike against video terminals; old Keighley sacked everyone but him. Best darkroom in Grub Street, eh, Alf?"

Alf did not smile, but perhaps he was too busy catching his breath. He had a Benedictine's beard clipped around the jowls and a manila envelope in one huge round paw.

"Looking for files, last time, right? On Lloyd's story, never located. But what I did get," Clift went on, pacing over to the window and back, his short words fading as he turned, "requisition slips for extra prints. From Harewood. Dated two days before his death . . . didn't get to me till a week ago. No one knew what to do about it. Forgot all about it, since . . . was something odd, though."

"Photographs," Penrose said, disappointment sounding in his voice.

"Yes. Well, sorry. You did ask."

"Can I go now?" Alf asked.

"Yes, fine. Leave the prints."

"You'll have to sign the form yourself, then."

"Oh, Christ, all right." Clift searched desperately through all his pockets, finally located a form, scrawled his name, threw it at the darkroom man.

"Cheers, Alf." The editor stubbed out his cigarette and ripped open the envelope as the big man puffed out of the room.

There were two eight-by-ten glossies, stapled to laser-printed caption sheets. Clift lined them up on the table.

"You never know," he said hopefully.

"See if clues revealed— Christ! Fuck all. File shots pulled for short takes."

Penrose, depressed, nevertheless leaned over to look.

The photographs, taken at face value, were boring.

Both were black-and-white shots of business functions. The one on the right showed four men coming down broad granite steps, all in business suits, all carrying attaché cases. Gothic statues of blindfolded ladies and ponytailed men protected the entrance. An igneous lintel bore the words SOUTHERN DISTRICT COURT. The caption was dated three years ago and read: "Officers of Wilmington Realty Trust leave federal court in New York after testifying on trust's takeover intentions concerning Lion Investment Holdings, Inc., of NY. From right to left, Howard Spengle, Marshall V. Willatt, Alan White."

The other photo showed some sort of awards ceremony. There was a podium with the logo "Peninsula Hotel." A bluff Colonial type was handing an award to a fat Chinese merchant. A row of men, both European and Asian, stood behind. Smiles all around. Flash-gun highlights propped faces in front of shadows. The caption was five years old and began, "Sir Yeo Lee Wan accepts the Queen's award for financial services on behalf of Eastern Holdings and Go-down Ltd. of Hong Kong."

"Eastern Holdings," Penrose said softly. "Bloody hell, Eastern Holdings! So it does have something to do with the insurance thing, after all."

He explained briefly what Harewood had told him at Jarry's the night before he died: how Eastern Holdings were both backers and owners of de Laune and Court. The editor sucked in smoke and surveyed the photos before him while Penrose talked.

"Of course, I still don't see what the hell it proves," Penrose finished, the first rush of excitement ebbing, "except that it seems to confirm that Harewood was definitely working on the insurance story."

Clift stubbed out his cigarette, readjusted the spectacles

on his nose and peered at the caption on the left, then at the caption on the right, then the caption on the left again. He turned back to the window, fumbling for cigarettes.

"Look again."

"Pardon?"

"The pix."

Penrose complied, holding one up to the light, then the other, and said, "I don't see anything— Hang on."

He compared the two once more.

"The second man from the left in the Hong Kong photo looks like, *is*, the same man as the one on the left in New York. He's got a mustache in Hong Kong, but he looks exactly the same."

"Correct. And there's more."

"He looks like my milkman in Cornwall, actually. He looks like everybody's milkman. And, yes, I've already seen it. You mean they don't carry the same name."

Clift turned back to the table. "Exactly. One is called 'Alan White.' The other is 'Vincent Dormier.' "

"It could be a mistake," Penrose said. "Maybe they're twins."

"Easy enough to check."

"A newspaper's not a research agency," Penrose mimicked Clift.

"Payment in kind always welcome."

"For example?"

"For example—" The editor gagged on a swallow of smoke, got involved in coughing and doubled up over the table. "For example," Clift gasped, finally collapsing into a chair, "what the story *is*—Oh, shit, forgot." Another spasm of coughing.

"Shall I get you a glass of water?"

Clift shook his head, speechless. After a small struggle he found a blue slip of paper in his hip pocket and handed it to Penrose.

"Forgot," he said again. "It's a credit-card record for a round trip to New York." He cleared his throat several times. "Harewood signed it. That's where he went before his death. That's what was so bloody odd. Never asked permission. Wondered about that."

Penrose stared at the slip of paper, which bore the carbon words: BRITISH AIRWAYS/T. HAREWOOD THE EVENING/

178

"Not just New York," Penrose said. "He spent twenty-four hours on Grand Tortuga Island."

For the first time since seeing de Laune he felt as if the great rockslide that had landed on him at Lloyd's had been pried off an inch or two, just enough to let him see a chink of daylight from where he lay, still trapped under its weight.

"It's the first real piece of evidence I have," Penrose breathed, holding the paper higher, like a chalice.

"Evidence for what?" Clift asked, getting off the chair and looking at the slip. "That's what I want to know."

"For why no one paid insurance on my ship."

"What?"

"Grand Tortuga."

"Come again? I don't understand."

"The reinsurance company on my policy. It was on Grand Tortuga Island. Look: Tim Harewood has some lead on a man who is linked to de Laune and Court. Harewood goes to Grand Tortuga. It could make sense."

"Goldfinger Posgate."

"Exactly."

"Has it ever crossed your mind"—the editor examined him, eyes squinting thoughtfully—"that there might be more to all this—to Harewood's dying, I mean—than meets the eye?"

"What do you mean?"

"Not sure. But Tim wouldn't have flitted off like that unless he'd found out something big. Big things can be risky."

Penrose looked back at the editor for a space of seconds.

"It's crossed my mind," he admitted at last, "but I'm beginning to realize how unlikely that is. Or, rather, how difficult to prove."

"*Evening* could help."

"Why?"

"Story seen in it? Owe it to Tim?"

"I'll settle for the insurance," Penrose said, a new species of hope strengthening his voice, and asked if he could take the prints with him when he left.

* * *

179

The porter at the University Club approached him immediately in implicit gratitude for the tip Penrose had left the day before.

"Two messages for you, sir," he added.

One was from Gunn, at London & Continental, confirming the phone call, asking him to take over command of the *London Princess* in five days' time, loading methane at the Isle of Grain terminal for a trip to St. Helier, in the Channel Islands. More trouble with premature babies.

The other was a telegram that read simply: LABORATORY TESTS POSITIVE. PLACEBO SUBSTITUTED FOR DIGITALIS TABLETS. SUSPECT PERSON UNKNOWN KNEW OF HEART CONDITION AND THREATENED VICTIM. INVESTIGATION REOPENED. PLEASE CONTACT ME SOONEST. RADETSKY.

The words sent a thrill.

He had a feeling once Radetsky had a real crime firm in his teeth he would not let go, come hell or high commissioner.

And there was something Penrose could do, as well.

"Can you make international telephone calls from here?"

"Of course, sir." Penrose wrote down the listing he wanted.

The porter came back five minutes later and said Grand Tortuga Directory Inquiries had no listing for Tortuga Insurance Company Ltd.

Penrose overtipped him, and thought for a minute.

"Do you make airline reservations here?"

"Of course, sir."

Penrose gave him the details before he had finished doing the cost-benefit analysis in his own mind.

It was a drastic step, but drastic things were happening to him.

He could not afford it, but the credit-card company did not know that, as yet. With a £13 million suit, it did not make that much difference in any case. He had just enough time before he had to ship out again.

When the porter finished making the booking, Penrose tipped him again and ran out the door toward the British Museum.

XVII

The colors were so bright they became translucent: blue lay on light blue and patches of deep, then blinding white, a fragment of olive swamp, all layer upon layer. Finally a black runway came up to meet the jet in a bouncing concrete embrace. Immediately the engines reversed and five seconds later the portholes streamed with condensation. For the first time since the idea entered his head, Penrose understood how close to the Equator he was traveling in coming to Grand Tortuga.

He had dressed light, to the extent that his duffle bag allowed, and that meant heavy cotton pants, a long-sleeved cotton shirt, wool socks, desert boots. When he stepped onto the boarding stairs the heat affected his winter-wound metabolism like shock, and with most of the same symptoms: moist palms, dragging respiration and accelerated heartbeat.

But the next sensation was pleasurable, as the organism sensed an environment where no extra effort was needed to obtain outside life support, with the possible exception of rum. Fog, ice, even rain already seemed improbable excesses of the atmospheric imagination.

The terminal was small, frontiers-of-flight style, made of corrugated tin and painted a harsh white: air conditioned but humble in contrast to a shiny new American-built control tower with smoked glass windows next door.

Penrose knew he had not officially left the United Kingdom, but even if the fact had slipped his mind, the customs and immigration formalities would have reminded him by their polite sadism, as if treading Her Majesty's soil, whether you'd left it or not, whatever category of British or EEC or foreign passport you bore, was a privilege to be paid for in time and dignity.

Notices warned that selling anything was forbidden to visitors in the Tortuga Islands, and dealing in drugs was punishable by long prison terms. The one traveler who looked as if he might know what the notices were about was a lanky Jamaican with greasy dreadlocks, a green, red and black cap and three abused guitar cases. He was cut out of the crowd and shepherded by immigration officials into a private room.

For his co-passengers—plump, bejeweled, blue-haired women with cabin bags full of expensive facial creams; men already geared in white madras jackets clutching ostrich-skin briefcases with combination locks—the notices were largely superfluous.

A butterscotch-colored man checked very carefully to see that Penrose had a return ticket and sufficient funds and/or a credit card. The loud post-travel silence of the arrival hall was underlined by the thump of rubber stamps and the call of unfamiliar birds. The man checked his name against a thick book and asked the purpose of his stay. Finally he stamped the passport for a seven-day visit. A large poster of a turtle with peg leg, cutlass and three-cornered hat said, "Sir Turtle welcomes you to Grand Tortuga," and pointed to complimentary rum punches. Penrose winced.

The information desk told him that the Bank of Labrador building was right on Post Office Square; he couldn't miss the glass-and-steel edifice rising lofty as a royal palm, which was as high as local law allowed. The fat, balding islander who picked him up in a prehistoric Riley at the taxi rank spent most of the time laughing or giggling but managed to tell him there were a couple of cheaper bed-and-breakfast places but the Tortugas were not London. "Mostly rich men are coming here, an dey go to beeg places like West Indian or Caribbean Club, and dey all full up now." He passed Penrose a brochure for what he claimed was a cheaper hotel, but "nice, man, very nice."

Penrose put the publicity on the hot vinyl beside him. It was a ten-minute ride from Robert Owens Airport, past hotels, villas, palm trees, to the center of downtown Georgetown, and it cost fifteen Tortuga dollars. The driver chuckled so much when he asked for the fare, as if nothing were so deserving of laughter as money going from you to him, that Penrose, bemused, handed it over without complaint.

He found himself standing by the curbside in what had once obviously been a sleepy colonial backwater, a Caribbean town of low buildings flattened even lower by a powerful sun. Just as obviously the modern world had caught it napping and transformed it all unawares: now Georgian relics in whitewashed pine raised questioning balconies at the cubed financial centers surrounding them. The sparse palms apparently suffered from reverse legislation, unable to grow any higher than the 430 banks of the capital. Fat American tourists buzzed by on mopeds, like bumblebees. Islanders hawked sugar-ice and brands of British cigarettes that no one in England smoked any more. Penrose bought a pack.

Opposite a central triangle where neat European road signs contrasted with thorny bushes, he found a café crammed between a photo shop and a car-rental agency. Umbrellas smudged black marks in the sunshine. He chose a place in the shade beneath an umbrella that read "Xing," put his duffle bag under the table and sat down to decide what he was going to do next.

He eyed the Bank of Labrador across the way, imposing, as the information girl had said, with its four stories of polarized windows. People came in and out through its varnished doors, in no great hurry, in no great numbers. It was noontime. Several dogs, scruffy but sane, hung around panting and sniffing each others' tails. Most of the Bank of Labrador's customers appeared to be either English or American.

No immediate solutions percolated through his jet lag other than to go to the building, find the Tortuga Insurance Company office, ask for the director, get his name and, when he returned to England, check to see if he was also on de Laune and Court's board. That, Penrose decided, should be enough to prove a fraudulent connection.

The only trouble with his plan was that it seemed pathetically amateurish, useless. Any fraud that dealt in large sums of money surely would have covered its tracks to the extent of disguising connections on the board of directors. But it was all he had to go on.

The heat was oppressive. Sunlight ricocheted off the pavement to lance his squinted eyes. Microscopic but voracious creatures that the waiter called sandflies kept him throwing slaps at his own face and neck like an idiot masochist. He lit a cigarette and ordered a planter's punch, hoping it would provide inspiration as well as an antidote for the bug bites and the twelve sleepless hours since he had left Heathrow.

His only inspiration was a resolution to purchase mosquito spray and a pair of sunglasses on his credit card as soon as possible, to find a cheap hotel that would take his credit card and shortly after that to pass out on the nearest available beach. The airline magazine had mentioned seven miles of beach near here; twelve square feet of it surely would be available, twelve feet of coral sand next to that translucent water where the body would cut off the circuits, one by one, till it shut down the quibbling mind.

The second rum drink brought no new ideas but proved mightily effective against jet lag. By the time he had finished a third, his original idea had almost recovered the bright optimism of novelty. A "tunny sandwich" he ordered turned out to be excellent peppered mackerel, which did not detract from his optimism. Even the astronomical bill seemed well within his capabilities.

He put it on his credit card anyway. Luckily, everyone seemed to take the card here—it was that kind of town.

There was a uniformed guard with TV cameras and telephones and lists of names who screened visitors from behind a desk inside the entrance to the Bank of Labrador. When Penrose told him he wanted the offices of the Tortuga Insurance Company Ltd. the guard consulted a list of offices that seemed roughly thirty times too long for the size of the building, and told him Room 218, second floor.

Penrose chose a handsome marble staircase in preference to the two elevators indicated by the guard. The air conditioning was so powerful that his shirt was actually less wet by the time he had climbed the two stories.

He found himself in a long, broad corridor that followed a square pattern inside the building. The only daylight came from the stairwell, and no outside noises could overcome the hiss of climate control. The carpet was an inch thick and the walls were covered with offset slats of real mahogany. The door with the number 218 bore a shining brass rectangle that read MCTAGGART, EBANKS, AND SMITH, BARRISTERS.

Penrose checked the doors to the right and left. They bore

184

only numbers. A quick trip around the corridor revealed that all the doors holding corporate names belonged to law firms, with the exception of two that read: BANK OF LABRADOR/TELEX OFFICE and DR. OWEN BODDEN GENERAL DENTISTRY.

He thought of going back down to check with the guard, but the duffle bag was beginning to drag at his fingers, his legs were getting tired and he had nothing to lose anyway. So he went around a corner, took a tie and his old gray jacket out of the bag, put them on and patted the wrinkles. He combed his hair with his fingers, hefted the bag once again and walked into Room 218.

Room 218 was a very large, completely circular reception room, with no doors visible and only one desk; the woman behind it was the most handsome mulatto he had ever seen. She had a face formed in a balanced oval, lips drawn in a bow shape, dark eyes that tilted slightly up. Her high cheekbones tied everything together without wasting any space. A demure cream blouse and a brassiere won Pyrrhic victories against breasts that had no need of either. Penrose felt like a piece of used-up and thrown-away jet trash in his rumpled jacket and sweat-sodden shirt. At least he had shaved on the plane. He was aware of his left hand rising to straighten his collar in an almost subconscious gesture of insecurity, and gave it up.

"Can I help you, sir?" the woman said in a voice sadly unable to keep up with the rest of her, nasal and high pitched as it was. On closer inspection, her eyes were lukewarm and a little greedy, her nail varnish was the same crusted-blood color as her lip gloss.

"I'm looking for Tortuga Insurance," he said, as if the name rolled off his lips every day.

"Can I help you," she repeated, without the question mark.

"Is this the right office?"

"Can I *help* you, sir."

"I see." He did see, too. "I have some insurance business that I wanted to take care of concerning assets I own in the Caribbean area. Tortuga Insurance was recommended to me in London. I wondered if you could put me in touch with one of its directors."

She appraised him for a second, while Penrose told himself hopefully that the knowledge in her smile had to do with older, more universal relationships than the one that had brought him to her office. She asked him to take a seat and lifted a telephone.

"Whom shall I say is calling please?"

"John Ethy."

He had thought up a cover story in the café. If pressed he would say that he had invested in a bare-boat charter firm in Montserrat, was thinking of shifting the boats to the Tortugas and would need to switch his coverage as well. A friend in shipping, back in London, had asked de Laune and Court for a recommendation, and had been given Tortuga Insurance's name and address.

End of story. It was just plausible and answered the obvious questions. Anyone who asked less obvious questions would want more than verbal answers, anyway.

The woman put the phone down, crossed a pair of legs that made you forget about her voice and pretended to shuffle paperwork, glancing up once in a while with an expression suggesting that men all belonged to a race with indistinguishable behavior patterns—which, in her case, perhaps they did.

Penrose pulled out his pipe and tobacco and absentmindedly worked at combining them. When he had got it lighted he examined the reception area, mentally pricing the abstract glass-and-brass table and the caliber of magazines thereon. The taste implicit in the wood slats (butternut here), the subdued shag, the authentic if out-of-place hunting prints denoted legal fees of corporate stature. A beautiful Haitian naïve in bold bright oils depicting a ship broken along a coral reef perhaps indicated where some of the fees had come from.

Ten minutes later the phone buzzed. The girl answered, smiled, hung up, nails flashing.

"I'm sorry, the partners are out at lunch," she said happily.

"I'll wait," Penrose said, smiling back.

"It might be a very long time."

"That's fine. I've nothing to do all day." Penrose picked up a New York financial weekly and settled back on the brass-and-leather couch. The smile fell from her lips like bad fruit, and she lifted the phone again. The office was so well soundproofed he could not make out what she murmured.

Twenty-five more minutes dragged by. Penrose leafed through *Fortune,* the *Economist,* and the Tortuga *Compass.*

New York's real estate boom was sagging, new dockland developments on the Thames were going belly up and Capt. Johns of the *Sunquest* had just landed a 240-pound dorado. Then an invisible door in the butternut slid open. A thin, middle-aged European in a light blue suit came out and said, "Mr. Ethy."

Penrose started to his feet. The man had a very dark tan, ravines in his cheeks and black eyes that stayed narrow in the antithesis of welcome. He did not come up to meet him or shake Penrose's hand.

"I'm sorry you had to wait. Unfortunately, Tortuga Insurance does not conduct person-to-person business from this office. I'm sorry." He jerked to the left, as if to leave.

"Yes, I understand." Penrose ignored the movement, waved the objections away with one hand that said this was the most obvious point in the world. "As I told this young lady, I merely wished to get in touch with one of the principals. Tortuga Insurance was recommended to me in London. Perhaps you could give me their business address, Mr.—?"

"I'm sorry," the man repeated, with no sorrow at all in his voice. His eyes remained hostile despite the crow's-feet. His nostrils lifted, as if Penrose were beginning to rot a little, and his mouth drew tighter around an accent that was Lincoln's Inn Fields with a hot dash of West Indies thrown in for zest.

"Surely as their representative you are authorized to give out their address or telephone or Telex number?"

"If they've been recommended to you," the man replied, emphasizing the first word, "you must know they do virtually all their business with the same steady clientele. They take very few new customers, and only then after extensive referrals and vetting. In any case, we merely act as legal advisers—" He pretended to quell a yawn.

"But I have been referred," Penrose insisted. "De Laune and Court, the underwriters, at Lloyd's in London recommended them to me."

The man turned away, his mouth decomposing into what looked like a sneer. Penrose began to get angry, and held his temper in check with an effort that stretched mental muscles.

"Could you not call them and ask them—dear chap? Mention my referral, and so forth?"

"I'm sorry Mr.—ah—Ethy," the man repeated, the sneer

187

becoming unmistakable now. He turned his back. "Desrene, please show Mr.—er—the gentleman out?"

The butternut paneling hissed shut on his back. A light on Desrene's switchboard winked yellow five seconds later. Penrose stood his ground for another five seconds, then swiveled, to find the receptionist standing beside the door and trying unsuccessfully to bite down her amusement.

He picked up the duffle bag and whispered, "I really hate your nail polish," as he left, but her smile did not crack even one fraction.

Penrose wandered around Georgetown for a while, getting hotter, more exhausted and more depressed.

He had flown three thousand exorbitant miles on spec and credit only to be defeated within two hours of landing.

The rum punches had worn off, and the canvas straps of the duffle bag were wearing ruts in his fingers. His clothes were damp and itchy, his cracked rib was beginning to hurt again, his eyes felt as if they had been rolled in glass splinters and then used as ball bearings and the bloody sandflies seemed everywhere.

He found a pub called the Israel Hands with a picture of a huge black-bearded pirate shooting another pirate point-blank on the sign. Inside, the decor included more pirate clichés than Penrose had ever seen outside a Douglas Fairbanks movie. Every spare corner was crammed with brass running lights, Jolly Rogers, conch shells, nooses, nets, ships' wheels, tin cutlasses, "treasure" chests, wood muskets, skulls, "gold" moidors, cannonballs and models of Spanish galleons.

A planter's punch cost Penrose $4.50, but the punch was freezing cold. The bar was empty and dark and afforded relief from the marauding sun; the bartender was friendly and inquisitive.

After four or five minutes Penrose let his guard down and mentioned he was a seaman, and they talked ships for a while. The bartender, apparently believing his own decor, described a schooner of notorious turtle poachers, the Diggory brothers, that had just come into the harbor.

Another planter's punch, and Penrose, weary of his cover story and overly grateful for even a barstool alliance, decided he had nothing to lose by telling a strange bartender he was trying to track down the owners of an insurance company that owed him money.

The bartender polished glasses and said, "Why don't you look up the owners at Company House? If it is a Tortuga corporation, they have all the company papers there. Anyone can look at them; that is the law. They are trying to change it, because the Americans wish to hide money here from their tax people, but it is still the law. Islanders have little enough control as it is, you know."

Penrose almost did not find time for a third planter's punch. He left a good tip, picked up his duffle bag and opened the door so quickly he nearly knocked down a young American wearing dark glasses and a seersucker suit. As he looked for a taxi he cursed himself for trying to be too canny, trying to avoid the obvious. If his brain had been working right, if he had been in London, a visit to Company House was the first thing he would have done. He should have thought about it—in fact, he had thought about it before he left, but in the haze of telescoped time zones he had forgotten the Tortuga Islands would be structured in the flexibly rigid mold of that skeleton of Empire, the British Civil Service.

The Tortuga version of Company House was located in government offices next to the police headquarters. Various side offices were occupied by heavy men in madras jackets holding official "board meetings" or signing articles of incorporation. The smell of cigars was strong; the occasional laughter chummy, intimate.

The secretary in charge of company records was as plain and fat and European as the receptionist at McTaggart, Ebanks had been the opposite. A folded piece of plastic on her desk read: MRS. C. FOSTER.

When he asked if he was in the right place to examine company records the woman began a long recitation concerning the variety and scope of the files kept here, chanting like a tape machine, her thoughts obviously elsewhere. Halfway through the speech, from a door that appeared to lead to a closet, came a sound that could only be an infant's wail.

He looked up, startled, and the women paled and stopped in midsentence.

"It's my son," she whispered, looking around, strain in her movements. "He's teething, and I couldn't find anyone."

"He does sound a little young," Penrose observed, "to be a civil servant."

She smiled apprehensively. "I'm not supposed to have him here."

"I won't tell," Penrose whispered back, "if you help me."

"Oh—just a minute." She disappeared into the file room. The wailing stopped, then resumed on a lower scale.

"Teething's horrible," Penrose said in sympathy when she returned. "They don't know what's going on."

"I know. I've tried everything—putting camphor on his gums, even little crumbs of aspirin, but there's nothing for it, I suppose."

"He'll need them later. The teeth," Penrose elaborated. "For chewing. Just a joke."

She laughed, dutifully, and returned to business.

Penrose explained his needs.

"You'll have to wait a day, of course. You know?"

"Er, no, I didn't. I'd hoped." He must have looked frustrated; she relented a little.

"Well, there's not too much happening today. People are getting ready for the Pirate's Festival, I suppose."

"I've come all the way from London."

"Ah, London," the woman said, losing track of business again. "What part?"

"I used to live in Willesden, when I was there. I'm from Cornwall, originally."

"I'm from Hounslow," she volunteered, as if that made them almost neighbors. "I do miss it sometimes, though it's lovely here of course. Could you fill out these forms, then? There's six of them."

Now that he was so close he began to have doubts.

"What if it's a London-registered company? Would it be registered here if it's not based on Tortuga?"

"No, only Tortuga companies are here, ones that are formed here in Georgetown only."

"But it's got an office here."

"Doesn't matter, you see."

"I'm sure it's a Tortuga company, though." He was aware of how wishful he sounded.

"Well, fill out the forms, then."

The forms were perversions of officialdom, asking for information that ranged from date of birth to passport number to business address and spouse's domicile "if different from above." The six forms gave Mrs. Foster time to quiet her baby to an occasional gurgle. Penrose left the forms on her desk and walked over to the windows while he waited.

Outside, the sun hid behind a cloud so white and convoluted it looked like you could sit in it. Cars droned. A light airplane dove and swooped around the horizon, seeming to give the ground a close shave as it released silvery fogs of insecticide. Death to sandflies. A hummingbird flitted in a hibiscus below, and a young American with a receding hairline and a seersucker suit walked into a gift shop down the street.

"They try to make it difficult," her voice came from behind him, "because there are so many companies here and some of them aren't too keen on people seeing the files, though I shouldn't say so. But it is still public record, and seeing as you've come all the way from London, I'll see what I can do."

She was back inside five minutes with a manila folder tied with purple ribbon. A label gummed to the flap read "Tortuga Insurance Company Ltd." The prospect of possible success dried Penrose's throat.

He sat down at a wooden table and opened the folder.

There were seven or eight documents, some of them stiff with ribbons and sealing wax. The first in the pile was also the most formal, double-edged, with a seal and palms, a lion rampant and three stars. Three stars for three islands, Penrose thought, vaguely.

"Certificate of incorporation," it read.

I, Robert Bodden Crosby, Registrar of Companies of the Tortuga Islands, do hereby certify, pursuant to the Companies Law Chapter 22, that all the requisitions of the said law in respect of organization were complied with by Tortuga Insurance Company formed in Grand Tortuga Island on 14th August 1983. This company was registered on 14th August 1983.

Given under my hand and seal in Georgetown, Grand Tortuga Island, British West Indies.

Nothing there. Penrose put the certificate aside.

The next two documents were articles of incorporation stating that the Tortuga Insurance Company had been duly incorporated and registered to undertake and carry on all or any of the business of shipowners, brokers or agents, and

191

insurance brokers, underwriters, ship and aircraft managers, tug owners, loading brokers . . . The documents were signed by R. Bodden Crosby and his deputy, on behalf of the governor of the Tortuga Islands.

The president and treasurer of the Tortuga Insurance Company had signed on behalf of the company. Their names were Duncan McTaggart (President) and Crosby Ebanks (Treasurer). Andrew Smith was listed as Secretary and General Counsel.

The attorneys, Penrose thought. How convenient, and how obvious. Not only did they act as a letter box for the reinsurance company, but they also acted as proxy for its actual directors. It had been Smith's name on the letter he'd received.

The fact that these legal false bottoms almost certainly existed to cover shadier dealings was outweighed by the efficacy of the camouflage. The former did not compensate for the latter, in exactly the same way as suspicions did not hold up in court.

He could only wonder in a peevish fashion what might happen in the unlikely event that the Tortuga proxies decided to take over the company for themselves. What recourse or safeguard would the hidden directors have?

The next two pages provided the answer.

The first limited the company by shares and ascribed five percent of common stock to Mr. Duncan McTaggart, Esq., Mr. Crosby Ebanks and Mr. Andrew Smith, all of Georgetown, Grand Tortuga Island.

The second gave title of the remaining ninety-five percent of stock to Mr. Vincent Dormier, Esq., of Victoria, Hong Kong Territory.

Vincent Dormier. The same name as the man in the news photos Harewood had requested two days before he left for Tortuga. The man who was also Mr. Alan White. The man who was connected to Eastern Holdings Ltd.

Eastern Holdings, whose directors, Harewood had said were both "names" in, and owners of de Laune and Court, Underwriters, at Lloyd's of London.

Penrose slammed his fist down on the table as hard as he could. Mrs. Foster looked up startled. The baby thought about the noise briefly, and began to cry.

"Shhh."

"Sorry."

"Found what you were looking for?"

"Yes."

"Down the hall, to the left, one dollar a copy," she said, forestalling the next question.

"A dollar?" Penrose said, shocked despite the elation, but he went anyway.

A portly Canadian in a plaid jacket led two quiet islanders past him as he copied his documents. "We'll have a good lobster lunch at that place down by the harbor," the Canadian was saying, "then I'll buy you guys nine holes of golf. It's on the bank."

Penrose left the government offices with a markedly lighter tread than he had when he entered. The air was just as oppressive but the duffle bag seemed to have shed twenty pounds. It would probably cost thirty quid, but he owed himself a lobster lunch, he decided.

He looked around carefully as he hailed a taxi, but the seersucker man was nowhere to be seen.

Wreckley's Dive Hotel and Grill had been recommended by Mrs. Foster. It consisted of three whitewashed clapboard buildings curved around a neat coral courtyard with scarlet flowers and a cistern at the back. Cocoa palms and cedars stifled noises from the road and a large beach hotel on the other side.

A very light-skinned teenager clad in tennis shoes and ducks took the duffle bag when he got out of the taxi, giving Penrose a chance to stare at the hired car that had been following him since Georgetown.

The second cab was stopped. Now it moved slowly, described a U-turn, and headed back down Seven Mile Beach Road toward town. The passenger in the back never graduated from being a vague blur in dark glasses. It was impossible to tell what he was wearing.

The kid introduced himself as Presley Wreckley. He asked, politely, for fifty dollars in advance and settled for a credit-card chit. He asked Penrose if he wanted to dive in the morning, so he could get some air bottles ready, and showed him to his room.

Dinner was offered up in the trellised rear section of the courtyard. The turtle steaks were broiled on and served from a stone grill near the cistern. The turtle was tough and overcooked, but if you sloshed enough hot sauce on it and washed everything down with rum punch it was edible.

The sempiternal trade wind had picked up and brought unhappy looking clouds with it, but it drove away the sandflies. A radio in Presley's corner mentioned village festivals in the east end that might be canceled due to worsening weather. The palms spoke sentences consisting solely of sibilants.

Darkness fell quickly. Presley came over and made a separate yellow planet of his table with a kerosene lamp. Penrose stayed there after dessert (runny custard), sipping rum, enjoying a fatigue so great it had fermented into an intoxicant all its own and watching the dodging stars. He thought about the man who was following him and what he was going to do about it, but he did not think very hard.

There were only two other people having dinner in the courtyard, a very short, attractive blonde girl and her consort, a tall man with a liberal beard. Penrose vaguely made up his mind that even if McTaggart, Ebanks, and Smith had somehow managed to have him followed from the Bank of Labrador building, they would not be attempting anything as drastic as the Antwerp incident. That would be up to de Laune and Court, or Eastern Holdings, or whoever, assuming they had truly been behind the assault in Skipperstraat. He was almost asleep in his chair when the bearded man came up and offered to buy him a rum drink. Penrose was too tired to refuse.

He was a free-lance journalist taking time off to work on a master's thesis entitled "The Novels of Thomas Pynchon as a Vehicle for Doggerel." She devoted high ideals to an environmental foundation in Vancouver. They were both here to dive the North Wall, where the Grand Tortuga reef fell into a five-hundred-fathom trough in a spectacular welter of niggerheads and wrecked ships.

They were pleasant and a little sick of having only each other to talk to. Penrose felt guilty that the only time he managed to show much interest in their inoffensive words was when they mentioned air tours of Tortuga Brac and Little Tortuga.

These, they said in answer to his questions, were two small islands about fifty miles to the north. They had tiny populations but lots of limestone caves, giant iguanas, frigate birds and some of the best coral diving in the Caribbean. Two planes left daily, at 10:00 and 2:30, and there was a tour guide to show you around the islands. All you had to do was make a reservation with Presley.

They called Presley over, and Penrose duly booked a seat.

He then made excuses about jet lag and went to his little whitewashed room that smelled of salt and hibiscus. He remembered to undress and pull the mosquito netting over himself. The sea wind breathed deeply through the slats serving as windows, and a lizard croaked amorous verses in the rafters. He was asleep within two minutes.

XVIII

He slept late, too late, but got to the airport in time for the afternoon flight, uncertain, in the departing traffic of a market day, whether he had been followed or not.

He waited in the airport bar, peering through the windows at the parking lot, but did not see the seersucker man. At the last minute he went to check in, and was told to hurry to the Tortuga Express Airways gate, where his plane was waiting. His presumed tail still had not showed up, and he climbed into the ancient C-47 feeling more than a little foolish at having blown a further hundred dollars on evading a figment of his paranoia.

Well, right now, that was the credit-card company's problem. And at least the photocopies were secure. Before he left he had pried Presley away from washing up after breakfast and filling the Canadians' picnic baskets to lock the documents away in the hotel safe.

The Dakota was a vintage prewar passenger model with Art Deco cabin designs that reminded Penrose vaguely of Paris Métro decorations. He could see only three Europeans: a broad man in shorts and a Kareeba jacket who knew everyone else and was obviously a resident, and two English tourists with burned knees and falsely diffident expressions.

The rest of the passengers were islanders of various hues, many clutching market baskets filled with very dead chickens and not very fresh vegetables. More crates thumped into the cargo section, explaining the delay.

At the last minute an American-looking man, with receding hair and a button nose, in yellow slacks and a seersucker jacket, rushed up the steps, took off his dark glasses and hiked up the crowded, sloping aisle to the last remaining seat. The door pressured shut after him, and the engines sputtered, then roared. They taxied lazily around the bright apron and took off in a pocket of bad air, jumping and shaking into the sky over the harbor.

The water was so clear Penrose could see a shoal of fish near the reef. There was an ancient fishing schooner anchored nearby, tubs of gear scattered around her gray-weathered decks: the poachers. A rusting, beat-up coaster, maybe 500 tons, was tied up at Government Quay, flying a grimy red duster and proclaiming her name, *MK Trader,* to an uninterested world. They leveled off, stood on one wing and headed northeast.

Partway through the forty-minute flight the clouds grew more frequent and changed color, but the pilot seemed to know how to dodge the worst pressure differentials and the turbulence never got very serious. They landed on a single strip scraped out of coral and stone only twenty-five minutes late and taxied to a Quonset hut and a wind sock—the terminal. The pilot opened the door, unfolded its built-in ladder, and the passengers filed out, through the hard sunlight and into the shadow of the hangar.

Penrose had reviewed his options during the flight and realized they were limited to two. Either he could challenge the seersucker man now, or he could challenge him later.

He decided to wait.

The Brac tour office consisted of a little wooden stand and a sign on wheels, attended by a small, middle-aged mestizo in a flowered shirt and a forage cap bearing the name of a company that made tractors. A card on his lapel read "Sam Ebanks," but Penrose had seen enough of the Tortugas to know that Ebanks here was like Morgan in Wales. The list in his hand, Sam told Penrose, held only two names signed on for the tour: a Mr. John Penrose and a Mr. David Smith.

It was absolutely no surprise at all when the little building drained of every other European save the man in the seersucker jacket.

"Meestah Smeet," Sam said, gesturing. "You Meestah Smeet!"

Meestah Smeet had his shades back on, but the rest of his body had nothing to hide behind. He nodded jerkily and tried to do something with his hands and feet. Penrose, with a start, noticed that his left armpit, unlike the right, showed no dark patch of perspiration. There was something else there—a shoulder holster, probably. Just like the movies.

"Oh-kee-ay, genmen," Sam said, "please step with me."

The island was pinkish sand and bugs; the stunning light got little discipline from scraggly trees and thornbushes. An Austin mini-moke—like a cigarette pack on marshmallows, hot metal covered with a fringed, striped canopy—stood at the place of honor by the Quonset door, glued immobile by the consistency of its own shadow. Somewhere a transistor radio finished threatening Babylon with the mighty suffer-ee-ay-shon of Ja Rastafar-aye. The Jamaican Broadcasting Corporation broke in with its own warnings of tropical storms.

Sam got in the driver's seat and beckoned to his customers, who played a tense silent game of no-after-you before jackknifing aboard. Penrose briefly thought about running straight back onto Tortuga Express Airways and waiting the two hours for the flight back, but before he could overcome the inertia of decision-making they were bouncing down the road at fifteen mph, Seersucker looking every which way but at him.

"Look." Sam did his job by pointing to the sky. "Frigate bird."

Penrose glanced briefly. Seersucker looked at his watch.

"You want to see dragons?" he went on. "Sheepwreck? Turtles? Pirate treasure?"

They trundled by a small cluster of neat boxlike houses tucked in bright gardens. ("Dese houses belong to men working on sheeps, tree, four months: captain, sailah.") A face from a nightmare caught light at the window of the last house: nose swollen to the size of a forehead, mongoloid eyes, a pink split mouth. "We see everything anyweeah," Sam continued merrily.

The road got better but their driver refused to come out of second gear. They crawled along the shoreline, around bays and points. The sea lay caged behind a barrier reef. Clouds stained it different shades as they passed, shuttering the westering sun, then restoring its shine. Sam pointed out more frigate birds; a cave where British soldiers had massacred a band of pirates; another cave where last year two children had found doubloons from Henry Morgan's treasure (the American snorted); a gully where refugees from Cromwell's governor in Jamaica hid from the reach of the Grim Protector. Penrose made up his mind to tackle the American verbally as soon as they got back to the airport. For the present he would enjoy the warm breeze in his hair; for the first time since he'd arrived, his thick cotton shirt was not sticking to his back and the sandflies were out of contention.

This could have been fun, he thought, if it had been Claire Thibodeault instead of Seersucker sitting next to him in the tiny vehicle.

Tortuga Brac was a long, narrow island built around a huge bluff that rose from sea level at the southwestern end, where the airstrip was, to a height of 140 feet at the northeastern point. Halfway along the southern stretch Sam drove up a track toward a cave opening in the limestone slope, halted at the entrance and turned on his brights.

A huge face from ten million years ago appeared out of the darkness, blinking eyes that were incapable of any social emotion and therefore the essence of horror. It was a huge lizard, a Tortuga iguana, at least five feet long, to judge by the size of its head.

Its tongue slithered once and it turned and tried to disappear in the diminishing crack of its shallow cave.

"Dragon," Sam commented. "Very shy, aye, Meestah Smeet." The American looked away with an exclamation of disgust and mumbled something rude, still avoiding any kind of contact.

"You can take piksha, indeed if you want. Look—" he pointed to the right—"more frigate bird." He let go the brakes and they moved on near the beach, swerving back and forth to avoid outcroppings of limestone.

The strip of beach grew narrower as the bluff to their left grew taller, crowding out the flatlands with their occasional cabins and scrubby vegetation. They came around a point and saw, for the first time, where the island came to an end, maybe a mile ahead, in a monstrous rash of jagged limestone towering sheer above the Caribbean. They could see more of the horizon, too, now strewn with purple clouds.

"Maybe you'll spend night on the isle." Sam chuckled, pointing at the clouds. "David Smith" sniffed.

As they drove closer to the shoreline to pass around

buttresses reaching out from the bluff Penrose noticed a medium-sized bay, where the reef curved inward and a tongue of sand curved out. A seaplane was moored in the lee of a crescent of beach. He pointed it out to Sam Ebanks, who nodded and said, "Trippers," as if that explained it all.

Then he added, more enthusiastically, "Pirates' cave up here; dragon too," and demonstrated by turning inland.

The wind was weaker on this side of the island, Penrose thought, or maybe it had dropped generally. If so it was not a good omen, and he wondered what kind of odd Graham Greene situation might develop if their return flight was canceled and they were forced to spend the night in some sandy beach cabana: two men, the shadow and his quarry, each of whom knew but would not admit the other's role, locked into the third persona of "tripper" on a flyblown island no one had ever heard of.

Sam drew his vehicle up in front of a cave partly obscured by the lip of windblown sand in front of it and pulled the hand brake. Limestone loomed for fifty feet above them. Footprints leading in and out of the cave's mouth confirmed the presence of other tourists. Neither passenger moved.

Sam pointed at the cave and repeated, "This is best place. Pirates' treasure was in here, Henry Morgan, och aye." Penrose looked at Seersucker, who was resolutely looking in every direction but his fellow tripper's, and began to laugh: the whole scenario was so absurd.

"Pirates' cave," Penrose agreed.

He stepped out of the little car, over the swell of sand and edged delicately into the limestone arch.

The coral hues faded into darkness ahead of him. He could feel warm moisture from inside. Heat reflected viciously from the rock. The sandflies, foiled till then by the car's slipstream, attacked with a vigor that indicated this cave was one of their strongholds.

"This is as far as I'm going, thanks very much." There was a sound of sand being scuffed and a long shadow drew up beside him. Seersucker was right on his tail. Penrose, swinging his arms again at the flies, turned and looked him right in the face, but he still wore dark glasses and his features were black against the sunshine outside.

As he stared at his companion, Penrose heard the ratcheting noise of a hand brake, an unprecedented leap in revolutions from the mini-moke's engine. Then Sam Ebanks was gone, spurting sand from his little tires.

Penrose strode around Seersucker and toward the mouth of the cave. He shouted something, but the car kept right on going, its striped canopy fluttering gaily as the driver shifted into fourth gear, heading south as fast as he possibly could.

The immediate vicinity of the cave was now dominated by four mixed-breed men in sloppy deck clothes. They must have come from one of the gullies near the cave, he thought. One of them was very large and carried in his left hand a long burnished cutlass with a brass hand guard, of the type that had gone out of style a hundred years ago in every place but the Israel Hands pub. The right hand hung, shriveled and useless, from a shrunken shoulder.

Another had a Colt .45, Army issue, stuck in his broad leather belt in such a fashion as to permanently destroy his chances of procreation should the gun ever go off accidentally.

The other two carried fishing knives. One had bright hennaed hair. The other had only one eye, and he squinted ferociously in their direction.

Behind them the seaplane they had come on turned in the breeze, heliographing nonsense from its windows.

"You goddam son of a bitch."

Seersucker turned to Penrose and slid his right hand under his left lapel. Penrose, suddenly convinced that he had been well and truly trapped, moved from deep instinct and grabbed the American in a rugby tackle.

They were roughly the same weight, but the dive caught the American off guard and he stumbled and fell. They rolled once, twice over the fine sand of the cave floor, Penrose's brain taking snapshots of the four men watching the floor show in astonishment. The American had Penrose's head in a lock, while Penrose had Seersucker's gun arm blocked with his right hand. They piled up against painful angles of limestone wall, spitting grit. Seersucker released Penrose's head, grabbed a piece of rock and tried to pound it against his opponent's temple, but Penrose deflected the blow onto his shoulder and attempted to ram his head into Seersucker's nose. There was an incredibly loud crash, and a red tear appeared on the American's shoulder.

A gentle rain of limestone chips pattered behind them, backed by a high, nervous hissing.

"Oh-kee-eh, dat's enough boiss."

Penrose glanced up and to the right and saw the Colt .45 pointed vaguely at the cave, fat smoke oozing from its muzzle.

"Bloody hell."

"Fuckin' shit."

Penrose realized he had only one chance, and that was to get his opponent's body between himself and the other men and wrest the gun from the American, to hold him hostage. Then he would force the Yank's henchmen to let him out of the cave, using the American as a shield. It was a ludicrous plan, but Kirsten's message kept ringing in the back of his mind ("learn karate . . ."). He wished he'd taken her advice.

He reversed his effort and pulled Seersucker on top of him, but that was a mistake, because it allowed the American just enough leverage to get his elbow on Penrose's Adam's apple and drop his weight behind it, cutting off the Englishman's air supply.

"Let go, Limey."

Penrose torqued his throat, jackknifed his body, but he could not get the elbow out of the way.

"Let go, you schmuck!"

Penrose loosened his grip on the gun hand, intending to hook his fingers into Seersucker's eyes, but the American was too quick. He had rolled back against the wall and had the gun out before Penrose could get back on top of him. He watched Seersucker whip out a small .38 Police Special and point it at him, and tensed his stomach muscles against the terror of pointblank insult.

He watched as Seersucker swiveled forty-five degrees, aimed the gun out of the cave and fired a shot at the four men who ringed the entrance.

"What?" Penrose croaked out in astonishment, shocked by the noise at least as much as the act.

Seersucker ignored him.

"I've got your man in here," he yelled, but the four men had vanished as soon as the gun went off, falling out of sight behind the curving lip of sand immediately outside the cave.

One of them was groaning in rage and pain.

Another shouted, "Ras mahn, watfa you no tee-ell eem haff pees-tol, mahn."

Seersucker pointed the .38 at Penrose again to encourage him, then shouted, "I've got your man in here. I'll cool him if you don't leave."

Penrose, blinking against the sand and sweat and flies, had his gaze fixed on "David Smith." But apprehension must have replaced the surprise in the set of his mouth.

"Whatsa matter, Limey? Get back against the other wall."

"It's not going to work."

"What?" The American spat sand from his lips with little rhythmic "tuts." The tear in his jacket was not bleeding— probably just a rent made by flying limestone.

"Holding me hostage," Penrose said.

"We'll see. Move!"

"No. Listen to me. They're not *with* me. I thought they were with *you*."

The voices and groans outside had subsided. One of the men made a quick dash for a small ridge and dived for cover like a stunt man. Seersucker kept his revolver trained on Penrose.

"Good story, wise guy. Then what are you doing here, tell me that?"

Penrose did not need to talk, because there was another .45-caliber explosion, farther away, but the cave reverberated with shock and ricochets. Both of them ducked, instinctively covering their heads.

Still wincing, the American looked up. "You wanna kill your boy?" he screamed.

"Mon, you keel eem eef you wahnt," came the reply, distant. Someone laughed.

Seersucker did not move except to bring his gun elbow back to a good angle of fire, take off his dark glasses with his left hand, shake them free of sand and put them back on. There was further discussion beyond the cave entrance. Penrose tried to catch what they were saying, and failed.

The American looked back and forth, measuring the cave mouth, weighing possibilities, measuring again.

"Get up," he said at last.

"What?" Penrose brought his attention back to the American.

"Get up."

"Why?"

"So we can see whose side you're really on." He flicked the revolver muzzle toward the outside, where daylight rose, corrugated by heat waves, from the beach. Then he aimed the gun at Penrose again.

"You're mad. They'll shoot me."

"Then," Seersucker said with a smile that wasn't really, "I'll know I made a mistake."

"Come *on*."

"I'm going to count to three."

"Come on, mate—how do you know they're not just thieves, pirates even?"

"One."

"The last pirate they had here was only forty years ago. I read it in a brochure."

"Two."

"Why on earth would I want to kill you, anyway? I don't know who the fucking hell you are!"

"Three."

"Okay! Okay!" Penrose jacked himself up in a crouch, complaining, "It doesn't make sense."

"Yes, it does," Seersucker explained. "If they don't plug you, I got myself a hostage. If they do shoot, I don't, either way. See what I mean? But don't worry," he continued in a consoling tone, "they're obviously lousy shots. They're turtle poachers, you know, so they're much better with knives. They'll probably miss you, or hit you in the shoulder or the balls or something."

"Oh, hell," Penrose said.

"Move!" The .38 jerked.

The American was just too far away to jump. Penrose raised himself cautiously to full height. Sweat streamed from every pore in his skin, and it wasn't only because of the heat. A black head ducked behind a limestone shelf thirty feet away.

"Move toward the entrance."

Penrose took one step.

"Move." The voice was implacable.

"No."

"If you don't."

"What have I got to—"

The air stirred near his forehead, followed an instant later by the crash of another magnum shell. Penrose dropped onto his stomach, unconvinced that he didn't have a large hole somewhere.

A faint low chuckle came from outside.

"I wonder who the fuck they *are* working for then," Seersucker said as he wiped sweat from his forehead, scratched his neck and pointed his .38 toward the entrance.

"I wonder who the hell you're working for," Penrose gasped as he checked himself with shaky fingers for bullet holes. He tried to translate the shock and indignation and failed. All he could come up with was a feeble "You nearly had me killed just then."

"We could probably make a run for it, but it'd be safer after dark." The American looked at his watch. "As long as they don't find any more .45s."

"They're probably radioing from the plane," Penrose pointed out.

Seersucker thought about it for a moment, looking at his watch. "It's about one hour till dusk. Worth the risk."

"Unless, as you say, they find more pistols."

The American gave him a look.

"Barrel of laughs, aren't you?" He craned his neck to check the beach again. "I wonder," he added, "if there's a way out the back?"

"Why don't you check?"

They exchanged glances.

"Maybe I will."

The American hefted his gun, hesitated, and slid backward on knees and elbows to where light was swallowed by rock.

"Shouldn't you leave me the gun?"

"No way."

A match fizzed, added backlight and faded out of sight.

But he was back inside a minute, the matches out and a definite catch in his voice when he dropped back onto his stomach and said, "We can't get out that way."

"What's the matter—ghosts?"

"Worse."

"What?"

"There's a lizard back there, a dragon. Anyway, the cave stops."

Penrose remembered the hissing noise when the first shot had been fired, but there didn't seem much they could do about it one way or another. Except wait.

They waited for five minutes.

The American was the first to break the silence.

"So who are you? Okay, John Penrose, I know. Probably an alias."

"Who are you?"

"You first."

"No, I insist."

"I've got the gun."

"You Yanks," Penrose said, getting his courage back, "always convinced guns solve everything, just like TV."

"They've certainly solved things today," Seersucker pointed out.

"All right. Only tell me—you've been following me, right?"

The American looked at him with an expression that said "Obviously."

"Since McTaggart, Ebanks?"

"Who?"

"To the dive hotel? That was you in the taxi?"

"What taxi?"

"Very clever. And then you just checked the register."

Silence.

"Unless that couple—no, they couldn't have been."

There was a slapping sound as the American launched a counterattack against sandflies.

"Hell," Penrose said, and paused to try to get these new data into processable shape.

Who were the men outside working for, then?

"On second thought," Penrose said, "I don't think I'll tell you anything."

"You may have to."

"What—you'll shoot me if I don't?"

"No. Extradite you."

"What?"

Seersucker sighed. He said, "The United States had good extradition agreements with the You-Kay."

"And?"

"Are you stupid or just pretending?"

"A bit of both, actually."

Seersucker looked at him. After checking the sand outside for enemy action, he pulled a wallet out of his breast pocket and flipped out a small plastic-sheathed photo identity card that read "United States of America Securities and Exchange Commission Office of the Special Investigator."

The name under the photo was Carleton Winslow Phelps. Penrose examined the ID carefully.

"Well, I'll be damned," he said at last. "The Seventh Cavalry."

"Don't get smart on me now, Mac."

"But I'm quite serious." Penrose smiled his relief, readjusted percentages and tried to figure out how much he should tell an agent of the U.S. government.

XIX

He ended up telling him quite a lot.

It was an unusual attitude for a speech, lying face down on the fine coral sand, itching, scratching and waiting for armed onslaught, but Penrose had thought about the variables enough and had explained them to Sir Norman, Radetsky and Claire enough so it came out like an oral dissertation. Now he could detach himself somewhat from the process, look out for turtle poachers while he talked, note how the clouds and a setting sun were being blurred in the mixer of sky to form a lurid cocktail that had never meant anything positive for mariners.

He even found himself relishing the situation in some out-of-the-way corner of his mind, even as dread sat in his stomach, heavy and toadlike; found himself thinking that what he had suggested to the American might not be so far off, and perhaps these turtle poachers made an occasional extra dollar from piracy, their clapped-out schooner coming down, all sails set, on an unsuspecting yacht like a vision from another, ruder, time: boarding with cutlasses, weighting the corpses, bringing the prize back to strip on one of the ten thousand uninhabited, mosquito-ridden cays of the Greater Antilles.

It was stretching the imagination a bit, however, to give the pirates an air force, even if it consisted only of one antiquated seaplane.

"Reinsurance fraud," Seersucker said when Penrose finished outlining the chain of events, as if he had just been told of parking violations.

"Well, I'm sorry. It's all I've got."

208

Penrose took out his pack of cork-tipped cigarettes, found one that wasn't crushed, offered another to the SEC man, as an afterthought. The American shook his head. While Penrose smoked the American took off his sodden jacket and shirt and checked the shallow scratch he had got from the ricocheting limestone, but the sandflies seemed to get worse as it got darker, and he had to rush his shirt back on.

No sounds came from outside except the lisp and suck of the waves and the rising "kriss" of wind on sand. Seersucker snaked forward for a quick look over the lip of the cave's mouth, slithered back and quickly checked his revolver, popping out five bullets, spinning the chamber, peering up the barrel to look for sand, working the hammer and finally clicking the magazine home again.

"Why don't you fill up the gun?"

"No more ammo," the American replied, casually.

" 'No more ammo.' And here I thought your type always wore a gun belt with little holes for extra rounds."

"Not on an airplane. Although I did get out of the security check this morning, if you noticed. Besides, I didn't figure you'd have friends on Tortuga Brac."

"You don't still think—"

"Just checking, Mac."

"I've told you my side. Now I'd like to know more about what the hell you're doing here."

The SEC man lit another cigarette.

"Nah, I don't think so."

"Why not?"

"Why should I?"

"Because"—Penrose was beginning to get exasperated—"*they* probably remembered to bring extra ammo out there. Because any minute they may get extra guns, and they already outnumber us two to one. Which means that one of us might not make it out of here at dark, and that one could easily be you, and in that case, how will I know who to explain all this to when you're dead."

"I'm not the one who's gonna snuff it—unless these fuckin' flies eat me alive."

"Bloody hell," Penrose said in disgust, and jammed his own cigarette out in the sand. Now light was hemorrhaging from the sky. The prospect of action had turned his stomach into a series of brittle ridges that made deep breathing difficult. "I'd appreciate your logistical support," Penrose added, "when we make a break for it, but after that you're on your own."

"If we make it."

"If we make it."

"We oughta have a plan."

They discussed tactics for a while, both knowing their major problem was how to survive the first rush out of the cave, knowing there was only so much they could plan for that.

Silence again.

"You'd testify, though," Seersucker said cautiously.

Penrose laughed.

"For what?"

"For the SEC. Against Tortuga Insurance."

"No bloody way."

"You'd have to. I know your type—you wouldn't fight a grand jury subpoena."

"You seem to forget—we don't have much empire left, but you're on one of the last remaining bits. Your grand jury subpoenas carry no weight here, Mr. SEC-man Phelps. In fact, I wouldn't be at all surprised if you're not supposed to be here at all."

Phelps sucked his cheeks in and out. "I can't," he said. "I'm not allowed to tell anyone."

"I won't tell."

"It's not that simple. It goes much further than just insurance."

"In fact," Penrose offered, "if you tell me, I won't tell Tortuga Government House that you're an undercover SEC agent. Since the Tortugas have made themselves rich by being an offshore tax haven for Yankee dollars, I'm sure they'd throw you out on your arse. Which, in turn, would not do your career much good."

The American breathed out hard through his nostrils. "You know, you're a real bigot."

"Eh?"

"You don't like Americans. The way you speak about them—"

"I don't like empires. I've got nothing against Americans, personally, except that you took over where the Raj left off."

Another long pause.

"It's a complicated story: I can give you an overview."

"No." The point about blowing the American's cover

seemed to have scored, Penrose thought: as always, the best leverage on Organization Man was one using bureaucratic politics as a fulcrum. He had learned that at Courtenay's. "I want the whole picture."

"You wouldn't understand. It's got to do with the New York securities market, heavy technical shit. Boring."

"Do you really want me to tell the governor general? Try me."

"Did you notice," Seersucker remarked in very bright tones, "how those men out there are deformed? It's because the Tortuga people inbred for so many years some of them got genetic abnormalities. It's such a stigma they hide their deformed kids, or send them to hunt turtles on the outer banks. Interesting, huh?"

"Tell me," Penrose insisted, "what you are investigating."

Seersucker rolled over to scratch fly bites around his stomach.

Finally he sighed and said, "I'm gonna get into all kinds of trouble for this."

"Daddy," Penrose imitated a childish voice, "tell me about securities?"

"I have to go into a lot of other stuff. I can't just start off; it's very technical."

"You're repeating yourself."

"Yeah. Well—it's a real volatile market," Seersucker began.

"Yes?"

"Also real profitable. Billions of dollars traded every day. Hundreds of millions worth of government bonds bought and sold. Like, Joe gets on the phone to Mac and says we want three hundred mil worth of that new Treasury or state hydropower issue. Bill says okay, and the deal's done. The paperwork comes much later, if it comes at all. You can make a fortune in a week, you can lose a fortune in a week. All of this," he added to reassure himself, "is public record."

"Sounds like reinsurance," Penrose answered.

"Same psychology. Jesus, I shouldn't even be talking to you."

"As you said, none of that's secret."

"No— You won't repeat any of this?"

"Why would I want to? You haven't said anything yet."

"Yeah. Well. Anyway, the background *is* important. A security is worth its intrinsic market value plus whatever it has accumulated in interest over its life span. Many of the companies make their money by trading the securities. Some of them do this by complicated arrangements known as reverse-repurchase agreements, where you borrow a security, pay only the interest that accrues while you have it, and sell it short as soon as it goes up in value. You then pocket the difference, and invest it. Get it?"

"Sort of."

"Don't worry about the details." The SEC man's voice was getting stronger as his brain got involved in the financial paper chase and he forgot where his body was. "The point is that you can make millions by stacking thousands of these deals on top of each other every day. The paperwork is so complex that you can also hide a lot of your profits from the IRS and the SEC. You can also lose hundreds of millions of dollars every day if you overextend yourself, if you don't invest enough of the profits right, or plow 'em back into long-term securities. Or even if you get the timing wrong, and have a liquidity problem. Then the whole castle of cards starts to fall. If that happens to a big enough company"—he almost shuddered—"the New York securities market crashes, because all those companies are fucking each other up the ass every day, trading with each other millions of times a day. If one crashes and starts calling debts, the next one will. It's a chain reaction, and where do they get most of this money from anyway? Huh? From the banks, that's where. See, there're not enough regulations to control all this; it's a mini–Black Friday waiting to happen. And if the securities market crashes, you gotta bank panic too. It's what the SEC's supposed to prevent." He remembered to look at his watch. "Another fifteen minutes till dark."

"Time enough," Penrose said, the adrenaline beginning to cramp his stomach.

"Yeah. Well. Now let's say one of the big securities traders, call it company X, overextends itself way, way over its head doing these reverse-repurchase deals, but they're making so much doing it that no one realizes they're not taking care of the long-term picture. The whole point is that those guys have only been around ten years; they're pirates; they're planning all along to skim the cream—they got buddies in the banks—and then do a Vesco. Now let's say a

212

consortium of foreign holding companies, mostly based in Hong Kong and Singapore, decides they want a share of this New York securities action. So they fly a takeover tender on company X, without realizing that the owners have been milking X and the banks for all they're worth. Or maybe they don't care, and let them keep doing it. Only, the consortium launders some of its own profits by paying huge but false premiums to a certain reinsurance company based on Grand Tortuga."

"Tortuga Insurance Company."

"You said it, not me."

"Which is why you're here."

"No shit."

Penrose rehashed the information for a moment.

"Would one of these Hong Kong holding companies be named Eastern Holdings and Godown Limited?"

"It's not impossible." Seersucker started playing with his revolver, thought better of it and put it back within easy reach on a flat piece of limestone.

Penrose chose his next words carefully.

"Would it be possible," he said, "for them suddenly to realize they've bought a ship that's leaking in every seam?"

"Leaking? You mean company X losing money?" The American laughed, but his legal soul was not amused. "The fucking ship has got no bottom! But yeah, it's possible. The paperwork is easy to fake, but not forever."

"And would it be possible," Penrose said, "for them to go broke trying to bail it out?"

"I've been trying to tell you—it's a castle of cards, man. The deals they do are worth tens of billions of dollars, if you take all their loans and reverse-repurchases and swaps and everything into account. It could bankrupt the Federal Reserve Bank of New York. But it's probably what's happened. The SEC has only heard rumors, nothing definite. It was the IRS who was first to tip us off, because of the fake premiums. And if you start gabbing about what I told you, Penrose"—the American's eyes stared at Penrose through the penumbra—"you could be responsible for the collapse of Wall Street. At least, the securities side."

"And the downfall of the American Way of Life."

"Oh, Jesus."

"Just joking," Penrose said hastily. "I promise I won't tell."

"We gotta go."

"It's not dark. Just one more question. Let's say this has happened—the consortium, including Eastern Holdings, is losing money badly by trying to keep company X afloat. Could they be losing so much money that even the reinsurance company Eastern Holdings owns cannot pay a paltry thirteen-million-pound claim on my ship?"

Seersucker nodded. "Obviously. At least for a few weeks. If they're trying to bail out Nastal they will have a short-term liquidity crisis that would make the South Sea Bubble look like a yard sale on a rainy Sunday."

"Nastal?"

"Oh, shit." Seersucker picked up his .38. "Looks like I'll just have to waste you anyway."

"You're joking, of course."

"I'm not joking about how serious this is." The iron he had noticed earlier in the SEC man's voice was back.

As if to underline his words, a solid cone of light splashed into their eyes, connecting the darkness in the cave to the gloaming outside.

The beach around the cave, however, was dark, except for a tiny bug of light in the cabin of the seaplane that blinked occasionally when the pilot shifted.

The searchlight was set on the beach. The angle of the cave's entrance was such that it blocked the light from where they were lying, putting it out of the line of fire from the SEC man's pistol.

"Trow-ott dee gon, mahn," came a voice from well beyond the searchlight. "We no wahnt to ehrt you."

"No," Penrose answered softly. "They'd like to kill us painlessly. Decent of them."

"It's you they want, you know."

"How the hell do you know?"

"Well, if what you said was the truth—they did cool your hack buddy."

Penrose interpreted for a minute.

"That was in London."

"So what?"

"Exactly—so what?"

"Well, we still gotta figure out how to blow this joint."

"Why," Penrose asked in exasperation, "must you always talk like a 1920s Hollywood gumshoe?"

"I do *not* talk like a 1920s Hollywood gumshoe. This happens to be colloquial American."

"You're the expert. You're the expert with guns, too. I thought you had it all figured out earlier."

"I had," Seersucker said peevishly. "There's new input." He pointed into the glow of the searchlight.

"Can't you shoot it out?"

" 'Shoot it out,' he says. It's got to be a good fifty feet away. With a .38 snubbie? While they plug away at me with that cannon?"

Penrose had been dodging the thought of flying bullets all afternoon. Now that darkness had come, his imagination was getting more active, the urge to change their situation growing stronger. He was only five or six feet inside the cave entrance, but even so it was getting to him.

"Let's just run for it then. Do the plan we agreed on. There has to be a reason they're simply holding us here."

"Run for it? With zero cover?"

"Sure. You know," Penrose said nervously, "Butch Cassidy and the Sundance Kid did it."

"Yeah, and look what happened to them." Seersucker stroked his bald patch.

Penrose rolled over on one elbow and stretched his retina muscles to search the surrounding area, but he could see nothing beyond the light.

He conducted a futile inventory in his mind of the objects available to them for missiles, shields or diversions, until a very soft sound, more imagined than heard, reminded him they were not alone in the cave.

He thought about it for a moment, then said, "I know where we can get cover."

"Huh?"

"About five feet and three hundred pounds' worth of armor."

"The heat's getting to you, Penrose. Or maybe it's the flies?"

"Self-propelled. Four-wheel drive." Penrose jerked his thumb toward the rear of the cave, and saw the American's head jerk back in alarmed response. "You said we had company, remember?"

"The—*dragon?* The lizard? No way. No fucking way, man."

"But why not?" The more Penrose thought about it, the more he liked the idea. "It would make one hell of a good diversion."

"I'd rather shoot it out." There was a wall behind the American's voice.

"We can just scare him out, then charge out behind him, with you shooting. They only have one gun at this point, and we know they're not very good shots. I think we'd make it. Both of us. I mean, I hope.

"Why not?" he insisted.

"How do you know he won't attack us instead?"

"They're very shy; that's what our friend Sam said."

"Yeah, our friend."

"You're scared of him, aren't you? The lizard," Penrose said.

"I'm not scared. It's just—oh, shit, all right, I'm nervous. I hate reptiles, lizards, iguanas, you name it. I always have."

"But you wear one on your shirt."

"That's not a lizard." He sounded aggrieved. "That's an alligator. Why don't *you* go scare him."

"I don't want to."

"Why not? You don't like 'em, either?"

Penrose began to laugh, helplessly, less and less softly.

"What *is* your problem?"

"I," Penrose said, between gasps, "I hate caves. I—am claustrophobic."

"Oh, very funny. Oh, just great," but there was a tremor of amusement in Seersucker's voice as well. "What a pair of fucking heroes. Great Caesar's ghost."

"Let's both get him. We can hold each other's hand."

"No way. I know you Brits are all faggots."

"You bet' not cohm oht, mahn," the voice taunted, a little closer now.

"Anything is better than doing nothing."

"Anything?"

"Anything."

They both fell silent, listening to the scurrying of bare feet just inside their range of hearing, running from left to right.

Seersucker's answer was to pull out his book of matches. He began to slide backward, propelling himself on elbows and knees.

Penrose followed him, the nausea coming on twice as strong as they slid deeper into the darker limestone hole.

Sweat pricked out on his forehead and pearled in the high humidity, delighting the sandflies.

When they were brought close together and out of range of even the backlight of the poachers' light, Seersucker struck a match.

Penrose felt even sicker.

The cave had narrowed to a tight esophagus in the wavering yellow glow that defined all they could see underground. The opening was about four feet in diameter. Beyond was the utter absence of light. Without thinking, Penrose put his hands to the arch: the rock was cool, granular and moist. His arms felt every ounce of the tons of limestone that lay above him.

"Where is he?" he said, working hard to get the words out against a dry mouth.

In lieu of answer the American brought the light closer to the hole. In the dying flare of the match they saw the cave disappear under its own floor fifteen feet away. Crouched at the dead end, its eyes glowing green in the refracted light, a full-size Tortuga iguana watched them, puffing its gullet out very slowly and sticking a long pinkish tongue in their direction—watched them without blinking.

"Jesus H. Christ!" It was hard to tell if the match was spent or if the trembling of Seersucker's hand had extinguished it before its time. Darkness closed its mouth over them, digested them, until in a painful spray of phosphorus he lit a second.

"I'm not going in after him."

"Bloody hell," Penrose complained, still holding the roof up with his hands. "Let's just get out of the way and fire the gun behind him."

"No."

"What, then?" he projected his voice to keep it from vibrating.

"I've got a better idea." The American's own voice was stretched with hysteria. "Ready?"

"Ready for what? Wait—"

All Penrose saw was a half-burned match brought next to the full book of its fellows. Fifteen matches blew into a single round of fireworks, which Seersucker tossed with beautiful accuracy, over, up, and on top of the dragon's gleaming saw-toothed tail.

The explosion of light encircled an explosion of movement

as the dragon panicked and streaked for the entrance of the cave in a liquid convulsion of scale and muscle.

There was a loud hiss of tongue, a cloud of thrown sand, then darkness. Penrose and Seersucker both leaped backward and fell over each other. The Englishman felt a heavy, cold, armored thing mash his ankle into the limestone, and the American made a loud gagging noise.

"Come on, man. Come on!" Penrose rolled to his feet, propelled by his fear. He saw a flash of his brother's face again, born of that same feel of darkness, of great weight.

The American almost overbalanced him, grabbing his shoulder to get up. They both ran in a full crouch toward the overexposed entrance. "The gun, man. The gun!" The searchlight kissed their heads and shoulders. A loud yelp of alarm came from outside. Penrose tensed himself for the bullet, but the cave behind was more powerful in the balance of terrors and he ran even faster.

Five feet ahead of him Penrose saw the dragon—till then only an unseen coil of moving sound—become a full black silhouette against the opening. There was a second shout, louder than the first, but the dragon kept running in a surprisingly rapid scuttle of muscles more used to rounded movements. Then a much bigger concussion mushed the air out of Penrose's left eardrum.

They burst, all three together, over the lip of the cave, Penrose immediately tucking into a roll out of the blinding silver of light, into utter shadow and a hard contact with rock and sand still warm from the sun.

He rolled twice more, stuck out a leg and came up on his feet. He was conscious of a narrow beam of light sketching quick lines across cloud and cliff as someone—Phelps, presumably—kicked the searchlight over. Penrose ignored it and pelted headlong up the beach, stumbling in his hurry to flee the confines of the last couple of hours. There was a shout from the American, and Penrose heard, or thought he heard, a body rushing in the other direction close by, but it never came toward him.

He continued running, changing direction every five seconds. Soon he realized that the only sounds were sea noises and feedback from his own pounding heart and lungs and feet.

Penrose jinked left in the night, tripping, slowing, as he

tried to get his bearings. He fell once on sharp shell or coral, cutting his knees, but he could only wipe the sand and blood away with his fingers and stagger on. He crossed over the tide wrack a second later and pulled up in damp sand at the water's edge.

He knew where he was now. The lagoon made licking noises all around him and the smell of salt water was strong. He could see the tiny orange dot that was the seaplane's chart light, one hundred or two hundred yards offshore, which meant that he must be standing near the end of the small peninsula sheltering the plane's anchorage on the south.

The wind had come up from the northwest since they had entered the cave. Penrose listened hard, filtering out the normal, organic noises of waves, wind, driven sand, every sense feeling for the rhythms of pursuit.

Nothing.

Breaking out of the cave had been the be-all and end-all of the plan he and Phelps had made earlier. Vaguely they had agreed that when they made it out—if they made it out—they should head in opposite directions up the beach, find a break in the limestone bluff, and hide from their pursuers in the back country till dawn came and they could summon help.

The sequence of sounds and impressions played back on his brain. The cry. The answering shot from Phelps's pistol. A subsequent yell. His impression of someone running, back toward the cave.

The night remained empty. The wrongness of it made Penrose feel lonely and vulnerable. He squatted in the moist coral sand, sensing the Caribbean's warmth soak through his trousers, opened his pupils wide to catch what stray light remained from sunset or stars now obscured by clouds. His eyes found nothing to focus on except the blacker black of cliffs and the single beacon from the seaplane, just as his mind could not quite grasp the ease of their escape, how their situation had so completely shifted.

He wondered what had happened to the poachers. There had been four of them only an hour ago, four poachers and a .45.

Penrose listened hard for another minute, his muscles beginning to ache a little as he squatted. Still nothing clashed with the sounds of sea and wind. Finally, when he reckoned at least five minutes had passed since they had broken out of the cave, he got to his feet. Orienting himself by the sound of breakers as well as the anchored plane, he set off toward the cliffs inland, stooping to keep his silhouette as low as possible.

The night seemed to have got darker. He stubbed his toes on a rock, and kept putting his foot wrong on coral, but it took him no longer than two or three minutes to reach the foot of the limestone bluff. He looked once more in the direction of the cave before turning southward and setting off along the skirt of shale and boulders by the side of the cliff. Then he stopped short, every muscle tensing.

A vague call had come against the wind, a shapeless sound in too low a key for sea birds.

"A-a-a-y, o-o-o," it came again. There was something human in its timbre, and even through the hiss of the wind he could tell the key was close to that of Phelps's voice.

Penrose turned, hesitated, then made up his mind. He set off carefully back toward the cave, straining his eyes to make out rocks ahead, trying to keep cover between him and his destination, feeling with his toes to avoid disturbing the scree. As he picked his way he went through the various possibilities in his mind: Phelps was wounded (but he had heard no shot, except from the American's own gun); one of the poachers was imitating his voice; they had caught Phelps and were forcing the American to call for him. Penrose held his breath as he moved and edged along more carefully. The wind would carry his noises forward.

"Penro-o-o-ose!"

He groped his way around a limestone buttress covered with guano, in time to catch the call's direction. He was almost certain it was Phelps, maybe fifty yards ahead and to the right of him. He edged out between two boulders, stepped onto clear sand and held his position.

He thought he could see Phelps now: an odd-shaped lump of darkness halfway between cliff and beach. The seaplane light still shone, to his right, making wedge-shaped reflections on the waves.

"Penrose! Where the hell are you? I got him!" Suddenly a light beam glanced down the beach, sweeping back and forth. Penrose stepped hastily backward, but his face must have showed in the backscatter, for the beam jerked toward him and froze him blind in its brightness.

"Christ. There you are. Where have you been? Come over here and help me out."

"I thought it might be a trap," Penrose called, not moving.

"Man, are you suspicious," Phelps yelled back. "No. They've all left, 'cept for this little fucker. I'm trying to persuade him to tell us all about himself."

"Shine the beam on him," Penrose shouted.

The light pulled back and around, illuminating a man lying prone in the sand, with one knee and the muzzle of the poachers' .45 pistol grinding into his very white neck.

"Satisfied?"

"Who is he?"

"Beats the hell out of me," came the voice over the pistol. "All I know is that we spent hours planning our little James Bond escapade, complete with a fucking *reptile*, just to run from this little shit, who didn't even have his gun out." He laughed, bitterly. "Christ," he said again.

Penrose went over slowly.

"Go through his pockets," the SEC man said, "while I hold him."

"Fuck you," the man groaned, and spat sand in Penrose's direction.

In the aura of the light Penrose could see he was very thin, his face scarred with ancient acne. He wore dungarees, a denim jacket with a shoulder patch that read "First Air Cav" and a loose Mexican shirt.

"That's all he knows how to say," Phelps commented, and leaned harder on the man's neck. "He's a disgrace to Air Cav. I caught him running as fast as he could go. He didn't even try to use the piece."

The man's pockets contained only cigarettes, keys, a candy bar, caffeine tablets and a wallet, whose contents Penrose spread out on the sand before him.

"He's the pilot," Penrose explained.

"No shit," Phelps said. "Ever heard of flying poachers?"

Penrose ignored him. "American. Michael O'Leary. From Miami, Florida. He's rated for two-engine commercial planes."

"Fuck you," the pilot said, for the tenth time.

"Anything else?"

"A card from something called the Veterans Administration. A driver's license, I think. Jamaican dollars. That's it."

"Okay, Mike," Phelps said, and shifted his weight on the

pilot's back. "Like I told you, I'm an agent for the SEC. I showed you my ID. I want you to tell us why you and your buddies were trying to waste us in the cave."

"Fuck you."

"Yeah, you should be so lucky. But you're gonna tell us eventually, soldier, so why not save us both a lot of time and answer the question."

"Fuck you. Whadda ya gonna do, arrest me here? Kill me?"

"Yeah." Phelps pressed the gun harder. "No one makes a turkey out of me."

"Fuck you, Jack. Then you'll be right back where you started. See? I'm calling your bluff, asshole. See? I can play poker too."

"Don't say 'fuck you' all the time," Penrose complained.

"Fuck you."

"Look, Mac," Phelps offered. "I won't kill you straight off. I'll shoot you in one knee, then the other. Finally the stomach. Then we'll dump you in the ocean and walk over the island. It would just be so much more convenient?"

"Fuck you, Mr. Federal Fucking Agent."

The explosion was magnified tenfold by surprise. The pilot jerked as if he'd been hit. A crater, five inches deep, appeared in front of him. The sand that had filled it now lay over his face.

O'Leary cursed, coughed, shook his head. He spat repeatedly, and worked his jaw between spits. The smell of gunpowder lingered in their nostrils after the wind had whipped it to leeward. Penrose had to swallow to get his heart back down near the aorta again.

"Fuck you," the pilot repeated, less confidently, but Penrose could hardly hear him over the ringing in his ears.

"What? What did you say, Mac?"

The .45 swung back to point at the pilot's right knee. In the sheen of light Penrose noticed a theatrical thumb work the safety on, then off again.

"That," Phelps yelled against the wind, "was the only warning you're going to get." There was something in his voice, something discernible mostly by its absence, that carried great conviction in Penrose's mind. He wondered how he could stop the American from carrying out his intentions.

The pilot believed him too, for he slumped, then recovered. "You wouldn't: you government agents aren't allowed to do that shit."

"Try me, soldier," Phelps suggested in the same empty tone.

The pilot thought about it. He cleared his throat once, twice.

"A guy in Mo' Bay," he began, and coughed. "He arranges charters for me. He arranged this the night before last."

"That's much, much better," Phelps said approvingly. "Go on."

"What?"

"Go on!"

"That's all I know!" the pilot protested. "I don't even know the name of the guy who called. The guys I picked up this morning had the cash with 'em. We were gonna get the rest when this fuckin' bullshit was finished."

"When we were dead, you mean, asshole."

"No."

"What happened to the rest of them?" Penrose put in, trying to clear his ears with his index fingers.

"They went back to get their boat. For supplies, he says," Phelps answered.

"Fucking scum," the pilot said bitterly. "They weren't all s'posed to go."

"How do we know he's not lying, and they're not behind the cliff there, waiting to fill us full of holes?" Penrose suggested.

"They went to— ow!"

"You expect me to believe that crap?" Phelps yelled out of the blue, and he pushed the muzzle of the .45 back into the pilot's knee, pressing the pilot's neck into the sand with his own knee at the same time.

"I swear to God I'm telling you the truth!" the pilot yelled, the tremor in his voice coming through strong, even half muffled by sand.

"I don't think I like your truth, flyboy," Phelps shouted. "You made fools of us once already. Maybe a bullet in the knee would improve your story."

"No!" the pilot shrieked. "I swear to you, man! They went to the boat, for supplies. They were worried about the storm. We never figured you guys would come out!"

A gust of wind blew at the next words. Penrose had to lean forward to hear what he said.

"It's the truth, man," the pilot went on miserably, shaking his head at the irony of it as well as to get sand out of his mouth. "They weren't going to kill you. I don't know why you guys didn't just stay in there."

He spat again and said, "Don't you get it? They weren't s'posed to hurt you. They were getting paid for every day they just kept you in the cave."

Penrose, Phelps and the pilot spent the rest of the night in a ravine a quarter mile to the south, listening to rats scurry among the rocks while the storm blew itself out of the west of Tortuga Brac.

Phelps only half believed O'Leary's story and bound the man's wrists and ankles with their belts. He had decided O'Leary was, if not a murderer, then at least a drug pilot, and passed the hours going over his story, trying to catch the pilot in a lie or half truth. Penrose soon grew weary of the endless questions and left to keep guard by the beach.

It got chilly around 2:00 A.M., the wind dropped by 4. First light found them stiff and exhausted. The seaplane was still safely moored in the lee of the little point, and there was no sign of the schooner on the horizon. They argued over what to do about O'Leary.

"Those people shot at us even if they weren't trying to kill us."

"You bring him in, then," Phelps said. "I can't. Like he said, they'll throw me out."

"But they can check his story. We'll never find out who paid him."

"He's telling the truth about that," the American retorted. "Apart from what else he says, he runs grass. It's written all over him. They never know who pays 'em. It's how these guys operate."

They finally left the pilot, still belted hand and foot, just inside the ravine. They took his wallet and the keys to his seaplane and set off cross-country toward the road, periodically hitching their pants up as they walked. A cook from one of the two diving hotels on the island picked them up at 5:30 A.M., and dropped them at the airport a half hour later.

In the blankness of fatigue the morning passed slowly. The Quonset hut was sticky with heat, and they spent the time scratching sandfly bites and checking every face that came through the door, but the pilot never turned up: either he had not freed his bonds or he was waiting for the schooner. They took the earliest flight back to Grand Tortuga and landed shortly before 1:00 P.M. Penrose's brain was beginning to stall from lack of sleep, and the bug bites were driving him crazy. But Phelps, apparently, was still capable of quick movement: he said an abrupt good-bye and dashed for the first taxi, holding his trousers, casting a glance that suspected Penrose of blowing his cover at the first opportunity.

Penrose gave him a mental shrug, then his mind shook off the dust and began to function.

His evidence—the evidence he had come here to get—was back at the hotel, which meant they knew where it was. Whoever "they" were.

He hiked up his own pants and sprinted after Phelps to the taxi rank.

He saw at once that the room had been searched: Presley said he had only made the bed, but his clothes were turned over in the unlocked duffle bag, his travel documents bent out of their staples.

No one had tampered with the hotel safe, however. In his relief Penrose said nothing about the search, just showered, changed, ordered one planter's punch, then another. When he had finished the rum drinks, he signed the credit-card slip and took a taxi back to the airport.

He thought the search might have been carried out by McTaggart, Ebanks's boys, or, rather, TIC's, or perhaps the friendly Canadian divers; it could even have been the SEC, or the person who paid the men to blockade him in the cave.

He didn't care. The planter's punches were having their usual therapeutic effect on fatigue, and the photocopies he had come here to obtain were folded safe in his jacket pocket, radiating a warmth in the area of his chest that blended nicely with the glow of the rum. While he waited for his flight, he even dared daydream a little about what his new ship might look like, but he stopped himself, superstitious, and went to charge cablegrams instead.

The net effect of one of the cablegrams grabbed Penrose by the collar as he stepped into the well of expectant faces outside the customs area of Terminal 1 at Heathrow Airport. Penrose recognized the timbre of the growl and its West Country origin before he turned and exclaimed, "Colin!"

The old seaman said nothing, merely took his bag and headed for the sliding doors, but Penrose thought there had been light in the blue eyes that he had not seen in a month.

"You look bloody awful, lad," Colin said conversationally as he pushed the Land-Rover into the underpass at a speed that made Sam Ebanks's seem blinding by comparison. "Tan, but awful."

A sports car tooted at them from behind, then roared to pass, a furred model at the wheel.

"Mm. Did you see her?" Penrose followed the Lotus with his eyes.

"Damn you, Penrose!" Anger flooded the lined face, then washed away again. "Oi've been cursin' your name for a month now, an' it's mostly because of your damned way with women."

"Come again?"

"Oh, the woman, damn you, the Welsh woman that started this whole mess." Colin swerved and shifted into third gear, never wavering from his grim concentration on the road ahead, even as a West German combi came within three inches of his rear bumper.

"It were so unnecessary, d'ye see. I couldn't talk to you because it was your sleepin' with her that sank my ship. But

I thought about it and thought about it. I finally realized it was not your seamanship, anyway. There's nothing I could have done either, d'ye see?"

Penrose grunted. The explanation did not make much sense, but it was the closest he'd ever get to an apology from the old man.

"She were a good ship. But I don't understand about the papers?"

"The papers?"

"The ones you mentioned in the cable."

"She was a good ship. And"—Penrose took out the folded photocopies—"we're going to get another. As good, or better."

Colin Lovell looked away from the road for an instant.

"You've sorted the problems out? For the insurance? Pengerswick did not say ought."

"I've got proof," Penrose said, keeping his voice as matter-of-fact as he could, "that the Lloyd's underwriters are not paying up because they've got their arse in a wringer of fraud. Fraud, man—they're bloody crooks." He went over the details.

Colin listened, the grim angles of his jaw doubly strong as he coped with twin tricks of skulduggery and M4 traffic. When he'd come to the end, Penrose offered to drive, but Colin said, "It helps me thinking."

"If you think as badly, we'll be here all night. Besides, you're heading north here."

"Aye. Are you not going to Priory?"

"No."

"I see."

"Where are you staying?"

"Hammersmith."

"Convenient."

"Aye. You're not back with Selina, then?"

"No."

"I see."

"No, you don't see."

"Sorry. I don't mean to pry my nose in," Colin insisted, "but I think you should talk to Sir Norman about all this."

"Why?"

"Because, d'ye see"—Colin came to a careful stop ten feet before a changing light—"he's a powerful man. He could talk to people you never could, at the police, at Lloyd's, in the government even. Your friend in the police sounds like a very under-underdog. And Sir Norman gives good advice, as well: he's your logical contact for this. If anyone can get the people in charge at Lloyd's to sit up and take notice and pay us money for a new ship, it's him."

"To tell you the truth," Penrose replied, "I'd rather planned not to see that family for a long while."

Colin came to a stop in the middle of the Westway. He turned to face the younger man.

"Women and ships, Penrose," he growled, and his eyes tried to throw light as far inside Penrose's skull as they could reach, "it's the old story. Women and ships, they do not mix, Penrose. Keep them apart. They're like oil and water; bad luck. Sir Norman is the most important man we know; we have got to use him, and never mind Selina."

Horns behind them were blaring so loud now that Penrose had to lean forward to hear.

"You sound like old Tregeagle. You've still got a Cornish-squire complex," he shouted. "Why are we sitting in the middle of the road? Why are we on the Westway, anyway?"

"Lord Ethy—"

"Fuck Lord Ethy," Penrose said violently. "He's in New Zealand."

"It's your precious little differences with Selina," Colin insisted, "or a new ship for us. Take your pick."

"It's not that at all. I don't need Sir Norman."

"But he could help."

"He could help, but—"

"There you have it."

"Will you bloody *drive?*" Penrose shouted.

"And we're on Westway," Colin finished, letting off the hand brake, "so we can take Marylebone Road to Holborn so you can find Sir Norman at the bank. I don't know London well, but I know that much. No time like the present."

"Whatever you say, Colin." Penrose sat back, too tired to argue further. But soon the feeling of success seeped back, and he smiled inwardly as he checked the cars behind them for the tenth time since Heathrow. He was reasonably certain the beige van that had followed them since the airport was no longer on their tail.

* * *

Old Ewing, the doorman, did a double take when Penrose got out of the Land-Rover's passenger seat at the Lombard Street headquarters of Courtenay's Bank.

"Bless me, Mr. Penrose?" he said, sniffing at how close he had come to giving this unshaven gentleman in wrinkled, jet-worn clothes his most disdainful offer of help together with the square-shouldered block that had been known to repel earls.

"Hello, Mr. Ewing," Penrose said, and checked to see if his photocopies were still in place. "Is Sir Norman in?"

"I believe he may be, sir." Ewing knew full well, but as a matter of policy never revealed how extensive his knowledge really was. "I believe I saw Mr. Drummond and Lord Askew go up as well. And Mr. Hilliard."

"A commission meeting, then."

"Perhaps a commission meeting. Should I—" Ewing cleared his throat delicately.

"I'll tell Mr. Fraser to make an appointment for me," Penrose reassured him.

The doorman opened a pair of glass doors four yards in breadth, and Penrose crossed the threshold. Marble steps and gold mosaic scaled the iced heights of the bank's foyer.

For a moment it was like going back in time. The same statue of Shuttlewood Courtenay glowered down on the same Persian carpets, the walnut paneling, tea services with the Courtenay arms in gilt, the shining brass scales that were, by tradition, used only to weigh gold sovereigns. He talked with Mr. Fraser, the porter, sat through one of the old man's interminable and senile philosophies and waited.

After a surprisingly brief interval Fraser beckoned him over and unlocked the door (varnished almost black) of the private staircase to the directors' floor.

They were sitting in full conclave when Penrose entered the room. Four financial eagles in the identical unflappable feathers of their ilk: Lord Askew, of John Glynnis, fat dripping over the wings of his armchair, the assurance of the financially obese; Alec Drummond, of Royal Edinburgh and Overseas, always grim even for a Highlander; a man he did not recognize—Hilliard, presumably; and Sir Norman. Their ties were Coldstream, University, a Churchillian polka dot and Royal Indian Navy.

Sir Norman presided at the head of the table, under the recurrent glare of an oil Shuttlewood, by Reynolds, in front of a carved fireplace that seemed too delicate to contain the swirling flames inside. The table was strewn with papers and silver dishes that held truffle sauce and salmon. The interior decoration appeared to converge on Sir Norman with the full weight of symbolism: Chinese wallpaper, Persian screens, Georgian candlesticks, portraits of HM ships that had safeguarded Courtenay investments in Bombay, Shanghai and the Argentine. Fire shadows underlined the geological folding of the banker's face and threw odd reflections into his eyes.

"Come in, Penrose. Not surprised to see you. We've just finished commission business."

Sir Norman's voice was forced to even heartier notes than usual. Askew burped and nodded distantly. Drummond polished the table in front of him with his napkin. Hilliard stared his lack of interest.

"No introductions necessary, eh? I must say, Penrose, you look a mess. Doesn't he look a mess? And that jacket! Where've you been? You look healthy, though—healthy, but a mess. At any rate, we'll soon fix you up. I knew you'd come back, you see."

"I've been in Grand Tortuga—"

"Grand Tortuga, eh? Fine place, fine. Royal West Indian Club. Went to sow his wild oats after leaving my daughter, eh? Long sabbatical. That's all past, though."

"I've not come for a job."

"No?" Sir Norman rocked forward. His jowls blew up like a dragon's, and a belch escaped with a soft hiss that coincided precisely with one of Askew's. "Pardon. No? Then you've come to gloat, I daresay. Not that I blame you. I was wrong, and I don't mind admitting it. Absolutely incredible!" He threw a copy of the *Evening* down on the table. It landed on a battleground of pâté and vol-au-vent with part of the headline legible: MYSTERY . . . DEAD . . . INQUEST.

Penrose walked over and opened up the paper. The date was yesterday's. A publicity shot of Tim Harewood stared out of the newsprint. The rest of the headline read: OF . . . NEWSMAN . . . REOPENED

"Radetsky."

"The long nose of the Jew," said Lord Askew, not altogether approving.

"Really," Penrose admonished. "And you in the sport of Rothschilds."

Sir Norman waved at them.

"Well, now are you satisfied? We've still matters to talk about, banking matters, and if banking doesn't interest you—"

"I didn't come to gloat either, Sir Norman. I've come to propose a barter."

"You mean you need a favor." Penrose's father-in-law tugged at his earlobe and glanced at his colleagues with what was meant to be a knowing smile.

"Only in return for something more valuable."

"What, then?" The jerking cheek movement, tiny though it was, betrayed larger tremors within the banker, and his eyes kept darting to a point behind Penrose's head. The man was as exhausted as he was himself, Penrose realized, or ill: perhaps his liver was acting up again, in which case he was mad to eat foie gras for lunch.

"Would it be better if we talked in private? I don't want to bore these gentlemen."

"No, no, quite all right." The others made forced noises. "Trust these men as I trust myself, if that's what you mean."

"I only meant—"

"No, no, go on."

"Right." Penrose paused, then said, "Perhaps you gentlemen could help, as well. At any rate, I wondered if you could possibly have another talk with the man you know at Lloyd's. In light of new evidence I have found—"

"New evidence of what?" Sir Norman interrupted.

"Yes, what?" Lord Askew said, opening a turnip watch.

"New evidence that makes it fairly certain that the reason the insurance claim on my ship—thirteen million, you may remember—was denied was because de Laune and Court had fraudulently reinsured the policy with another company that they in fact owned. So that when my ship went down, they were caught short."

"Posgate," said Askew, and "Howden," said Drummond, simultaneously, like a church response and with as much excitement. Hilliard stood up to examine a model of the new Tilbury docklands development Courtenay's was sponsoring: upscale waterfront condominiums complete with monorails and STOL airports for Maggie Thatcher's new plastic Britain.

"Proof," Sir Norman said. "Penrose, I can't simply—"

The captain walked up to the head of the table and laid out the news photographs and the photocopies. Once again he went through the chain of evidence, plowing through Sir Norman's interruptions. Despite their boredom Drummond and Askew got up to ogle the documents carefully. Sir Norman gave up interrupting, and listened. Askew vented occasional belches. An aroma of salmon and cream mingled with that of birch smoke.

"Circumstantial," Courtenay commented at last.

Askew nodded. Drummond walked to the mullioned window and gazed out at the dome of St. Paul's.

"But impressive, Penrose."

The captain sighed.

"Wouldn't hold up in court, of course. But then, it may not have to. They'll pay attention at Lloyd's, you know." Sir Norman's eyes wandered over to the window and Drummond. "They're very fussy at Lloyd's. Isn't that so, Alec?"

"So you won't mind."

"Not at all, dear chap. After all, how will we be able to foreclose on your ship mortgage in a week's time if you don't get your insurance?"

Penrose felt his facial capillaries expand, drawing blood upward while the shock punched lower down.

"Look, he'd forgotten all about it," Courtenay said, delighted.

The mortgage—hell, the mortgage, Penrose thought.

Sir Norman opened a scrolled cedar humidor and passed cigars to his three colleagues. One of the ancient stewards who waited on the board room trembled in with Armagnac and crystal snifters. Penrose remembered vaguely how, when he was at Courtenay's, he used to make up stories about the stewards: how they slept in crypts in the cellar, living on parchments and fried silverfish since the early days, succubi of financial tradition.

"You weren't expecting us to accord you special treatment? Those were your own terms, when you took out the mortgage. You'll have to abide by them."

"No, of course not. It had simply slipped my mind," Penrose answered quickly, isolating and controlling this new anxiety. He had, in fact, forgotten all about it. His bank usually made the payments automatically, but every penny in his own account had gone to pay Brian, Tommy and Malinson. If you reeled once, the blows never let up.

He continued, "I'll be making the payment, of course."

The *Salope* was attached, but he could sell the Land-Rover; buy time until Lloyd's considered the evidence, until the Welsh surveyor came back and told them his ship had in fact been inspected, until he got the money for a new *Witch*.

"The name of the securities company?" Sir Norman asked finally.

Penrose hesitated.

"Well, come on, Penrose. Your information is useless without it."

"Not quite."

"Yes, quite. You spoke of a trade. I'll not be talking to the chap I know at Lloyd's. Neither will my friends here. Not on that sort of barter, as you call it."

Penrose began pacing again, assurance coming back into his words. This board room, after all, was where he had learned to string arguments together under pressure. He helped himself to a cigar from the humidor and took a taper from a box near the fireplace. Sir Norman glowered, the others frowned.

"When I was in Grand Tortuga," Penrose said, "I got involved in a bit of trouble, probably because I was looking into the reinsurance company concerned." He grabbed the decanter from the steward as he tottered by and poured a generous helping into an empty glass.

Askew looked sick.

"I won't bore you with the details, but in the course of getting away from a group of thugs on Tortuga Brac I ran into an American agent—"

The cigar was a Havana, the Armagnac old enough to have acquired different and delicate layers of flavor that massaged each other on the tongue. Somehow the combination allowed him to talk fluidly, concisely, better than he ever recalled doing under Shuttlewood's sneering eye. Sketching in the chain reactions of financial collapse, he could enjoy observing Askew and Drummond begin to cast glances in each other's direction and lose the expressions of excruciating patience that had dominated their faces earlier. Only Hilliard remained aloof as Buddha in the coiling incense of his Havana.

When the captain finished, there was no sound for a long time except the spitting logs and the occasional blurt of traffic far below.

Askew whispered in Sir Norman's ear.

"Don't—get—sarcastic."

"The name of the securities firm?" Askew added.

"The SEC bloke did not want to start a run."

Drummond laughed mirthlessly.

"A run?" Sir Norman spat incredulously. "My God, a run!" he went on. "Assuming what you say is true, you can't begin to imagine, Penrose. Do you have any idea what you're talking about?" He started to hoist himself out of his seat in agitation, but subsided, defeated by the pâté and salmon.

"Everyone's known for years the New York securities market is a bomb waiting to explode," he said. "It's not new, but the latest administration has been too busy deregulating and rearming capital America to worry about it. When it blows up it will take half of Wall Street with it, which in turn will knock the world banking system for six, because I daresay there's not a bank on this planet without its nest egg in New York, in one shape or fashion. It would stop Wall Street dead. A run! My God, did you hear that?" Sir Norman's voice cracked through his normal top range. "My God!" His face grew dark as he looked at his colleagues. With a swing of his forearm he swept a crystal decanter of port off the table, into the hearth. The crash made the bankers jump. "It would be a catastrophe for us, for the world. It's impossible to believe, but you may have saved our bloody arses with your ridiculous little ship!"

The banker was practically screaming, his face twitching a comedy routine of alarm. The other bankers were staring out the windows, or at the ceiling. Drummond muttered to Hilliard.

"I'm sorry," Penrose said into the pounding silence when his father-in-law had run out of breath.

"You were talking of a trade," Askew said, as if it had become his business.

It was time for the information, Penrose thought, if he wanted his thirty pieces of silvery influence. He owed Phelps nothing, he'd promised him nothing.

"You won't start pulling out too heavily?"

234

"Mr. Penrose." Hilliard spoke for the first time. His voice was high, very soft but beautifully modulated. Background noise seemed to fade when he talked. "We of all people have a vested interest in avoiding panic on the Street. Surely you can see that. The name, please."

"Nastal." It was out almost before he'd decided to speak it. Sorry, Phelps, he thought.

All four men continued looking at him, just as they had before.

"Nastal, of course," Askew said finally, looking at Hilliard.

"Can we keep these papers?" Drummond added, reaching for them.

"No. I need them, for now."

Sir Norman took a deep draught of Armagnac to facilitate normal speech and said, "I'll need them if I'm to talk to Lloyd's."

"I'll get you copies." Penrose picked up the documents.

"Who are you showing them to?" asked Drummond.

"A journalist I know."

It was as if he'd told the department head of MI5 that he was just popping over to lunch over at the Soviet Embassy. Askew belched twice as fast in outrage. Drummond repeated, "No, no, no," and polished his shiny spot of table even harder.

Penrose began walking away.

"But you expressed concern," Drummond said, a Scots burr showing through in his *r*.

"You mustn't, Penrose," Sir Norman called out in a cracked voice.

"But I won't, Sir Norman. I won't tell them about Nastal, or Wall Street. I assure you I am only interested in the insurance angle of this thing. That's what got Tim Harewood killed. That's what will get me another 'ridiculous little ship.' "

"If you're not careful, I shan't talk to Lloyd's—"

"Listen." Penrose walked back to the table, braced his fingers against its mirrorlike surface, thrust his head forward. "I have absolutely no interest in bringing Wall Street crashing to the ground. Or even merely the securities side of things. Please remember this is all hearsay, in any case. That's something you should take into account in any measures you may take. I, for one, will not mention any of that information to anybody: I only traded it to you because I needed your help."

"Rather mercenary, aren't you?" was the dry comment from Drummond's corner.

"If that means that I pick my wars—"

It was not the greatest exit line, but the old revulsion was returning in force. Penrose swiveled and walked fast toward the door.

Downstairs Fraser let him use the private telephone because it was "just like old times," and old times, to old men, formed the most pleasant of excuses.

At London & Continental, Gunn had left for the day, but there was a message for Captain Penrose, the receptionist said, if he'd wait while she found it.

" 'Join *London Princess* BPM Dock Greenhithe soonest ETA loading LPG canisters Isle of Grain LPG dock 1900 March 21 ETD Jersey ASAP Gunn.' There's a lot of initials," she said doubtfully. "Did you get it?"

"That was fine," Penrose replied, speeding up a little at the prospect of shipping out. That and the nervousness left over from the meeting upstairs had woken him up to the point where he was only dog tired.

He would have to take the train to Gravesend, yet he found the energy to telephone Claire's hotel. The trip to St. Helier and back generally took up to five days, including turnaround and assuming they came back to London, an assumption you never made with coasters. He wanted to see her before he left.

But when he got through, he found she was busy, and a little distant, even when he told her he had found something in the Tortugas to celebrate. Academic politics had got her down, she said. She would try to call him tonight, or tomorrow if he could tell her where his ship was, and perhaps she could join him for a drink before he sailed. She told him to be careful, and have a drink on her.

He then called Selina, but all he got was her answering machine, the one with the Aragon quote. He told the machine where he would be (old habits died hard), then picked up his gear and headed for Liverpool Street, kicking himself mentally for getting involved again. What would a woman like Claire see in him no matter what his background? What kind of a life could he offer her anyway, and wasn't that a prospect any woman looked at first no matter how tentative the relationship? The childbearing imperative, no doubt, he reflected, with ancient male jealousy.

The gray ride to Greenhithe in a train compartment scarred with football preferences only helped insofar as he dozed off for ten minutes between Deptford and Woolwich. He had borrowed money from Colin so he could take a taxi to the berth, but by the time he had picked his way down the endless pier over the slimy river, humping the duffle bag across tracks and planking made treacherous with wet clay, he felt as if the last protein fumes of his body fuel had been burned one hundred miles ago.

No one came to take his bag when he threw it aboard and climbed down the ladder (it was quarter tide) to the stern deck. He dragged his gear down the companionway, uncaring, a casualty of time zones, and a head poked out the half-open door of the galley.

"Fuck me, it's the guv'nor!"

"Brian?"

The astonishment he felt was mostly due to the crease of memories created by the sight—Brian in the galley was a *Witch of Fraddam* image. The memory shoved away fatigue, reminded him of hope.

"What the hell are you—" Grins and handshakes.

"Wotcher my lord," Brian said. "You gave 'em me moniker, dinyer, so you wouldn't have to keep payin' me wages? Their deck hand decided to prolong his vacation, so they called me up yesterday. 'Ow was the sunny Caribbean?"

"Interesting. I'll tell you in the morning."

Penrose pushed his surprise and delight back for future consideration, and set the alarm in his cabin for 4:00 A.M. His dreams were few and far between, and he remembered not a one.

XXI

The crew of the *London Princess* woke to a pregnant
silence very early on Sunday March 21, with an ETA for
loading methane for the Channel Islands at a berth twenty
miles eastward down the Thames estuary.

The vernal equinoxes Penrose had experienced seldom
lived up to their symbolic significance, but this one was an
exception. There was an apt feeling of reserve power, as if
the infinity of programmed acids poised to ripen on this day
could with tiny electricities polarize the very dawn, setting
off motions that would shift planets.

The captain clutched his tea mug like it was the last link to
functional reality. He walked out on the starboard bridge
wing, wombed in his donkey jacket, fighting the spatial
hangover of jet fatigue.

Flat-arse calm.

Color leaked into atmospheric moisture to the east, a
sickly wash of pink spreading into gun blue. Closer by, the
river had woven a skein of mist that mercifully clothed
varicose channels exposed by the low tide of two hours ago.
The huge rotted lumber pilings of the pier jutted and gaped
and stank among the shadows like an old set of giant
dentures. Across the Thames, he could make out the warehouses and locks of Tilbury Docks.

Fifty years ago those docks had been a warren of enter-
prise and haste as ships of every size, shape and description,
from spanking three-stack White Star liners to crack three-
castle freighters to rusty and steam-wheezing tramps,
queued and jostled in their lust for new cargoes: dry goods
for Dar es Salaam, generators for Mandalay, lumber from

Göteborg, coal for New Orleans, ore from Duluth, steel for Lima, wine from Bordeaux, tea from Shanghai, grain from Montreal, needles and shoes and railway tracks for Bombay and Rio and Perth.

Then the British Empire had existed to provide its banks with investment opportunities and its fleet with goods for trade, the terms of trade being usually negative unless you included the cargo rates and financing. The oceans of the world had become the domain of the red duster, which flew relatively unfettered despite Plimsoll and Parliament. A plethora of smokestacks and derricks, dark and white faces similar in their need for tonnage and their thirst for destinations.

London's dockland was a sepulcher now. Courtenay's and others were whiting them with apartment buildings, in the hope that the men who both created and satisfied desires would sip wine where the scum of the earth once whored and brawled. The great warehouses echoed and crumbled, empty of all but skylights and memories; the England of Drake had succeeded to the Euro-Britain of insurance regulations; the unemployed of Lancashire rioted not for food but against monotony. The road to the modern Wigan Pier led through hovels of the old Empire and Lagos and Calcutta and Soweto.

Mel interrupted his dawn dreams.

"Ready."

"Checked the oil? Primed?"

"Aye."

"Ballasted?"

"Aye, your honor." Teach your grandma to suck eggs, Mel was saying in effect, his eyes flashing in the cargo lights.

"We can discharge on the way down." He went below for another cup of tea, then back to the bridge to notify Gravesend traffic control on the VHF and to stand by the wheel as the ship trembled to life. Mel and Sean went up forward; Brian, as the junior deck hand, got on the pier. The *Princess*'s bow was facing upstream, toward London, the same way as the tidal flow, so he told Brian to loose all the lines except a spring line leading from the port bow. Pushing to slow ahead with full port rudder, he allowed the current to catch her stern and slowly drift the ship perpendicular to the pier, picking up Brian and the spring line while she was still levering herself off a fender Sean held on her port cheek. He rang for half astern, slowly kissed off the pier and backed out into the full rush of the Thames gently, to miss a string of barges moored upstream. When he was far enough into the iron river he put her slow, then half ahead, and brought her in a wide swing to port toward the increasing flush of the dawn.

They headed, still at half speed, down the stretches of river named long ago for the difficulties they presented for sailing ships, or their angle to the prevailing winds: Fiddler's Reach, the Long Hope, Mucking Flats, Sea Reach. Seabirds moaned. The ship's heating system hissed. Pat made noises in the galley. The mist thickened a little past Shellhaven and Canvey Island, but the radar worked well for once; there was no wind or sea to interfere with the reception and the line of buoys could be followed like a modern rendition of Plato's cave by the shadows they made on a cathode-tube display.

Brian came up to the bridge with the captain's breakfast, and Mel went down to the saloon to get his.

"By Christ, skipper," the deck hand said, "it feels bloody odd, dunnit? As if we'd been swizzed by a ghost or summat."

"What?"

"Fooled. Oi mean we're on the wrong ship, know that oi mean? But oi still feel like 'enry's dan below writing 'is mum, and you've taken over from Malinson because you never trusted 'im in a fog."

"He wasn't that bad," Penrose said, changing the subject.

"'E was all right, wiv radar. But me great-uncle, the one wot had the Thames barge, he lived on the daughter orl 'is life and 'e could tell where 'e was on the Thames just by the color of it. Or sometimes 'e'd put tallow on the lead and taste the bottom and he could say, 'We're two miles sarfeast of the Knock.' Or by the way the birds were flyin' 'e'd know which way Marsh End was. Oi went wiv 'im once. I remember 'im tastin' the water once and lookin' up and sayin', 'Alter course half a point to the northeast or summat and we'll be on the Nore in five minutes' time.' And there it was."

"Now," Penrose agreed, "you just punch in the fucking Decca. Or the satnav. But I've news for you—I think I'm going to get the insurance money. I *am* going to get it," he corrected himself under his breath as he remembered the cards he held.

240

East, and southerly around Grain Spit. The mist was starting to lift, and they could see the red-painted signs and buoys placed in a wide circumference around the sunken ammo ship SS *Richard Montgomery* on Sheerness Middle Sand. The signs read: DANGER. HIGH EXPLOSIVE. KEEP OUT.

They rendezvoused with the Medway pilot boat south of the warning buoys and just north of Garrison Point.

The pilot was an old coasterman with a roving eye named Knocker Oakey. Penrose had used him before, taking cement up the estuary to Gillingham. Knocker was no exception to the crazy pilot's rule: he had been known to take naval craft down the channel at night at twenty knots to see how fast they'd go on their way to Chatham dockyard. Gravesend traffic control hated him. But by the same token he was skilled enough to get away with it.

Penrose went below for a second helping of eggs and fresh chips and tea. Mel, already on his second beer, went to the engine room to check the deballasting as they lightened ship in anticipation of her load.

When the captain came back onto his bridge the mist had completely streamed off inland. The sun had come up high behind an armor of clouds, which had to be the trough the weather service had predicted. There was still none of the wind usually associated with a front, however: the water lay flat and uninspired as ever, a little oily from upstream abuse.

They came around the southeastern tip of the Isle of Grain. Knocker reduced speed to a quarter as they approached the massive concrete-and-wood jetties that served the British Gas refinery.

Penrose had never come this close to the refinery, and he looked about in the disbelief of someone who had looked for a city and found only a stage set.

He knew that officially the BG refinery was working at "reduced output," due to the fact that there was too much oil nowadays and too many refineries to process it, both in England and on the Continent, in places like Europoort and the Schelde. Still he'd assumed that for a refinery that covered a good four square miles of sedimentary peninsula, reduced output could only mean a few polymer crackers shut down, some winterized pipelines, fifteen hundred men laid off. The view you got from the Thames did nothing to dispel that notion, for at a distance the refinery looked like a teeming metropolis built for a race of very narrow and fluid petro-creatures, a Gotham of pipes and tubes piled vertically or horizontally, braced by five-story-high scaffolding, clustered around chimney cathedrals, bent into U's and shot into the ground, connected by other pipes and tubes to the brigades and regiments and divisions and armies of two-hundred-foot-high storage tanks that occupied all the fields around. The landscape itself could not challenge the refinery's domination: it was as flat and low as any land could possibly get without actually submerging.

But close up, Penrose realized this was a metropolis that had been abandoned long ago by the petro-creatures, leaving nothing but corpses propped to the battlements. Paint flaked off color-coded pipes. Whole acres of tubing, valves, pumps, meters and gauges lay rusting. Chimneys crumbled. A clock on the headquarters building pointed, now and forever, to the eternity of one arrested moment: 1:36. Weeds grew among the storage tanks and the mysterious bends and alembics of the downstream plants.

There were some signs of survivors, however. A faint flame flickered from the methane plant, far away toward All Hallow's marsh. A fresh division of LPG tanks, shiny with care and new paint. Two flat railway wagons of methane pallets stood on the western end of the jetty, as well as a mobile crane. A handful of men in blue jackets and hardhats hung around waiting to take their lines.

The *Princess* rubbed her cheeks against the huge tanker dolphins of the second jetty, where a pilot launch lay waiting to take away Knocker Oakey. Sean threw a heaving line ten feet up and over, and they took the spring line so Penrose could pinch her stern into the jetty and make fast while Brian protected their rust with a couple of old tires on a rope.

The set routine of loading began. A pudgy dockmaster came aboard with the manifest (no insurance forms, Penrose noticed, grateful). An agent from Strood dropped by with customs documents and the Lights List and left quickly. The pilot hung around the bridge hinting at a second helping of breakfast. In his spare minutes Penrose made quick calculations, balancing the overall weight of cargo against the coaster's righting lever, her center of gravity. He flicked on the red "Dangerous Cargo" light, and asked Sean to bend the red pennant on the after signal halyard. Mel produced two portable NO SMOKING signs to complement the big red notices on the dock and looked pityingly at Penrose when the captain reminded him to make sure all vents, portholes and companionways to the accommodations and the engine room were secured in the closed position. Then Penrose went to check the cargo—six hundred-odd tons of liquid propane gas, sealed under great pressure in four-foot-high canisters of tubular steel painted a glaring white, with a lip underneath and a steel mantle on top to protect the gaskets and O rings. The canisters, standing upright, were sandwiched inside crates made of two pine pallets belted and nailed together with four-by-twos. They were heavily built, Penrose noticed approvingly, and fastened with three-inch nails.

The dockers stood around idly, like dockers the world over, except that they were not smoking. One of them, a curved figure in donkey jacket and hardhat like the rest, was ambling down the jetty for a tea break. Penrose explained to the dockmaster, the loading foreman and the crane operator how he wanted the load placed: pallets—midships, forward, aft—all chocked and battened in such a way as to avoid the slightest shifting in the kind of seaway they were sure to encounter when the roaring tides of the Channel Islands met an opposing wind.

The dockmaster explained that because the eastern end of the jetty was unsound the crane would have to stay in the same area and Penrose would need to move his ship back and forth to distribute the load.

Negotiations completed, the crane's big diesel began to make little preignition sneezes that eventually connected into a chain of noises and thundered into life. Dockers began slipping wire cradles under the first batch of pallets.

Penrose watched them hook the cradle up, signal the crane to hoist it a foot or two above the dock, signal to put it back down, readjust the cables till the pallet sat level in its cradle, hoist again and shepherd the explosive load carefully into the air with a guiding line, over the old concrete and the half-rotten timbers of the dock, to lower it safely thirty feet into the *Princess*'s waiting hold. Three pallets, and the men warmed to their work, shooting rough comments back and forth.

Penrose continued his patrol, nevertheless, checking to make sure all the pallets were as well assembled as the first batch. He pulled his donkey jacket tighter: it was not all that cold, but very damp, with the smelly breath of Kentish marshes all around them.

He would look at all the pallets, entrust the rest of the loading to Mel and catch a bus to Strood and a train to London for a meeting with Allan Clift.

The crates near the crane were all solid. Penrose moved on to the rows of methane canisters stacked between dockside and the flatcars, choosing his way carefully among track and disused fuel lines and fittings whose original purpose he could only guess at. Mel called to him from the bridge window at one point, but Penrose held up his hand and continued his inspection.

"Fucking *Navy* man," the mate scoffed, and shut the window with a bang and a hoarse laugh, but Penrose did not mind.

For the rest of his seagoing life he was going to check his cargoes as carefully as he possibly could because bad freight contradicted the whole point of carrying cargo: you never got where you were going.

The crates were wedged close to each other next to the first flatcar, and he had to squeeze sideways to check them, ducking down to peer down the different rows of methane bottles. Yet it was only a glimpse he caught from one angle at the corner of his eye that made him hesitate, push himself back, squeeze into the gap and peer among the scrap and darkness to locate the pallet with the anomaly—a glint of exposed copper, which was a little out of place, and a square of bright pink next to it, which was even odder.

The gray light above was obstructed by the stacked canisters. Down here the smell was even more potent, a contradiction of sweet fresh pine boards and Medway muck. Whatever it was lay crammed tight in the middle of four rows of canisters, deep in the darkest shadows in the center of the sandwich of pallets.

Curiosity was the first dominant impulse. Maybe someone had left something behind? Idle curiosity which became less idle, more serious, then seemed to fall off a cliff.

It took him a full five seconds to put the various patterns together. Six long pink logs, wrapped in a cylindrical arrangement of tight polyethylene, with a glint of copper coming from a chink in the middle of the central log. The cylinders appeared to be wrapped with electrician's tape that fastened them to a plank of Bakelite.

Three boxes were wired together on the Bakelite plank. The largest, black, had a clock face of some kind. The smaller middle one was of transparent plastic. The third was all matte-black metal. A battery with bright wires ran into the center of the sticks, into the rear of the black box.

It was ridiculous, a Hollywood touch, but when the crane's diesel huffed slower as strain came off its cable back in the overcast world of sanity only forty paces away, he could hear a measured, minute ticking coming from the device in the center of the pallet.

A bomb.

He recognized it dispassionately, but the horror of its implications overwhelmed his frozen calm. If it went off, it would blow open the methane canisters around it, and the gas they contained would explode. When the LPG exploded, it would blow open every other canister on the dock in a chain reaction so rapid that the different blasts would all meld into one.

When the dock went up, the ball of flame created by the expanding gases would envelope the *London Princess*'s hold, and the canisters there would join the party. So would the gigantic holding tanks only one hundred feet away. The horror stories about tiny methane tanks, a teacup's worth, vaporizing large seagoing yachts, could be multiplied a hundred-thousandfold here.

The exploding propane would melt the flesh off the bones of every man, woman and child within a kilometer, char the bones so dry they cracked. And when the storage tanks went up, they would create a fire storm that would ignite every volatile compound still stored in four square miles of refinery, vaporizing the refinery and the power station behind it, leveling the town of Sheerness, only a mile across the river, not to mention the quiet farmhouses with dovecotes in the eaves in the villages nearby.

Penrose was racked with horror, bent, frozen, as the possibilities rolled through his brain.

And the ammunition ship—dear God, the ammo ship, twenty thousand tons of amatol growing less and less stable as the years went by and the tides rolled in and out. They had stopped diving, stopped salvaging it, as soon as they'd started, as soon as they'd seen what her hold looked like; prohibited even small boats from going within a mile of the wreck, because they reckoned if her cargo of aerial bombs went off it would wipe out southeastern Kent, Gravesend and Tilbury—and that was before they built the other LPG depots, at Canvey Island and Shellhaven.

Penrose realized he had spent what felt like an eternity but was probably no more than thirty seconds with every muscle rigid. Now he deliberately straightened up and looked around at the doomed section of world he lived in.

Nothing had changed. Only he knew. The flat horizon stubbed its toe a little on Garrison Point then killed time all the way to Holland. A fancy varnished motorboat puttered out in the Channel: naval chaps on an outing. A sea gull stood on a dolphin piling ten feet away, sharpening its yellow beak, looking at the funny human, sharpening its beak, watching Penrose again.

"You'd better piss off," Penrose said to the sea gull, his voice shaking a bit. Only then could he move. He slid himself very carefully from between two pallets, sidled faster and faster through the ranked canisters, finally leaped clear of the freight and began bounding over track and pipes and oil-covered planking back to his ship. It was difficult to do with absolutely no breath in his lungs.

"Mel!" he croaked when he reached the crane and could see his mate standing by the hold.

He spotted the dockmaster at the same instant and beckoned him urgently over. His hands were trembling slightly, he noticed, so he stuffed them in his pockets, the old reflex.

Bloody hell, he had absolutely no idea how much time they had—seconds, minutes, hours? His stomach told him one second, at the outside. The death toll would be horrendous, and it was all in his hands, but there was no use shouting "Bomb" or "Fire." He was that much in control.

"What's up?"

"What's the matter? You look ill—"

"Come with me," he said, and began moving so fast back toward the flatcars that he slipped on a patch of tar and nearly fell on his face.

"You first," he ordered the dockmaster when they had all weaseled between the lined-up pallets. "Squeeze in there and look in the middle of the left-hand pallet."

"Come on, mate, is this a joke?" the dockmaster asked hopefully. "You coastermen are right ones for a barney."

"Just look—*now!*" Penrose yelled, feeling the urgency rushing to his face. Mel watched him oddly. The dockmaster started to protest, but something in Penrose's eyes stopped him, and he jammed himself into the gap. He had a lot of trouble squirming his bulk around the corner of the right-hand pallet; then he was clear. "Next one down," Penrose told him, and he stepped sideways along the pallets. All that could be seen now was his bottom. All of a sudden the dockmaster froze, just as Penrose had.

He stayed in that position for ten seconds before pushing himself backward in a panic, ripping his jacket on a protruding nail on the corner, banging into the next pallet as he swiveled to face the other two men.

"Jesus, be fucking careful!" the captain screamed. Mel looked at him with visions of straitjackets in his eyes.

"A bomb!" The dockmaster's eyes were staring. "My Christ, it's a bomb. I saw 'em like that in Malaysia, I tell you— No, it's not. I mean it could be anything, right? But we'd—"

"Fuck off," Mel said in disbelief.

"It's a bomb," Penrose said. "What else?" He cleared his throat.

"What else? Of course it's a bomb," Mel mimicked, expecting a hoax.

"Go look."

Mel went.

"But it'll all go," the dockmaster said, "I mean everything. My God—" His hands opened and closed, spasmodic, helpless. "I'll ring Security."

Penrose held his arm as he turned to leave.

"Let me off, man. I've got to get help."

"Wait," Penrose said, trying to think against his own fear, which was rising with the dockmaster's. "Wait!"

"Why? You idiot! My God!"

"First of all, there are things we can do." He caught up again with the furious thoughts in his mind. "Get the crane here. Get the pallets out from around it so we can isolate the bomb. Get one of your men to call Security; tell them to call the Navy. Mel?"

The mate was back; his swarthy complexion had become as gray as the clouds above.

"Get a Mayday to Gravesend radio. Then call Chatham dockyard on the VHF to see if they have bomb-disposal people."

"I've got to call Security," the dockmaster interrupted,

robotlike, his eyes fixed on some bureaucratic horizon where following the rules was an absolute guarantee of long life and pensioned leisure.

"Get one of your men to go. Get the crane. *NOW!*" Penrose roared, letting panic escape through his mouth. "Get a fuckin' move on, or we're all going to fry; GO!"

In the country of shock the loudest voice was king. The dockmaster plunged and twisted off toward the crane, Mel hard on his heels. Penrose contorted himself back deep into the space between the ranked pallets and deliberately shut his eyes to let them get acclimated to the darkness, as well as to give him a chance to control the fear that compressed his lungs and made jelly of his stomach and had dismantled the governor on his heart.

When he opened his eyes again he could see details on the bomb that he had missed before. Pressing his cheeks deep into the cold angle between two canisters he could note how tightly the various components had been wired and taped together, how difficult it would be to tamper with a part without disturbing the whole. Not that I want to touch it at all, he told himself, but should it become imperative—

The crane diesel idled—presumably the dockmaster was explaining the situation to its operator—and the ticking started out of the relative silence like it was amplified. Penrose wiped sweat off his eyebrows and peered harder at the central element of the bomb.

It had bright white dashes arranged in a full circle around a one-eighth-inch hole. It was not a clock face, as he had first thought, but a kitchen timer of the kind that counted out minutes until the *quenelles de brochet* were done to perfection. The final setting, all the way on top, looked like 1200, but that couldn't be right. He blinked his eyes and looked again, a little away from the dial this time, a trick that helped when searching the horizon for stars or buoys.

The numbers grew more visible now: 120 space 0. Across the circle from the 120 was the number 60. The gradations had to be ten-minute intervals. The maximum delay you could set the timer for was 120 minutes, or two hours. If the knob that both set the mechanism and indicated how long it had run were still there, he would have known exactly how much time he had left, even halted the countdown by jamming the dial; but the person who had set the timer had removed the knob as well.

Penrose turned his attention to the Plexiglas box. The more he looked at it, the more difficult it became to breathe calmly. He could only just make out the contents, but what he saw looked like a single copper bar, hinged about two-thirds of the way down, with little bumps of copper and solder on both ends. The bar was set at an angle of maybe thirty degrees to the horizontal. The single hinge was set onto a copper terminal with a piece of gray metal wired beneath. Obviously, if the box were tilted or shaken enough, the hanging end of the hinged bar would touch the unconnected copper terminal and complete some kind of circuit.

With six sticks of gelignite or plastic explosive or whatever taped below, it was not hard to guess what kind of circuit it led to—a trembler device. He had seen them in a Navy mines course.

"Boom," Penrose said. Naming the terror should have brought definition and, ultimately, understanding and domination, but the spell did not work.

The box below the trembler was a typical flashlight casing, but if it held batteries, what purpose did the big six-volt cell also wired (upside down) to the Bakelite play?

The dock began to tremble, and the diesel sound grew louder and louder. They were bringing the crane over, ten tons of throbbing Perkins and gears and pulleys on creaking treads crossing a jetty that had seen its better days before Suez.

Fascinated, feeling a queer sort of intimacy attach itself to his unique knowledge of what was going on, as if the bomb brought everyone affected into an intimate relationship of destruction, Penrose watched the copper bar tremble delicately with the jetty. It only had a quarter inch to travel, less if the current was strong enough to spark. One particularly strong shudder, as the crane operator slowed one tread and speeded up the other to adjust his course, and the bar actually dipped a fraction toward the waiting terminal.

Penrose slid out of the gap as smoothly and quickly as he possibly could, jumped to his feet and held up both hands, palms out, paddling air at the crane operator in an international signal of slow down, go back, stop.

The operator looked confused, but braked to a halt.

A docker was ambling up the quay, oblivious. "Telephone," he yelled, "for the skipper." Penrose ignored him.

How long did they have? he wondered again, and suddenly caught an image of the docker who had left as soon as they'd tied up. The stooped man—hell, stooped!—like the Chinese on Skipperstraat. He would have left time for himself to escape, a half hour, even an hour—twenty minutes at least.

It had been at least that since they'd tied up.

"Slow down—go as softly as you can," Penrose said.

Mel was running up from behind. The crane operator hadn't heard. The dockmaster was in the cabin as well and he leaned out the doorway.

"What is it?" His voice cracked a little.

"Slow down! Go softly, softly, softly. There's a trembler: if it shakes too much it'll blow."

"Blimey." The dockmaster looked sick and bent himself back into the cabin. The crane operator shook his head, gesticulating. Penrose noticed a handful of dockers running past the flatcars down the dock, taking with them the man who had brought the message. The gesticulating stopped, the diesel wound up again, the treads began to jerk forward, slow, uneven, but a little smoother than before.

Penrose gulped and quelled a very strong urge to follow the dockers. Then he squeezed himself in next to the bomb again.

This time he didn't bother looking death in the face but winkled a shoulder in before his head. After he took off his wristwatch there was just room to fit his left arm between two of the canisters. With his fingers stretched all the way out, he could feel the edge of the Bakelite, touch the slick stretch of electrician's tape securing it to the rolls of explosive. He shut his eyes tightly as he probed with two of his fingers. When he had tensed his arm to the point where the trembling was ironed out, he gripped the Bakelite as hard as possible between the outermost joints of his longest fingers and tried to steady the device against the ever-increasing sag and shiver of the jetty.

But with his eyes closed and the bomb out of sight, a deep fatalism set in, even his wishes seeming to be powerless against the determinism of electricity and detonator. Doubts poured into the breach: what if he destroyed every man, woman and child in southeast Kent out of the infernal arrogance of command? Killed his ship, his crew? He wondered what the blast would feel like for the tiny sliver of a second he would have to experience his own death.

The trembling had eased in the interval. The diesel was idling. Penrose unpinched his aching fingers, gingerly let contact slip away from the bomb where it rested and pulled himself to his feet, blinking salt from his eyes. The crane derrick hovered above, and Brian was perched on the flatcar, looking as ill as he'd ever seen him.

Surely any action was better than none. That was a lesson the sea had taught.

"Mind your plate of bread," Brian muttered with a sick grin.

"Yeh." Penrose took a deep, trembling breath. "Where're the dockers?"

"Scarpered."

"We need the sling."

"Brought it."

Penrose climbed up to the flatcar and looked over the pallets.

"We'll get that one out of the way, then that one with the paint on it, then that one. Then we can get at it."

"Nah—that one first, to get around the flatcar; it's easier."

"Fine."

"'Op it."

"What?" the dockmaster yelled.

Penrose explained what they needed. Then he and Brian rigged the sling under the first accessible pallet in the square of crates sitting around the bomb, pulling the greasy, stiff cables under the pine baulks, connecting them with a Black-wall hook.

When they had it fast to the lifting cable the operator began winching slowly, as Penrose had asked, as slowly as his lowest gear would allow, his face a white knot of concentration.

The pallet came off the dock a little unevenly but with only a tiny jerk as the released planks whimpered back into place. Brian guided the pallet manually, dragging it against momentum ten feet to the side.

The crane operator was a Paganini of the throttle. The next two pallets were lifted off even more smoothly. Penrose began to consider lifting even the booby-trapped pallet, bomb and all—except that would not solve anything. He wished his brain worked better under panic conditions, but at least it was not obeying its natural inclination to shut down entirely.

On the last crate, Penrose pulled the sling cables a little too close to the edge, and all nine bottles canted sideways when the derrick took the strain. One corner of the pallet came down, the upper edge just missing the pallet with the bomb, the lower hitting the deck with a thud that almost hurt his feet. Brian yelled "Shitfuckin" and Penrose, idiotically, closed his eyes to ward off the million or so pounds of blast as the trembler fell and completed the circuit and sent a jolt of six-volt electricity into the fulminate of mercury cap—

Nothing. Still nothing.

He opened his eyes.

Nothing had happened except that the dockmaster had got out of the crane cabin and come along to help him readjust the sling. No one looked at anyone else's eyes, Brian signed to wind up the cable. The pallet was hoisted up, the deck planks groaned, the booby-trapped crate barely shivered at all, and Penrose fell to his knees and peered at the device.

The trembler bar was exactly where it had been before. No way of telling if or how much it had moved. The ticking seemed softer, but that was the relative proximity of the diesel. It also seemed slower, but that had to be in his own mind. Had to be.

"Hammer. Wot the bloody Jesus is wrong wiv me?" Brian said.

"Do you need me any more?" the crane operator shouted from where he was running, thirty yards away.

"Crowbar, as well."

Brian ran in the other direction.

"How—er—Christ, how long before—you know?" the dockmaster said, from the window of the crane.

"I've no idea," Penrose answered, peering between the methane canisters, thinking that any emotion usually seemed to carry its own anaesthetic; the longer it touched you the less it hurt, but that did not seem to be true of this fear. The effort of holding that one feeling of terror—holding it like an opera note without breaking—carried with it no agony of release.

Mel came back with Brian and hammers, crowbars and screwdrivers from the engine room.

"Did you get the Navy?"

"I told 'em what's going on. They sounded upset."

"Upset. Well, fuck 'em."

"Yeh."

"Gently, handily now." Penrose picked up a crowbar, jammed it very hard but carefully into a thin crack that separated the top pallet from one of the four corner posts that held it together. Brian put his shoulder against another corner post to steady the unit. Penrose applied pressure, gently at first, then harder. As the gap increased he rammed the bar in deeper and put his full weight on the other end.

The corner of the top pallet came loose with a screech, resting on the ends of its three nails.

"Now what?"

"The other three posts on the corners. Then we can pull the top right off."

"Now what?" Brian said again when they had finished.

"The crane," Mel said. "Bloody hell, the crane man: he's gone!"

"I can run it," the dockmaster said, from where he was still bracing one of the corner posts. The man's eyes were very white, just this side of panic.

"Then run it."

"The 'ook'll fit in the 'oles," Brian said. "Oi tried it."

The dockmaster was not as delicate as the crane operator. He was slower and maybe more nervous, but he got the hook down to canister level without incident.

"We just need the one out," Penrose told him.

"No, it won't fit now," Brian said, trying to jam the hook into one of the perforations in the mantle around the canister's neck. "Shit. Must be different—"

"The back one, near the valve," Mel said. "Quick, where they put the gas hose in; it's bigger."

"Roight."

"Where's Sean?"

"Don't know."

"Got it!"

"Tell him to hoist it— Wait wait *wait*," Penrose shouted, stretching his arm in between the two back canisters. "Wait."

"Got it?"

"Got it," Penrose said, half lying now on the dock,

gripping the bomb as tightly as possible so that it would not fall when one of the four canisters it was wedged against was removed.

"Ready?"

"Mel, steady the bottom with your hands."

"The bottom of the bomb?"

"No, you twit: the bottom of the canister that's going out."

The diesel chugged. Penrose saw the looped cable straighten against the clouds. Brian held the hook in place in the canister. The loop disappeared too fast.

"Slow down," Penrose roared, and held his breath, certain that the dockmaster was going to jerk the canister into the sky, bumping the bomb, dipping the trembler and sending them and northern Kent into a fiery kingdom come.

At the last minute the revolutions diminished but the cable still took the strain roughly, and the canister jerked, rotated, swung against all Mel could do to steady it, even though he was bent like a spring with his feet braced against the lower pallet. Penrose could feel the Bakelite plank compress a little as the canister squeezed against it, and then it was jerking up—

"Damn!" Penrose shouted, desperately compensating to keep the Bakelite level with his fingers against the upward pressure of the lifting canister. Just as suddenly the canister spun and swung the other way, and he was holding the whole package with his fingertips, jamming it as hard as he could into place, two or three inches above its previous position to keep it from falling back.

"Mel! Let go of the canister. Get the bomb!"

"The bomb? Christ!"

"Hold it *level*."

"What?" Mel's voice cracked.

"The bomb—here, like I'm doing: hold it absolutely steady."

"Hang on."

"Hurry *up*. My fingers are slipping!"

"Hold on." Mel slid his arms into the gap left by the canister they had pulled out. "I've got it."

"You've got it?"

The canister was swinging up, over and then back and

forth as the dockmaster put in the brake and killed the engine.

"Got it."

"You're sure? Don't let it move one millimeter."

"Right."

"I'm letting go now."

"Right."

Penrose slowly loosened his fingers, dragged out his right arm, came around to where Mel was frozen in a position of supplication, his powerful hands gripping the device through the space where the canister had stood, keeping it level against the three remaining canisters it had been packed against.

"Oh, God, now what?" the mate whispered. "It's *ticking!*"

"Now comes the tricky part. Now we ease it out of there, walk it as far away as we can and drop it off the dock, I think."

"You think? You're joking. My God, it's ticking."

"Yeah," Penrose agreed. "For God's sake don't move."

"Why can't we just brace it and wait for the Navy?"

"Because it may go off any second."

"Aye. Well, why can't we leave? It'd be better than blowing up as well."

"Because we couldn't run fast enough or far enough. Believe me."

"Well," Mel said, blinking sweat from his eyes, "okay. Then why can't we just run with this fuckin' thing?"

"What do you mean?"

"You know, just chuck it over the fuckin' dock."

"Because you see that plastic box? The transparent one?"

"Aye."

"See that little copper bar?"

"Aye. Oh, my God."

"Exactly. Congratulations, me old son. It's you and me have got the prize job. Now can you lift her up, very, very gentle like, absolutely level all the way, and bring her to shoulder height so you can see the bar all the time."

"Aye."

Far away, out of the corner of his eye, Penrose could see a Navy crash boat churning down the Medway toward the Isle of Grain. Much closer, the fancy motor launch had come inshore till she was only a quarter mile off, near the channel to the refinery dock.

"Now I'll grip the other end."

"Where are we going?"

"All the way down, away from the methane tanks."

"It's easier if you let me carry it alone."

"If you tilt the copper bar, that's it," Penrose warned.

"Aye." Mel's breathing was low and fast, "Got it."

"You're sure you can do it?"

"It's easier with just one."

"I'll lead you. Back now. Easy." Mel took a step back, delicate as a ballerina, removing the weight from one foot, balancing, putting his weight on the other. "Love-ly."

"Fuck me, it almost moved."

"Is it still ticking?"

"Aye."

"If it stops, try to throw it off the pier first thing."

There was a crack of sound from offshore, but Penrose ignored it. The Navy signaling, probably.

"Now forward. One step. Perfect. Three steps and you've got a rail. How's the copper bar?"

"Fuck me."

"Some other time," Penrose said. "Track now."

"Right."

"Step high: it's a tall one."

A whuffling of air came over their heads and a clang from the crane. Then another crack of sound. Penrose forced himself not to put it all together.

"What the bloody?"

"He's fuckin' shootin'," Brian yelled from behind the crane.

Penrose tried not to look, but out of the corner of his eye he could see the launch offshore, a tiny figure raising its hand, a puff of smoke.

"What the?"

"Careful. He's using a pistol—never hit us at this range. Just trying to scare us without getting too close."

"Fuck me."

"They can't know about the ammo ship."

"Did you have to mention that?"

"Watch out now—pipes here. Step. And step."

"It moved—ah, fuck it—Penrose me arms are trembling."

"Easy, Mel. Another twenty feet to the edge."

256

"Christ."

"Softly."

A thud, and a long score of white wood appeared like magic on the jetty, ten yards to their right. Then the sound of the shot.

"Take it. *Take it!*"

"You're doing beautifully. Watch the plank."

"My arm—"

"Now turn—no, this way, away from the gas— How's it doing?"

"—is trembling."

Another whuffling of air; nothing to indicate where the bullet landed. They edged delicately down the quay, the captain guiding the mate from behind with his hands at his waist, Mel's eyes never quitting the mess of wire and batteries and death with the shivering copper bar four inches in front of his nose.

Much closer, much louder, the noise of air being battered aside at 650 feet per second came sudden and so loud that Mel flinched involuntarily. The toe of his deck shoe dipped and caught on an uneven plank. He lurched forward, all muscles rigid, with a hoarse gasp, then thrust the bomb out level, both arms stretched out at the edge of the dock, letting the device follow through on the descending arc of his body and arms, in front and over the timbers before he fell in turn. Penrose threw himself full length, grabbing at the mate's shoulder to keep him from rolling over the coaming after the bomb.

For a long second there was nothing.

Then the world blew up. A vast wall of white-and-black water soared fifty feet into the air. The jetty heaved, slamming into their stomachs with the force of a locomotive. A gigantic piling shot heavenward, slow and elegant as a ballistic missile. Cement, splinters, mud, track ties, pipes, valves, gratings and seaweed seemed to vomit them up with other debris.

In the suspended calm of such irresistible force Penrose felt himself do a slow somersault in thin air, accompanied by a chunk of rotten wood, broken off in the shape of a chicken. He could see Mel to his left, an expression of great surprise on his face.

Then gravity reasserted itself and everything came crashing down around them, mixing in a soup of broken water and

257

mud. They felt themselves falling, glancing off the subsided dock, then rolling, helpless, faster and faster, sluiced in a shute of rubble and other elements of which noise was the most awesome component, until with a mighty hiss and a roar they joined twenty tons and a huge section of jetty in eight fathoms of dredged water in the Medway estuary.

XXII

In the calm after Armageddon Penrose felt nothing but the bubble of cavitating liquid and a mortal cold that robbed him of air, congealing the blood in his limbs, dragging him deep into the rotting chambers of the current. He had shut his lips and eyes in a reflex older than cognition but he remained completely disoriented after he opened them. Kicking his feet was a reflex of optimistic panic; the increasing light as buoyancy took hold, a geodesic fluke.

Then he surfaced, his lungs convulsing in a backward retch in their thirst for oxygen. He floundered, gasping, toward a piling hanging half on and half off the ruins of the jetty, kicking into other wreckage that surfaced to him as he swam. Once, a surfacing plank caught him painfully in the crotch, and he kicked with his legs together after that.

When he had crawled onto the piling and up a couple of adjoining planks he could look up.

The sky was still gray and unchanged. His ship was still floating and intact, a good eighty feet beyond the broken section of the dock.

A full thirty yards of jetty had partially collapsed, its outermost pilings swept away by the force of the explosion so that the dock's structure, reinforced by steel rods, had bent downward under its own weight, the pattern of splintered planks curving underwater, a gangway for submarines.

He pulled himself farther up the planks, toward Mel, who was lying spread-eagled, his donkey jacket rucked up and his neck at a crooked angle, pinned by something underneath. The captain thought he was dead, but a voice he had somehow illogically assumed was in his own head became Mel's as he drew nearer.

"Bloody fuckin' bloody hell," the voice repeated like a litany. "I'm alive, I think I'm alive. It's too cold to be fuckin' hell. Bloody fuckin' bloody hell. I'm not dead, I'm not dead, I'm not dead." And the chant degenerated into soft chuckling.

"You all right, Mel?"

He had to repeat the words. The mate's ears were still ringing from the force of the blast, as were his own. Penrose's mind started catching up with his body and did a quick, automatic damage inventory, but everything appeared to function, around and despite a multitude of little cuts and bruises from falling cement. Only the deep cold of the water had permeated his bones, like a premonition of dying.

"Is that you, skipper?"

"You all right?"

"Aye. Me jacket's caught."

There was a very loud rumble of an engine, very close by.

The pilot launch came up. Next to the wheelhouse Knocker Oakey was literally hopping up and down in his excitement.

"Come on, come on, come on!" he was yelling.

"What the fuck does he want?" Mel said.

"I don't know. He seems very excited about things in general."

"Leave us alone," Mel called, then held his head and said, "Ow!"

"Come on!" Knocker jumped onto the gunwale, hanging onto the tiny cabin, where a white-faced apprentice was nervously edging the pilot boat in through the debris. "It's that fancy launch that set off the explosion—sabotage! Get on! Let's get her! Oh, Christ! Come on!"

Thus it was Knocker who had control of the aftermath. White whiskers stiff and bristling in the breeze, his roving eye poking this way and that, he manhandled Penrose and his groggy mate aboard by sheer force of will, put on full power and took over the wheel. Swerving around chunks of dock he headed north and east down the estuary, toward Garrison Point.

"There he goes."

Penrose was still reeling from his brief flight, and shivering so hard from the river's chill he couldn't focus properly, but there was a dot of white wake intruding at thirty knots into the dark flat tones of mudbanks past Green Spit. He looked aft, at the Navy crash boat still lumbering a mile away, then to port at the comforting familiarity of his ship, riding calm and unhurt as they went past.

Too much had happened too quick and hard to process fully. His brain would have to file information while it worked on the action at hand, reserve the excess data for future analysis.

He said, "You'll never catch him."

"I've got an Allison on this launch. She'll do eighteen, twenty sometimes. Almost planes, sometimes."

"I *thought* this thing was awfully loud."

"Hard on petrol, though."

"But that launch was a Riva."

"I know."

"It'll probably do forty."

"I know."

"How do you know so much, Knocker?" Penrose squinted at the tiny plume of spray way forward and failed again to cope with the enormity of what the Riva had tried to do. Some anger was building, undefined, but he could not focus that either.

"I thought we could follow her on radar. I radioed Gravesend and asked them to call the coppers. So she'll probably be intercepted before he gets to London. There's a spare jacket below"—he nodded to his apprentice—"and some tea."

"How do you know he's going to London? He could be going to Southend."

Penrose was shivering so hard it seemed his muscles were jigging around independently.

"Because I've seen that launch before. In St. Katharine's Docks, next to Tower Bridge. I used to teach at the merchant navy school there."

"Are you sure? Who's on it?"

"No way of telling. They hire it out."

"Take me back then." Penrose's mind was beginning to work.

"No. We'll be there at the kill." Knocker fumbled in a

drawer full of glasses and pilot books and hauled out an ancient brass Very pistol. He pointed it at Penrose with a toothless grin.

Penrose exchanged his sodden jacket for a dry one two sizes too large.

"Piss off, Knocker. Are you sure that launch was from St. Katharine's?"

"I saw him close up. I was watching him with glasses. It's got a little blue ensign on the port windshield. It's the same one; there's not many of them. I may be old, you know—"

"If you let us off," Mel spoke up from the bench where he was embracing himself in back of the wheelhouse, "we can wait for him when he gets off. In case the police miss him. We'll never catch him in this tub, at any rate."

"Watch yer bleedin' mouth," Knocker snarled in Mel's direction.

"You seen the back of your head recently?" Penrose asked Mel, conversationally.

Mel put his hand to his head, and it came away red. Then he fell off the bench, to his knees, as Knocker swung the wheel hard to port and headed the pilot launch back the way they had come.

"Reckon you're right, damn it," he shouted, conveying morosity even through the volume. "But it's best to catch that nutter before he gets his hands on a cruise missile or summat."

They charged into Rochester Harbor at fifteen knots, under a bridge heavy with Victorian tumors. The pilot launch laid a wake that elicited threats and shaken fists from breakfasting yachtsmen on an antique steamboat on the other side.

Knocker brought the launch into a dock behind ten laid-up Crescent coasters, moored side by side in marine euthanasia off hurricane buoys.

Mel wanted to go with Penrose, but the captain convinced him to stay with the pilot and talk to the police or the Navy, who were certain to be on *London Princess* by now: let them in on what he was doing, assuming he knew what he was doing.

Strood British Rail station was only five minutes from the public jetty, but he had to wait twenty minutes for the next train to London Bridge, and he paced the platform to control the chills. The clouds had thickened, a small breeze had come up from the west and a few tentative raindrops splatted onto the platform, dripping down the timetables and their graffiti, which read "National Front" (with swastika) and "Gravesend Punks."

The train arrived a minute late, a blue-and-yellow worm that lived in two-minute suburban bursts punctuated by the arrhythmic slamming of compartment doors. Only when he had sat for a full quarter of an hour, shivering by the token heat duct, watching the flat countryside slide by without a single redeeming feature of relief, as if too geologically bored to do anything about its own lack of interest, did the facts begin to assume any kind of proportion or pattern.

They had tried to kill him—again. "They" and the hunched Chinese from Antwerp.

But not just him: his crew, the ship, the refinery, the Isle of Grain, Gillingham and Chatham. Maybe the stooped assassin had not been aware of how volatile the ammo ship was, but ignorance was no excuse; the enormity of the possible chain reaction made it criminal. The man had to be a sociopath, and those behind him worse, to commit mass murder simply because their lucrative little swindle had come unglued. Men like de Laune, companies like Eastern Holdings had killed for centuries to preserve their little webs of power, but they had usually done it abroad, by proxy, letting the Royal Navy fire the shells at funny-colored natives.

Antwerp. Tortuga. Kent. How the hell did they always know where he was?

The clear blue flame of anger did not burn any duller by the time he got off the train at London Bridge station. It was 10:15. St. Katharine's Docks were just across the river. If the Riva could do a steady twenty-five knots, say thirty with the current, it would be coming up on St. Katharine's about now.

The ten pounds Knocker Oakey had given him would pay for a taxi and to spare. Penrose ran headlong through the station, jumped the cab queue as a chorus muttered "Oi, 'elp yourself" and "In a rush, mate?" The driver told him he "shouldn't ought to have done that" and muttered at the shortness of the trip, until Penrose offered him a fiver to make it in five minutes or less.

He got out of the cab at 10:22, under the nostrils of the Tower Hotel porter, who held the door open and immediately wished he hadn't, as he stared at Penrose's grimy face, donkey jacket and sodden work clothes.

The St. Katharine's Docks complex was a preview of what all London docklands could look like by the end of the century. Its centerpiece was a huge hotel and convention center faced with russet stone and panoramic windows. It had three different bars. Business people could look out at the Thames, a mothballed cruiser and the tower where Anne Boleyn had her pretty neck ventilated with an axe, as they munched peanuts and sipped gin and discussed realtime access and greenmail.

The hotel dominated a few tall, restored brick warehouses that long ago held freight for the East Indies and were now filled with galleries of naïve art and antique shops selling "nautical" lamps of teak and brass and sennet. The ship basins sheltered yachts and a number of restored vessels, including the *Discovery*, the ship that had taken Sir Robert Falcon Scott on his last voyage to the Antarctic.

Penrose dodged the doorman and a picket line of strikers bearing signs reading NO REDUNDANCE and COME BACK MR. ROBERTS ALL IS FORGIVEN. He skirted the hotel complex, around St. Thomas More Street. On his left Jack the Ripper's haunts were replaced with staggered high-rise offices.

The Riva's berth, Knocker had said, lay at the eastern end of St. Katharine's, next to *Discovery*. St. Thomas More Street led around to the east, closed in by ruined brick walls and unrenovated depots, to a palisade fence and a parking lot marked "Number Seven Gate."

The old ship's spars and single buff smokestack rose among the forest of masts and parked cars, dwarfing even the wrecked foundations that encircled the eastern complex. Tourists, businessmen and parties of Sea Scouts walked around the black water, gazing at craft of every shape and size: tubby catamarans, a gleaming white trawler yacht, an ancient steam coaster, launches, dinghies and a Thames barge.

The berth was not hard to find. A big plywood panel reading YACHTS FOR HIRE stood on the dockside, with the blue pennant Knocker had recognized. A twenty-foot Magnum speedboat, an old, straight-stemmed party boat and an empty rectangle where the Riva docked lay hard by a deserted reservations booth.

Three cars were parked in a chained-off area for guests'

parking: two luxury sedans and a four-cylinder compact.

Penrose circled the area, searching the basin in case the Riva had moored elsewhere, then walked back and forth among the farthest rank of parked cars to keep warm. The rain had let up, but the clouds were cruising by fast and thick and darker than before on a strengthening wind that cut right through his clothes.

After five minutes he decided he was too conspicuous and went to skulk behind a tumulus of huge pink granite stones piled next to the gatehouse. Five minutes later he got nervous about not seeing enough of the entrance lock where the launch would first appear, and alternated between shivering while walking and shivering in place.

After half an hour the antidote of frustrated expectations, as well as the debilitating effect of continuous trembling, had counteracted his previous urgency and left him feeling completely washed out, foolish, an organism stripped of the illusion of science and whose only purpose in life was a hot bath.

The hunch that had brought him here—Mel's hunch, he thought vindictively—seemed very old.

First of all, he told himself, any assassin capable of the planning and detail required to booby-trap his cargo would probably ditch the Riva in one of the thousand mudholes up and down the estuary and make good his escape overland.

Second, even if he tried to return to St. Katharine's, perhaps to pick up a car, the police would surely have blocked the Thames by now.

Third, where were the police that Gravesend was supposed to warn?

Penrose checked his watch. He would telephone the police, he decided, and return to spy on the basin until they showed up. Then he would go find a bath at Brian's. He jumped up and down, flapping his arms like a cormorant to get the blood circulating again, and walked around the gatehouse and a troop of Sea Scouts lining up for the coach ride home. He strode toward the basin for a last check of the berth. A figure in a green trench coat, thin and heavily stooped, with his head so swathed in a long white scarf it was impossible to guess his features, hurried along in the same direction.

Penrose, conscious of an extraneous presence, turned his head to glance behind him, registered the short height and

265

speed, turned more sharply and caught the deep stoop, the watchful slitted eyes.

He stopped and whirled around.

Twenty-five feet behind him the man in the trench coat stopped as well. His hand came out of the right pocket and flattened against his chest, pure temptation in his stillness. Then he swiveled and ran straight through the line of Sea Scouts, knocking over two of them.

Polite criticisms from the scoutmaster. Passionate insults from the scouts. Penrose had been frozen by cold muscles and the amazement of coming face to face with the man who had been trying to kill him since Skipperstraat. By the time he lunged after the stooped man, the figure was fifty feet off and pulling away.

It was not easy to run. The cold was bad and his ribs were aching again—he must have fallen on them when the explosion knocked him overboard. He tried to get his arms swinging and lower his center of gravity into a steady sprint, pushing his breath deep into the area constricted by the pain in his chest: dodging tourists as he charged down a brick walk, through an archway, under a warehouse.

He looked around. The stooped man was nowhere in sight. The archway led to a second yacht basin, which held four Thames barges, all advertising wine-and-dinner cruises. Postcard shops and convoluted lampposts lined an arcade of wrought-iron girders.

The man in the trench coat could not have gone right, where a raised drawbridge signaled an open channel. Penrose pushed himself around to the left, braked and ducked immediately behind a column: he had caught a glimpse of a man with a stoop, in green, raising a piece of overlong metal in his general direction from behind a column twenty paces away.

Penrose realized he was a sitting duck if the man decided he no longer cared about witnesses. He could not wait here. He got ready to make a run for it, back the way he had come, but he saw the hunched figure, now with twice the lead, loping on disproportionately long legs past a man taking snapshots of his girlfriend and across a second drawbridge to the left.

Penrose followed, more cautiously now, over the gratings of the drawbridge.

The green trench coat had disappeared behind another line

of pickets, in front of the Tower Hotel's kitchen entrance. He sidled leftward around a fat concrete column marking a drive-in arcade beneath the huge hotel. He peered around, flinching almost, but there was no one on the shiny tiles except a security guard in a booth.

There was nobody in the driveway leading between the embankment and hotel to the street either, just a rank of taxis, engines rattling patiently. His quarry could be anywhere, blotted against the whimsical statue of a naked girl and a dolphin, or hidden behind a pinkish buttress.

Or he could have gone through the wide glass doors to his right and lost himself among the tourists schooling inside the Tower Hotel. There was a doorman next to the taxi rank but no one at the doors, so Penrose strode in as if he owned the tall, glassed entrance hall, the sick green carpeting, the reception desks of stained wood, the concrete columns bracing a first-floor balcony.

A Nigerian woman wrapped in jungle-colored silk moved like a windjammer up the twisting carpeted stairs connecting the two levels.

A Singaporean executive with a zoom lens was trying to fit HMS *Belfast,* Tower Bridge, the Tower of London and the new arts center into one shot. An American tour group milled around in a rash of bright colors and an aroma of spearmint.

Beyond the national clichés, beyond the potted trees that hid the staircase, a spot of green cloth moved swiftly into an entrance labeled "The Picnic Basket," waving at a proffered menu, shoving through clusters of people who groped in a bucket of after-dinner mints. Disappearing again.

Penrose followed at a slow trot that speeded up when he noticed a porter moving to intercept him. The Picnic Basket's maître d'hôtel was still staring after the stooped man, so he had no trouble slipping behind his back into the restaurant.

It was a bright, circular room that had made some interior decorator very wealthy: fake lattice crisscrossed lemon-colored walls hung with brass palm fronds; dark green chairs and a matching carpet set off bamboo tables. It was lunchtime, and waiters hovered over striped ties and lizardskin handbags, servicing meetings and contacts and affairs.

A commotion came from behind a centerpiece of palms, bamboo and serving carts. A Kensington resident flew gracefully backward for a distance of four feet, followed by a table, forks and plates of Wapping Scampi and Veal Cordon Bleu.

A siren began to yelp.

Penrose was the only moving object in the hush that followed. He jumped down two steps, followed an aisle between tables, shoved aside a waiter and found the scene of the outrage: a capsized chair, a young secretary in bright lipstick and clashing frock rising to her feet, her mouth a perfect *O* of wonder as she stared at her employer where he sat on the floor with his tie facing sideways and color rising to his cheeks. Behind them an inconspicuous door marked FIRE EXIT swung slowly to.

Penrose said, "Excuse me," and jumped the table. As he burst through the door, briefly forgetting that there might be a bullet waiting on the other side, he heard the woman with the bright lipstick trying unsuccessfully to stifle a giggle. Then the door closed behind him.

He was in a dark concrete stairwell facing a second fire door. There was no one here, no sound of steps upstairs. The siren was much louder. A smell of spices. He eased open the second fire door, squinting against the daylight.

No shadow, no saboteur. He edged out carefully, just the same, and moved onto the brick, scanning the embankment and finding his man almost immediately: he must have run the length of the hotel forecourt to where it abutted Tower Bridge and was now very coolly climbing a massive set of stairs with bright blue banisters leading onto the bridge itself.

Penrose ran to the stairs as soon as he was out of sight, but the quarry now seemed confident he had lost his tail and took no great pains to conceal himself as he crossed the Thames under the ornate castle-and-cable arrangement of the old drawbridge.

Penrose doffed the borrowed donkey jacket to make himself look different. The man in the trench coat circled around the second huge tower of the bridge to search once for followers, but Penrose was far enough away and must have looked unfamiliar enough, for the stooped man continued at exactly the same purposeful stride as before.

They reached the south side of the Thames. The stooped man turned immediately left, down a narrow street of decrepit brick factories bridged with pipes, catwalks and lifting beams. Penrose gave the man more of a lead, so he could follow from corner to corner, as far as possible. They passed a brewery and a pub, right, then right again, Penrose's heels beginning to blister in his damp leather boots, back onto Tower Bridge Road.

He hung even farther back at this point, certain that the man must be doubling around on him, but when he turned the last corner he found he had almost lost him. The Chinese had gone straight across the bridge approach road and a long way down a quiet thoroughfare of trees and turreted houses.

He had slowed down a bit, checked back less often, but Penrose was beginning to find tailing excruciatingly difficult work, not at all the simple job hinted in police movies: the art of hiding and the act of following required two diametrically opposed modes of behavior, concealing yourself behind or under things while somehow staying close enough to cover every possible escape option open to your target. The only way to reconcile the two ideals was by long sprints from one hiding place to the next, sprints that hurt his ribs and heels and made the housewives stare.

The hunt became the kind of physical grind that left the mind free to wonder why he was tailing the man in the first place. They came to an elevated railway line pierced by a very dark, curved tunnel with a sidewalk: he had to move very cautiously here, hide behind a Morris van in a place he only wanted to flee. There was no way, Penrose reflected, that he was going to tackle the man; he was too quick with the side arm. The only hope was to follow the Chinese to his destination without being detected, which would give him either a clue to the man's identity or time to telephone the police. They had to be near London Bridge station by now, which meant the stooped man might be going back to North Kent. Hell, they might have been on the same train coming up.

He wondered where the coppers were. In the time it had taken to reach the Tower Hotel they could have surrounded St. Katharine's Docks three times over. Perhaps Gravesend had decided this was one of Knocker's little pranks.

The Chinese was not checking at all any more. They went past two road tunnels under the railway line, where warehouses had become modern office buildings. There was a

British Telecom repair truck, lots of parked cars to hide behind, a bakery, another underpass, a high rise on the left and another huge glass office block down the street.

Passersby were more numerous and he did not have to hide so often or run so hard, so he did not miss seeing the hunched figure enter a small parking lot opposite the glass building and go through to the tunnel beyond.

Penrose hugged the wall outside, immobilized by logical apprehension as well as his illogical dislike of underground spaces, but it was the history behind this chase that finally drove him on, determined to finish with the unpredictability. The tunnel itself had been turned into a parking lot. Neon shone on honeycombed cement, red-and-white entry gates, cobblestones and air ducts, the eerie geometry of vaults whose original function had long been subverted. A bulkhead bore a sign: WRM CONTROL.

There was only one other exit. Penrose felt the yellow gloom closing in on him; the roof was too high to brace his arms against. It was the perfect place for an ambush, but there was an old man checking tickets on cars behind the bulkhead, and there was Penrose's conviction that the Chinese did not know he was being followed at this stage, and that he would lose him if he did not move.

He ran across the cobblestones at full tilt, into a second underpass, filled with exhaust fumes, traffic and nothing else. He looked around, desperately.

No one.

Any direction was better than none. He chose right at random and because it was the shortest way out of the tunnel. The corner curved around a tiled ladies' WC and he almost knocked over a veiled woman in a black *abeyah*, clutching an *A to Z* guide to London as she came out the door.

The Chinese was sauntering leisurely only twenty yards beyond her, opposite a café, checking the price of sandwiches as if he had nothing better to do. He glanced quickly up the street, away from Penrose, then drifted into an entrance in the railway wall and did not come out.

After a full minute, Penrose followed.

Two big, black, nail-studded doors opened wide on what looked like a darkened crypt. Soft moans of agony escaped from inside. Hooded black figures stood paralyzed in attitudes of pain.

A notice read: PLEASE DO NOT FEED THE RATS and ALL HUMAN REMAINS ON VIEW IN THIS EXHIBITION ARE GENUINE. A sign on a half-opened portcullis read: LONDON DUNGEON. ADMISSION £3.

Penrose did not have three pounds. He went in anyway, past skeletons and fake cobwebs and a plain girl in a spiked cage who screeched, "'ere, not you too"; but the guard who normally checked the tickets was not at his post. Penrose parted the thick drapes and entered the dungeon.

It was quite well done, he thought, pushing his fear of the subterranean away while he searched the penumbra. A greenish light gave the old railway arches a good Hammersmith Studios mood. In front of him a wax witch dangled at the end of a gibbet, near a sign that explained how torture and sadism were an integral part of London's past and no one had fully documented their history until this museum had thoughtfully filled the gap.

Isolated knots of people gaped at exhibits in the ghoulish light, or else gaped at a man in a guard's uniform who stood in the longest transept and yelled in a broad Glaswegian accent, "Cum back here, Jimmy, eh! Ay, yu! Stop! Och, *sod* the *bas*tard!"

The girl in the booth had come in behind him and was yelling to attract the guard's attention. Penrose slipped into the nearest archway and walked rapidly among the exhibits, trying to come around to where the guard had been looking.

As he walked he saw: Druid sacrifices dripping with scarlet blood and plastic mistletoe; Becket stabbed and gouting blood on the steps of Canterbury; Anne Boleyn with the axe about to dig into the back of her neck ("The King being in his jousts at Greenwich," the sign began); a man being boiled to death in a cauldron, tendons standing out most realistically while his taped screams wafted around the exhibit from hidden speakers; a mock-up of plague victims, churls rotting and vomiting blackness ("Then there was no love, faithfulness or trust"); live caged rats, labeled descendants of the plague carriers; a model of Execution Dock at Wapping, where pirates had hung while three tides washed under them; iron gyres, men impaled with blood streaming from their mouths, naked revelers in a devil's coven.

The audience was mainly tourists, a few little boys trying to see how scared they could get without becoming actively terrified. He saw no green trench coat in the gloom, no stooped shoulders, although he had occasional glimpses of the guard running back and forth between different archways, and once he had to dodge behind an axe murderer as the ticket girl ran past, looking for him as well.

He walked faster and faster, beginning to feel queasy as he grew conscious of the weight of bricks and milk trains overhead.

"Little Ease," a life-size facsimile of a tiny hole in the deepest bowels of a dungeon, a cell too tiny for a man to uncurl in, made sweat flow freer on his brow, but now he began checking inside the various exhibits, behind pillories and guillotines. There, fighting the impression of having been down too long, too deep, he heard a shrill "Here he is," like a signal of freedom, and "Got you" followed by a scream, the sound of a blow, a fall.

It was close, behind his back, but not directed at him. He sprinted toward the sound, around the devil's coven, through a crowd clotting around the Scots guard. The guard, who was lying on the cement floor among all these other visions of horror, was staring at the very real chocolate blood pulsing from a wound in his thigh, at the display halberd that had made it.

A woman began a long, fluting scream, so real it turned all the contrived agony into proofs of human shallowness that made the reality so much worse.

He had been spotted.

Penrose paused for only an instant before continuing toward yet another swinging fire door. He ran hard through an empty eating area, a gift shop, another set of doors and out onto the street, which was empty except for a BRITISH RAIL-LONDON BRIDGE sign next to a doorway in the same railway embankment he had been following all along.

Fatigue washed back over him as he ran halfway up the stairs. He had to slow down to a walk, take one step at a time; his ribs hurt now at every breath and his feet were slippery in leaking fluid from his blisters. When he got to the top of the staircase, in the open forecourt of London Bridge station, he had once again lost his man.

There were few travelers this time of day. A flower stall stood, colorful but unfrequented, next to the first set of entrance doors. There was no one in a green trench coat across the whole broad expanse of road and court. Pigeons flapped back and forth while Penrose hesitated, then went inside.

He was in the new railway station, built on the bones of the old, a Meccano structure of yellow girders and brown vinyl floor with suspended black-and-white departure displays. A couple of people were making phone calls against the right wall, one or two were watching the signboards flip around.

Penrose began trotting, a little aimlessly, a little weakly, down a ramp to the train platforms, past a ticket collector who let him go by, for whatever reason, with a wave.

He took the first stairs up, to tracks five and six, and stumbled out onto a platform that was like all the others. There was a view of more warehouses, cranes, Tower Bridge, and one commuter train waiting on the next track.

He could almost sense the odds clicking lower, flipping against him like the automatic signboards in the station. To save what he could of his chances he jogged back down the stairs, over and up to the next platform. As he crested the top of the staircase he heard a whistle. The train was fifteen yards away and beginning to roll. He threw energy he could not spare into his legs and raced the last compartment, reaching the door and opening it as the train attained a speed he could barely match. He dragged himself in with a grip on the doorjamb just as his legs began moving too fast for his feet, and fell rather than stepped into the compartment, pulling the door shut behind him. There was no one there but a red-faced man in British Rail workclothes, fast asleep in the opposite corner.

The train rattled quicker, past council houses with blue trim and identical lace curtains, a cookie factory, a brewery, a football park—all the necessities of life, he thought—then slowed down sharply to pull in at an elevated station: Deptford.

Penrose opened the windows on both sides, checking against hope to see if the Chinese got out either on the platform or the tracks, with no luck.

On to Greenwich and ground level. Again he checked, again with no success. The dropping sensation of failure took over. He felt angry, too, ashamed at being duped by a coward of this caliber, a man who killed by proxy or at a distance or from behind.

But when there was nothing left to hope for, there were still motions to go through. This time he moved up to the next compartment, interrupting a young man and a flushed plump woman on his knee.

It was the same story at Maze Hill and Westcombe Park. At each stop he moved up a compartment, checking for anyone getting on or off. There were few passengers. It began to rain again, thick drops that ran dirty fingers in streaks down the windows. At Charlton he was pulling his head back to shelter, about to slide the window shut, when he saw a door toward the front swing open. The Chinese jumped out, nimbly, looked back once at the train he had come on, then headed up the steps to a walkway leading to the ticket office and the street.

Penrose waited as long as he dared. When he opened the door and jumped out, the train was moving at what he judged to be sprinting speed, but he must have overestimated his own running prowess. The slick platform seemed to catch both his feet, and he tumbled flat and fast, with barely enough time to curl and protect his head and sides. The concrete slammed his shoulder, rolled him over, skinned his palm and barked his knee. Then he was up and running, looking at the overpass, where the top of a green trench coat and a white scarf were visible for an instant.

From the window of his booth the ticket collector had seen him fall. Penrose gave him a pound. The man was a Sikh, turbaned and very respectful of British Rail regulations, and he looked at Penrose with contempt and said, "You are a silly sod." The captain stepped carefully out on the street.

Again he worried about the gun, and again there was no need. The Chinese was loping along in that incongruous style of his, down a low-rent High Street with an off-license, greengrocers, a building society.

Limping a little from his sore knee, checking his ribs with one hand, trying to run in a forward position to favor his heels, Penrose followed.

As he did he tried to think in rhythm with his jogging pace, tried to locate and identify something he felt was odd about the Oriental's behavior, but physical misery was gaining the upper hand and soon he concentrated solely on keeping up.

His quarry took the first right, down a street of row houses that curved past a lumberyard, left under the railway line.

The Asian seemed, when they shared the same field of view, to be flagging as well, so Penrose remained the same distance behind.

The road became a cul-de-sac for cars, a walking street for split-level council apartments that opened on a main road. Oxygen and nicotine fought a painful battle for the last remaining spaces in his lungs. The rain was now splatting down with unashamed vigor. Far ahead, seen through rain dripping from his eyebrows, the Chinese turned left past a petrol station. The road he turned into bent slowly around trucking company depots and brick walls capped with barbed wire, a neat café with green trim closed for the weekend. A sign said they were entering a "trading area." The curve hid his quarry now.

The road ended in a T junction with a pipe store on the right and a garage, its horseshoe driveway full of Italian cars, on the left. Penrose looked up and down and saw with an absence of surprise that the Chinese had disappeared.

He stood in the crossroads, swaying, breathing harshly. The bar on the T was an industrial road, like the one he had just run down. Blue flat-bed trailers were parked down its right side. To the left were more flat-beds, a pub, and much farther down a vast, well-lighted factory building. Beyond that, nothing, or, more likely, the river.

He took a few tentative steps to the left, fueled by an affective conviction that he could not choose wrong at this stage of the chase. The street remained empty.

It seemed impossible that the Chinese could have achieved the speed necessary to reach the street by the pub. It seemed equally far-fetched that he could have scaled the brick and barbed wire that fenced everything in this area. That left hiding places, such as the parked trucks to his right, the Fiats and Lancias at the garage behind him.

Behind him a light pinching of gravel came over the splat of rainwater, telling Penrose the garage had been the jackpot choice.

He spun around. The Chinese was standing by the corner, his left arm almost straight and aiming at Penrose, his other hand bracing the gun, whose muzzle seemed much too big and black. A silencer.

The Chinese had lost his face. That was Penrose's first impression. The scarf was still around his mouth, but the rest of his head, even his hair, had faded into a pastiche of tan blobs. He soon realized the man had a stocking mask on, and that he was going to kill him. Or, more probably, wound him, at that range, with a silencer. Then close in for the *coup de grâce*—unless action came first.

Action beat hesitation. He had told himself that story enough today; he was beginning to believe it. So he moved, ducking in a panicked scuttle to his left, then his right in a parody of all the World War II films he had ever seen. He expected at any moment the hiss of a bullet, but the man did not fire, or else missed very badly as Penrose ducked behind the nearest flat-bed and took off at a blister-ripping pace down the sidewalk.

His next impression was that he had figured out what was odd about the Oriental's behavior. Question: When did a man with a gun let himself be charged by an unarmed man? Answer: When the man with the gun wanted to lead the unarmed man to an area of deserted warehouses to finish him off silently and with no witnesses.

Penrose cursed himself with what little breath he had to spare. He cursed the rain, too, and the dreary surroundings, and in a crazy surge of will to live swore not to die here if he could help it, not in this gray road in this gray town when at last he at least had a chance at a new ship and every sparkling clean piece of water he chose to point her bows at.

Fifty frenetic strides down the road he risked a glance from behind a blue Luton van. The Chinese was in full view and loping again, a little shadow in a stocking mask appearing and disappearing with every reversal of breath. The gun was back out of sight in its holster.

Penrose resumed running, past the pub, past a corrugated fence, under the loom of the factory. Nothing left now but the task of running, and suddenly nowhere left to run. He had come to the end of the road. A dead end.

Factory fence stretched in front of him and to the right. Corrugated fencing, then a new, spiked iron affair that ended in a freshly painted gate. The gate had a sign: TTB. GLC EMPLOYEES ONLY. KEEP OUT. DANGER. It led to a massively landscaped lawn and futuristic-looking buildings that held Penrose's attention for all of a quarter of a second.

The gate stood open. The Chinese was a cable's length behind and closing. He went in. There were trees lined up in prim rows, a big grass-covered dike on the right. An empty tour bus was parked by the dike. Approach roads and walkways covered a good acre yet were dwarfed by a six-story structure that looked as if it had been designed by a committee of soya-silo designers and airport-control-tower architects. Beyond it was the Thames, and spanning the Thames was a strange series of gigantic stainless-steel eggs cracked and broken and giving birth to gawky yellow-legged creatures all kicking upstream in unison.

The largest movable flood barrier in the world, Penrose remembered. The huge shells were built on piers sunk deep in the riverbed. Under the piers, in massive cement sills, were housed arcs of black steel, two hundred feet long, that could be rotated upward to block the flow of the Thames should flood conditions threaten. The arcs were moved by the long yellow rocker beams, partially visible inside the "cracked" shells, hooked up to hydraulic engines underneath the housings.

It was the last monument to a vanished welfare city-state. The Labour-dominated council that built it had been abolished by the Tory government while the barrier was being completed. But Penrose knew the place was manned and guarded twenty-four hours a day. He had taken the *Witch* several times upriver past the barrier's hydrodynamic shapes.

He ran toward the main entrance, where floodlights and yellow windows promised protection.

The main entrance lay beneath the control tower: a wide, long ramp leading below ground level to a braced and light-drenched passageway. A glass booth guarded the ramp, and a guard in a blue jumpsuit with hardhat and walkie-talkie guarded the booth.

Penrose moved onto the approach, into the circle of lights. As the guard stepped out of the booth, Penrose turned, and stumbled and fell to one knee as his muscles released prematurely.

The Chinese was thirty feet away. He had slowed to a walk, but was still advancing. Penrose got to his feet and staggered toward the guard, who stood waiting, legs spread, hands on hips.

"You're trespassing, *sir*," the guard said.

"Yes. You've got to call the police—"

"Who might you be? Sir?"

"I'm being chased—"

277

"'Ow'd you get in here? Sir? This is private property."

"—by that man. Listen!" Penrose yelled. "He's got a gun."

"You're trespassing," the guard repeated stonily. "I'll call the police all right—about you, sir."

The man's hostility was pathetic. Penrose turned around, fear, anger and a sense of the ridiculous vying within him. The man in the green trench coat, incredibly, still wore his stocking mask and now he stepped within the circle of floodlights, his hand slipping underneath the coat for his gun.

Penrose felt his belief in consistency slipping. None of this made sense. He turned back to the guard. The man was in his fifties, with ample white hair, a thin face and pale blue shore-patrol eyes.

"Will you do your fucking job?" Penrose yelled. "Call the police, man!" He began to edge backward, but the guard shot out a hand and grabbed his elbow.

"You'll stay right here. And you, sir, can take that thing off."

The guard stopped talking. The Chinese pulled the gun from under his coat, the length of the silencer making it an interminable gesture. Penrose steeled himself as he saw the muzzle coming into view for the third time that day, but it was angled away from him, ranging up the guard's body, pointing granite-steady at the man's chest, and locking there.

From the corner of his right eye Penrose noticed that the guard's features had gone completely white, then flushed purple in the space of a second. Faced for the first time by a bullying power greater than his own he seemed petrified, his eyes knowing only the gun.

The words came lower than a hiss from a wet spot on the stocking mask. "You are dead."

It was the first time Penrose had heard the Oriental's voice.

In the guard's booth colored lights winked on and off in futile fashion. Penrose broke and used the only reflex he knew for these situations. He threw himself headlong down the ramp, expecting to die immediately, his back braced for the explosive shock; rolling to his feet in a convulsion made up equally of pain and desperation, he staggered down the rubberized surface, swerved left and right, ignored a series of darkened offices, a pair of lifts. He plunged through an open steel door.

The Chinese had missed again. He wasn't complaining, but that did not make sense, either.

He was in a tiny enclosed spiral stairwell, half the size of the one he had chased the Chinese through in the Tower Hotel. The same surface covered steel stairs whose rails were painted a bright industrial green. The stairs led only down. The air was pervaded by a deep electric hum that did not mask the rapid squeak of approaching feet on the ramp outside. Penrose began leaping down, four steps at a time, sliding his bruised hands forward down the handrails, using them to vault another four steps, gritting his teeth against the messages his nerves were sending.

This time the Chinese was gaining, indicating that, unlike Penrose, he possessed reserves of strength that had been kept untapped. Why he had not used them earlier, to lose or catch him in lonelier places than this, was already becoming part of the awe Penrose felt toward his faceless pursuer. The way he poured massive effort into devising complicated methods in complicated places to damage or kill Penrose, then let him follow in deserted parking lots or darkened wax museums—it was an irrational yet irresistible force that was catching up with him now, and this combination of power and irrationality formed the root of the terror sprouting in the neocortex, terror that grew with every leap that brought him further under the crushing weight of fourteen thousand tons of steel gate and one hundred thousand tons of concrete and hundreds of thousands of gallons of river that now lay above his head.

The Chinese was only ten or fifteen steps above him. He could hear his breath rasping between jumps. He had to keep control, deviate from the headlong rut of panic. The next landing had a bright blue bulkhead door, similar to others he had passed, with a lever handle that locked it into its frame.

Penrose wrenched it open, breath sobbing, jumped over the coaming—and stopped dead.

He was in an endless, tight tunnel, lit by strips of dull neon, the kind of tunnel he hated most.

It went on out of sight, a little taller than a man, one of the two maintenance tunnels linking the separate piers and shells under the river. All around it was the thrumming of electromagnets and the trembling of concrete and bedrock as the mighty river thundered by only a few feet overhead.

Sweat prickled out all over his body. The clang of feet on the stairs grew very loud. Dread behind, and dread before, but there was nothing he could do to a man with a gun. Yet it was a measure of his respect for the Chinese that he could swing the door to (there was no locking handle on his side) and race blindly down the tunnel and through the first watertight door he found, one hundred feet later.

The Chinese was behind him, must have seen him, but Penrose did not turn around again. He was in a smaller stairwell than the last, but this one led upward. He climbed as fast as he could, three, two, then one step at a time, hand over hand up the railing two uninterrupted, gasping flights, to a square room with one lift door and three watertight doors painted different colors: yellow, green, blue.

The hum of machinery held in reserve was stronger here; it was louder even than his thumping heart, his tearing breath, the rush and roar of water almost a tangible presence. He wanted to try the lifts—lifts were now the lesser of three evils—but they would never come in time; they could be immobilized too easily, and he would be trapped. All in all he had run himself into as neat and final a rathole as any game gone to ground, with a pistol at his back and more tunnel waiting for him behind one of those three doors.

He took a little longer now, the fatigue interfering with his mental discipline, but was able to force himself to open the door—the farthest, the green one—to prolong the inevitable, to step over the coaming and try to close it behind him.

A light, flush in the door, came on when he opened it. When he turned around, still crouching from the low entrance, he saw he had come to the end.

He was in a narrow, wedge-shaped chamber, standing in one of the angles of the wedge. The wall to his left was nearly vertical, smooth except for two shallow grooves that ran its full height of fifty or sixty feet into shadows the door light would not reach. The wall on his right was much more gradual, rising up a twenty-degree slope and tapering off maybe eighty feet away to darkness. Thin metal pads broke its continuity at five-foot intervals. The pads were sprung, a half inch off the surface, and connected with electric cables. The wall in front of him was sheer and flat and only five feet away.

All these walls were of concrete, thickly smeared with

grease. The roof, however, was of solid metal, painted a light yellow, and there was a gap on every side that indicated it could move. Would move, if the right buttons were pushed.

Penrose recognized it instantly.

The rocker arm. One thousand tons of high-tensile-strength steel that could be pivoted in the center and hydraulically rammed through an arc to bring the flood-control gates to the "up" position. When the upper end of the arm lifted, the lower end came down, down through this compartment where he was standing, forty feet below the surface of the Thames. Down against the greased hydraulic pads, one of which he was standing on.

No matter that the Thames was not flooding. No matter that the barriers were never shut to navigation without a lot of warnings and ballyhoo. No matter that there might just be a gap at the edge of the lowest hydraulic pad, down near a drain that was probably a grease sump, where a prone human body might escape being crushed too flat.

It was the second time in his life he knew he was beaten. The combination of weights and stresses, whether intrinsic or potential, was going to be too great for his control.

Penrose spun around and pushed open the door to throw himself to his death on the Oriental's gun.

He did not have to go far. The door was open and the stocking mask—it, too, drawing terror from the lack of logical patterns—was framed in the oval steel opening. The head looked up and around, examining the chamber, examining Penrose. The knot where the stocking was bunched and tied at the top looked like a Samurai's hairdo. The arm stretched out, a little short of stiff, and once again Penrose faced the nothingness of the silencer, aimed straight at his forehead.

He had nowhere to run. He let his arms fall and tensed his leg muscles for their ultimate spring, but the Chinese made a funny little hissing noise and pulled the trigger before he was ready.

Fascinated, even as he sent the "jump" signal to his leg muscles—too late now, far too late—Penrose could watch the hammer work back, then snap forward. He heard metal strike home as he pushed himself forward. He could be surprised at how you heard the hammer before you heard the powder, and he was astounded at how you could pathetically slip on the grease underfoot even for your last jump on earth, one more proof that life was only a scene by an amateur playwright.

He landed well short of his assailant, on his knees, ridiculous, striking his forehead on the coaming, and began to realize that the bullet had never fired. He looked up at the bland hissing mask, at the mouth of the silencer still pointed at his head, at a gloved hand pulling the trigger through again, one foot away.

Click.

Click.

Click. Click. Click. Click.

The hissing became a high chuckle, and then a lisping whisper that echoed back and forth around the sump chamber.

"Empty gun. The whole time, Mr. Penrose. But no one knows that. No one will know when I force them to start the machinery so that you will be very slowly crushed to death here. Oh, yes."

With a contortion of shoulder muscles under the green trench coat, the stooped man slammed the heavy watertight door shut, just as Penrose, driven by a panic quicker than his brain, jackknifed in the direction of the coaming.

The light went out.

There was a smell of spices.

The slam reverberated up and down the chamber.

The feeling of confinement took over his mind.

Darkness, great weight— What had his brother *done?*

Penrose pushed himself with all his strength against the door, sobbing against closed mouth while he struggled, slipping on grease, trying to push the door open.

He'd never tell on him. (If only Benjie would let him out.)

He did this for a number of minutes, letting the panic feed and bleed through muscles, straining his ribs and back with the effort, hearing only the harsh sounds in his throat and the roaring of great black waters overhead. The roaring became louder and louder and louder, the rumbling of the pier became more and more powerful, until it had communicated and then invaded his entire body.

No room to move, no space to breathe. The memory came from much deeper than consciousness, but its blackness pervaded the part of his brain he could control.

"Let me out," he found himself shouting in his own mind.

"Benjie," he pleaded, hearing the echoes reverberate in every corner of his brain. He held his breath, crucified on the sealed door, listening to sweat drip off his brow, listening outside his head, because the noise *was* louder.

There was a new element now, a high-pitched whining from everywhere and nowhere that rose until it practically went out of range.

Something rang high above his head, a clang that hurt his ears, a rumble that shook the walls and built louder, louder, louder. Now even the screams in his head could not compete.

A second clang, softer than the first, preceded a new, very gentle grinding noise that was accompanied by sounds that might actually have been sense perceptions of closeness, of air being squeezed out from above.

The walls around him trembled harder.

The rocker arm was moving.

Electromagnets the size of motorcars had polarized into a spin at the flick of a switch, activating two gigantic hydraulic motors that were now pistoning a thousand cantilevered tons of steel around a circle that ended where he knelt.

Penrose stood up and stared through the black dark, every muscle trembling, feeling the chamber tighten around him.

After a while he sat next to the hydraulic pad, clamped his arms over his ears, shut his eyes tight and tried with all his might not to cry out loud.

He stayed that way even when he realized that the grinding and rumbling had stopped, with the rocker arm still a good twenty feet over his head.

He stayed curled for hours. At 10:40 P.M. a technician came to drain the hydraulic overflow sump that had been filled during an unauthorized start of number five floodgate's motors and found him by the sensor springs, almost unable to move.

Light from the opened door lifted the darkness, diluted the weight, and the technician's frightened curse spoke of rescue.

But the voice inside Penrose continued to plead, even then, with a brother who could not hear, about a terror he could not face.

XXIII

The flashing lights that came afterward seemed to pervade the next two days and two nights.

The maintenance man summoned a rescue crew, who observed Penrose's ashen features, his listless movements, and treated him for shock, stating first-aid rules like spells out loud as they worked.

The first blue lights came from a St. John's ambulance waiting for him on the grassy forecourt of the tidal barrier. Then came the Metropolitan Police cars and vans, pulling up in cumulative squawks of sirens and loud-speaker static, disgorging constables, sergeants and detectives as connections were made by radio.

One set of flashing blue lights took him to a clinic; another drove him to Charlton police station. More blue lights and sirens transported him to police headquarters. When he stepped out on the curved driveway in front of New Scotland Yard there were five men from the wire services and newspapers popping flashbulbs at him. On page one of the morning editions his face would look chalky, rigid, a death mask.

The police did not use an actual interrogation lamp, but the habits of technique were strong and they did shine a gooseneck lamp his way so they could see him better than he could see them. The TV people made no bones about lighting him up: Penrose perceived the press conference set up by the *Evening,* in cooperation with the police, only as a storm of relentless glare and questions from men and women he could not distinguish.

Lights and questions—forty-eight hours of them. They

found Brian's mother's phone number the first day. They tracked him down on the *London Princess* at Dreadnought Wharf, in Greenwich, on the second. Mel had taken the ship there after offloading the methane, which was now "evidence" instead of cargo for St. Helier.

The tabloids were not satisfied with the news conference and organized a pool of reporters, who camped out by Dreadnought's security gate with more lights and questions. One of the brasher West German magazines even hired a motorboat and tried to board the coaster at dusk the same evening.

At three in the morning of the third day Penrose rousted out his crew, started up the engine and quietly slipped his moorings. By doing so he broke all kinds of rules: he did not file a trip plan with Port of London control in Gravesend; he kept his running lights off during the first five minutes of the run in direct contravention of the International Convention for the Prevention of Collisions at Sea; and by changing wharves for no good commercial reason he was committing barratry, the misuse of someone else's vessel for private purposes.

Penrose did not give a damn. Amid the glare of spots and the interruptions of reporters he could never come to grips with the blackness that had dominated his mind since the Chinese had turned the lever on the watertight door.

BPM wharf and the complex of mill works behind were bulky enough to shield *Princess* from inquiring eyes ashore. There were usually enough coasters docking there, waiting for tides, to provide anonymity, for a while at least.

He stayed in his bunk most of the day, leaving the ship only to make phone calls, one to London & Continental, a second to Colin, the third to leave a message at Claire's hotel. He found that he needed to see her, because the lack of interruptions gave the blackness free rein in his mind. He started hitting the unbonded liquor at 1600.

By 1800 he had given up and joined the rest of the *Princess*'s crew in the Peeking Duck.

"Another pint for the hero," Alfred said, cheerfully sarcastic, as he edged a cloudy glass of third-strength brew on Penrose's crowded table.

"Fuck off, Alfred," Penrose answered.

"Good lad," Mel approved.

"Leave 'im be," Colin remonstrated.

Claire Thibodeault said nothing. She had said very little all evening, just sent violet looks at the captain and sipped at endless miniature bottles of a sweet champagne drink. In her own quiet way she was getting as drunk as Penrose.

Alfred had ears that would have done an African elephant proud. He had a mangy mustache, few teeth, less hair. He had worn a red bow tie since the General Strike, above a waistcoat usually stained with ale and sausage juices.

Alfred didn't mind Penrose cursing him, didn't mind that the crew of the *London Princess* had gone to ground in the Peeking Duck to get away from the press. It was the first time his moldering little pub had had a genuine celebrity in the public bar, and word had got around the waterfront that the men who had saved Kent were hiding out in the Peeking Duck today. For thirty years Alfred had not had a crowd like this; he'd had to hire Pat as extra help behind the bar. He shuffled around the brown light and cigarette smoke, the discarded salt-and-vinegar-crisp packages, the sawdust, like a man who had just seen the Holy Ghost.

"For God's sake, what's the matter, man?" Colin said into the depths of his whisky. He put the glass down empty, swayed briefly but recovered, and straightened his tie. "You should be happy. You're—"

"—the toast of London," Penrose completed. "I know." Colin looked hurt.

"You've said it ten times tonight," Penrose explained.

"What about me?" Mel complained, pointing at the bandage on his head and looking at Claire for sympathy.

"You, too, of course." Colin lifted his glass, glaring at the woman.

Claire got to her feet, and Mel jumped to his and pulled out her chair for her. A trifle unsteadily, she edged around the crowd and the big bronze propeller by the wall. Penrose and two-thirds of the bar watched her go, approving the tilt of her chin and the flow of her hair, the way she filled tight jeans and the blouse above them. A sheepskin-lined vest and boots added a spice of challenge to her way of walking.

She had come in two hours ago with her overnight bag and sat down at Penrose's table without fanfare or explanation other than that Brian's mother had told her where they were. Mel had taken his eyes off her only three times since.

"Here's to Claire," Mel breathed, for the sixth or seventh time that evening, reaching for his pint and knocking over the foot-high stack of dailies in front of him. The tabloids spread like gulls over the wet sawdust, opening headline wings as they unfolded.

THAMES SAVED AS BOMBING FAILS
MYSTERY LOONY BOMBS KENT GAS SHIP
EVENING EXCLUSIVE. GAS SHIP HERO SAYS HE WAS
   TARGET: 'I WAS TRAPPED IN TIDAL BARRIER'
LLOYD'S LET FRAUD HAPPEN, CAPTAIN SAYS
INSURANCE FRAUD PROMPTED MURDER, SUICIDE
LLOYD'S SUICIDE SAID HE HIRED BOMBER

Penrose kicked the papers under the table.

"It's not your fault." Mel put a fraternal arm around his shoulders. "He would have killed himself anyway. The guilt, you know." He slavered a little. "God, I hate insurance people."

"Think of what he did to us." Colin leaned forward, his merchant navy tie askew, gray eyes intent. "Just because of his little reinsurance trick. He was taking his chances; he lost. Even the Lloyd's people said he deserved it."

"It's not that," Penrose said, and roared "Alfred" because his pint was empty.

"Then what is it?" Colin spread his hands, palms up, in amazement; normally undemonstrative, the whiskies had shaken his hand language free. "We're going to get the insurance money: that's what those Lloyd's people told us. We're going to get our insurance, do you hear?" He was shouting. "We're going to get our new ship."

There were laughing comments from the dockers and mill workers, the suburban call girls.

Colin's aberrant delight winkled Penrose out of his depression for a minute; he looked at the old man's joy and drew vicarious pleasure from the memory.

All it had taken was a bomb. The bomb spawned publicity, and publicity achieved within twenty-four hours what Penrose, Colin and Pengerswick had failed to attain in a month. One of Sir Norman's friends had contacted Brent the same day. The vast intelligence structure of Lloyd's had been switched on, and somehow they had managed to locate the Welsh surveyor, in Salvador, Bahia, and obtain his assurance that the *Witch of Fraddam* had been surveyed before she left Port Garth.

To give them their due, the Lloyd's committee moved swiftly once set in motion. They had convened the next morning and agreed to cover his claim and investigate de Laune and Court. Brent had tracked Penrose down through Gunn.

De Laune, however, had put himself beyond reach of investigation. They found the underwriter the same morning, swinging below Vauxhall Bridge with a note in his pocket and a length of clothesline creasing the Eton tie around his throat. The domestic details of suicide, Penrose had reflected at the time, were what caused the pathos: as if when it came to the crunch the closest relationship a man had was to inanimate articles of toilet and laundry, like clothesline. Like Harewood's dental floss and spices.

Claire returned, watched by thirty eyeballs. Instead of sitting down, she came around the back of Penrose's chair, wrapped her arms around his neck, put her head on his shoulder and tried to strangle him.

"Hello," Penrose said.

"I have to talk to you."

"Then talk."

"I can't—"

"What's the matter?"

"What's the matter with *you?*"

"I asked you first," Penrose said automatically, familiar with the rituals of squabbling. He caught himself. "The matter with me is I wish everyone would stop asking me that question."

"I just want to talk to you. Alone."

"We'll go back to the ship."

"Captain Penrose," Alfred shouted from the pay phone. He lifted the receiver.

"No," Penrose shouted back, waving his arm back and forth, thinking the press had finally tracked him down in revenge for giving Allan Clift the exclusive.

"It's Captain Gunn at London and Continental," Alf shouted, covering the phone.

Claire unwound her arms and stood back against the wall, stiff and uncomfortable.

Penrose got up, using the chair as a cane, collected his balance, then made his way to the phone.

When he came back he said, "Mel."

"Wot?" the mate asked from behind a tiny Gravesend shopgirl who had climbed on his knee and was telling him how he reminded her of wossisname that parachute colonel who had been killed at Goose Green.

Her friend was the size of a number one sea buoy, fat bobbing freely under a print dress. Brian had to sit on her lap to get anything accomplished.

"We've got a trip—this morning's tide," Penrose said when he came back.

"Where?" Brian asked.

"Treg. China clay."

Colin looked up, shocked. His tie was loose, Penrose noticed.

"But that's our contract."

"*Was,* Colin, was. Get the lads back on the ship at closing time, Mel."

"He's not moving," the Gravesend maid grinned, winding her arms around him.

"It's free beer, John," Mel complained, his eyes suddenly serious. Brian told the sea buoy she could come back to the ship.

Claire said, "John." Colin glared at her again.

"Coming."

The door to the pub burst open. A waft of low-tide odor and mist came in from the dark and the cold, cutting channels in the cigarette smoke. The paper-mill security guard followed the chill inside.

Every coasterman in London knew the guard. His name was Adam; he was six feet seven inches tall, a Barbudan and black as the Earl of Hell's waistcoat. He was a former drum major in the Coldstream Guards, with the bearing and confidence to match.

Some of the men said he was a witch doctor who did things with pins to little cloth dolls. Partly for this reason he was never short of duty-free Scotch.

The guard came through the doors backward and bare-headed, hunched over to get under the lintel. He swiveled into the brown light to reveal what he was carrying: Sean, naked, wet, covered with harbor slime, with a long knife in one hand and Adam's uniform cap clutched in the other to cover his private parts.

Adam's stoop reminded Penrose briefly of another man's posture, and he realized that the Oriental's hunch might be there to disguise the fact that he was very tall.

Adam straightened, almost scraping the molded tin ceiling. The white of his eyes flashed. He lifted his right arm, the one not holding Sean. The huge fist was closed around the neck of a large and dead goose. Tar smeared its tail feathers, and blood dripped from its beak and a gash in its throat.

"Captain Penrose," Adam said in a deep and dire tone.

The pub, which had gone silent when he entered, began to fill with a menacing rumble.

"Sheila," said one mill worker.

"Christ," said another.

"He killed our mascot," said a third.

Tears flooded the eyes of the part-time prostitute on Mel's lap. The sea buoy said, "'e shouldn't orter 'av dun that, 'e reely shouldn't."

"This deck hand of yours killed the company goose, Cap'n Penrose," Adam said.

Two men smacked their pints down on the bar in unison and walked over to the guard. They examined the goose. One of them stroked its feathers.

"Let's take 'im outside, Adam," they urged.

"Easy on, lads," Penrose said. "I'll deal with him."

"It's not your business, Mr. Hero."

"I know how you lads felt about him, about the goose: we'll pay for him. Her, I mean."

"But why'd he do it?"

"Yeh, why'd he do it, fuckin' hero."

"Yeh, and why's he naked? What was he *doing* to her, naked 'n' all?"

Sean had stopped struggling when he came into the light. He tried an ingratiating smile, but he was surrounded by large mill hands, Adam's grip was none too gentle, and it was easy to see he was scared. And very cold.

"Why'd you do it, Sean?" Penrose tried to push through the unyielding circle of men.

Adam said, "I found him crawling around the pier after Sheila. He was on the rafts. I told him to come up but he would not listen."

"I had the knife in my mouth," Sean protested. "I was

tryin' to balance on the bluddy float. I couldn't talk. I just thought it were a normal goose. For dinner."

A Scotsman bayed, "Bring his body doon tae the river."

"Aye, bring him outside."

"No," Penrose said.

"We'll teach the little bastard."

"Poor Sheila."

"Bring his body *doon*."

"No," Penrose said. "I can't let you do that."

"Let us have him, Adam."

Everyone looked at the tall security man.

"No," Adam said regretfully. "I don't think I can let you mash this kid up."

The Scotsman jumped out of the circle and stood in front of the black man.

Penrose lifted a ten-pound note out of Colin's wallet. "I'll help you buy another goose. Come on, mate, he's just a lad."

"Then take yurr ship and get oot." The Scotsman swung around.

Penrose looked around at the circle of hostile faces.

"All right, lads, okay," he said finally. "We'll go back to the ship. We'll be gone before dawn."

They filed out the door, the sea buoy towing Brian behind her. Claire stayed rigid against the wall until all the crew had gone but Penrose, then motioned she would follow.

Colin, still upset because of the china-clay contract, refused to go aboard with them for a final glass. He got into the Land-Rover and drove, more slowly than usual, into the stinking night.

They followed the old path, around the rotting barges, across the stinking tidal creeks, around the propeller factory, by the flood wall, picking their way across the bits of decay that the river, a big old gray tomcat, had dragged up and left on London's doorstep.

Halfway there, Claire caught up to them and tugged at Penrose's coat.

"There's someone following us."

Penrose looked around. A floodlight from the propeller factory cast reflections on mudflats that crystallized in the mist.

"I don't see anyone."

"I saw him twice, I'm sure. In the shadows."

"Probably someone from the newspapers."

"I hope so."

"What do you mean? Who else would follow us now? Everything's finished."

"You say that with such conviction."

"Oh, hell. You're the one that seems despondent."

"No, I'm fine."

"Forget it, then."

When they got to the gate barring entrance to the paper-mill dock they found the press already there. Adam had sneaked Sean back in the BPM van, but when Mel and Brian and the woman weaved up, five men turned a glaring TV light on them and began to stick videocams and microphones in their faces.

"What is your reaction to de Laune's suicide?"

"Why won't John Penrose give us an interview?"

"Tell us your feelings when you first saw the bomb."

"Where's Penrose?"

"Why did he hide his ship?"

In the confusion Penrose and Claire managed to skulk around the shadows surrounding the cameras. Behind the TV lights the quay was twice as black, with only a glowing lamp on *London Princess*'s upper deck to guide them. His legs were a little unwieldy, and he slipped twice on spilled mineral. Claire fell behind, and he heard her being ill over the side of the quay.

It always seemed to be low tide at BPM's dock, which meant to get aboard you had to climb eight or ten feet down a steep ladder to the maindeck. Claire took one look at the forty-foot drop into ooze and Thames water, the crabs and eels waiting expectantly, and said she was going to be sick again and perhaps she'd go back to the hotel.

Penrose told her the trains did not run past ten and threw her bag down to the deck.

After she made it down, he went to the galley to heat coffee. When he brought it to the cabin, she was coming out of the shower, looking small in a long silk robe from her overnight bag.

"You're going to stay," he said.

"I brought champagne," she replied, the eyes very big in her pale face.

"Well, by Christ, let's get it," Penrose said in mock jovial tones. "Bring on the dancing girls."

"What *is* the matter with you? I've never seen you like this."

"I'm the toast of London. It's affecting me. Where's the bubbly?"

"Pat was sweet. He put it in the fridge in the kitchen."

"Galley."

"Galley, then."

He brought the champagne back in mugs and they drank it in silence, without any more toasts. There was the wail of a harmonica from the crew's cabins: Sean consoling himself with music.

"Is it what Mel thought?" she said, counting bubbles in her mug.

"What?"

"Because de Laune killed himself?"

"That bastard? No. Not that I feel good about it. But I don't feel guilty, either."

"I forgot—you're not Catholic."

"Good old Henry the Eighth."

"But your life is good now, isn't it? Lloyd's found the architect—"

"Surveyor."

"Surveyor, then. In Brazil. So they know your claim is good?"

"Well, there's their bloody *Inchmaree* clause—but no, they can't prove negligence; it simply isn't there. They were denying my claim because they couldn't come up with the thirteen million quid, for the whisky. I think they will pay. They are," he finished bitterly, "Lloyd's, after all."

"So you'll get your new ship, as Colin said."

"I saved them fifty times my claim by finding the bomb."

"So you should be happy."

"But I am happy."

A series of clumps came from the deck above: shouts, a feminine giggle, feet tramping aft.

"No. There's something wrong," she insisted.

"Damn it, will you stop prying!" It came out close to shouting.

"I'm not prying. It's you who's trying to tell me something."

The eyes.

He poured more champagne for himself, feeling at the rot that had set into him since the episode in the barrier's sump chamber. He was drunk enough to stand outside himself and observe it, sober enough to realize that keeping it hidden through all the interrogations and debriefings and interviews had done absolutely no good at all.

He thought of the World War I prayer his grandfather had once taught him: "Dear God, if there is a god; save my soul, if I have a soul."

Selina had a name for what was affecting him.

"If you must know, I lost control," he muttered finally.

"I'm sorry?"

"Lost control." He got up, emptied the champagne bottle into his mug, paced to the porthole, back, to the porthole again, stared at its round hints of barnacles, seaweed amid darkness defiled by the deck light above.

"I don't understand."

"When that Chinese bloke tricked me into the tidal barrier. It—did something."

"Go on."

"I am going on. But you can't understand. He chased me into the chamber, compartment really, where the hydraulic arm came down. Way under the tidal barrier, under the Thames. He shut me in a hole. Then he went up to the control room for that section of the barrier. There was no one there. He had knocked out the guard. God."

"You don't have to," she said, leaning forward. "I read what you told the *Evening*."

"I do have to. I didn't tell them what it did to me. You know, he switched on every button he could and started the rocker arm coming down. It was madness. I mean, who would do something like that? If he wanted to kill me, there were so many easier ways. Luckily, one of the switches, they said, was the hydraulic safety drain, so it stopped automatically. Otherwise it would—I would have been—crushed. And of course there was an override." He tried to laugh.

"Anyone can be afraid."

"It wasn't the fear. It was what the fear did to me. There were things I could have done. They might not have done any good, but I remember there were electric wires in the chamber that I could have ripped out or shorted out; I could

294

have tried yelling, for fuck's sake, in case someone else was around. Instead—I curled up in a fetal position, covered my ears and fought not to yell. You see; I had lost control."

"But I do know what you're talking about."

"You can't. And if you did, it would not be as important to you. But to me, for my job—if I lose control like that I'm not fit for command, don't you see? The Navy was right."

But when he was in the Navy he'd had Selina to back him up, Selina to trust.

"I do know." She shook her head. "I do understand."

"When has it happened to you?"

"It must have happened to me. I fear it as well, the loss of control. All fear is of something inside yourself. It's why."

"I'm sorry. There's none left. You can finish my cup. Why what?"

"Why." She put the bottle back, hoisted her knees up to the settee and hugged them with her arms. The long damp curls made ring marks on the silk. "Why"—her voice was muffled—"I don't do well with relationships. Why I don't think this one will work. John."

"What?" he said from the porthole. "Not you too."

"What do you mean, me too?"

"We haven't even given it a chance."

"I felt fear for you, you know," she said from her knees. "Retrospectively. My God. You know I called the refinery right when the papers said it was happening. Luckily they couldn't find you; it could have made the difference right then, instead of—"

He remembered the message: "Telephone for the skipper."

"It *was* right then."

"Jesus," she continued. "And that Chinaman. He would have killed you—you say he was crazy—I don't know how he avoided it." She shivered. "Already it does something to me—it's not good."

"Why?"

"I have too many things to do."

"What," Penrose said, "is more important?"

"More important." She lifted her head until her eyes shone above the level of her knees. " 'More important,' he says. What's more important to you, your new ship or your new relationship? Which would you choose if you had to choose?"

"That's not fair." The rot inside was only compounded by the anticipation of loneliness that had begun as a small doubt so short a time ago.

Loneliness, however, he knew, and knew he could deal with being alone. Betrayal: now that was something else. Someone had told them where he was.

"I can't believe we've given this enough of a chance."

"You really don't get it at all." She sniffed once, looked at the bulkhead. "I told you, but you didn't hear me. I didn't grow up like you, bred for power, as you were, no matter whether you rebelled against it or not. I grew up on what we call the wrong side of the tracks. I don't remember a winter when I wasn't cold way deep down in my bones somewhere. There were eight of us. One of my brothers died of pneumonia one winter."

"But for you that's changed now, hasn't it?" Penrose said, to keep her talking.

She jerked her chin up. "Changed? By God it has changed. But I can never escape from it. I can only understand the scars it left. From having the rich Yankee kids in town scream by on their snowmobiles yelling 'Hey, Frostback!' From having to move three times one winter when the lumber company decided the housing was too much to maintain. From my father spending all his money on whisky and beating up my mother because he was so humiliated. He broke her chin. It never set right. From having him leave all of us, at the end."

"I can understand that."

"No, you can't except intellectually, which doesn't count."

"And you almost a shrink," he said, clicking his tongue. "Okay. Maybe I can't. But you do seem to have dealt with it."

"Yes, I have," Claire said. "I've embraced it, even joked about it. It's the only way to control it."

"Jokes," Penrose said. "I'm all for that."

"You don't understand. Good psychology is about restoring communication with yourself, your subconscious is a lazy kid who thinks he can cover up his own mess by pulling the rug over it. But then it starts to go bad, and the only solution is to bring things out in the open, restore the communication. I'm trying to tell you something."

"But I agree. It applies to communications. Between people."

"Does it?"

Penrose felt a terrible sense of sadness and affection for Claire, for himself. The feeling pushed him toward her. "Damn it, Claire, if we're so alike," he said urgently, "why can't you give us a chance?" The booze was drying up his words, he knew, but she was in no better shape.

"You really can't quite get it, can you?" she said again. "Because I've found something that will forever keep me away from Brunswick Falls. From Maine. Something that will bring me enough power, and money, and respect. And nothing can get in the way. Nothing. I won't let it."

"Power? In a psychology department?"

"Don't."

He knelt down to come level with her eyes, but his balance was not up to the task, and he had to use her knees for support. He kept his hand there and said, "You don't know what you're trading in yet."

"Yes, I do." She jerked her chin again, looking at him squarely.

"Come to Cornwall. Take a couple of days off."

"You smell of beer."

"Sorry. Well?"

"I can't."

"On the ship. It's allowed. I promise I won't pressure you."

She dropped her forehead on her knees. Her hand crept out and found his. He squeezed it hard.

"No commitments, no promises," he continued, encouraged. "Just two days to learn more about each other. Maybe you can tell me how to come to terms with what happened. We can part friends at the end."

No answer.

"Please, Claire."

"And here," she said from the folds of dressing gown, "I thought you Brits were all cool and phlegmatic."

"It's a front," he confided. "The upper classes made it up to scare the French. Underneath we're much more passionate and romantic than the Frogs are."

A small laugh escaped the silk.

"Will you come?"

"I have to lunch with someone at University College tomorrow."

"Fuck University College."

"Okay," she said, "fuck 'em. If you promise me one thing."

"What?"

"Promise me you won't bullshit, about emotions, that stuff."

"I'll do my best."

The weather started out misting and mediocre. The Internav man had fixed the radar quite recently, and they made decent time, south and west around North Foreland and Dungeness. At sunset the next day, abeam of Beachy Head, the clouds began to thin.

The wind stayed steady at ten to fifteen knots from the west, the swells easy. The night was clear, purple and beautiful. Dawn raised pink curtains on a perfect spring day. Penrose could smell the buds from the quiet hills of Devon, opening in the sunshine off their starboard side.

In all other respects the trip was a disaster.

The long swells they caught after South Foreland, combined with an overdose of sparkling wines, threw Claire's stomach into a turmoil; she was sick in the captain's bunk all the way to Cornwall. She lay with her face to the bulkhead and spoke only in monosyllables when Penrose came in or when Pat brought her tea. Penrose slept, when he was off watch, in Mel's cabin.

They closed the cliffs of Treg Bay on the evening of the second day. Merlyn Carn sulked off Blackbottle Point; behind the hills the clay pits rose silver above the long shadows of sunset.

The familiar sight made Penrose feel a little better. He could see the trees beginning to shade green as they drew nearer, and he went below to rouse Claire.

The sheltered waters of the bay had settled her stomach by the time Penrose brought *London Princess* to the Cornish China Clay berth in the harbor. She came onto the bridge, pale but fresh from the shower, with an air of getting things over with, but the sight of a maroon Bentley whispering to a halt by the gangplank stopped whatever words were coming in her throat.

"Who's that? In the fancy car, I mean."

Penrose turned from the chart table, where he was filling in the logbook, already certain in his own gut when he went over to the starboard window.

"Sir Norman. My father-in-law. His car, at any rate. It's his dock."

Old Mukerjee got out of the front, looking like death on holiday in his long black suit.

Penrose went back to the logbook.

The lines were doubled and the gangplank secured. Shortly after, Mukerjee clambered up and knocked formally at the bridge door. Claire opened it for him.

"Hello, Mr. Mukerjee."

"Mr. John." The old Punjabi was out of breath. "Miss. I wish to bring you an invitation from Sir Norman. For dinner, at Restormel House."

"When?"

"Tonight, of course. Sir Norman wishes to congratulate you on your heroism. He also wishes for you to congratulate Miss Selina."

"Selina? Why Selina, Mr. Mukerjee?" Penrose snapped the parallel rulers open and shut, open and shut, click, clack, click.

"For Miss Selina's new engagement."

Clack. Penrose saw, with annoyance, that he had snipped a piece off the inside of the ebony rulers.

"Miss Selina's engagement. That's not bad, given that we haven't even divorced yet."

"Sir Norman would like the Miss to come, as well."

"Would he now, Mr. Mukerjee? Well, that's certainly bringing everything full circle."

"Pardon?"

"Full circle." Penrose slid off the chart-table and went to stand by the wheel, looking forward, where Brian and Sean were uncovering the donkey engine. "Wrapping everything up so bloody neatly. Me, Selina, our marriage, my life up to now, as if we were all pieces in his board game. You can tell him to stick his invitation right up his bloody arsehole."

Claire said, "John."

"What?"

"Remember what I said."

"What?" Her face was very beautiful, he thought, when it got so drawn and pale.

"You have to embrace these things if you want to control

them. It's like your claustrophobia: it will always dominate you until you cut open the abscess within yourself, the infection that caused it in the first place."

"I thought we were talking about claustrophobia."

"But we are."

"No."

"Think, John." She tossed her hair back. "Do you want to flee from these things all your life?"

He looked at her very long and hard, realized he was breathing too fast and forced himself to breathe deeper.

"Doesn't it bother you? Seeing my wife?"

"No. Why should it?"

"What do you think?" He swung around on Mukerjee.

"You should come, sir, of course." The Indian shrugged his neutrality.

"Will *you* come?" he said to Claire.

"I think you must go."

"That's not what I asked."

"If you like. I'll come, if you like."

"Maybe this is rubbish," Penrose told her, "but I read once that acrophobia comes from a secret desire to fly. Do you think claustrophobia is a secret desire for the womb? Do you think my not wanting to attend this dinner stems from a secret desire to hit rock bottom, doctor?" He did not wait for an answer, but said, "What time, Mr. Mukerjee?"

"Seven o'clock. I pick you up, Mr. John," the old Indian replied, allowing a thin smile to crack his features.

"Very well," Penrose said. "Tell Sir Norman we accept." Then he went forward to talk to Mel.

The mate listened in silence while Penrose explained what he wanted.

"I don't understand," he said finally, watching Mukerjee get back in the Bentley. "You want us to do what?"

"Follow us. I'll call a taxi for you, or hire a car, or borrow one even."

"But why?"

"A precaution, call it. One or two things that don't add up."

"About the bombing? But the silly git's dead."

"I don't know, Mel." Penrose shook his head. "I may be all the way off, of course. Perhaps I'm shutting the stable door. But I've been waltzing along merrily with my eyes shut all this time, and I'm getting bloody sick of being on the receiving end of things. Bombs. Guns. Thugs. So call it insurance. If you take Sean and Brian, we can all be back by eleven. We can get up early tomorrow to sweep down the hold."

"Oh, I'm not complaining, skipper. It's just that there's all the lovely scrumpy cider in this town."

"I'll make it up to you," Penrose promised, "tomorrow night."

"On one condition."

"What's that?"

"You give me a job on your new ship." The earring sparkled.

"Done," Penrose said, and shook the mate's hand to seal the bargain.

XXIV

The stars had come out by the time the Bentley crunched up to the vast portico of Restormel House.

Off to the left, on the lawn that, the last time Penrose had seen it, held some of the best horseflesh in western England, starlit statues brooded in the blue light, meditating revenge on the species that had locked their forms in stone. Behind them the Restormel River escaped over a dam, past the "Pantheon," down a "grotto," through the trees to the sea, playing water music all the way.

"Jesus," Claire said, looking around.

"Quite."

She turned to stare back down the long drive. "The car didn't follow us here."

"I told you: he wasn't following us at all," Penrose replied. "There's only the one road from Penquite to Chark."

"And Mel and the rest—"

"They're already here. Nearby."

"This way, please," Mukerjee said. Aqbar came down to take their coats. Penrose straightened his gray jacket and merchant navy tie.

The huge Murano chandelier in the entrance hall had been turned up as high as it would go. Two umbrella spotlights were mounted, one on each of the two staircases that curved from the second-floor balcony. Selina emerged from behind their glare, wearing a dark green dress that trailed a little behind her ankles. Her hair was tossed up, so it fell back over her face, artfully casual. She was squinting into the eyepiece of a video camera.

Claire gazed upward at the apparition, lips tight.

Penrose turned aside to Aqbar. "Where is Sir Norman?"

"He's in the Italian Room, with the others." Selina's words carried bell-like in the marble acoustics.

"We'll join them, I think," Penrose said, to everyone and no one.

"Wait."

Carefully Selina lowered the camera, took a powerpack off her shoulder, rested it on the balcony and came down the steps, not too fast, not too slow, head high. Penrose allowed her the entrance.

"Your wife," Claire whispered.

"Not for long." Penrose reached for his pipe.

Up close he saw she had put on makeup, something she rarely did: coral lipstick, white powder, purple eye shadow. It did not suit her. She looked levelly at him to demonstrate her discipline, and only he could tell what it cost her, because the high spot in her cheeks was burning, even through the face powder, as it always did when she was on the point of losing it.

"I'm Selina Penrose," she said.

"Claire. Claire Thibodeault."

Penrose experienced his usual awe at the horrifying honesty with which women looked at each other in situations like these. He knew Claire would feel upstaged in her short skirt and long sweater and funky blue beret.

Selina looked back at him.

"I'm sorry," she said, not sorry, "could we talk for a moment, alone?"

"About the weather?"

"Please."

"I don't think," he said, "that we have anything left to talk about."

"It's important."

Sir Norman saved him further embarrassment by appearing stage left. He was dressed in a morning suit and looked even more bloated and unhealthy than the last time Penrose had seen him. The tic did not seize his cheek any more, but the nerves now came out through the eyes, which blinked rapidly and darted back and forth, left and right, as if he were expecting guests to emerge from the paneling. Still, he gave Claire his most charming smile and shepherded them all, with smooth phrases, down the hall, through the library, into the Italian Room.

Penrose was as glad as he was surprised to see they were not the only guests. Lord Askew, Drummond and Hilliard—the entire banking commission—were grouped around the sculpted fireplace with the ubiquitous Hawkes, all in black tie. Askew was folded into an armchair; the rest stood, at ease or attention, interrupted in the middle of a discussion.

"Busman's holiday," Sir Norman chortled. He grabbed Claire's arm and introduced her around. Selina followed them in and stood poised by the chess table, trying to catch his eye. Penrose fielded the cool compliments and half-hearted congratulations: when a part of the financial main went under as de Laune had, every man in the City felt his own mortality. The men were more interested in Claire anyway.

He stayed at the fireplace, gazing at the large tableaux by Imperiali and Ricci, the marble Venus, avoiding Selina's eyes, fiddling with his pipe. Mukerjee brought him a whisky-and-soda, then another. Claire answered questions with great aplomb, though he could tell she was nervous. The presence of a peer was enough to rattle the most cocksure American.

Drummond finally turned to him and said, a trifle reluctantly, "And what's your opinion, Penrose?"

He said he hadn't been following their dialectic.

"The old chestnut," Askew said. "Drummond here still believes we should have kept out of the Common Market. We seem evenly divided."

"Oh, I'm just a simple mariner. You'll not want my opinion—old boy."

"Speak as a former banker, then."

There was a flounce of silk as Selina left the room.

Penrose shrugged.

"The EEC," Drummond interjected. "For or against?"

"Of course," Penrose said ignoring him, "speaking as a humble mariner, there is the effect on the coasting fleets."

Hilliard said, "And that is?"

"Requiring licenses for officers on coastal freighters."

"I should think you'd be for," Drummond said, adding, "Single malt," for Mukerjee's benefit.

"No," Penrose said. "What the EEC is doing is substituting an examination for experience. I've seen what it can do."

"Surely," Askew said, "you need some test of proficiency."

"No. It used to be that coastermen knew the language of the coast much better than they knew the English of EEC exams. Until we joined the Common Market, they proved they could do a job by doing it. Now we get men coming on as mates who've spent two years at school and can't tie a bowline. I had one like that on the *Witch*."

"But that's coasters," Hilliard said softly. "Not real, deepwater ships."

Maybe it was the things Hilliard said, Penrose thought, rather than the way he said them, that created space around his words.

"With all due respect, Hilliard," Penrose countered just as softly, "you don't understand the sea. Any fool can sail deepwater, and many do. It doesn't matter where you are in the open sea."

He pointed at one of the massive Imperiali tableaux, showing an ornate shipwreck surrounded by sea monsters; a fantastically complex wreckage and half-naked people being dashed to pieces against a rock. "It's the coast that's perilous: it's the coast that will trap you on a lee shore, or tear your bottom out on a rock. It's the coast that separates the men from the boys. We're usually happier out of sight of land."

Mukerjee doddered in at that point and said, "Telephone for Mr. John."

"What?" He couldn't hide his surprise.

"Telephone."

"But no one knows I'm here," he said, wondering if it was Mel.

Mukerjee just stood at the door. Penrose followed him out.

The telephone room was off the entrance hall, nestled under the curve of one of the marble staircases. The receiver was on its rest. Selina sat in the leather armchair beside it.

"Oh." Penrose saw her, stopped dead and turned to go.

"John, please." She came out of the booth.

"No, Selina. A clever trick, but no."

"You don't look well, you know. You're too thin." She always had a knack of making the most irrelevant comment carry meaning. "I must talk to you about something very, very important."

"What? Your marriage to Quentin? Or other forms of betrayal?"

Since he was unable to stand still, he walked off. Her heels clicked behind him.

"What are you talking about? That was ages ago. Why don't you stop? Why can't you talk? *Damn* you, John," she cried, and knocked a Rysbrack bust to the floor.

The party was moving into the dining hall when he got back, but only Claire acknowledged his return. He took her arm, formally escorting her in.

The dining hall was lined on one side by the highest French windows in England, looking over the urns and balustrades of the terrace to lawns and *pièces d'eau* and the night beyond. A broad white hearth at one end held a small fire. Two of Sir Norman's favorite beagles slept on a rug nearby. Above the mantel hung the massive portrait of Selina's mother, who had died shortly after George's birth. It was a tapestry of primary colors, abstract and strong, that managed to hold its own in the Italianate decor, perhaps by reaching almost up to the frescoes on the ceiling. The resemblance to Selina was marked.

Crystal candlesticks on the table mimicked a vast crystal chandelier overhead; thirty candles bounced off a thousand facets of glass on one side, mirror on the other. There were even candles in the minstrel gallery, across the length of hall opposite Lady Courtenay. A side table held eight or nine serving trays over flickering blue flames. There were place cards. Penrose was seated between Sir Norman and Hilliard. Claire sat across from him, and Selina sat beside Hilliard.

Selina was the last to come in. She walked slowly past the serving table while Mukerjee and his wife buzzed around transferring food from platter to plate.

"Beans," she intoned in a very high voice, "beans; these are old beans, has beans. And that's not Brie; that's debris. Shame on you, Mrs. Mukerjee. Ah, moussaka," she went on, "if moussaka be the food of love, play on. If love be food, then we can consommé our relationship."

"Selina, do come and stop clowning about," her father said crossly.

306

"Asp—ic, Cleopatra's favorite dessert. And this piece of cod passes all understanding."

Hawkes looked around the table with a professional expression, pushed his chair back and went over to Selina.

Penrose, like everyone else, pretended to ignore the scene while listening hard to Hawkes's mutters.

"Absinthe makes the heart grow fonder," Selina interrupted, and laughed.

Hawkes slapped her.

Penrose jumped to his feet. "Hang on a minute," he began, turning around, but the slap appeared to have worked. Selina was walking around to her place, saying, "I'm sorry, I'm sorry."

"Sit down, Penrose," Sir Norman shouted, pulling at his ear.

"I'm all right, John." Selina sat down, watching him.

"Who the hell do you think you are, Hawkes?"

"Her therapist—old chap."

"Here, Penrose," Sir Norman said, more calmly, "sit down and have some of the curried aspic with grapes. It's Jalal Singh's specialty. He gets the turmeric flown specially from Delhi; he knows how much I like fresh spices."

Penrose started to sit, wondering idly why the word "turmeric" had such a familiar ring to it. Then he froze. His mind made connections as if it had already made all the groundwork. He looked at Sir Norman. His knee remained half bent in a ridiculous posture.

"Well, sit down, Penrose," Sir Norman insisted. "Stop staring at me like that. Come on!"

They were all looking at him, vague and surprised. Askew even interrupted the story he was telling Claire about the American congressman he had caught in the kitchen cutting bacon to fish for trout at his lodge in the highlands. Only Hawkes was actually listening.

"Turmeric," Penrose said, "fresh turmeric."

"Yes. It's very hard to find, Penrose. Sit down."

"Harewood," Penrose said. The name dropped like a rock in the stillness of the room. "You were a friend of his. He had invited a friend of his for dinner that night, the night he was killed."

"Norman," Hawkes said, looking at Courtenay.

"What are you going on about, Penrose? Sit down," Sir

Norman said. His cheek jumped, and he rubbed it with his left hand.

"I wasn't sure," Penrose said, beginning to feel the horror, knowing this horror would only temporarily dominate the self-hatred he'd felt since the Chinese slammed the door shut in his face. "I wasn't sure until now. But look at the eyes: you're not questioning what I say; you're dealing with it as a problem."

"You've gone right around the bend, Penrose."

"Have I?" Penrose brought his breathing into line. "Have I? Well, I admit that until just now I wasn't too sure of my suspicions, but now I'm more certain."

The certainty built: all the discordant events that had been ringing in his head since the flight to Holland fell into place at once, making a pattern like free electrons around a molecule.

Claire was looking at him with panic on her face, aghast at his carrying on so in front of Lord Askew.

"Don't be such a cliché, Penrose," Hawkes said, as he filled his glass with wine. "So boring. Such classic symptoms of paranoid schizophrenia: it's as if you'd read the textbooks. Is this a show?"

Ostentatiously Drummond asked Hilliard something about clearinghouses and Threadneedle Street.

"No," Penrose insisted, feeling his face flush and his stomach quiver.

But he was on the defensive. It was an old board-room tactic that could be neutralized only by stubbornness. There was too much wrong. "It's not just intuition," he said in Sir Norman's direction. "Listen."

He paused for an instant to collect his thoughts, then said, "Item: Tim Harewood was killed, somehow, by someone he knew. Someone who put a placebo in his pill bottle and then went over to search the place when he died. The killer had been invited, he knew about Harewood's condition—therefore, a friend. But what a friend! A friend who showed up for dinner, and smiled, and smiled, and then pulled a gun on him and literally scared him to death when he knew Tim would not be protected by his medicine.

"Item," Penrose counted on a second finger, "Harewood was clutching a spice jar full of fresh turmeric when he died: your favorite spice, Sir Norman, as we've all just heard. Tim

308

Harewood's last message, perhaps. You probably gave him the spice.

"Item three"—Penrose did not look at Selina—"what happened to me over and over again, in Antwerp, in the Tortuga Islands, in Kent four days ago. I made no secret of going to those places, but it was not public knowledge either. And only one person besides myself knew beforehand that I was going to all three places. My loving wife, soon to be my ex, who tells her doting father everything."

Selina shook her head, once, twice, did not stop, her eyes enormous.

"Penrose," Drummond said, "stop it. You're not well."

"The Lloyd's man confessed," Sir Norman said in a low, intense voice. "He confessed, John. Do you understand?"

Penrose got up, kicking his chair out from behind him.

"De Laune? Very convenient. But how would de Laune have killed Harewood? He didn't even know him. And then there's why."

Mukerjee came up in the background to serve the first course. Penrose waved him away, pacing back and forth behind Hilliard and Selina.

"De Laune had a reason, certainly. But so did you."

"This has gone on long enough," Askew called, cutting a slice off the aspic. "Miss Thibodeault?"

"You'll find it hard to cut with a ceremonial kukri," Sir Norman said. "Mukerjee will do it, while we let Penrose rave. He'll tire of it soon enough."

"John?" Claire said.

"John." Selina was trying to flatten her face between two trembling hands.

"Oh, I hadn't figured it out. Not when the American agent mentioned a consortium of banks connected to Tortuga Insurance: how they stood on the verge of catastrophe. I wasn't even sure when I saw all you gentlemen here tonight. But Harewood must have found out something in New York or Georgetown: something that would have finally blown the lid off Nastal, which you and Courtenay's, and Royal Edinburgh and Overseas, and Johns Glynnis own with Eastern Holdings. Right, Lord Askew?"

"Damn it, Penrose, stop it! Stop it now!" Sir Norman's face was pink from shouting. "Stop it now," he repeated in a quieter voice, "or leave."

"I still wasn't sure," Penrose continued, "till you mentioned turmeric. But the piece of information that first made me really wonder about my father-in-law was the fact that he was losing money in the Tilbury docklands project. I remembered that, after the bomb. After all, who in their right mind would gratuitously wipe out half a county when a bullet would have sufficed, unless he had something to gain from it. And who, for that matter, might tell his hired gun that the most sadistic way to kill me would be in a place like one under the tidal barrier."

"But I didn't want to kill you," Sir Norman replied. The jumping shadows of candles made the spasms in his cheek that much deeper. The high collar was dark with moisture.

"It's all circumstantial," Drummond confided to Hilliard. "It would be laughed right out of court."

"It doesn't have to go to court," Hilliard hissed back. "All it would take is a word to his friends at the *Evening*."

"I didn't want to kill you." Sir Norman smiled sadly. "Just keep you off balance, you see. Doesn't that make—"

"Shut *up*, Courtenay!" Drummond said.

Penrose was taken aback for a moment.

Then he saw Sir Norman's eyes begin to check his position relative to Mukerjee and the door, flicking back and forth, assessing distances.

"I'm sorry," Penrose said aloud, remembering a new resolve to act rather than react.

He leaned over Selina, quickly grabbed the kukri from the platter of aspic and brought it back against her neck. In the same line of movement he put his left arm around her shoulders, bent her sideways and dragged her out around her chair.

His wife went rigid in his arms.

The knife made a clear line of sauce at her throat. Pink gravy dribbled down under the lace and green silk between her breasts.

"Stop right where you are, Mukerjee," Penrose said in the silence. "Remember," he continued a little ridiculously, "most killings are between family members."

"John—" Selina's eyes rolled up white against the tears— "please."

Hawkes got to his feet.

Sir Norman picked up his glass and flung it to the floor.

"Don't think I wouldn't. Claire," Penrose said, but his

voice quavered, and he had to repeat himself. "Claire, get behind me."

The American did not question him. His eyes probably looked as mad as his father-in-law's. No one tried to stop her when she passed behind Sir Norman to his back.

"Let's go."

Selina would not move. He had to drag her in reverse, squeezing her against his chest, while he faced the frozen table.

He checked behind him. Claire was at the Italian Room door, staring.

"Out," he said, "quickly," facing the table again. He took three strides back, dragging Selina, careful not to let the knife slip. He bumped into Claire.

"Damn it, open the door!"

Instead, he felt her hand cool at his neck and a loud hiss at his ear. His automatic intake of breath drew the gas deep into his chest. It felt like breathing fire. His lungs turned themselves inside out, and seized up as they tried to evacuate the pain. His eyes burned out, even against shut lids. He couldn't breathe. Tears streamed; his stomach heaved. He kept Selina against him as he fell, kept the knife close by her throat, but rough hands grabbed his arm and twisted the knife away. Another pair of hands twisted him, where he lay on his side, helpless.

At that point it didn't matter. Nothing mattered but to somehow sneak some oxygen past the firebreaks in his abdomen. To make matters worse, he began to throw up, and the vomit got tangled in the gag reflex. To cough was agony, yet he had no choice but to cough, to burst his lungs and cough and retch, cough and retch, his throat rattling when he tried to draw air back in. His chest felt like it was being flayed from inside with every choke. He managed one breath, but the fresh air revitalized the Mace inside. After another bout of coughing he got a second breath. Success of a sort. More whisky-and-soda came up, after which he managed a third breath, and a fourth.

When he finally got to the point where he had time to care about what was going on around him he found he was still lying on the cold marble floor. Aqbar and Jalal Singh stood in front of him with kukris in their fists.

Sir Norman and Mukerjee were struggling with Selina. Drummond and Hilliard sat talking at the tables as if nothing

311

had happened. Lord Askew hovered nervously. Hawkes came in through the library door with a black satchel, shifted the beagles and deposited it next to the hearth.

Claire stood at one of the French windows, looking out. Betrayed.

"No-o-o," Selina yelled, and kicked Mukerjee in the stomach. Her hair had fallen in blond monster claws over her face.

Hawkes pulled a bottle of alcohol, a blue box of swabs, a belt of hypodermic syringes and two little rubber-topped vials from his bag.

"John," Selina shrieked again. Her mother looked on from the wall, indifferent.

He tried to get to a kneeling position, the breath rasping in his throat, but Aqbar kicked him in the sternum, and he collapsed.

"You can come out now," Hilliard called.

Hawkes pushed the needle through one of the little vials, pumped in a couple of cubic centimeters, used the other, tapped the syringe, squirted it, then walked over to Selina with the hypodermic in one hand and cotton in the other. Drummond joined him, grabbing Selina's left arm. Hawkes cleaned her shoulder with alcohol, injected the substance, swabbed the area once more. Selina jerked and collapsed, crying again.

"Woss in—" Penrose tried to say. "What's in—what the hell are you giving her?" he gasped.

Behind Penrose a door opened. It was the door leading to a spiral staircase giving access to the minstrel gallery. A figure in a plain business suit walked over to the table, keeping his back to Penrose.

Sir Norman joined him, closing his fists very tightly, opening them again, closing, opening.

"You heard?"

A nod from the figure.

"He guessed. Damn it all, he guessed." Sir Norman looked at Penrose squirming on the floor, while Jalal Singh held the kukri over his temple. "You had no facts."

The figure did a quarter turn and glanced at the captain. Through the tears that continued to stream from his eyes Penrose saw an unremarkable face, a sort of bread-pudding visage that looked exactly like his milkman in Treg: only this time he had longish sideburns and no mustache. The man

312

from the *Evening* photos. The man who "owned" Tortuga Insurance. The man who worked for Eastern Holdings.

"Dormier," Penrose gasped, holding his stomach.

"You are lucky, I told you." Dormier turned back to Sir Norman. "But you should have got rid of him right at the start."

"Don't lecture me."

"Who else would Eastern turn to for financing but the bank commission? He was bound to guess."

"Don't lecture me!"

"I can lecture you," the other retorted in an odd, transatlantic sort of accent, "because I'm right."

"Right, wrong," Sir Norman said, "it's all so very relative from up here, don't you see." He went to stand over Penrose.

"I tried, you see, Penrose," he said, wiping sweat from his jowls. "I really tried. Never liked you, of course, because of Selina, but I did get used to you. We're not unlike, you and I. As I said."

"But you said you wouldn't." It was Claire's voice. She had turned from the window and was hugging herself.

"And I didn't. Well, I admit, I did want to scare you. Just rattle you enough to keep you from pushing the Harewood thing. Only for a week or two, till we got New York straightened out. I told him not to kill you, at first, because of my daughter. Damage you. Give you a chance, an actuarial—" Sir Norman had trouble getting the adjective past his twitching cheek—"an actuarial chance. If you died, so much the worse for you, so much the better for us. Rather clever, eh? Actuarial: considering all the trouble started because of Eastern's bloody insurers, their being too cheap to pay their own loss premiums."

Penrose's father-in-law knelt on the marble, bringing his face close to the captain's. Aqbar, ever protective, put his knees on Penrose's head and let the point of the kukri rest next to his right eyeball.

"Of course, you could have died, which would have saved us all the trouble. Statistically, in fact, you should be dead several times over. Hold his arms." Aqbar dropped his knife and pinned Penrose's elbows to the floor. Jalal Singh sat down on his ankles. Mukerjee left Selina, who was seated in Sir Norman's chair now looking pensively at the plate, and held one of Penrose's wrists.

313

The other bankers trooped over to stand around Penrose's field of vision like curious penguins on an Antarctic ice floe. Hawkes followed them, holding a syringe.

"We're not taking any chances now, of course."

"Not this time," Hawkes agreed.

Part of him cared, Penrose realized—the little life bug inside him was desperately unwilling to be crushed. The little life bug also cared desperately, of course, about Claire's foreclosing on his emotional loans. But another part of him was indifferent: there would be so much effort involved in continuing to live while he knew he was at the mercy of that shuttered fear lodged deep inside his unconscious.

"Why don't you—" he said, still trying to force his lacerated lungs—"why don't you—just use the word. Say what you mean. Kill me."

"You said you wouldn't," Claire said. "You let me telephone him at the gas plant. And you didn't kill him in the barrier."

"I did try," Hawkes said with a self-effacing smile. "If he hadn't died he should have had a breakdown. He was tougher than we thought." He squirted clear liquid into the air. A tiny drop fell on Penrose's face. Penrose looked at the psychiatrist's face as if it were the first time he had seen him.

"You?" he said in disbelief.

"At your service." Hawkes knelt and rolled back Penrose's sleeve.

"I say," Lord Askew grumbled.

"But that's not—"

"My part-time job, old boy." Hawkes had lost his neurotic air and looked very distant and assured. "Much more lucrative, I assure you, taking care of, shall we say, problems that the banking commission can't solve through ordinary channels."

"You're not—"

"No, actually." The alcohol was cool on his arm, the needle unnoticed until he pulled the syringe out again. "I'm a professional."

"Tenth Hussars, seconded to the Special Boat Service, don't you know." Sir Norman chuckled and sat down beside Penrose's face in cozy fashion. "Ah, my stiff joints. I can't count the number of times I put Hawkes and his men ashore well behind Jap lines. Best explosives man in the business:

he blew up dams, bridges, tracks, roads, petrol dumps, ammo dumps. Remember that Irrawaddy one?" Sir Norman chuckled fondly. "We saw it twenty miles out."

Hawkes kept swabbing.

"But you're not," Penrose repeated.

"Chinese?"

"Show him," Courtenay commanded, grinning.

Hawkes packed his syringe, removed a couple of tiny plastic bags from the satchel and turned his back to Penrose. His elbows worked, like a squirrel from the back.

"Let's not make the same mistake," Dormier said. "Let's get rid of him now."

Askew said, "No one mentioned getting rid of anybody."

"You were saying"—Hawkes turned back to Penrose—"that I'm not an Asian."

Penrose gasped. The psychiatrist had swiveled ninety degrees back so only one profile was visible. One cheek was distended and his skin had turned orangy yellow. He had hunched way down, concealing his height, and pulled up the collar of his smoking jacket.

It was the Chinese. Padding under his cheekbones was accentuated by a squint that gave him a touch of epicanthic eyefold. The change of character, when he turned full face, was translated in the eyes. Instead of the hurt and vindictive look Hawkes usually wore, a cool and passionless man lived behind those irises. Penrose had no doubt in his mind at all that Hawkes was mad.

Hawkes straightened, stuck two fingers in his mouth and removed a piece of wet wax. He put the wax in one of the small plastic pouches, replaced it in the black satchel and pulled out the other pouch, which was filled with yellow powder.

"Fresh turmeric," he said, rubbing his face, and laughed. "Instant wog." His hand came away yellow. There was a smell of curry.

"Always the ham," Sir Norman commented ingenuously.

"I can't. I won't allow it." Askew pushed himself between Hawkes and Drummond, wedging them apart with his bulk.

"Won't allow what?"

"To make him disappear. You never mentioned anything like this before. Threats, spying, stealing, why not? Everyone else does. But this is—"

"Murder," Penrose offered. "Call a spade a spade."

315

"Shut up."

"You went along with it last time," Drummond pointed out.

"He's repressed it," Hawkes explained.

Askew pulled hard at two or three of his chins. "That was going to be one exception; we had no choice. You said the bomb was an accident."

Hilliard took out a gleaming lighter and lit a cigar with such a flourish that everyone looked at him—even Penrose, eyes straining up from under Aqbar's knife.

"Do you think we have any choice now?" Hilliard asked softly.

"Yes," Claire said from the window. She threw back a mass of curls with a twist of her hand and strode over, very straight, as dramatic, in her own way, as Hilliard.

Penrose felt a curious thing happen then. Everything in the room jolted, as if it were part of an elevator, and shifted a foot lower. The colors paled, people's voices became slightly fuzzier.

"And what might that be, your ladyship?" Hawkes said nastily.

"Keep him. Keep him hidden until we can get out from under Nastal. Sir Norman says only two days more and the loan clears. After that it won't matter. After that he can't prove anything."

The man in the plain business suit—Dormier—laughed. His face looked like a pudding with a hole in it. He looked at Claire and ran his tongue over his lips, left to right.

"Don't be ridiculous," Hilliard hissed. "He's not the average sailor. He's not even a lonely journalist with no family, few friends. He's a celebrity now, thanks to Courtenay's soft heart, and too many people know he came here tonight, his shipping company, his crew. This is the first place they'll come looking."

Claire said, "Um," and glanced at Penrose. Her eyes were shielded, impenetrable. He tried to say "Don't" with his own, but could not tell if she understood. He tried to form "No" with his lips, but his brain was having an inordinate amount of difficulty getting through to his mouth. The injection, he thought, was taking effect.

"If you don't kill him—" she began.

"There are ways," Askew said, too loudly. "People can be bought—"

A thud came from the table as Selina slipped sideways and fell off her chair to lie prone on the floor.

Dormier laughed again and looked at Claire's breasts.

"I won't allow it," Claire said.

"Dear, dear," Sir Norman interjected. "And you were telling us how much you wanted to—no, needed—that treasurer's position. You won't get it at this rate, you know. Pounding the streets of New York again, I daresay."

She looked around the ring of faces: Hawkes sneering; Drummond harsh; Askew sweating; Dormier grinning; Hilliard impassive. She ended with Sir Norman, who forestalled her.

"He's not worth it."

"You said I wouldn't have to get involved in this kind of thing," Claire whispered. "But all the time, the methane plant would have killed him, even if I hadn't called. You said it was a mistake."

"Yes," Askew said, and belched.

"You can't make an omelette," Sir Norman said, "without breaking eggs. Isn't that right, John?" He patted Penrose's cheek. Penrose tried to jerk away, but his head was far too heavy.

"Royal Edinburgh and Overseas have a Singapore subsidiary," Drummond said vaguely. "It's going to get a lot more business after nineteen-ninety-seven. We need a new director."

"Now there's an offer," Dormier said, smiling, "you really should take. It's very generous."

Claire looked at his mouth and looked away with no expression.

"And as for you, Lord Askew," Hilliard said, "I commend the words of Miss Thibodeault's countryman: 'We must all hang together, or most assuredly we shall all hang separately.'"

"Only two days, and Nastal will be out of the woods," Drummond reminded him.

"It's not too long," Hilliard added.

"You know—" Hawkes stifled a yawn—"we can't just make him disappear. We have to make him disappear with a reason, or the press will get after it. Which means like Harewood. An accident. And it has to be tonight."

"I hope you do better than with Harewood," Hilliard hissed. "They'll be looking."

"That's funny, Hawkes." Sir Norman blinked furiously. "I've been thinking about that. And I've got an idea." He lurched to his feet, then looked down where Penrose lay.

" 'Have hope, O friend,' " he recited. " 'Yea death disgraced is hard: much honor shall be thine.' " He drew Dormier, Drummond and Hilliard to one side and began gesticulating.

Hawkes knelt down and jabbed a finger at each of Penrose's eyes in turn and said words to Aqbar in Hindi.

Aqbar followed Claire out of the room.

Hawkes joined the conversation. Askew helped himself to wine. Selina lay still on the floor, twenty feet from her husband. No one paid him any attention. The life instinct inside Penrose urgently wanted him to pull himself together, but the death bug, sure of its ascendancy, was quite content that all contact had been lost between muscles and mind and there was absolutely nothing he could do to affect what was going to happen to him tonight.

The night and western England rushed by in an eighty-mile-per-hour breeze broken only by the ticking of the Bentley's clock and the occasional tense murmur from Aqbar, Hawkes, Dormier, or Claire.

At least Penrose assumed it was western England, but the sedative Hawkes had given him padded his consciousness in layers of cotton wool a foot thick. Everything stood at four or five or six removes, including what few deductions he had left to make. After a year or so of this he let his mind have its way and drift around, serenaded by the rush of slipstream, rocked by the slow curves of the M3.

Occasionally words or noise came like heaving lines to what was going on in the place he used to call the real world.

The clink of crystal and the smell of Scotch from a fold-out minibar in the rear seat.

"Not even Exeter yet. He's got to get a move on."

"A mixture of sodium pentothal and a half milliliter of curare. The pentothal sedates; the curare's a muscle relaxant." It was Hawkes's voice, and presumably his hand that picked up Penrose's, held it a foot above where he lay sprawled on the car's rug and dropped it. It fell with all the tension of custard. "He'll need another injection in an hour or so."

"No, that was Yeovil. Better than I thought. We'll be there before five."

"Plenty of detonators from the clay pits." Hawkes again.

"Will fit in nicely with his comments about Lloyd's." (Dormier?)

A jolting series of curves stood out in this endless time of complete helplessness. Aqbar uttered a lot of words in Hindi, and Hawkes twisted around to look back in urgent fashion. The sharp movements slid Penrose back and forth enough to rug-burn his ear. He was glad he had thrown up his whisky-and-sodas, since he knew there was no way he could control his bladder in these conditions. After a while the jolting stopped, but there was a note of nervousness in Dormier's voice that had not been there before.

"You're sure?"

"We've lost them."

"Who were they?"

"It wasn't the cops."

"What the hell did he do?" A heel jabbed into Penrose's bad rib. He didn't even flinch.

"Just kids on a lark."

Aqbar said, "They were there for at least an hour."

"They've gone, anyway."

Three times Penrose felt himself lifted, adjusted by small but strong hands, hands that smelled sharp and delicate. Twice he felt less uncomfortable. The third time someone held his arm up for the injection.

"Paid off that Welsh surveyor, you know, to go on holiday early. Talk about false bloody economies—"

When he awoke, the Bentley was slowing, stopping, accelerating, turning. Lights blinked and faded in the smoked windows. This went on for another endless period, until the Bentley came to a final halt. The engine stilled. Doors opened into a crusty silence. The car rocked.

Someone—it had to be Hawkes, because he smelled of curry—dragged Penrose feet first out the door onto a cold sidewalk and leaned him against a wall.

Penrose's eyes were hard to aim but they focused quite well, which was odd, he thought, when you considered they were muscles like the rest.

They were parked under a vast arcade that looked quite familiar to Penrose. The roof was two stories high, glassed in over bow-shaped steel girders. Fluted columns held up the beams and separated the shops between. In the canary glow of streetlights all the shops and columns seemed painted in cream and blood. Even the car appeared to radiate an evil rouge color.

Penrose wondered how he knew this place. The arcade split four ways: a pub called the Lamb formed one corner;

an oyster stall, a butcher and a restaurant called Bulevants supported the others. Everything was shut and dark. A bus growled several streets away in the predawn hush, the call of a red predator in the jungles of the city.

Hawkes and Dormier both bent over Penrose. The psychiatrist had darkened his other cheek with turmeric and put his fake cheekbones back in. The Chinese had returned, with a slur in his speech from the wax pads.

"We'll pretend he'sh jush drunk."

Penrose suddenly remembered the booby-trapped fence during the Courant. Hawkes must have rigged that as well, he realized.

"Put the scarf over your face," Dormier snapped.

Claire had her beret back on. It gave him a little pang to see it. She had worn it in Antwerp, where she had waited to snare him. She did not look at him.

"Okay."

"Right."

"His other shoulder."

They hauled Penrose to his feet like a sack of vegetables and hoisted him in a fireman's carry.

Aqbar got in the driver's seat of the Bentley. Claire started to climb in the rear door.

"No!" Dormier shouted.

"Shut up, for God's sake, man."

"No one's about."

"Miss Thibodeault," the psychiatrist continued. He walked over to her and fastened the top button of her coat, like a father. "We want you to be a full partner, my dear. Let's go."

Claire shivered. She shut the door of the Bentley very slowly.

"Put your scarf over your face," Dormier repeated, adjusting his own.

They started down the arcade. Their footsteps slapped below the arches; Penrose's shoes made a long scuffing noise.

The arcade ended fifty yards farther on. They turned under some complex scaffolding and then into an alley that led between bowed walls of very heavy sandstone, six or seven stories high, cut with tall, curved windows. A single wooden door with a round recess above it gave access to the wall on the right. Dormier left Penrose hanging off Hawkes.

321

He produced a heavy circle of keys and opened the door. Hawkes looked up and down the alley, but no one was in sight. The movement folded Penrose's neck sideways and back, so he caught sight of a rectangle of night sky, orange and black with a satellite or planet shining to one side of clouds. It was very pretty, he thought, to be leaving behind.

They dragged him up steps, and his head flopped forward again. Down a long corridor, surfaced in marble; recessed lighting glowed dimly at the edges. The walls were covered in very dark, polished wood, with railings. The swinging doors had brass portholes. The whole place felt, even smelled, like one of the old Cunarders. Penrose knew he had been here before.

The last set of swinging doors came out on the second-floor balcony of the Underwriting Room at Lloyd's of London.

No one was visible. Through the glass at the balcony edge he could see the Lutine Bell in the gray-blue ocean below. One or two of the wooden booths had green desk lamps shining like running lights across the vast expanse. A teletype chattered to itself and was still. Most of the light came from a large round recess in the roof. It reflected off the square-cut columns and made them look even more like shiny cheese.

"Where to now?"

Dormier waved for quiet. Far across and below, a man in a cloak with an ermine collar walked up to the distant teletype. The thin noise of ripping paper came quite clearly. He went back to the lobby, silent on the blue carpet.

Hawkes motioned that he wanted to put his end of the load down, and they laid Penrose in the middle of the balcony. Claire was standing against the wall, beside a display cabinet and a shining steel door. Her beret was pulled low over her eyes.

The psychiatrist took off his coat. An army musette hung on his shoulder. He unstrapped it and looked around.

"Where'sh the guard?"

"Not to worry. They don't patrol much at this hour."

"You're sure of our line of escape?"

"Absolutely."

Light shone copper on Hawkes's fat cheekbones. He had readopted the Chinese role. He squinted and stooped as he looked around the huge room; walked to the balcony and back, shrugged his bowed shoulders.

"Anywhere'sh azh good azh any other, I shuppose."

"The roof," Dormier said, with the air of someone who did not want to let a good thing go to waste, "is largely unsupported. Surely you can do something with that."

Hawkes shrugged again.

"I would need a shaped charge. I'd need to get closer. If there was a confined space, I could multiply the blast a factor of twenty or thirty. But all we have to do ish take care of our shacrificial goatsh here."

Dormier glanced sharply at Claire, but she was far away, staring at the ceiling. "Shut up."

Hawkes shrugged.

"But there's one right here, you know."

Penrose, through his haze of sedation, found himself feeling very sorry for Claire.

"What do you mean?"

"A confined space." Dormier walked to the steel door. "The Nelson Room," he went on. "It's totally encased in steel. Walls, roof, floor, because of all the silver inside. The guard will open it."

"What do you mean?" Hawkes repeated. "I mean, what will you do, ashk him nicely?"

"There's only one in the lobby." Dormier grinned at the psychiatrist. "Why don't you give me the pistol?"

"There'sh no need," Hawkes objected.

"But we should do it properly," Dormier countered.

"Do you—"

"I can handle it," Dormier interrupted. "I was in Cyprus. I can handle it."

"What rank?"

"Lieutenant. Rifle Corps. And you?"

"Major. You Blackbuttons"—he smiled—"were generalists, in my experiensh. Indifferent at everything."

The smile disappeared from Dormier's face.

"We did more than you people ever did. You're still the Cheyne Ten, in spirit if not in name. Give me the gun."

Hawkes did not move. He stared at Dormier through narrowed eyes. The door opened behind them.

Aqbar slid into the room carrying an insecticide sprayer with hose and nozzle attached, and held himself at ease by the entrance.

323

"We haven't got all night."

Hawkes reached under his camel's hair coat and pulled out the gun and silencer. He hesitated, then surrendered the gun to the younger man. Dormier hefted it and disappeared past Aqbar through the swinging door.

Time passed. Hawkes prowled restlessly. Aqbar played sentry. Claire watched the ceiling.

Penrose was feeling sorrier and sorrier for Claire, in an abstract, drug-enhanced way that could have included anyone and everyone. He was feeling very sorry for himself in the same way. His lips were almost immobile; in fact, his head was canted over and he could not prevent himself from drooling onto his collarbone. He could roll his eyes and try to wink in Claire's direction to attract her attention. Maybe he could wink an SOS at her, he thought, although what good that would do was beyond him; it was quite obvious that he was in distress. There was always the Morse letter G—"you are standing into danger"—but the odds on her getting that were about the same as those of being rescued by George Armstrong Custer or Nelson himself.

Dormier was back quite soon with a second set of keys. He went straight to the door and fitted one into a hole next to the frame. A little red light blinked off above it. Two more keys went into keyholes. Hawkes asked what he'd done with the guard.

"He's in booth 101, resting. I turned the fire alarm override on," he confided, winking at Claire.

"What about the others?"

"They won't come back till their watch is over at six."

"How do you know?"

"I used to work here, remember?"

The door swung open with a deliberation that spoke of great weight. Hawkes dragged him in by the heels and rolled him onto his stomach against a wall.

"The Nelson Room," Dormier said when he had swung the door to. Neon flickered to sterile life behind wood paneling. "Built, so we are told, to the exact specifications of HMS *Victory*'s day cabin. Containing a priceless silver service donated to Admiral Lord Nelson after the battle of Copenhagen."

At the moment all Penrose could see was paneling and gray-painted floor. All he could feel was the presence of huge steel panels that turned this room into an airtight, fire-tight box.

"Donated by a grateful nation to the man who kept the seas safe for British merchant bankers."

"Shall we get on with it?" Hawkes said, taking off his coat.

There was a lot of scurrying around while Penrose lay face to the wall.

"The hose screws the other way."

"Here let me do it."

"Why do you have to do that? I thought you used plastic. Even in your day—" Dormier said.

"By vaporizing, it will become explosive, eshpecially in here. Then it will make a nice hot fire. It should have thirty or forty times the power."

"Courtenay will hate to have missed it." Dormier chuckled.

Claire rolled Penrose over.

Her eyes were dry, her face very pale.

"I'm so sorry, John," she said. "Sorry for both of us."

Not as sorry as I am for you. Politely he tried to semaphore back with his eyelids, but her lip dragged to one side and she rose abruptly, leaving him with a view of the room.

It was fairly narrow, the oak colors lightened with cream paint. Most of the walls were taken up by glass cabinets that contained silver platters, soup tureens, spoons, trays, cups and punch bowls, sparkling with the improbable clarity of good and well-buffed silver. There were also medals, dress swords, an early nineteenth-century admiral's uniform (slightly used, with one sleeve pinned). The display between Claire's espadrille and his head was given over to brown documents pinned on cork.

"No, thoshe are Navy-type. It'sh got to look azh if he stole them. Crimp that one, you twit. And that one."

"I hope you're doubling them."

"Obviously. The detonator goesh in lasht."

"I'll pump out the naphtha."

"Not yet, man. Let Aqbar do it, when everything'sh set."

"Christ, you're cautious."

"It's my show. If you don't like it, shtuff it, Lieutenant."

Above Penrose's head Claire cleared her throat nervously.

His eyes got tired of watching her face. He let them track down a display of documents near him.

"Your wine is found so good that I desire you will send me twenty dozen of the same port wine," read the document closest to him. It was signed, "Horatio Viscount Nelson."

Dormier said, "I'll just check on the guard."

Below was a detailed bill listing all the purchases of wine for a carriage trip from Naples to England.

The only passengers in the coach-and-four, according to the manifest, were Nelson, Sir William Hamilton and his wife, Lady Hamilton.

A cozy little *ménage à trois,* he thought, but his mind was distracted by the smell of naphtha that was now pervading the room.

The total bill for wine consumed during the trip was £3,300. Not bad, Penrose reflected, considering a pound bought so much more in those days. Had adultery been nourished or drowned in a sea of Loire and burgundy and port, Penrose wondered, but his thoughts now focused on the white flesh of Claire's hand where it gripped a small cylinder of silvery metal.

"Another fifteen pumpsh," Hawkes whispered to Aqbar.

Penrose, by straining his sluggish eye muscles as far as they would go, found he could follow Claire's feet past the loom of his own nose as they left the wall and took one step, two steps, three steps into the center of the room.

Hawkes stood with his back to Penrose. Aqbar's shoes protruded from beyond. So did part of his coat and a single elbow, pumping methodically at the handle of the weed sprayer. As Penrose watched, Aqbar picked up the canister, strapped it on one shoulder, walked fully into view and turned a valve. His other hand held a hose and nozzle, which emitted a fine spray of whitish mist. He began to walk around the room spraying the vapor in every corner.

Claire took another step. She was only two or three feet from where Hawkes checked wires, without touching a bottle filled with clear liquid. A pen-shaped object was wedged in its mouth. Beside the bottle lay what must be the timing device. Wires linked the pen-shaped object with the timer.

A black shoe entered the picture, much closer to Penrose's head. It nearly blocked the view of Claire's espadrilles.

Claire raised her right arm and shifted balance, shaking curls out of her eyes.

The dark gray pants belonged to Dormier. So did the dark gray sleeve that lifted high and to one side. The fist at the end belonged to Dormier as well, but the gun it gripped was Hawkes's. In the no-time of pentothal, Penrose watched his thumb check the hammer was uncocked and return to grip the barrel. Then gun, fist and sleeve crashed, incredibly fast, straight into the mass of chestnut curls.

Claire crumpled and fell backward. Her head bounced off Penrose's shins and onto the floor, leaving a strand of hair resting on his pants. She shook a little and lay still. The little cylinder of Mace fell from her limp fingers and rolled across the wood.

That hurt, deep down below the anesthetic. The command to yell came strong and clear, the precise signals that would move the tongue against the roof of Penrose's mouth for the hard *c*, the liquid *l*, but his lips only twitched once.

Hawkes jerked around in surprise.

"She was going to spray you," Dormier said.

"The bloody bitch."

"I knew it," Aqbar grumbled from the other end of the room. "Sir Norman told me she is trouble."

The other two ignored him.

"Is it time yet?"

Dormier shrugged. "There's no guards as yet. It's just four-fifty-five."

"Is everything ready?"

Penrose suddenly imagined what it would be like when they closed him in this steel-walled mausoleum. Him and a roomful of vaporized chemicals burning to combine with oxygen.

The pressure, for a brief second, would be enormous, until the expanding gases blew out a steel plate. Confinement echoed around him, and he closed his eyes against the dread.

He could feel the pressure already, in his bladder. He had an enormous desire to relieve himself. For the moment, control still lay with the automatic side of his cerebral switchboard, but when the pressure came— For some reason, it bothered him that he would go out wetting his pants.

Hawkes straightened up from the bomb, looking at his wrist.

"The timing's set for five-ten. It ish now four-fifty-six. Shynchronize your watches."

Dormier checked a digital watch. Aqbar fiddled with a massive gold contraption on his forearm.

"Fourteen minutes," Hawkes said. "Let'sh go."

"No."

"What do you mean?"

"We shouldn't leave yet," Dormier said.

Aqbar's eyes strayed to the Molotov cocktail, back to Hawkes.

"We've thirteen minutes and twenty-five seconds."

"There've been too many fuck-ups by you Special Boats lot. All this pissing about with bombs and harassment. I'm not taking any more chances with this one."

Hawkes smiled. "So you'll shtay?"

"There's too much at stake."

"Suit yourself, Lieutenant," Hawkes said. "Just remember that'sh a Special Services bomb. Can't rely on it to be completely accurate, eh? Let's go, Aqbar."

When Hawkes and Aqbar had left, Dormier went straight to Penrose's side, grabbed his pants and rolled him away from the wall and across the floor. A nerve in Penrose's cheeks began jumping as his jaw caught and slid on the parquet. Perhaps it was a sign, he thought, that the curare's hold was lessening, but when he tried to shift his left arm the fingers barely moved.

At least his view had changed. Now he could see the open fire door and a square of the Underwriting Room it framed.

Dormier turned to Claire Thibodeault. He took her wrists and dragged her next to Penrose, cutting the captain's view in half. Her head flopped loosely and a drop of blood scurried down her forehead and splatted on the floor.

Dormier stepped over Claire and moved to look out the door. He checked his watch, came back and stooped over Claire, letting his eyes run up and down her body. He checked his watch again and then stooped and lifted her short skirt up above her waist.

"Mmm." The groan started deep in Penrose's chest. He could feel his fingers twitch, a reflex of atavism.

"You don't like it, sailor man? Just watch what I do with your crumpet."

Dormier's hands moved toward Claire's thighs. She was

328

too close to him for Penrose to see beyond her rucked-up dress. He groaned again, then stopped in surprise.

In the rectangle of doorway he saw a fat figure in top hat and ermine cloak tiptoe idiotically around one of the roque-fort columns and disappear again.

From behind the same column a head edged out, then an eye. Penrose felt his own eyes staring, and lowered them as quickly as he could. He looked at Dormier, but the man was on his knees, fumbling at his belt and staring downward at Claire.

Rage surged in Penrose's chest. His stomach heaved.

The head edged out, followed by a hand with a short-barreled revolver. A blue-and-white-striped jacket came next, with a blazer patch that read "Groton." Plaid pants. The figure strode soundlessly across the carpeted balcony outside and took cover behind the door frame, leaving only one eye and a swatch of blond hair in view.

Dormier had his pants unzipped. He checked his watch with a turn of the wrist, then put his gun on Claire's stomach. His hands dropped and lifted. There was a sound of tearing silk.

The head at the door grew bigger. Penrose thanked his stars he could not react to the surprise he felt. Two blue eyes checked the room, right and left. They took in the incendiary bomb and returned to Dormier.

Then Seersucker hopped full into the doorway, dropped in a crouch with both hands together over the .38 Special, which was trained directly on Dormier's head.

"Freeze! Don't move! I gotta gun!"

Dormier gasped. His head swiveled, and he fell back on his haunches in the same movement.

"Hold it!"

He held it for half a second. Then his hand snapped at Claire's stomach, picked up the gun. At the same time he rolled sideways, his hand finding butt and trigger and rotating to aim as he moved.

"Drop it! Freeze!"

The air split down a fault line of sound—once, twice. The paneling shattered white to one side of the door. Dormier's body lifted a foot off the ground and shoved backward. A pinkish mist spread downwind of it.

The smell of gunpowder wrapped itself around the pervasive odor of lighter fluid.

Seersucker held his breath for a minute, then he rose carefully to his feet, both hands keeping the barrel locked on Dormier's body. He extended one foot, delicate as a dancer, and sent the Webley skittering across the gray floor. He brought the toe back, put it under Dormier's shoulder, lifted his knee and rolled him over.

Then he put the gun under his jacket and walked over to the bomb.

"Don't touch. You must wait."

The top-hatted guard stared in from the doorway, white hands raised in claws of apprehension.

The American pushed the hair back over his bald patch. He took out a red bandanna and wiped his forehead.

"Cool it," he said. "I'm trying to think."

He continued staring at the bomb. He put one finger on the timer, pulled it back. Stared some more.

Then he gripped the bottled chemicals with one hand. With the other he grasped one of the red wires between two fingers.

The guard vanished.

Seersucker did not even look up. Very slowly, very gently he eased the anode out of a hole in one end of the incendiary pencil. He bent the wire carefully into the air and eased the cathode out of its hole; bent that one out of harm's way. He fiddled at the timing box for a while, then took out a pocket knife and pried the detonator out of the bottle's mouth.

When he had separated the various plastic, glass and metal mechanisms from the chemical they were designed to fire, he took out the bandanna again.

He got up and stepped over Claire's body to where Penrose's eyes stared from the swamp of numbness.

"How's it goin', Penrose?" he said. "You know, I'm really beginning to believe you're innocent."

The cat was not interested in musical comedy and led him into a bombed-out tenement. A girl held a baby on her knees, rocking it softly. She looked at him and said it was her fault her baby had been crushed, would die.

A phone rang among the rubble. It was the fire brigade, but they rambled on and on about the "circumstances" and would not come to get the baby. He had to relieve himself. He went out back, into an overgrown garden, where a huge man with no face attacked him with fists. He fended off one onslaught, then another. The huge man ate blueberry pie in between attacks, but confided to Penrose that he would throw it up later.

The garden disappeared, and Penrose knew he must have escaped. He got on a horizontal elevator that took him to a room with no view, where he was supposed to demonstrate a radar flashlight for the blind. The flashlight was defective—it kept switching ranges—but it worked well enough to tell him the room was getting smaller and smaller. And still he had to relieve himself—

Penrose woke up with his bladder bursting. He lay flat on his back, pinned tight under coarse sheets. The ceiling above his head was the color of dirty pistachio sherbet. Light came from his right, so gray as to be almost shadow: but it was daylight, to his relief.

A hospital, somewhere in London. The air smelled of sticking plaster and alcohol. He was lying on a National Health steel bed—not uncomfortable. There was a plastic curtain to his left, from behind which came an occasional sniff, or rustle of sheets. In front of him was a wall with a frosted-glass window. Below the window the pistachio hue gave way to paint the color of pus. A bell rang, far away. Voices rose and fell, in vaguely familiar intonations, behind a wooden door.

Still alive. The feeling of celebration bloomed.

His mind was slippery from the run of dreams. It traveled back through the events that had led him here: the rush of lights and two-tone horns when the ambulance carried him from Lloyd's; young faces, bright with emergency and stethoscopes; men in top hats and ermine cloaks bustling with stretchers and brass fire extinguishers; Seersucker's face; the smell of naphtha. The awareness of pressure sat on his chest and the feeling made him squirm. The squirm rocked the bed, which creaked. The noise told him he had control over his muscles again.

He moved tentatively at first. He pulled the sheets off and swung his legs over the side of the bed, one at a time. Every signal got through, every muscle obeyed, the feedback checked out. The drugs had worn off. He became conscious of what the voices outside were saying.

"You can't," one voice said. "I'm a law-enforcement agent."

"In America, Mr. Phelps. In England you are only another visitor. A visitor who shot a man with an unlicensed firearm. I know the murder rate in Los Angeles, but we take these things seriously here."

The voice was known to him.

"Wait till the ambassador gets on the horn is all I can say."

That voice, too.

"I will. In the meantime, let's go over this again, if you don't mind. You say you used a signaling device to follow them to London? Do you know you require a permit for this device?"

"Hello," Penrose called, and winced.

The door opened. A thin and lugubrious face peered into the room, nostrils flaring.

"Inspector Radetsky," Penrose said. "Where the hell is the loo?"

When he came back from the WC they forced him to get back into bed, more, he suspected, to keep him in a vulnerable position for questioning than out of any great concern for his health. Seersucker stood by the wall, dressed in a tweed hat and a leather coat, under which strange colors clashed. Radetsky sat stooped over his black note pad, looking like a raven in his long coat. A third man, in a nondescript jacket, took notes on top of an attaché case.

They told each other stories about what had happened. After a while the questions got sharper, the anecdotes more specific.

"They all got away?" Penrose said at last. "The lot of them? Now that's what I call fantastic police work."

"We've got the RAF looking, and the French have been notified," Radetsky answered. "We'll find them."

"And Selina's disappeared? You're sure she's not with them?"

"I told you—the others were seen boarding *Selina*, the yacht. There was no woman with them."

"And you lot are sitting at the foot of my bed looking concerned!"

"The Cornwall CID's been through Restormel House. They found her brother and some Indian servants—"

"You know," Seersucker interrupted, looking at Radetsky, "she could have been in on it. There's a way."

Penrose also looked at the inspector.

"Will you intern this idiot, or deport him, or something? The man's sick. I'm sure he still thinks I'm guilty. Selina, I told you, had no part in it."

Radetsky fumbled for his pastilles.

"Please be reasonable, Mr. Penrose," he said. "Remember, if it were not for Mr. Phelps's suspicions we could not have found enough of you to fill a teaspoon."

"It's not an argument."

"Yeah, buddy," the American said. "Now I've saved your ass twice, just by being suspicious."

"By having me followed since I got back from Grand Tortuga. It's the old dilemma: is security worth the price?"

"Jesus!" Seersucker ran his fingers through his hair. "How was I to know? The first place you went when you got back was Courtenay's Bank. That's when I first thought Courtenay's might—"

"If you hadn't been so bloody Nixonian," Penrose retorted, "you would have told the police, then Sir Norman wouldn't have got away. And you wouldn't have had to play shoot-'em-up with the man at Lloyd's."

Like watching a movie in his head, Penrose could see Sir

333

Norman kneeling on the floor reciting Kipling. He felt his insides grow even colder.

"Why *did* you visit Courtenay's, sir, at that time?"

"To ask my father-in-law to use his influence with Lloyd's. I have to go now."

"We haven't finished with the inquiries."

"You two sit and interrogate each other and confiscate each other's side arms. I'm worried about Selina." But he rested back on the pillow, aware of how much stuffing the drug had knocked out of him.

"She may also have left on her own. There were three cars missing from Restormel."

"Three?"

"One was the Bentley you say they took you to London in. One was a Daimler. We found that at the harbor." He shuffled through notes.

"What was the third?"

"I can't seem to find it."

"A Jaguar," the third man said. "Green, five years old. XJ6."

"The Jag. But you don't know Selina. Even if they didn't harm her, she's quite capable of—" He kicked off the covers, and winced. His ribs were acting up again, though the night he'd injured them, in Antwerp, seemed an eternity ago.

"You cannot leave like this," Radetsky said. "You must be checked out."

"Can't I?" Penrose replied. "Just you wait, kommandant. But I think I might know where she is."

"Then where? The Cornwall CID—"

"I'll call to check, but it's better that I go," Penrose said. "I don't need your help—for this. Not if she took the Jag."

The policemen looked at each other smugly.

"Where the hell are my clothes?"

"You may not find it so easy to leave as you think, Mr. Penrose."

"Give me back my clothes. I'll call my solicitor."

"We have them, and you can have them back," the third man told him. "It's just that the ward's been cordoned off. The press is waiting at every entrance. You're big news, and they're very pushy, are the gentlemen of the press. They'll tear you to pieces. It would be much simpler," he finished, "to let us sneak you over to New Scotland Yard. Then you can go where you like."

On his way out he asked to stop by the room where Claire Thibodeault lay.

Two constables and a nurse led him down dingy corridors and metal stairways. People in light green smocks with apologetic eyes dodged orderlies across the green linoleum. Heating pipes wheezed vainly and battled the damp. A third constable sat by a plain brown door with a yellow quarantine sticker.

"It's not visiting hours," the nurse said, "but since you're a VIP—" One of the policemen winked at her. "That's all right then," the other one said.

"Why is she under guard?"

"For her protection, sir. Like you."

Claire looked completely defenseless in the gray sheets. Her curls were limp and without luster even where her head wasn't bandaged. He felt gut shot just looking at her.

Her eyes were open, staring at the ceiling. They gave the wound a twinge, like bad weather.

The walls in this ward were painted the color of rotted apples.

He walked over and looked down at her face. She was very pale, and her lips had split when she fell.

"How are you feeling?" he said.

Her eyes flicked toward him, and away.

"Are you all right?" he insisted. "Claire." He prodded the barrow of blanket where her arm was buried.

"Wonderful, thanks."

"She has a concussion," the nurse said from the doorway. "We're keeping her under observation."

"Thank you." Penrose went to shut the door. The nurse stabbed him with a look as he closed her out.

"Why did you come here? Please leave me alone."

Penrose paced back and raised the window shade. The window looked out on a brown courtyard that kitchen exhausts were slowly staining black. The grayness outside joined with the dinginess in. He felt tired to the soles of his shoes.

"I came," he told the kitchen fans, "to get something analyzed, though I'm probably as much of a psychologist as

335

you are. To analyze a process. A process, you see, of cutting out a piece of my insides to give you on a plate. You pretended to accept it, you pretended to reciprocate. In fact, you were selling it all—me, even yourself—all to the highest bidder. So I want to know how much it all was worth. What do you think, doctor?"

The laugh that came from her bed was crystalline, broken, very sharp.

"Poor John."

"Yes," he agreed, "poor John."

"What happened to the British stiff upper lip."

"I told you—it's a front."

"I didn't betray you," she said at length. "I was *always* working for the consortium. I'm a vice-president of Harrison Bank, in Boston. It's theirs."

"And so are you—theirs. But you dealt with me under false pretenses."

Her laugh cracked the room again.

"It's called business."

"It's called lying."

"Words. Only words."

"You underestimate words. They're not just words. How you speak is the same thing as how you think. How you think and speak is identically equal to how you cope with the events of the world around you. It's a basic survival function. Once you start lying you interfere with that survival function."

"Don't talk to me about survival!" The sound of bed sheets made him turn. Claire had hoisted herself up on one elbow: there were dark half moons under her eyes. "I told you. I made my decision years ago. It allowed me to survive under conditions you've never met, Mr. British aristo-*cat*."

He looked at her.

"Was it worth it?"

"Oh, fuck off," she said, and rolled onto her back again.

"No, I'm serious, Claire. Once—on the *Princess,* do you remember?—only four days ago, you told me the only way I would ever control my own fears. You said all fear was of something inside oneself, which is true, it seems to me."

"I don't remember."

He ignored her.

"You also said," he went on—"I can remember very well because it made a big impression at the time—that good

336

psychology was all about restoring communication with yourself. That your subconscious is like a lazy child who thought he could cover up his mess by hiding it. That the only solution was to uncover things, restore the communication."

"I did my homework."

"No, you believed it. I think. I hope you believed it. You convinced the hell out of me."

"Believe it, then. It's a free country."

"I can use it," he said. "It's not much to ask."

She did not answer. She turned her head to look at the wall.

"But it could be true of you, as well," he insisted. "What made you cover up your own hurt? When your father hit your mother, when the kids called you—"

"Shut up."

"We could have—"

"Shut up!"

"Why are you crying?"

"I'm not."

"What are you going to do?" He reached over to put his hand on her shoulder. She shook it off.

"Perhaps you should go back to Maine."

"Will you shut *up?* Why are you doing this to me?" She was not trying to hide the tears any more.

"I'm sorry."

He walked to the door.

"Penrose," she said into her pillow.

"What?"

"Fuck off."

"All right."

"No, wait. You're such a sucker for big-sounding phrases; you want another one?"

"I don't think so."

"Yes, you do." She took a deep breath. "You once mentioned love to me. You want to know where love starts? With trust in yourself that is put inside when you're too young to know it. Fear is the reverse. It'll get you, unless you cut it open, like I said. But sometimes you have to cut too deep."

"I'm sorry," he repeated, feeling sick.

"I can't go back to Maine. Even if they don't lock me up."

She looked like a hurt child, Penrose thought, doubled up

337

in a fetal position now, snuffling against the wall. He turned back despite himself, approached the bed again. From this position he could see the blue beret and her short frock on a stool beside her bed, folded neatly over tights and flowered underwear.

"Claire."

"Don't. Please go now."

"But you shouldn't—"

"I'm not. I'm not crying for you. I'm crying for me. Because I'll always miss my dad. Because I'll always be hungry. Because I have a goddam right to feel sorry for myself. Because I'll go back, when all this blows over, to be a treasurer and a board member in Singapore or whatever. Hand me my clothes."

"You can't. You have a concussion."

She rolled back and buried her head in the pillow. Her neck looked very fragile and white, like a child's.

He turned once again. His hand was on the doorknob when she whispered, "They told me they wouldn't kill you, John. They let me call you, at the refinery. And I tried to stop them, at the end."

"I know."

"With the Mace—"

He looked back for the space of several heartbeats.

He said, "As far as the police know, you're just my friend. You can go anytime you like."

He shut the door softly behind him.

The constables looked at him curiously, and quickly looked away.

Penrose got through to Jack Tomkyns at three in the afternoon.

The Special Branch men pretended to be busy as they listened to him. Radetsky, more sure of his future these days, offered mint pastilles to their chief inspector. Between the metal blinds of New Scotland Yard you could see the towers of Parliament rising through the rain. Closer by, people queued under umbrellas, waiting for long-distance telephones.

"She's there," Penrose said when he'd hung up. "It's what I thought. She's done it before."

"That's all right then." A Special Branch detective with a thick mustache made an entry on a time sheet.

338

"I'd like to go to Cornwall on the night train."

Papers rustled on metal desks. A video display terminal blinked. The detective checked the ends of his mustache and said, "We have more questions."

"He doesn't seem to realize," the chief inspector told Radetsky, "just what's been going on."

The chief inspector was very wide and Scots. He had washed-out blue eyes, close-cropped hair and huge ears, which he rubbed constantly, like a cat with mites. He was halfway through a takeout steak-and-kidney pie, soggy with brown sauce, which he attacked periodically with a plastic fork.

"This Johnny defuses a bomb that almost blew up London. They find him trapped in the Thames tidal barrier. The press goes wild. Next thing, he shows up beside an incendiary device that could have demolished Lloyd's. The bomb was allegedly set by his father-in-law, one of the top merchant bankers in the city. The press goes wilder. It turns out the CIA knows more than we do about the whole affair. Can't you *understand*, Mr. Penrose"—he opened his eyes wide—"why we might be just a wee bit curious?"

"SEC, not CIA," Radetsky muttered.

"What?"

"Securities and Exchange Commission. SEC."

"You can question me just as well in Cornwall. And I've got to get back to my ship."

"No, you don't."

"I'm sorry, I do."

"We got a message from your shipping company. To see how you were," the detective with the mustache said. "A Mr.—Gunn, I think. He said he was glad you were safe, but not to worry, he'd found another captain. I think"—the detective stroked his whiskers to a point—"he thought you a little accident-prone—"

"They had you all set up, you know," the chief inspector interrupted. "We just heard. The *Evening* got a night cable, with your name attached. Saying you did it for revenge; Lloyd's was an institution destructive to independent shipowners, you said. They only gave you your money because of all the publicity."

"I didn't send it."

"Why did they leave, if they had him set up for it?" one of the uniformed men asked.

"A good question indeed. What do you think, Penrose?"

"I don't know." The captain shrugged and sat down heavily. "Just in case."

"Och, you're a stubborn man, Penrose," the chief inspector said, and poured more brown sauce over his pie. "Peterson."

"Yes, sir."

"Drive this man down to Cornwall tonight. Take him to this place—Restormel House. Get an on-the-scene deposition, with the St. Austell people. Make sure you get all the details we don't cover here. Then take Mr. Penrose where he wants, but *after* you have all the info."

"What," Penrose asked, "happened to habeas corpus?"

"Habeas what?" the chief inspector said, his mouth full. "It's been a terrible long time since my Latin O levels."

"It's a joke," Peterson reassured him. "Would you like some coffee? It's going to be a long day."

They got to the long tor overlooking St. Winnoc at five the next morning.

Clouds drooped low over the little valley. They hung the tall pines on the hilltop with deep mist. The river took its colors from the sky and curled like a snake of lead. Far below, Jack's farmhouse and the church lay peacefully between trees and water. The Jaguar, the car she took only to visit this place, was a dull glint by the churchyard gate.

The lane downhill cut deep through hedges. It was wide enough for two cows walking abreast, or one police Rover driven by a skillful but increasingly impatient Peterson. By the time Penrose got out and restored circulation to his legs, the detective was gone, with nothing but a diminishing scale of gears to remember him by.

A rook cawed in the dawn silence.

The tombstones were rotting teeth in dark green gum disease.

Smoke penciled from the farmhouse chimney. Jack's black-and-white mongrel yapped from the barn. The hills glowed with hints of morning.

Mrs. Tomkyns saw him coming from the kitchen window. She opened the door and pointed a spoon behind him as he came through the yard.

"She's by the graveyard again. She won't listen. Like last time."

"Thank you," Penrose said.

"She came in last night, for tea, when we told her you called. But she's out now with that damned camera thing again, excuse me."

The gate creaked as badly as ever. He saw her only because of the movement. She was sitting with her back to a willow, way down by the riverbank. The video camera was propped nearby, next to a stack of tape cassettes. As he drew nearer she picked it up, hoisted it to her eye and focused it at him.

"Hello," he said.

"Howdy, stranger," said the voice behind the camera.

She had on blue jeans and Wellington boots and the thick sweater he had brought her back from Norway when he was running on the Norsk Hydro contract. For some reason he saw that as a good omen, and then realized why: it was different from the Ophelia outfits she so often favored.

"I've come to apologize," he said.

"Hello, then."

"Can you put that thing down?"

"I'm experimenting. I'm filming every living thing that turns up in this graveyard. Mudpies, snails, the heron, Jack, cats, worms. You, too."

"Selina."

A nightjar churred, well upriver.

"What brings you to these here parts, pudner?" she said in a terrible American Western accent. "Wah dontcha take off yer boots and stay awhile."

"Selina!"

"But I know what you're thinking." The accent was gone. She tracked left to the river, released the trigger and, lowering the video and powerpack gently to the ground, looked him full in the eyes.

Even in the blurred blue light he could see the hollowness of her eyes and cheeks.

"Sit down." She patted the grass.

He sat on a patch of moss that immediately soaked through his trousers.

"You're thinking I was going to do an Ophelia." She picked a dandelion and tossed it at him. "Here's rue for you—oh, you must wear your rue with a difference. Don't look at me like that."

He looked at the river instead.

341

"It's still as beautiful." She followed his gaze. "It never changes. I hope after the hydrogen bombs it will still look this way.

"When I got out from under that horrible drug," she said, as if this were all the same subject, "when I finally could make my muscles work again, I went all over the house. Looking for you, for Daddy. No one was there. Uncle James had left with his black bag." She shivered slightly. "So had that man in the minstrel gallery.

"I wandered around for a long time, taking pictures. I think I went mad, a little—yes, like George. He had broken through his door, by the way. I finally found him in a room under Daddy's office. You get into it through the chimney. It was a room I'd never known existed, an old priest's room in the oldest section of the house. Crucifixes everywhere. Just like there was something under Daddy I never knew existed.

"It was filled with Japanese uniforms. Machine guns. Old pictures of Daddy and Uncle James dressed like Malays, with darkened skin. George was loading one of the machine guns. I filmed him while he shot away the white ensign on one of the walls. It made a terrible noise and it threw out heavy brass cartridges everywhere. We laughed and laughed. George kept laughing. For all I know, he's laughing still. Halfway through, though, I began to cry."

He looked back at her, assessing.

"The next thing I knew I was here, at Betty's grave. Absolutely alone."

Penrose swallowed. She had not called her by her given name since she died. It had always been "the child."

"Mrs. Tomkyns came out to tell me you were all right. I was very glad, John, but frankly it didn't matter all that much. You see, when I went mad in the secret room with George, it was pure self-defense. When that stopped, I had no defenses left. For the first time I was face to face with the fact that I was alone. My mother died of asthma. My child died of no-one-knows-exactly-what. My husband went to sea. My brother's a junkie and lives in his own private place. My father's gone. All I have left is myself."

"Selina."

"What?"

"Easy."

"Don't coddle me."

He fought the surge of annoyance and said, "Okay."

She opened her hands in a gesture that said "It's simple."

"But I don't mind myself so much any more." He followed her gaze now. She was looking at a heron picking at the slate banks on the river's edge. The cracked colors of her eyes seemed to accept the river colors and become part of them. "I'm different from most people, in ways you know, but last night, for the first time, I accepted that."

She glanced at him, at the bird, looked at him again.

"The hole in your soul's gotten bigger, hasn't it?"

"I'm all right."

"Poor John."

The words reminded him of Claire, and he felt himself go numb. With difficulty he pushed the numbness away.

"I'm okay," he insisted. "It's just an old—er—preoccupation. I was worried about you. I thought you might need help. I thought I ought to tell you. Hell, to apologize for holding a knife at your throat. For thinking you had helped your father try to get rid of me."

"But I did."

He stared.

"At first." She picked another dandelion, threw it in the river. It rested on the surface, turned and eased downstream. "You always told me where you're going. It's one of the nice things. I wondered why my father was so interested. He kept asking where you were, where you were headed. I thought at first it was because he wanted to woo you back to the bank."

"So *that's* how he knew I was in Antwerp? In Grand Tortuga? In Kent?"

She shook her head. "Not Kent. You see, by then I knew my father had killed his friend Tim Harewood." She picked yet another dandelion and examined it with great concentration. Using two fingers she plucked out petals, one by one.

"You knew?" he repeated stupidly.

"Yes."

"How?"

"The video. Quentin's improvisation. He showed me the whole thing again. He was very proud of it, and the way it made you look silly."

Penrose rescued his left foot, which had been conquered by pins and needles.

"Go on. I don't understand."

"It's one of the things that turned me off him, in the end. Anyway, you remember at Jarry's he got your face and spliced in the wave shots through his magic box. He panned across the table several times. I noticed the bottle of pills in front of Tim's plate, of course. Then I noticed it drift, sort of, stop-frame by stop-frame, in front of my father's plate. In the next shot of that area it had disappeared."

"He switched it then."

"Apparently."

The "apparently," Penrose thought, spoke of a respect for evidence that was new to his wife.

"Why didn't you tell me?"

"But I tried, John. Oh, I wasn't absolutely sure, and for a long time I tried like hell not to believe it, but it fitted too well with the way he was acting. And the bank was in difficulties. It fit. But then you had left, then you were on the boat, then you were hiding from the press, then you were at sea. Then you were walking into Restormel with your girlfriend. The one who was faithfully relaying everything you told her to my father."

"She tried to stop them in the end."

"From killing you?"

"Yes."

"Jolly decent of her, don't you think?"

"Yes."

"Is that what's wrong with you? What she did to you?"

"No."

"The death bug strikes again."

He had to smile.

"The old one?" she said.

"The old one. Only this time it really bit."

Selina lay back against the tree and closed her eyes.

"This feels," Penrose said, to change the subject, "like we're back at the university. You know, the river, the way you're dressed."

"It does, doesn't it? Only, we thought we could never possibly need help in those days."

"Never." He smiled.

"I don't know what you think. Maybe we've got too much in the way. Betty, poor little thing. Other things."

"Eh?"

"You heard me."

"You're talking between the lines again, Selina."

She opened her eyes, reached out two fingers, closed her eyes again and continued the dandelion genocide.

"Okay. I don't know how long my own life bug will be dominant. This newfound equanimity of self. I can always use help, therefore. If you're interested."

"Stop it."

"What?"

"It's just your way of offering help to me."

Her eyes opened again and looked at him, very level.

"Okay. I know you. What's wrong with that?"

"Nothing."

"And I do need help. I'll never get over my mother—I don't mind admitting it, the way you do."

"Last time we were here you wanted a divorce."

"No, *you* wanted a divorce. But we can still get divorced. It doesn't have to stop us from helping each other."

He shrugged.

"Why did you leave, anyway?"

"You mean, why did we grow apart."

"As you like."

He thought of all the distances and frustrations, and the deeper lack of contentment and finally said, "Do you want the shallow reasons, or the structural ones?"

"I know the shallow ones."

"Well—" He drew a deep breath. "I've thought about it a lot recently. And I think it was the code."

"Pardon?"

"The code. We all spoke the same way, thought the same way. I needed to get out. Talk differently. Think differently. Spike the learning curve again. Intellectual claustrophobia. What about Quentin?"

"My God, John," she said, "we should at least be friends again. You're as crazy as I am."

"What about Quentin?"

"Quentin." She giggled. "Poor Quentin. Last I saw of him, he was being devoured alive, purple hair and videos and all, by some pop singer with huge teeth who kept keening the same idiotic song, over and over again, in his ear. Quentin Leap. Bad pun. Sorry."

"But Mukerjee said you were getting married."

"Daddy lied," she said simply. "I'd called it off weeks ago. It's not the first time. The first time he lied was when he told me boys had germs." She giggled again.

Penrose felt his energy flagging. "How do we start, then?" he said.

"I don't know. A little bit at a time? We could spend the day together, for instance. We could go to Malpas."

"Okay," Penrose said simply, and closed his eyes.

Penrose and Selina had something to eat at Jack Tomkyns's, then they drove the Jag into the hills and walked the woods near Malpas ford.

The clouds never lifted but the wind was westerly and comfortable if one wore a sweater. Neither held any expectations for the day. Because of this they talked with ease, even about Sir Norman and Claire. Penrose noticed how Selina's face seemed to have sweated off its turmoil and become more serene. The quality of her skin had changed, somehow: it shone as if from an incandescence within. The ethereal look this gave her, paradoxically, increased the physical attraction he felt for her. Every movement she made seemed charged with dance and electricity.

None of this tapped the blackness, but it made it possible to forget at times. He dozed off in the early afternoon and slept for two hours under a stand of oaks, uninterrupted by dreams of anything. Though he felt twice as tired when he awoke he knew that he had charged essential batteries.

The car radio told them the *Selina* had been found, moored and abandoned, in Morlaix, on the Brittany coast. The bankers were at large in France.

Selina did not want to return to Restormel.

They got back to Wheal Quay a little after dusk. There was a note from Colin on the countinghouse door, saying he had checked the *Salope*, her stuffing box was leaking and she needed her diesel run; he had been trying to get in touch with Penrose about something important and would Penrose please see him before he blew up Cornwall.

The old hatch had warped further, and he had to kick at

the sliding top to loosen it against the tracks. A faint smell of stale tobacco rose from the cabin. Selina asked, "What's that paper on the mast?" and looked dismayed when he told her.

Her eyes were wary but soft. She had not been on the *Salope* in over a year. He gave her an exaggerated bow and let her lead the way down the hatch.

She went down the companionway backward, turned around, drew a breath—and screamed, a piercing, wailing sound that had not one single thread of control resting on it. A sound from a different world, where the things that happened were beyond ken.

Penrose grasped the hatch coaming and swung down, not using the steps, tweaking his ribs, bumping her roughly out of the way as he landed on all fours on the saloon deck.

The light he kept in the forward cabin was still on, but the door forward was closed, leaving the saloon in darkness.

A single light—one of the *Salope*'s—had been propped on the bookshelf in such a way as to aim its beam at the little Norwegian stove next to the forward bulkhead.

Claire Thibodeault's head stood propped on the stove, spotlit by the torch. Black blood had seeped onto the metal and coagulated around her severed neck. The skin of her throat was pure ivory.

Selina's scream cut off. She gagged, choked and coughed. She fell against Penrose, held him in a steel grip. He put his arms around her instinctively. Her whole body trembled. He felt his own stomach flop upside down as he fumbled for the switch.

She sensed what he was doing and said, "No, don't put the light on." Her voice was more than half a sob. "Let's get out," she croaked, and pulled away. "He's still here— Oh, *God*." She gagged again.

"Run," he whispered. "Get in the woods till I call."

She lost no time clambering up the steps, but he boosted her fanny over the coaming anyway. She was immediately sick on the deck.

Penrose stood frozen for a second. His eyes were magnets, Claire's head a pole. The horror welled up, mixed in pity. With a mental wrench he dragged his eyes away, closed them and concentrated on listening, but all he could hear was the boom of his arteries and Selina throwing up topside.

His fingers found the switch, and he flicked it downward. Colors leaped to attention. The blood around Claire's neck turned ocher. Her face became bruised and blue.

Someone said, "Hello."

He leaped straight into the air, yelling, "Hah!" in his fright, and landed half-facing the door to the pilot's cabin, where the voice had come from, loud, friendly and amused.

The cabin door was open. Sir Norman sat on the narrow bunk, aiming a shining Purdey sporting gun at Penrose's chest.

Selina had stopped being sick. He hoped for a moment she had got away into the woods. Then he heard her scream again. The sound set rooks complaining in the trees above the river. It broke him free of this new shock.

"You're not in France," was all he could think to say.

"Good lord, no," his father-in-law answered. "Can't stand the plumbing."

Penrose looked at the hands on the shotgun, expecting to see blood.

"You sick *bastard!*" Penrose spat the words.

"Dear, oh, dear," Sir Norman said, and smiled. He was still dressed in a morning suit. His bow tie was tightly knotted. Only his face showed signs of being up and on the lam for twenty-four hours. The lines and wrinkles there were so tightly drawn they hampered the jumping nerves in the banker's cheek.

There was a sound of scuffling on the deck above. Selina cried "No!" once, then a fist connected and someone fell. Penrose put his hand to the ladder, his foot on the first rung. Sir Norman leaned to follow his movement, tracked him with the shotgun and fired.

Penrose was beginning to get used to the sound of close-range firing but this concussion was beyond belief. The shot passed inches from his head and tore a fist-sized hole in the coach roof. The force of sound and broken air made him slip and fall against the ladder.

Selina was crying again, saying "No," over and over.

"One more cartridge," Sir Norman said jovially. "This one's for the kidneys. Sit on the bunk."

Numbed, his head ringing, Penrose did as he was told.

Selina's Wellingtons and jeans came into view in the hatchway. When she touched the deck she swiveled, looking around the floorboards. When she found Penrose sitting on the bunk, alive, she was beyond surprise. She looked until she found her father.

"You."

Her features, except for the one pink cheekbone, were as white as the dead face on the stove. Her eyes were enormous. They were drawn to Claire Thibodeault. Her throat seized up.

"You," she choked up again. "Daddy." She put her head in her hands and covered eyes that would not close.

"Ah, Selina," Sir Norman said. "Pity about all this. Still. Can't be helped."

Another morning suit came down the companionway, facing forward. Very long pants with a silk cavalry stripe. A white hand holding a pistol. The muzzle compensated to stay pointed at Selina's spine.

"Daddy," Selina said through her fingers.

"Sir Norman," Penrose interrupted hopelessly, "let her go. Let her not see any of this. She won't say anything. She's your daughter."

Hawkes's face came into view. He put the pistol to Selina's spine.

"My father," Selina said. Her fingers descended, an upside-down portcullis, to reveal flooded eyes.

The door to the forward cabin opened silently. Hilliard stood in the entrance, holding a stubbed-out cigar, wrapped in a fur coat that made him twice the size he was.

Selina ignored him. "You're not well," she told her father, and took a single hesitant step in his direction. "You need help."

The shotgun flicked from Penrose to Selina.

She stopped short.

"Don't come near me, Sela," Sir Norman warned.

"Courtenay," Hilliard said.

"But I am fine," Selina's father continued in a friendlier tone. "I'm just in a bit of trouble. Isn't that right, John? We can still handle it. There's no proof. Or, rather"—he pointed at the obscenity on the stove—"there's the proof. We were damned lucky she sneaked out of that hospital."

"Circumstantial," Hawkes agreed. "Based on the American. Anyway, it was Dormier."

"Courtenay," Hilliard repeated. "I'll have no more of these perversions. Put them away. Now."

"Hilliard wants to commandeer this boat," Sir Norman

explained, pointing the shotgun at Penrose again, "to join Askew and Drummond in the land of Turkish toilets. We shall let our barristers face the music till everything blows over. Isn't that the plan?" he asked, his face abruptly puckering in concern.

"That's the plan," Hawkes said, with an encouraging smile.

"Take care of them now. Then we can bury them wherever you want."

"I told you," Courtenay insisted, "no."

"You're mad, Courtenay." Penrose shivered. "You've gone right around the bend. And you, Hawkes."

Sir Norman laughed. "Mad," he said, "perhaps. By most people's standards. But that's just to say I make my own rules. It's always been that way. Civilization depends on men like me; we are the only ones educated enough, philosopher-kings enough, to—"

"Now," Hilliard interrupted. He had exchanged his cigar for a tiny automatic pistol that he pointed at Penrose. In the same instant Hawkes was on one knee behind Selina. His pistol followed his body movement to aim at Hilliard.

"No."

"Now James, on the other hand," Courtenay said cheerfully, "may be a bit unstable; because of Burma, don't you know. He enjoys playing Chindits more than I do even."

"There is a reason," Hawkes said. "He deserves to be punished as well, but it won't make any difference."

"And let's not forget there is the off chance"—Courtenay wagged an admonishing finger at Hilliard—"that we may be stopped before we get rid of him properly. If he's dead, we'll be worse off. The odds are good, right now, but logically we must keep him alive until we can make him disappear."

"And the girl."

"No." A concrete wall in Courtenay's voice. "I'll handle her."

"You played with him twice before," Hilliard said, keeping the pistol aimed at Penrose, "and look where it got you."

"There will be no mistakes this time," Hawkes said.

"The explosives," Courtenay added happily, "are primed."

Hilliard put the revolver back in his coat.

"Penrose was right," he said bitterly. "You *are* mad. I wish to God I'd never got mixed up with you."

"You'll see," Courtenay replied. "It will be more interesting this way."

The Daimler was hidden in Bodrugan's barn. Penrose and Selina were prodded by shotgun and pistols into the back, then Hawkes took the wheel and followed Courtenay's directions, past Chark and Treska.

Hills, fields, nestled villages gave way to moorland that grew higher and starker. They passed the turnoff to Restormel. Arc lights shone in the distance. Hedges became stone walls. Behind them streaked a quarter moon, and in the intermittent light Penrose saw they had entered the pits country.

The clay pits occupied twenty square miles of blasted countryside between Tregoss Moor and the sea. Three-quarters of the pits belonged to a northern syndicate; most of the rest were the property of Cornish China Clay, in which Courtenay's held a controlling interest.

The open-pit mining went on twenty-four hours a day, seven days a week. Bulldozers, pressure hoses, earthmovers and Rome plows carved and recarved the terrain on a massive scale to extract the fine white mineral. Conveyor belts lifted the clay into three-story refining plants, where it was powdered, compressed or liquefied. Silos held the finished product until it was ready to be hauled or pumped to the nearby coast, to Treg or Charlestown or Par. There it was loaded on coastal freighters, bound for paper mills in London, potteries in France, or factories in northern Germany that turned the clay into lubricant for North Sea oil-drilling rigs.

In the daylight, Penrose knew, the clay country looked like the surface of an alien and hostile planet. Huge volcanoes of white slag rose three or four hundred feet between vast mountains of tailings and craters that were correspondingly deep. Rain had sliced this unnaturally arid soil into sheer arroyos and escarpments, wadis and canyons that had no place in England's green and pleasant ecology. The road itself ran by sufferance only where the land had been mined long enough ago to allow gorse to fix.

Everywhere the clay shone an unearthly silver in the moon rays. The arc lights of refining plants and the headlights of earth-moving units winked and moved all the way to the horizon.

It was a landscape from hell.

They passed a tiny hamlet of squat gray stone houses shut in by walls of slate. A miners' village. It reminded Penrose of Port Garth. The only sign of life and light came from a single tiny pub, hunched against a wind that came undiluted off the eroded slopes surrounding it.

The pub belonged to CCC. So did the village, and so did ninety-eight percent of the people there, Penrose knew. It was the only game in town.

A quarter mile past the village Courtenay pointed left, and the car turned into a track with a chain link fence on one side. They pitched and rolled uphill, under the shoulder of a particularly large clay volcano, and stopped by an open gate with a sign that read: DANGER NO TRESPASSING NO ENTRY CCC LTD.

Courtenay pressed a button on a small box over the sun visor; the gate swung slowly open. They ran down a graded tailing along the volcano's flank and stopped in the lee of a tall structure of corrugated sheet metal. Courtenay got out, followed by Hawkes. Penrose and Selina obeyed the encouraging gestures of small arms.

No lights shone in this section. The sheet metal hid hoppers and conveyor-belt machinery that were no longer in use. The wind brought a ceaseless roar from distant diesels and the smell of smoke from the miners' village. It was damp and cold.

Aqbar stepped out from the shadow of a hopper, holding a pair of beagles on long leashes.

"All ready, sir," he told Courtenay.

The dogs sniffed suspiciously. One of them started a long, disconnected growl that raised hackles on the back of Penrose's neck. Aqbar whacked him with the end of his leash.

The Indian was dressed in puttees, an Afghan jacket and a hardhat. He disappeared behind the building and reemerged with a bolt-action carbine across his back, leading a horse with a cavalry saddle and a coil of rope attached. The saddle blanket had "CCC Security" on it.

"After you, Hilliard," Courtenay said.

"For God's sake," Hilliard snorted.

Aqbar tied Penrose's wrists behind his back with the end of the rope. He gave him fifteen feet of slack, mounted the horse and tied the rest to his saddle horn. Selina yelled at

353

him, and Hawkes slapped her. Then they set off across the clay rubble, single file, Hawkes and his pistol at the rear.

The going was murderous. The ground was a cross between sand, gravel and clay, quite soft, cracked and crumbled by erosion. Clumps of gorse and bracken, more or less dead, constituted the only vegetation. Large chunks of corrugated iron and tar paper lay scattered about, as if the demon who made this place had entertained himself by ripping all man-made materials into shreds.

Down an arroyo, up a tailing, around another clay mountain; at times they had to scramble over landslides or across gullies, Penrose struggling to keep his footing. The beagles snuffed at his heels, and Aqbar's horse lunged close behind on every steep bit. Once, he slipped, fell and rolled down a slope of scree until he was pulled up short by Aqbar's rope. The Indian simply kept on going, dragging him on his back to the top. Selina yelled angrily, but it was not as brutal as it looked.

Selina was sandwiched behind Aqbar, in front of Hilliard. There was no way he could scheme or even talk with her. Perhaps, he thought, he had already spoken the last words he would ever say to his wife. The thought of losing Selina was bitter, but the idea of death itself wasn't so bad. The death bug welcomed it, Selina would have said. Certainly he felt, without being too melodramatic about it, as if death was only a little worse than a life ashore, knowing he was a coward, knowing he was at the mercy of a fear greater than himself. And it was so much easier not to struggle; to give in to the inevitability of the guns and men around him.

But without him, Selina would be helpless. Sir Norman might protect her this time, but who would warn her the next, when Hilliard came back on his own?

Twenty minutes passed. They were going roughly south, Penrose knew, but to make any kind of progress southward meant constantly turning east and west to avoid pits or canyons or mesas of clay. The only advantage in the rough going was that the exercise kept them from freezing.

Finally they crested the flank of a mountain and saw the moon glint on cliffs and a broad wedge of sea, surprisingly close, perhaps a third of a mile away. On the right lay a long ridge that did not shine in the night. They had come to the edge of the clay country.

The ridge line was marred by a tall finger of brick pointing at the clouds; a chimney, with a hut at its bottom. A delta of tailings ran downhill from a square black hole in the ridge. A ruined tower stood to one side. Hunks of corroded machinery, much older than the clay hardware, lay scattered around a terrace next to the chimney.

They filed down the flank and left, up the ridge of an old cutting. The unease he felt when he first saw the square hole grew, but the sense of fate made him keep his peace till they reached the terrace.

An old sign on the ruined building read: KERNOW TIN #12: SILVER WHEAL. One of the chunks of machinery was an ancient steam pump, another looked like a capsized trolley cart; both were mostly rust. A panel of scrap clanked sporadically in the wind.

The square hole was shored vertically and horizontally with balks. Railway ties paralleled each other into its depths, but the tracks had long since been removed, probably in some wartime reclamation drive.

Penrose stopped dead. The dogs sniffed his knees. Hilliard drew Selina aside with an arm twisted up her back. Sir Norman came alongside and grinned at him.

"Silver Wheal. Oldest tin mine in this parish," he said. "You're going all the way down it, Penrose, old son."

Penrose's face must have shown his refusal.

"But yes." He brought the shotgun up. The bores were two tunnels, one for each eye.

"Then *shoot* me." Penrose threw himself at the shotgun, twisting to kick it away, but Aqbar had already taken up the slack and he was jerked, ridiculous, out of the middle of his leap, and landed painfully on his back across a discarded spike, his head banging on the horse's fetlock.

The horse whinnied, shifted, and he had to push himself away from its hoof. He had never really thought it would work.

"Get on with it," Hilliard called. "I'll take care of her."

"No," Courtenay said. "We must all go together."

"That's ridiculous," Hilliard scoffed.

"He's right," Hawkes put in. "But I can see Sir Norman's point, Hilliard: he doesn't want any accidents to happen to his daughter."

Hilliard shrugged. "I won't touch her, if that's what you mean. She's your problem, Courtenay."

The hole was black as nothing. Penrose knew these old mines by reputation. The old Cornish miners had followed seams wherever they led, through increasing heat and artesian floods. Their workings spread out for miles, deep underground. Some of them led under the seabed itself.

"No," he said desperately. "For God's sake, Sir Norman, why are you doing this?"

"For the same reason as before," Sir Norman answered.

"Yes," Hawkes said. "Because we know that if it doesn't kill you outright, it will make you completely psychotic. Of course, that would have served our purpose in the tidal barrier, but now," he said in tones of sweet reason, "we have to kill you as well."

"Then kill me," Penrose repeated. "Go on." He struggled to his feet and would have run at the psychiatrist, but Aqbar had him roped in even closer. One of the dogs looked at the tunnel entrance and whined.

"You've bolloxed things up, dear boy," Sir Norman said. "You have to pay. And this way no one will ever, ever find out what happened to you."

"Come on," Hilliard yelled.

"He's right. Aqbar?"

The Indian dismounted and came around in front of his horse. Penrose hung on the rope and kicked both his legs. One of his feet connected with Aqbar's belly. Hawkes slipped in from behind and grabbed him around the Adam's apple. A beagle took his ankle in its teeth and worried it, growling a warning. Aqbar grunted, but held onto his right ankle. Hawkes's finger found a nerve ganglion in his armpit and a piercing pain shot down Penrose's left side; his entire flank went numb, in a very painful way.

Behind the horse, Selina screamed.

They wound the rope around and around his kicking legs and pulled it tight. Hawkes kept his fingertips on the nerve endings, and Aqbar took his other elbow. They dragged him bodily into the tunnel and paused while Sir Norman opened a padlock on a thick wooden door covered with hasps and red notices.

The door groaned open like something in the London Dungeon. They went inside the shaft.

Immediately the old feeling came back, as if the horror of the tidal barrier had reamed out wider and smoother channels for his fear to rush in through.

Darkness pressed in and around his head. His chest constricted. He had trouble breathing. Despite the residual numbness from Hawkes's fingerhold, he dragged his knees up until he was hanging off Hawkes and Aqbar—consciously to hinder the two men as much as possible, less consciously to return to the fetal position—but the psychiatrist squeezed with his fingers again, the nerves leaped into flame down his side once more and his muscles let go almost involuntarily.

The light Sir Norman held was very strong. In the backscatter he could see a jumble of old lifting machinery, what looked like cages and pulleys surrounding a wide shaft that led downward. The roof was supported by wooden beams. Above the beams wet rock hung drooling in anticipation.

The track ties led around the shaft and into tunnel beyond.

In the glint of light he could see that tunnel close, becoming narrower. Twenty feet away it left the horizontal and plunged downward at a twenty-degree angle, rough with ties and black wood support beams, till it vanished in the depths of the ore formation.

They dragged him around the shaft and into the tunnel.

Benjie, the voice in his head sobbed, Benjie. Penrose pressed his lips tight and shut his eyes as he was forced downward.

The tunnel was bad and got worse.

Even over the noise in his own head he could hear Aqbar and Hawkes gasping and cursing. He could not open his eyes, but his toes crashed repeatedly into pieces of broken wood and rock. Twice they pushed him over what had to be partial cave-ins, rolling him over the piles of rubble and splintered wood. Once, he bashed his forehead on a timber hanging out of the roof. Another time, his ankles caught on a loop of rusted cable, and he was pulled out of Aqbar's grasp and fell into a freezing puddle on the tunnel floor.

Water dripped on their necks and arms and splashed out of pools between the ties. The only sound above the labored breathing of the men who carried him was the ceaseless drip of water as it patiently worked its way through the limestone faults and disappeared through cracks in the slate floor; seeped and probed with chemical fingers, rubbed and abraded the rock using rock it had rubbed off before: wore and condensed and penetrated until it had undermined the artificial vacuum of this puny shaft, rotted the supports, softened their beds and reestablished balance in a thundering collapse of stone. Just to imagine it made him sweat harder than the rock.

But not yet. The rhythm of dripping water counted out seconds in geological time. The hundreds of thousands of precarious tons of rock poised above their heads contained the slow patience of eternity.

And eternity was what it felt like to Penrose, hours and hours in affective time as they dragged him deeper and his stomach knotted tighter to fight off geological fate. After a day or so of this kind of time—which was probably only a half hour—Penrose began opening his eyes.

Not because he wanted to see. In fact, the glimpses he did catch made him want to vomit, cutting what breath he had. The shaft was only five feet high at this point. Hawkes had to stoop like the old Asian persona he had once adopted. The chiseled vault of the tunnel roof gleamed with the pasty residue of decay. A good third of the supports were useless, either cracked or broken outright. Crumbled rock broke their stride now every ten or fifteen feet.

Penrose opened his eyes because his ankles had separated a little. The cable that had hooked one of his feet had loosened the rope around it. By working his knees up and down, slowly, so Hawkes's light would not catch the movement, he was gaining an extra fraction of play every time he pulled his feet apart.

The voice in his head was now punctuated by a hollow booming. He was going crazy, Penrose thought, just when he needed his wits.

They passed a blocked side shaft. Once he noticed through slitted eyelids the skeleton of a pony. Here and there was the odd crushed lamp or rusted pickaxe, looking like relics of some disaster much more serious than fallen tin prices.

The tunnel leveled off somewhat, and they dragged him another hundred feet and stopped. The voices—and the booming—were much louder. Despite the damp and the chill he was sweating more than Hawkes or Aqbar. And he had only a half inch of play between his ankles.

They let him drop and chatted among themselves.

If only he could unwind the rope. He would run and run, back up the shaft, till someone shot him: Hilliard, probably. No matter, as long as he died on a vector back to the sky. He was beginning to see that the other side of his fear was a passionate love of sky, a fondness for sun and birds and wind and the clean horizon of the sea.

He opened his eyes again. Aqbar and Sir Norman were peering down the tunnel, into the blackness. Hawkes was gone. Sir Norman saw him looking. He was very flushed in the shine of his lamp. White surrounded the pupils of his eyes.

"Thalassa, thalassa," he said. "The sea, Penrose, the sea. You love it so much. Even more than my daughter. It's right over our heads. Do you hear it?"

He should have realized that booming was not really in his head, Penrose thought; it was so resonant and deep, and yet just a measure away from regular.

"The waves. We're about fifty yards off the cliffs now. Listen to them!" Sir Norman cast his eyes upward as if in prayer, then looked down at his captive again. Aqbar shifted position nervously.

"We're going to bury you, old boy. Under hundreds and hundreds of tons of rock. We'll seal off the entrance. The sea will come in. You'll be trapped in this tunnel. Think on it. Think on it! It's so perfect!" He laughed, using only half his face.

Penrose squeezed his eyes tightly shut and levered one foot as hard as he could off the other. Benjie's face drifted in and out of his vision centers, familiar as the taste of his own terror.

He realized that he felt a little better, because the booming was not in his head. If he could maintain one grasp on reality, he might maintain others. It would be a comfort in his last three minutes.

When he peeked again he saw a spot of light winking far down the shaft, hindered by fallen supports but reflected on sweating rock. It wandered closer, brighter. Hawkes came up behind it. He was wet through and seemed very much on edge. His face was streaked with mud.

"The uphill one, now," Sir Norman said.

Hawkes nodded. "There's a dead man down there," he said. "It's nasty, very soft."

"Don't be frightened," Sir Norman said in mock sympathy.

"Stuff it, Courtenay. He's not a miner. It's recent."

"The other charge, James."

Hawkes looked at Penrose, and nodded and squelched back up the tunnel. "Three minutes," he called back.

Sir Norman squatted again. His eyes stared down the lantern beam, but Penrose got the feeling he saw nothing of substance.

"Three minutes, Penrose," he said. "It's a delay pencil fuse. Five two-pound charges of cortex in three-ring mains, and *boom!* The whole tunnel."

He got to his feet.

"You could have had it all, Penrose," he whispered. "You could have been my son. But you weren't strong enough.

"Good night. *Don't* dream," he quoted.

Then he was gone.

Light dappled fewer and fewer facets of the tunnel walls. The booming seemed to intensify. The backlight of Sir Norman's lamp went up the steeper angle and stopped next to Hawkes's, fifty yards away. Then both lights disappeared.

"No!" his mind yelled, but his lips stayed shut.

Total blackness settled in.

Penrose's body reacted without him. It arched and strained; his calf muscles bucked furiously at the rope. The skin on his legs, already raw, grew sorer and bled. Still he kicked; he pulled and worked at his hands as well, but they were tied too tightly and would not come apart. Sweat poured off him, and his lips mouthed the words in his brain as he struggled.

He worked an extra half inch of slack around his ankles, but then the knots tightened solid. He gave up kicking and began rubbing his legs against each other, jamming the loops on one anklebone as he tried to tug the other ankle free toward his knees. A voice in his head screamed his own name, but he paid it no heed because he had just got the right anklebone past the lowest loop.

It had to be close to three minutes since they had left.

"Joooohn."

It was a woman's voice. As far as he knew, his head did not speak in a woman's voice.

"John," it wailed again.

"Selina," he shouted. "No!"

Bits of light were dancing back on the roof of the shaft.

The fear had filled every cavity in his gut. Selina's presence somehow doubled it past the cracking point. Her light was approaching the angle where the plastic charge was buried.

"Go back," he roared. "It's going to cave in."

He closed his eyes, gritted his teeth and galvanized every fiber in his legs in a paroxysm of effort, beyond the strength of his muscles, beyond the endurance of his nerves. The skin on his right ankle tore loose. The extra room let it slide past two of the coils, lubricated by blood.

The voice in his head had changed its tune. It was shouting, "Selina," over and over.

"No, Selina," he yelled aloud. His right knee heaved again, and his foot tore loose, ridiculously fast. He kicked the rope clear of his ankles. He rolled awkwardly to a standing position, using the walls of the shaft to support his bound elbows, kicked the rest of the rope away and plunged back up the tunnel.

He cracked his forehead on a roof support almost immediately, whiplashing the neck muscles. He fell, got up, raced forward and tripped. He fell headlong again, bruising his knees, scraping his face on the rubble.

"John?"

"Go back!"

"John? Quickly!"

"Go *back!*"

He got on his knees, sobbing for breath, lurched to his feet. There was more light now. Selina was directing the beam in his direction, and he could see and avoid obstacles. The dip in the tunnel was forty feet away. He could not see his wife behind the glare of her light.

"Selaaa!"

Another, weaker, voice chimed in. It was a wail from limbo, Sir Norman's voice, confused and wild.

"Run, Selina!" Penrose yelled. He was close enough now so that he was dazzled, rather than helped, by the light. He stumbled on a fallen timber, collapsed and knocked his head on a rock hard enough to daze him.

Light was all around. So was the booming. Selina's hair fell over his face, and her hands took hold of his left elbow.

Light wavered stronger from up the tunnel.

"Come on!"

"Go back. I'm coming." He shook his head, rolled over.

"Selaaaa." What *was* that movie?

"Run, Selina." She kept pulling at his shoulder. He tried to get to his knees.

A flash of his brother's face, untouched by the years.

"Seli—" he began.

There was a fat "woomp."

The light up the tunnel switched off.

The shock wave boxed their ears, drummed on their chest cavities. The roaring that followed it was at first soft by comparison. Then it swelled, vibrated, punctuated with rocky explosions. Wood cracked. Water poured. The roar grew. The rain of rock chips on their heads became a downpour.

Selina still dragged him sideways, and with her help he managed to get his feet under him.

"Daddy," she cried now. Her light was almost invisible in the dust.

Guided by pure instinct, they started running back the way they had come, away from the rockfall. But with no warning the roof fell in on their heads, smashing them to the ground. The roar seemed to become alchemized into pressure, on his head, on his chest. Pain lanced from his ribs. He screamed back at the pain, at the terror, at the darkness.

The black weight was familiar: he was going to die in this place. He could not breathe. It was every nightmare he had ever dreamed.

"Benjie!" he screamed. He could not see. He could not hear. He roared for his brother, despite the ache in his head and the grit in his mouth. It had been almost like this. The old house had a hole, a priest's hole.

Penrose realized he was moving, but it was involuntary, his brain had no control over the muscles. His body tried to roll a bit, to allow his lung muscles room to work, but a giant hand was pressing down on his spine.

They had been taking Benjie to school. The old lady who smelled of lavender had come to take care of him. Benjie had wanted to take John's favorite bear with him, claiming it was his. It was *not*.

Short of oxygen, he inhaled while he was still spitting out grit. More dust entered his mouth, choked his air passages. He coughed. The pressure ground harder into his backbone, and red pain flared in his rib cage again.

He had hidden the bear, whose name was Bozzie, so Benjie could not take him. Benjie had been furious. Benjie had locked him in the priest's hole, forgetting that no one else knew he was there. It was black dark and only two feet wide. He stayed there all night and the next day, screaming his terror, while everyone searched the wells and woods and gypsy camps. He knew he was going to die.

He knew he was going to die now, but in a strange way the screaming of Benjie's name, out loud, had made him realize it was not his brother's fault. He knew he was going to die, but somehow he also knew that the pain in his right elbow came from the death grip of Selina's fingers. He reflected, quite calmly, that it was sad she would not have a chance.

He pushed up with his stomach muscles and thighs. The weight grew again. He tried to roll. He was suffocating. Lights flashed before his eyes. He convulsed, pushing against the top of his head, and gagged on dust again. He kicked out with his legs and felt them push through into thin air.

His brain, starved of oxygen, was working very slowly. There was air behind him. If he worked his legs back and forth hard enough, he should be able to winkle out. A good theory.

No air. They would suffocate eventually, of course. He accepted that and, doing so at last robbed fear of any great hold over him. Welcome, he said to himself, to rock bottom, and almost laughed at the feeble pun. He was going to die. He repeated it over and over. It seemed to help.

Dreamily he began working his hips around, in an almost sexual movement. Sex and death, he hallucinated, Eros and Thanatos, both returns to the primal cell. After three or four hip revolutions he felt the weight on his back shift to the left a bit. He rolled left very hard, ignoring the agony in his chest, and it shifted farther.

Now he could brace his knees and worm out. The first time he tried, his shoulder blades caught on rock. The second time, he got past the debris. The third time he dragged his torso out, and a kind of pressure locked around his waist, helping his efforts. The fourth time, he scraped his face between a couple of boulders and fell backward out of the rubble, choking and gasping as he inhaled the air that was more dust than anything. It took him awhile to realize that a lot of the gasping and choking came from Selina, who

363

had both arms wrapped around his stomach and was coughing and retching into his back and holding him as if she would never let go.

She was still holding him, and they were both still trying to get a clean breath of air, when the rumbling started again, two or three minutes later.

No "woomp" this time, just a deep and steady increase in sound, from the very lowest frequencies up. The air vibrated like a drum. Selina groped for her light, which showed up like a glowworm in the cluttered atmosphere beside her. She played the beam around, but although some of the heavier particles had settled, visibility was still less than four feet.

"What?" she said. Her voice trembled. Her face, hair and clothes were powdered gray with limestone dust, as were his. It was hard to read her expression in the penumbra.

There was no point in hiding what she would realize soon enough.

"A second charge," Penrose said. "Farther underground. Under the sea."

"But—"

"It must have slipped his mind. He forgot to mention it. Unless a rockfall was set off by the first."

"Oh, my God, John. What this must do to you!" She looked at him, then brought the light closer to his face. "Your forehead's bleeding. And your mouth."

He laughed at that and doubled over, coughing at the pain in his lungs. They were both going to drown in a flooded mine shaft within minutes, and she was worried about his cuts.

"Untie me," he said, when he could.

She had trouble with the knots and cursed when she broke a nail, but she had them undone within sixty seconds.

The roaring grew. When his hands were free he took the light and pulled Selina to her feet. The rockfall that had almost buried them was solid, complete. Granite boulders were visible among smaller stuff sloping to the roof.

From here to where the charge had been set would be thirty feet of solid debris. And somewhere under it all was Sir Norman.

He turned back in the direction of the sea. There was nowhere else to go.

"Daddy," Selina said once, like a childhood prayer. He

took her hand, and they began moving down the tunnel, toward the advancing water.

The roaring grew louder. Dust from the rockfalls clogged their little light.

"What are—" she cleared her throat, coughed—"what are we looking for?"

"A way out."

He said it lightheartedly. He had barely realized he was moving, acting, planning again, but he was. The fear was an old scaly dragon, wounded by his acceptance of death, held off by his remembering what had happened in the priest's hole. Claire had been right, after all. The realization brought a sharp taste of grief.

He continued. "There may be another way out. Side shaft. Ventilation tunnel. Anything. Otherwise we can try waiting till the tunnel floods. If we get to the rockfall before we run out of air, maybe we can swim out when it stops flooding."

"You're mad."

"Crazy as a coot," he agreed. "But I don't want you to die."

The fear dragon's eyes opened a slit. He had to remember it was not completely dead.

"And you?"

"You heard what your father said. Statistically speaking, I should be dead many times over."

If he started to care about living, the dragon might stir and his fear could start again.

"There was a side shaft way up the tunnel, past the fall," she said. "I hid in it when they went by."

He looked as carefully as he could. The first rush of water came thirty feet down the tunnel, cutting channels in the rubble, covering their feet. The smell of iodine melded with the tang of stone.

The dust got worse. He used the light to look at one side of the tunnel and felt the other with his fingers. The water quickly rose to their knees. It was black and cold. The hole the explosion had blown in the ocean floor could not be very big or they would be up to their necks by now. He was breathing very fast: he could not seem to fill his lungs to the brim any more.

The booming was much louder here. It combined with the

365

roar of flooding and the ring in their ears as seawater compressed air in the mine.

Selina gasped. She felt at her knees and cried out. "It's a *man*—oh, *God*."

He directed the light downward.

A corpse bobbed in the current, awash on air trapped inside its desiccated flesh. Its face—what was left of it—rose and fell in the milky current. Its eyes had been eaten out, probably by rats. Three or four feet of braided beard teased out behind the remains of a turban. White skull shone on one side of its head.

An Asian. Sir Norman must have used this tunnel before, Penrose thought. He pointed the light away and up, to erase the sight in darkness, and it was then that he saw the shaft.

It did not lead sideways and back, as he'd expected, but up. It was narrow and rough: a ventilation shaft.

He would never have seen it were it not for the dead man. It was small, and opened between two closely spaced timbers that would conceal it from up and down the tunnel.

"Look!" Selina had grasped the implications quicker than he. "Quickly!" She jumped up, her hands scrabbling for purchase, and fell back down in the water.

If it was a ventilation shaft, if it led straight up, Penrose thought, then Sir Norman had been wrong. They were not under the floor of the ocean. That was why the booming had increased as they went down the tunnel: they were getting closer to the cliffs, not farther away. Surf only crashed in shallow water.

So maybe she did have a chance. Determination hardened in his stomach.

"I'll give you a leg up." He found Selina's calf, fumbled down it, laced his fingers under the instep. She understood immediately.

"Where's the light?"

"Here. One. Two. Three." He lifted her up, and the pain in his chest made him stagger and groan.

"Nothing!" she yelled.

"What?" He could barely overcome the noise of water with his voice.

"There's nothing. No handholds. I can't get up," she wailed.

He set her back down and fell against the side of the tunnel, holding his ribs.

"How far did it lead?" he gasped.

"What?"

"How far?"

"I can't tell. Oh, John, what are we going to do?"

"We shouldn't—keep looking. We'll be trapped."

"But it's too sheer. We can't climb."

"Easy. We'll float up."

"You mean—just float?"

He nodded.

"But what if—?"

He shrugged and closed his eyes against the pain. If the shaft led nowhere, they would drown later rather than sooner. He felt nauseated. She felt for his hand and held it. The water was high enough that she had to hold the light at shoulder level. They looked at each other in its glow, leaned into the current and waited.

It did not take long. The flood reached Selina's breasts. When she could no longer stand against it she held onto Penrose and floated, gasping for air as the brutally cold water sucked warmth from her skin.

A few minutes later he had to do the same, holding onto one of the roof supports. For him, though, the cold water felt almost good: it seemed to dull the pain in his lungs, and fit in with his shortness of breath.

He could measure the rate of flooding by how fast the water crept up the black grain of the support. In less than a minute after he floated, the wood had vanished. They were bobbing in the vent shaft now, kicking occasionally, bracing themselves against the walls. The booming of waves, the singing of pressure, the bursting of their own breath echoed loudly around them.

He could not tell if it was fear or damage that compressed his lungs so. Their light showed only dust above them. Selina's trembling was making ring marks in the water; her lips were purple as Claire's had been. Claire was dead. Selina would be soon.

He could examine every pick and drill mark that had sunk this shaft, till the water blotted them out, one by one. The water slurped and gurgled at the walls, as if licking its chops in anticipation of victory.

"Why?" he said at last.

His voice resonated over and over in the shaft.

"Why what?" Her eyes flashed.

"Why did you—come down?"

"Hilliard—let me go."

"The—bastard." Penrose had breath only for phrases, not sentences. "Wanted you—dead."

"I know."

His teeth began chattering, like castanets, like hers.

"How long—can we swim in this cold?" she said. "My legs are dragging, John."

"Half an hour," he reassured her, though the truth was somewhat less. "Keep your legs—together. Don't get—face wet."

"I wonder if we're near Merlyn's Carn?" she gasped a little later. "That booming—sounds just like it."

"I'd not—thought of that," he said. "It could—just be surf."

Ten more feet. Five more minutes. Every foot seemed different, with little angles of rock, odd pick marks; once in a while, a tiny spiral ammonite, an occasional vein of tin ore. He kept hearing voices, very tiny, in his head. He tried to hug himself to keep the warmth in but he felt strength flowing out with his body heat.

After a while she said, "What?"

"I didn't—say anything."

"But I thought—I'm so cold, John. My arms are going now."

"Swim harder." He demonstrated, but his own movements were pathetically sluggish.

"I don't know—how long I can—"

"Here," he said. "Hold your knees. Lie a bit—on your back. Keep your—face out. I'll steady you."

"John," she whispered after a pause, "I hear voices."

"You too?" He coughed, and his lungs glued up. He coughed again, to free them, and tasted blood, warm and musty on his tongue. "Knackers," he muttered.

"What?"

"Knackers." They were the evil spirits in tin mines of Cornish legend.

"No—I'm serious." She took the light from his hand and played it upward. The beam wavered fitfully; her trembling was almost of spastic proportions.

"There's something up there. Some k-k-kind of shelf. We can rest on it."

Penrose felt his rib cage. There was a lump on the side that had not been there before. His breath was coming in rough, rapid wheezes that barely gave him enough air. Selina, intent, did not notice.

"Shit," she said. "I th-think it's stopped. That's th-the same—corkscrew thing—I've been looking at—f-f-for ages."

A bark echoed, very distinctly, down the shaft. Tregeagle's "Yellhounds," Penrose thought.

"Did you hear that?" she said.

"He-e-elp," she yelled. The echoes ricocheted about, mocking her, then subsided beneath the periodic boom of waves.

"We must b-be at sea level," he gasped.

"Oh, no." She brought the light down. He noticed the air was less heavy with dust. "Oh, no."

"What?"

"You're bleeding again—your mouth. It's not—a cut. It m-must be—your lungs."

He looked at her.

"Don't look at m-me like that, damn it."

"I'm not," he said. "How far is—the shelf?"

"Not far. Four or five feet."

"There's a way—get to the shelf."

"What? What?" she said.

"Chimney," he gasped. "If I can do it."

"I'll do it."

"Can't—too narrow."

He had tried it once, when he was in the climbing club at university.

"I'll try to—brace myself. High as I can go. You climb up. My shoulders. Okay?"

He had no breath for more explanations, and was relieved when she nodded. He pushed himself sideways against one wall of the shaft, nudged Selina aside with his legs and rammed his feet against the other wall. With his legs extended all the way out he could brace the top half of his back against the other side. He reached down with his hands and found a small purchase, braced with his feet and heaved upward, ready to ignore his ribs.

The pain duly came. His back scraped up three or four inches. He only barely had enough breath for this. He wormed his left foot up the opposite wall, then the right. Repeated the process, blowing like a marine mammal.

The pain worsened. It became a red fire in his brain he could not ignore, only grapple with, trying not to imagine what was happening to his insides. He was dripping, almost out of the water. "Now," he groaned, through clenched teeth.

She pulled herself across his stomach, using his shoulder and the wall for support. His stomach muscles trembled with the strain of her weight. When she tried to stand on his knee his foot slipped, then his back gave. They both fell in. Miraculously, the light stayed on.

Wordlessly he started again. His mind shut off all thoughts that were not about pain thresholds and increments of inches. Both of them knew he could not do it a third time. His breath sawed shallow, back and forth, back and forth. When she stood up this time she placed her foot on his lower stomach. The muscles jumped with tension but he did not slip.

"Oh, no," she said. Her voice broke. "This is where it ends."

He barely heard. He could feel his stomach muscles weakening despite repeated orders from his brain to tense up. His back was beginning to lose its friction hold, when her weight diminished. So did the light as she stuck it on the ledge. She put her right foot on his shoulder and pushed off. The shock tore something inside. It jerked him down and broke his grip on the wall. He splashed back in the freezing water.

When he came up to the surface, his mouth full of blood and seawater, the light had disappeared.

Her voice came, mysterious and full of hope.

"There *is* a way out. Oh, God, there's a way out. Behind the ledge."

She flashed the light at him.

"John." Her eyes came out of the darkness. "You must concentrate. I have to find something to pull you out with. I'm going down this tunnel."

"Go," he said, and coughed.

"John," she insisted, shouting against a particularly loud boom. "Listen to me."

"What?"

"Keep swimming—do you understand? Keep swimming."

He kept swimming.

"For me."

She froze for a moment, and said "Voices" in a small tone, and vanished.

Darkness. Black darkness without Selina. Black darkness, red blood, blue cold. The booming grew; the cold spread. The kicking of his feet was becoming almost imperceptible. Screams echoed. He was fighting for air. His mouth went underwater, and it took three times the effort to paddle his way back to the surface; so much effort, in fact, that he thought he wouldn't bother next time.

Boom, the waves went. Boom. They beat the same rhythm as the waves in his head that rushed, ever higher, over his brain.

He only knew his eyes were closed when everything went a uniform red. He opened them and was blinded by white light. Voices shouted at him. The water splashed over his head, and somebody wrestled with him, trying to drown him faster than he was drowning on his own. A voice shouted in a strange tongue. He went down a second time, swallowing sea water with the salt blood from his lungs. He struggled weakly. They had a line around his shoulders. If he was going to die anyway, he wondered, why go to all this trouble. A force hoisted him out of the cold, into the air, onto the rock, constricted his chest, blue under red under black—

When he opened his eyes again tears were streaming down Selina's face and Poodle Crocker was cursing him up, down and sideways.

"Damn, damn, damn," he said. "Damn him. Yes, the planks, the planks, the bloody *planks,* not the blanket, you silly little wog."

Penrose got a view of Poodle's long nostrils quivering with indignation, anorak and jeans below.

"The b-b-blanket too," Selina said, sniffling. "Hurry!"

Her face had been washed off in the flood, but now it was powdered white with limestone dust again, except for the tear streaks.

"He's awake."

Five brown faces, all with mustaches, two with turbans, bent over his stomach. Above them, the roof of a cave jumped with shadows.

"He's awake? If he's awake, why can't he wait?"

"He can't wait. Look at him."

Their voices subsided.

Penrose tried to sit up, but his head spun so badly he subsided.

"Oh, for God's sake," Poodle shouted at last. "All right. Go!"

Ten hands lifted him gently onto a pair of boards. Then the boards themselves were lifted into the air, and he saw the roof supports of a long horizontal tunnel beginning to flick past him. The old black timbers were braced with newer wood. In some cases they had been replaced altogether.

With the luxury of release came the realization that he had almost no strength left at all.

"Gently, very gently," Selina called, already out of breath.

The men who bore him exchanged sharp comments as they trotted.

Poodle ran ahead, holding a pair of Primus lamps to guide the way. Limestone dust rained from above, shaken loose by the wind of their passage.

"Damn it, Penrose," Poodle shouted, "I'll never be able to use this tunnel again. Do you hear me? I'll have to clear out. You've put me out of business. Left, Morarji, you bloody monkey. Go easy. Currency, man. There's fifty thousand quid's worth of French francs in those ammunition boxes—"

The tunnel wound on and on. Every jog brought a new knife stabbing into Penrose's chest.

"I hardly smuggle people any more—not much anyway. It's currency, man! I was getting rich! A public service—out of the hands of Froggie socialism. Down with Big Government! 'They seek him here, they seek him there,' " he recited, " 'those Frenchies seek him everywhere.' "

He could hear Selina panting as she ran alongside. Once in a while she would look at his face and make a noise like a mother cat.

"And they don't even pay that well. I use the Pakis to exchange franc notes. Talk about"—Crocker was winding himself—"subverting the capitalist system."

He could feel the blood level rising in his chest as each gasp grew shorter. He wondered how long it would take to drown in his own blood. He wondered if the weird stamping and jingling that had replaced the sounds of hurrying feet and crashing surf were part of the unfamiliar process of dying.

They stopped. Balks were stacked. The stretcher was lowered to the tunnel floor.

"All the way."

"No."

"All the way," Selina insisted.

"No. I've got to clear 'em out before."

"He can't."

"But he must."

"No."

"It's only twenty feet, woman! Here's your light. Good-bye, Penrose," Poodle whispered, bringing his mouth close. "You're home, damn your eyes!"

Someone slotted heavy boards back into place.

Selina bent over him. He could see the vault of a narrow tunnel overhead. He did not care if he never saw a tunnel support for as long as he lived.

"Just a little bit more, John," she said.

"Ghost," he said, meaning she looked like one.

"The tunnel ends in a house. We're almost there."

She put her arms around him and pulled him to a sitting position. The blood in his chest gurgled in disgusting fashion. He coughed, and the dust on her breasts turned pink.

"Oh, God." Her voice broke. "Please. Just one more effort."

Everything swam but he had somehow got to his feet. Selina was practically carrying him, holding the light with her free hand.

The tunnel ended as it had begun, in a thick wooden door. She pushed away the bar that locked it, heaved the door open and dragged him into an old-fashioned cellar whose walls were lined with hogsheads, tubs, barrels and cases of cider.

The stamping and jingling was over their heads now, very loud. Men's voices rose and fell.

"Stairs," Selina gasped, "please."

There were ten of them, and he knew every one. By the time they got to the top he couldn't see very well for the lights in front of his eyes. His muscles had gone right through his reserves of air and consciousness, and he could no longer replenish them fast enough. She pulled a second door open, and the stamp and jingle was all around them for a second, with the smell of ale and tobacco and firewood. Then the sounds frittered away to nothing as Selina stood, covered in chalky dust, holding an equally white Penrose and her light in the middle of a circle of clog dancers.

Silence. Then a bloodcurdling shriek.

"The Lady with the Lamp!" he heard Old Tregeagle scream. "She's come for Penrose!"

Penrose passed out cold and, dragging Selina with him, fell on the floor of the Anker.

The nice thing about Treg's hospital was that it had no courtyards or rooms without windows, so the first thing he saw when the anesthetic wore off was sky; a gray sky with clouds and herring gulls in it, a dark gray horizon where ocean met atmosphere. It was the most pleasant sight Penrose had ever seen.

They told him later that he had been injected with curare so that his lung muscles would relax while they patched the hole in his left lung. This accounted for the familiar flaccidity of his muscles the first day, but he felt no great desire to use them anyway, not with catheters and saline drips intruding on his flesh, their tubes hooked up to bottles and bags hung on adjustable chrome gibbets.

His eyes did work, and this allowed him a good view of Selina, who spent much of the first week fast asleep in an armchair by the window.

Sometime early in the week the police came. They told them her father was dead, that Hawkes and Hilliard and Aqbar had been apprehended on the *Salope* ten miles out, when her rudder chains broke and she started going around in circles.

They said that the tunnels between the Anker and the coast afforded evidence of a well-organized smuggling operation, whose perpetrators—including Jenkins, the landlord—had disappeared, leaving behind a lot of French currency and a number of small pedigreed dogs.

The corpse they had found in the mine tunnel was one of Poodle's charges who had died of an Oriental disease and had been dumped down the vent shaft.

Colin came by, evading the nurses. He had pictures of a Dutch coaster in mint condition in Hamburg that was going for less than the insurance money because freight rates were down again. Colin pinned the pictures of the coaster by Penrose's bed before he left.

The doctors told him he could have no more visitors after Colin. They said he had pneumonia and he was lucky to be alive. After the doctors left, Selina cried herself to sleep.

Penrose decided he agreed with the doctors. For the next ten days he spent a lot of time looking out the window, looking at Selina, looking at the photographs Colin had left.

Life resumed.